HIGH PRAISE FROM TINSELTOWN FOR
THE FREIGHT TRAIN OF LOVE…

"…Hollywood Hyphenate John Klawitter continues to amaze!"
  Bran Heath

"Takes you inside the lives of the City of the Angel's rich and famous show biz elite!"
  Anna Rhett

"An action and mystery drama that extends back from present day Holmby Hills to Saigon of the 1960's."
  Margaret Murphy

"Unexpectedly romantic, with twists and turns to keep readers guessing and an ending nobody could see coming!"
  John Warren I

OTHER BOOKS BY JOHN KLAWITTER

NOVELS
Crazyhead
Hollywood Havoc: The Trouble With Fat Boy
Hollywood Havoc: The Llama Goes Up
Devils
Foul
DoubleSpin
Orange Glory

NON-FICTION
Tinsel Wilderness
That Ain't No Shit (Stories of the Old Spooks & Spies)
Headslap: The Life & Times of Deacon Jones
The Book of Deacon (Afro American Oral Wisdom)

More about John Klawitter, his books and films at
www.johnklawitter.com

The Freight Train of Love

John Michael Klawitter

The Freight Train of Love

All Rights Reserved © 2010 by John Klawitter

No part of this book may be reproduced or transmitted in any form or by any means, graphic, electronic, or mechanical, including photocopying, recording, taping, or by any information storage or retrieval system, without the permission in writing from the publisher.

ISBN: 978-0-9830372-1-7

Printed in the United States of America

Dancing Bear Publishing
A division of Dancing Bear Ent., LLC
Paw it right.

For Lynn,
who found ways to bring me back.

And for my brothers
The Old Spooks & Spies

CHAPTER 1

Me, I'm the girl who hung around too long. I'm standing barefoot in my Haynes underwear on the sandy little mound next to my bungalow, focusing on the Mini Cooper tire I've hung from my Jacaranda tree. I dig in my heel at the mound and focus on the strike zone, and just then I spot Jack's crazy Vietnamese gardener hiding in the bushes, probably hoping when I go into my windup he can snap a crotch shot to put up on YouTube. I'm not taking the risk. I whiz one his way. He yelps and is gone in a flash. I don't know if I actually hit him and I don't care.

I pick up another ball and concentrate on the hole in the donut. I tell myself I don't give two hoots about the perverted old fart. But then I spot the dirty black silk of his pajamas. He's hiding behind the corner of Jack's Place. He thinks he's safe. I take my time with the windup and my curveball slides around the edge of the house and rips into Ong Vung's shoulder, knocking him ass over teakettle.

"Fuck-round-eye-witch!" he screams. He scrambles to his feet and scuttles away like a sand crab.

I figure the crazy bastard is gone for now, but my concentration's gone, too. I just stand there in the faint rosy glow of dawn, thinking about my life. I should be moving on, but it's getting harder and harder to throw down my glove and walk away. Hey, I'm not being greedy; it's just that I've gotten too involved with Jack, and maybe if you'd been through what I have, you would be, too. All I want is what every other woman I know has…a good man and maybe a few kids running around. But, you know, here I am, chugging on past my mid-30's and so far I've got *nada*.

I sling a cut fastball in the direction of the rubber tire. I hear the sound of wind off the stitching. *Over 90 for sure.* But I miss, high and to the right. And then I miss three more. Clearly, the Holmby Hills Ace has lost her concentration.

Maybe you don't know how to calculate *the lady's life*; let me give you instruction and guidance, little fly on the wall: The immortal Cy Young, the winning-est baseball slinger ever, had 511 wins, but that was an exception. A superslinger like that old hardballer Nolan Ryan has 324 lifetime wins. The great Lefty Grove had 300. If you're keeping score, and we ladies all do, the average woman can count on 360 shots at being a mom, 360 times that magic bit of life is going to come down the tube. Maybe a rim-shot chance at 400, but don't count on it.

So what makes you think it's easy? Real hardball slingers don't rely on just one pitch, and real women don't just go around spreading their legs, not if they have any self-respect.

So, here's my situation: On the one hand, I live in a world that is, in the local vernacular, *to die for*. And yet, I feel, I think—I *know*—I deserve more. Why shouldn't I get what I want? I work hard. I'm a good person, within reason. I have patience and a sense of humor; you have to have those things to survive in Jack's league.

Why, you ask, do baseball metaphors just seem to trip from my tongue? Well, I was a pitcher in high school. I've got a great fastball, I'm told, *for a lady*. Looking back, those were the times of my life, people cheering in the stands, my curls tucked under my baseball cap, and me mowing down those kids at the plate.

Over the last decade, I've certainly done my time with Wild Jack Larch. I should have put myself on extended waivers a long time ago. All these years, and he still won't get off the dime. Maybe he can't. There are times I don't even know how to bring it up any more.

Jack Larch. He lives in his own world. He's a Hollywood success story, a bit of an icon, you see, and he's just too damn successful. He's got time for his agent, the studios, the up-and-coming directors, the greedy little starlets, his press releases, his adoring fans. *Time for everybody but me.* I'm great and handy to have around like a wine bottle opener, a calculator or a back rub, but should I dare to bring up *the subject of us* and he gets this haunted little boy look, like he's really frightened. He says he loves me and I'm really special, but he's screwed up every relationship he's ever had. And maybe that is it. I honestly don't

know. I'm out of ideas here, and I've shown you the score card.
I'm clearly running out of time.

My name is Clair Moore. I live in a pleasant but uncertain
world, in my own bungalow on the other side of the big swimming
pool behind Jack's Holmby Hills estate. Clair Moore is not my
real name. I made it up shortly after the happy tryouts when I was
selected as an alternate cheerleader for the Dallas Cowboys.
Kolinowski is a squatty center or a gross bummer of a defensive
right tackle. It's not appropriate for a top-level sports bump-and-
grindster such as I was. This is America, land of opportunity.
Anybody can change their name. Changing your luck is another
thing.

However, I did start lucky with the Cowboys. Three
months after I made the squad, one of the regulars bumped up with
a new baby-kins and bummered out of her first string slot. In fact,
going preggie got her kicked right off the Rah-Rah team. Looking
back, I almost wish it had been me. Almost. You see, our born-
again star wide receiver bought her a ring, she had the kid and he
divorced her three months after the happy birth of his little
daughter. We all told her to get a pre-nup, but you know true love
never listens to well-meaning advice. Anyway, one week after she
adios-ed the squad, that was my own sexy butt steaming up the TV
sets on Sunday afternoons. Yes, even though I'm a slim chick, I
have a famous ass. One year, it even made the swim suit edition of
Sports Illustrated, how's that for rear end celebrity?

Dallas Cowboys. Sis Boom Bah That's where Jack first
saw me. Well, not exactly in Dallas, but on TV. He was watching
a Cowboys-Redskins game at a sports bar, and I came on doing the
hip swish in my skimpy white-and-blue outfit with the stars on it,
and Jack bet his drinking buddies he could take me out on a date.
This is Jack Larch, quasi-famous Hollywood author of the Dunk
Stingray men's adventure pulp novels and co-writer of several
Dunks adapted to the silver screen. Actually, the bet was for four
letters stronger than the word *date,* but Jack's long-suffering
literary agent Connie Abart, who caught the dubious assignment of
contacting me, assured me it was on the up-and-up, a date with the
famous best-selling author to *do up Tinseltown,* and she would
introduce me and everything.

Hey, the one big dream every NFL cheerleader has is scoring a movie. Empty-headed young me, I was no exception. The Cowboys were in San Diego when Connie caught up to me, but the Cowboys went into overtime and lost to the Chargers and by the time she we cabbed from LAX to Jack's place, he was asleep at his desk, which was a wash of unopened fan letters, unread Hollywood Reporters, uncashed royalty checks and unpaid bills.

It's now over a decade later and I'm his sweet girl next door. My house, Jack's old guest house, is built into the landscape behind the pool, constructed close up against the sandstone bluff in a way that coyotes occasionally leap across and settle in on my roof. They like it up there; the roof tiles retain the heat on our cold Holmby Hills nights when the onshore wind blows in from the Pacific Ocean, which is only five miles or so to the west. So, you see, I went from being Jack's date-that-never-happened, to his on-again-off-again relationship, to somewhat of his concerned neighbor and friend.

I don't know exactly how I got to be so good with money. I just *am*. I'm one of those girls who hocks the diamonds and puts the cash in REITs and TIPs. And don't think cheerleading in the NFL is peanuts, either. Maybe you don't pull in big buckos on the front end, but with commercials and endorsements, nobody complains about the gig. And a few years later when cheerleading played out for me, I persuaded Dina & Debbie, two of my ex-Cowboy hip-swishers, to toss in with me. They had been on the smart side about the pre-nups, and both had big alimony cash-outs from their own blissful relationship disasters. Our real estate company, Gal Pals, Inc. came to own a small handful of multi-unit apartment buildings at the nice west end of the San Fernando Valley. Besides that, I stay busy trying to prevent Jack from blowing his money on everything from Nigerian scams to young film starlets.

The good part is, Jack trusts me. The bad part is, it's less because of his good judgment and more because I live just across the pool and he can come screaming and carrying on about any old thing that bothers him any time he wants. It's usually about his money and the mystery of where it's disappeared.

Jack's vast and steady intake of royalties and option money dissolves like mist in hot morning sunlight, and to tell the truth, after all these years even I didn't know where a lot of it goes. He's a dear man, a hard head with a soft heart. He has dozens and dozens of hanger-ons, and he gives a lot to cancer, widows and orphans. His mother died of cancer, he tells me. And he considers me an orphan *and look how good I turned out.*

I am jealous somewhere in my flinty little heart, about the time and energy Jack wastes on his good time buddies and fare-thee-well young wanna-be actresses. Jack knows how I feel about this, too. He's always trying to make it up to me, telling me I'm the only person he can talk to. That is progress, of a sort, in our relationship.

When we first met, he said he could use the extra cash I would pay him for rent money. At the time, I needed a place to live, so I rented my bungalow. And then, about a year later, his good intentions went into a serious decline. For weeks on end, I dreaded meeting him on my way to my place. He'd be awash in booze and drugs, and what with the divorce from his second wife (I found out later it had been over me living in the guest house) he'd been more desperate than usual for the pocket change (about a thousand a week) that he would blow around town. I didn't mean to take advantage of old Jack, but when opportunity beats you over the head with a Louisville Slugger, that's hard to ignore.

What did I do? Well, my dear old undependable dad had been a Realtor in Plano, Texas in the Go-Go oil boom days, and the third thing he taught me was real estate. (The first thing was how to throw the cut-finger fastball, and the second, men will always run if you treat them like dirt. Well, I guess my mom helped with that lesson.)

Anyway, I'd save up my pennies from my pro cheerleader days, and I knew how to be inventive. A few days in the Los Angeles assessor's office and I came to the Larch-ster with a plan to save his ass—we ended up splitting his property and I bought the key lot behind his. That bailed Wild Jack out and left him about two and a half acres of useless grass and overgrown trees and a tiny coach house fronting Sunset Boulevard near the front end of the property. And he got the main house, a glass-and-concrete monster that he'd built after knocking down a graceful old

Spanish style manor. Overall, what remained to the Larch-ster was big spread with an eclectic flavor. The interior decorations were splendid with trophies from Dunk Stingray movie props. Dunk Stingray? We'll get to that. Suffice it to say, Wild Jack's fashionings were a cross between James Bond's basement and the Chicago Museum of Science and industry.

And, to top off the flavor of *Jack's Place*—or more appropriately, mow it all down—there was Jack's disgusting smelly old gardener. Ancient, crippled, one-eyed Ong Vung. Old slant-eyes never took off his conical straw hat, and, from the scent that followed him wherever he went, he never took a bath. As part of his pay, Jack let him live free in the coach house fronting Sunset Boulevard. The creepy old guy was something of a local legend for falling asleep while driving the lawn mower. One time, the police had famously corralled him while he was sound asleep, his mower cutting circles across all four lanes of Sunset Boulevard. That one made the local news, thanks to the power of cell phone photography. After that, Jack persuaded one of his show biz stuntmen pals to rig a dead man bungee cord release to the steering wheel. From then on, when the derelict from Ho Chi Minh City drifted off into dreamland, his mower would go in circles until eventually it might hit a tree or snag on a bush and stall out.

I told Jack a million times he should get rid of the lazy old creep. I'm right about that one; he can hire a squad of South-of-the-Border vegetation assassins for what he pays his guy, but stubborn Jack doesn't listen to me. I wasn't very quiet about it, and old cone head must have overheard me, because he is always giving me the evil eye.

My split of my real estate deal with Jack turns out to be what second string quarterbacks and over-the-hill receivers call *the butt end of the pig* when they warily eye their contracts, in other words, the left-overs. But the price is right, the location terrific, and I was happy for a while. I got the three bedroom guest house, which was still in the classic old Spanish style. *Some back end!* And the steep and useless hillside behind it, plus a barren hilltop strip of land behind that that runs for about 400 yards and ends fenced off from a nearly vertical gully. And half the swimming pool.

It is a key lot, which meant I own a small strip of land connecting my property to Sunset Boulevard. I put in a side road so I can drive back to my bungalow. That works out okay for me except that, every now and then Jack forgets and blocks my drive with one of his cars. Or, if he is in a particularly pissy mood, he says I can only use my half of the pool. Once he tied a rope across it, so I had to dive under it to get in a full lap.

Does his behavior sound maybe just a little bizarre? Believe me, Tinseltown is a wacko place, full of egotists, oddballs and an occasional genius. Since variations of the three stooges come in all sorts of combinations, I've found I have to stay alert. You probably know; in show biz, you have to push back to earn respect. And if you're a woman, you have to push back twice as hard.

When it comes to Jack's car blocking my drive, the answer is to have it towed a hundred feet or so to Jack's four car garage on the other side of his house. Since I am a regular paying customer at the Union 76 gas station over near Wilshire, and since I handle Jack's finances anyway, the towing service puts it on his tab. As for his roping off the pool, he stopped doing that after I dragged it soaking wet up to his bedroom. He must have really tied one on the night before, because I was half way down the stairs and giggling like a schoolgirl when I heard him half-asleep, snuffling and cursing about his fictional hero Dunk Stingray in a life-and-death struggle with the Loch Ness monster.

I think you get the picture. I'm here, he's right there next door, we're always running in and out of each other's homes and we're really close in a lot of ways and we look like a solid item, but really, we're not. We share just about everything except our beds and that weird gardener of his.

About the beds, we'd been there and done that a time or two. Once we even ran off to Vegas in the customary manner, got stony-assed drunk and maybe even married, I couldn't remember for sure, and Jack wouldn't say, probably too embarrassed to tell. Right after that we had another of our volcanic disagreements, so I put it out of my mind. *Couldn't have been—not me married to that nasty old fart!*

A little more about Jack's ancient Oriental weedwhacker. I once caught the weirdo peeping in my bathroom window. Sure, he had his hedge clippers, but he was just standing there, making them go snip, snip, snip like he was taking off my fingers one by one. At least that's what I thought when I saw him. Since I was butt naked at the time, you can imagine how I felt. The minute he knew I'd spotted him out there, he scooted away like some old bug, and that didn't make me feel any better. *The guy was guilty; I'd caught him in some sort of a dark moment, something like that.* I told Jack, but he just scoffed. He wasn't going to fire the nasty creeper-peeper, but I made him promise the fellow would stay off my property. After that, I hired my own gardener, an illegal alien from Southern Mexico who charges way too much, but at least I don't catch him masturbating in the oleanders.

Now about the Larch-ster, himself; he really is a mess in every way and every direction except one. That unpredictable old scamp can write, I'll give him that. Remember I was telling you about the three Hollywood types—fat-heads, weirdos and geniuses? Well, Wild Jack is nine tenths brilliant genius and the rest of him is totally screwed up. *Write fast, write good,* that's his motto, and generally he lives up to the first half, and if the second half isn't exactly *literature,* at least it hits the boffo box office high mark and sells big-time.

Over the years, Jack has earned the publishers and the studios tons of ducats. He's also blown more money than I'll ever make, and I see my mission as keeping him from the jaws of total financial disaster. This involves saying No to financing his pals' loser movie projects, No to his mistresses' soft palms eternally stretched out for another hit of cash and No to his ex-wife Dorothy's crabby demands, as well as No, No, No to the whims-of-the-day, anything from ultra-light flying to buying a WWII PT boat that he might be able to tow north from Argentina put in a new engine and turn into a sports fishing boat.

Since Jack put me in charge, I've managed to squirrel some of his cash away for the hard winter of his old age, which has been moving in for some time, and him unaware as ever. Jack, happily playing with his nuts, while the leaves turn brown and fall off the trees. The image amuses me for a moment, but then I feel guilty, and even depressed. He really is a hopeless shit. And yet, for all his problems, I can't help myself, I like the unredeemable scamp that he is. He annoys me in at least ten thousand ways, but he also brightens my days. Nothing boring ever happens around here

What is Wild Jack's public Tinseltown life like? After his early morning writing sessions, he mostly tours around the studios and watering holes in one of his classic cars. He wears his shallow, show biz How ya doin', Guy? personality. It has to be a strain, because underneath he isn't really like that. Hidden away deep in there somewhere there is a real person. Wild Jack would give you the shirt off his back, and just thinking about that impish and untamed rascal manages to warm my heart. I know, I'm a hopeless case. Okay, so what? What do you expect, Clair-of-the-classy-rear end to turn into a nun of the holy cross and give it up for Jesus? Not likely.

I remember this one day, the day I mark in memory that Wild Jack—or maybe it was both of us—took our first beginning steps toward growing up our relationship. It was morning and I was in my all white-and-blue bathroom in my pool house. I tossed my short, curly honey-blond hair at the mirror and gave myself the last look over. Lean and keen and not looking forward to 36. I'd recently had my tit-lift, and the girls were looking mighty fine. Not the big bazoomie implants, just the tricky little packets engineered to fight sag and put the perk back. From the general reaction I'd been getting from everybody but the Larch-ster, I'd decided they were doing their job. And I'd even observed his majesty giving me the friendly once-over when he thought I wasn't looking.

And, okay, since I'm going on about it here, I'd also had the little tuck around the eyes. I don't think Jack ever knew. He was writing Dunk 23 at the time…that's the one where Mormon terrorists take over a French nuclear sub and then Dunk takes over the terrorists after whacking an incredible array of bad people and stimulating three or four gorgeous hunks of feminine super-fection with his rock-hard…err, muscle. And yes, the terrorists were from Utah, don't ask me how writer-boy-wonder got to that.

So I was one of those lucky slim ladies, still winning the fight against sagging boobies, wrinkle-butt and gut-flab. Not that it was easy. But when all you've got is looks and brains and a bit of money, it would be a shame to let any of it go to pot, wouldn't it?

Wild Jack was pretending to hang tough in the good fight against evil father time, too, but he had his own set of rules. He played racquetball and had intermittent workouts at that exclusive club he belonged to over in Century City, and he went on and off the latest fad diets…but he smoked cigars and drank a lot. Wild Jack was never worried about personally crossing over. He was an expert at dispatching the evil-doers in his novels; when it came to his own exit from this mortal coil, he didn't have a clue. Actually, if you have a talent and also get lucky, there's nothing wrong with that. He didn't seem to worry about anything. From what I'd seen so far, about as far ahead as Wild Jack ever wanted to look was the next Dunk Stingray exploiter.

Bright and early this particular Sunday morning I'd put on my face and I was sitting outdoors at my glass table reading my laptop when himself staggered around to my side of the pool, looking a little worn and haggard.

"Hi, Clarity Malted," he said, squinting down at me, his iron grey hair sticking up every which way and his face a mess of wrinkles. "Jesus Christ, it's damned bright to be so early."

"Something like that," I agreed. "Night on the town?"

"See and be seen," he said.

"And pay the price."

"I want a sermon, I'll go church—which isn't about to happen." He took a closer look at what I was doing, "What the hell? You writing a script? As if I don't have enough goddamn competition in this screw-ass town?"

"Don't worry. Just taking a few notes on the financials."

"Oh," he said. That was okay, just so long as I wasn't competing with him. "Let's go get coffee. I'm buying."

That brightened my day. I liked my alone time with Jack. Sure, maybe it was the left-overs, the five minutes snatched here and there to go over the bills or whatever, but for some crazy reason, it was the best time for me. I couldn't help grinning up at him. "You sure look messed up, Wild Jack."

"And you look pretty as a daisy, Clair-Bear."

So we headed for my $150,000 dark grey Porsche sportster, the one known to all Jack's friends as 'Steve's Porsche' because the dealership that sold it to Jack swore Steve McQueen used to own it. That McQueen must have owned every dark grey sportster in town because you hear dozens of film biz fat rats claiming the same exact thing. Anyway, for sure, that was why Jack bought Steve's Porsche; another link to the great ones, the Hollywood Legends. Jack was always impatient to get up there on that select ledge himself, but I kept telling him, You have to die first, and that's a steep price.

Still, I did say *my* sportster, didn't I? Jack sold it to me for 30 cents on the dollar, yet another time when he really needed the cash. Only problem with the deal, he has his own set of keys and he drives it more than I do. And I get to pay the insurance.

"Gas costs more than lattes," I reminded him.

"Don't go crazy on me, Clair-Bear," he said, tipping his hat to Ong Vung, the battered old Vietnamese gardener, who was staring at an azalea bush as if it might be wired with explosives.

"There's the real meaning of the word 'crazy.' You should fire him."

"What, again? Why? Because he wears a cone hat? You're showing extreme racial prejudice."

"Don't give me that Hollywood correctness crap. That creep does a days work in a month, if that.'"

"Come on, Clair. He doesn't go on your property any more."

"I wish you'd put a shock collar on him, just to be sure."

"He cuts the grass," Jack said.

"He lives free in your coach house and you actually pay him, too."

Jack shrugs, but says nothing more about it. He's not going to change his mind. Like I've said, he lets me handle his finances, but he doesn't take me seriously. At least he respects my particular form of magic that keeps his money from flying out the window faster than it comes in.

We occasionally were an item in Hollywood, but that shows you how little they really know on Extra-Extra. Macho man that he is in public, the inner Jack is afraid to bring up our relationship, to try to explore just why we imploded and became dark stars orbiting each other without intertwining. Maybe you think that's the normal skittish male behavior, and sometimes I think so too. But, to tell the truth, I was afraid as well. I'd lost too much in my life, from my mom who ran away with her slippery divorce lawyer to my dad, who'd disappeared when the real estate market dried, to the awkward pile of romance rejects who showed up with flowers to date a real NFL cheerleader and then pulled on their pants and straightened their caps with the little emblems on them and glided on out the door before sun up.

After the Vegas debacle, Jack and I drifted apart again. After that, I found myself skating along from day to day, because I figured Wild Jack in my life in a limited way was better than life without the damn old Larch-ster. And that was when Joanie, the wanna-be blues singer hooked up with him for their two week marriage-fling. C'est la vie.

We pass Ong Vung, and Jack suddenly takes off at a dog trot, sprinting for *my* Porsche. I could beat the bandy-legged oldster, but I let him win. By the time I get there, he is already behind the wheel, grinning like a little boy. He's a generation older than me, but no mold grows on the boy, as he likes to say, talking about himself in the third person.

Jack guns it, and we shoot past Ong Vung, who is now head down on the mower, performing his usual aimless circles on the grassy lawn. We roar onto Sunset, heading east toward Wilshire for our jolts of caffeine. We argue about the stock market, which he understands about as well as blackjack, another game of chance at which he isn't very good. He looks over at me and his hands fly to illustrate how nuts I am not to be into solar power which he calls the new plastic, while I worry about him keeping my car on the road and if my auto insurance works when a crazy man is driving.

Physically speaking, Jack himself is wire-thin and dapper. He has a shock of stiff iron gray hair that he tortures into a stand up punk style, and a jet-black pencil moustache that lines his upper lip below his lumpy nose. He also sports a big dagger-and-heart tattoo on his left arm, something I figured he'd probably picked up from a drunken weekend in the good old days when he was a trooper in Saigon. The artwork is very fine and detailed, but typical of Jack's desire for uniqueness within the ordinary, it is skewed about 30 degrees off center on his arm. There's a little banner under the point where the knife pierces the heart. This reads, 'Death Before Dishonor,' a slogan that rings hollow in this town, I don't have to tell you.

The gossip rags believe old farts who try to look like young guys are fair game, and they've taken Jack apart a time or two. Still, he does manage to look like somebody—enough like present day Bob Dylan's frumpy brother to get second glances at Gelsons or Jerry's Famous Deli, and enough like himself so young soccer moms pull their kids aside and point him out as a bad example—a rich and nasty old bastard out of harmony with his time and place, or whatever young moms tell their kids these days to warn them not to grow up to write men's sick macho adventure novels. Wild Jack never minds any of that; he likes the froth in his life

He drives like a maniac, and this Sunday morning is no exception. A couple of years ago he won racing driver lessons, a prize in the annual Writer's Guild of America golf tournament, closest to the hole, he made sure to tell me. Anyway, after he wasted three days endangering the wild life at a Driving School for the Stars somewhere in southern Arizona, our Jack picked up enough rotten habits so he knew how to do all the stuntman getaway moves really badly. Winning that prize made him even more of a menace on the streets of West Hollywood, where he was already on his way to notorious. From the mountains to the sea, look out, Jack Larch is on the road!

I have good reason to cringe. His terrible driving—and his squinty, myopic vision—makes our morning motors to the favored Starbucks on Little Santa Monica Boulevard something of an adventure. Yes, unfortunately for me and my sweet little sportster, our café of choice is quite a ways from his glass-and-concrete slab home and my pool house hacienda. That's because the Starbucks frequented by Wild Jack and others of his ilk is located directly across the street from the biggest talent agency in the world. See and be seen.

That morning, we don't spot any of his big-time pals nursing their hangovers while waiting for their Vente Moccas. Jack signs a few autographs for the UCLA film kids hoping for their big break and we head back to Steve's Porsche.

"Candy-assed Pitt," Jack mutters to nobody in particular as we peel rubber out of the Starbucks parking lot and shoot north across big Santa Monica Boulevard, heading back home. He is talking about Dirk Pitt, another writer's leather-skinned hero from the old blood-and-guts school. Dirk isn't Jack's guy, so of course he's a bad hero.

"He sells, Jack," I say, stating the obvious. "He sells big."

"Dirk Pitt has fought in every fucking god damn war since Troy got sacked. He's a hundred and forty six years old."

"And not a scratch on him." I'm trying to humor Jack out of his funk.

"Yeah. Invisible armor." The Larch-ster lapses into an unhappy silence, and pushes my dark grey 911 along. The gearbox protests as he downshifts and we thump heavily through a cross-street rain wash, what the diamond-shaped yellow-orange signs proclaim is a DIP.

"The real dip is Cussler," Jack says. He's talking about Clive Cussler, author of the dozens of hugely successful Dirk Pitt novels.

At least, I'm thinking to myself as we rocket along, *At least Jack can still read the big yellow-orange signs.*

"Fuck-head like that snuffs the genre for everybody else. They become the genre, and that's what kills it. No room on the shelf for anybody else."

"You think?" I ask. It's a purely rhetorical question; Jack is going to tell me, anyway.

"It's just greed. Louis L'Amour killed off the Western. Stinking Hondo isn't enough, he's gotta do Londo and Fondo and 47 Sackett pulpers. Robert B. Parker polished off hard-boiled detective with his Spenser and that cute New York haiku tough-guy talk bullshit."

"Boston," I mutter under my breath. It's no use, Wild Jack's on a roll.

"Now days, if you want to write detective, you practically have to bring on a dike cunt bitch with some sort of high concept profession like tattoos inlaid with zirconium dust or inbred dwarf horticulture banana tomatoes. Unbelievable crap, but you put a million bucks in advertising behind anything and readers suck it up like cheap Algerian red. Then somebody else will come along and kill that one. You wait and see. Evanovich is already doing it with that Plum bitch. She's the next L'Amour."

That's the thing about Jack. No mincing words.

"You think Clive killed off Dunk Stingray?"

"I hold the fuck personally responsible."

Dunk Stingray is Jack's creation, and, hence, a good hero. Like Dirk, Dunk has saved the world dozens of times. He has fought his way through every deadly combat mission since World War II. I guess that would make him 95 years old at least, but young Miss Clarity Sweet-cakes knows her role. I hug what remains of my latte and I don't say another word about ageless heroism.

CHAPTER 2

You may think it's some kind of heaven on earth, being a cheerleader for a pro football team—I did make a pile of dinero, but in the process I seemed to have lost what little self-esteem I had left after momsy ran off with the lawyer. With the Sis Boom Bah bunch on the Dallas Cowboys, my A Game was all about getting that CB Beauty Shot, you know, my Cute Butt full screen right in America's face. I swear there was a direct relationship between the number of seconds my ass was on the screen and the extra dollars I made through commercials, mall openings and the like. I once told Jack how I felt and he just snorted, 'We all do that, Clair-Bear. Old Dunk Stingray is just a cheap sell-out, me selling the only bit of my sorry scribbler's ass the lit biz is interested in.' Once I got my head around that one, I started to think maybe Jack and I had more in common than I would have believed when we first met.

But now is no time for reflection. My eyes widen, the 911 wails and Jack swings us left onto Sunset Boulevard. He hits the gas; the sturdy little sportster roars, and I cringe in my seat as a fancy parade of posh homes whips by. I'm managing to get in a church service after all. Praise the Lord, Sunset is fairly deserted. Count your blessings. I just wish I had time to confess my sins. Jack blasts past an old purple Dodge Caravan loaded with tourists and happily flings Steve's Porsche into the first available curve.

"So, what do you think?" He looks at me, owl-like through his thick glasses. Jack is blind as a bat without his glasses, and nearly as blind with them. I know what Jack is asking. He can only be talking about one thing.

"I don't think you're happy," I said.

"That obvious, huh?"

I never lie to him about money, his work, or what I think of him and his antics. This time he is talking about "Stingray in Baghdad." At the moment, he is about half way through adapting "Baghdad," one of his later novels, into a screenplay. He's working with Eddie Barth, a professional adapter also known around town as 'the Goy Ghost.'

Jack is rotten at adapting, otherwise he'd never use Eddie. Jack's screenplay scripts always end up longer than his books. At some point he will just give up, toss Eddie a CD and a huge and unworkable 350 page first draft, and mutter, "You know what I'm thinking," or "Okay, it's all in there." Then 'the Goy Ghost' will slip away and quietly earn his fat fee by chopping off two thirds of what they have written. But that is still a few weeks in the future.

"Fucking 'Sahara,'" Jack fumes, referring to one of Cussler's popular novels that some years before had been turned into a costly screen epic that, in turn, had badly bombed at the box office. "They had nothing, Clarity."

"I know, Jack."

"Nothing," he repeats. "That's why they played the star-fuck game."

I shrug it off, "Penelope always takes her male lead down."

"The woman has no restraint."

"Method acting."

Jack snorts and then is quiet for a few beats before he starts up again.

"Connie tells me there's no room on the shelf for both Dirk and Dunk any more." Jack has shifted mental gears. Now he is talking about long-suffering Connie Abart, the lady who had introduced me to him.

"What does she know?"

"God damn right," he grumbles. Jack acts like he hates agents almost as much as he hates other writers. He only puts up with Eddie Barth because in his mind Eddie isn't a real author. You won't find his name on anything, so he doesn't exist, he is a ghost writer. And Jack thinks Eddie is closet gay, to boot. *Edward, the candy-ass gay ghost. No threat there.* As for Connie, she may look soft on the outside, but inside she's all razors and spring steel. And one final aside about Eddie, I know for a fact that Jack is 100% wrong on that score.

"I told her to get off her lazy ass. Get out there and sell something." Jack lays on the horn and zooms around a yellow school bus. "They have school on Sundays?" he asks.

"Faith Methodist," I read on the side of the bus. "Sunday school."

"Oh, yeah," he says. "Well, there ought to be a law."

A law against Sunday school. I allow myself a faint smile.

"Clair," he says.

I am surprised. Jack has used my name without any funny additives like 'Rare Clair' or 'Clarity Supreme.'

"I'm worried about you. About me. About us."

"What's to worry?" I ask. I guess the uninitiated might call me Jack's long time girlfriend, ten years, at least, but this is news. Jack never worries about us. This has my interest up, like I'm in purgatory and I spot the Pope selling special absolutions.

"I don't know what to do," he says in a low mutter that is almost lost in the growl of Steve's Porsche's powerful engine.

"Do? What do you mean, do, Jack?"

"Look at me, Clair. I'm born to fuck up relationships. My life's a train wreck; three ex-wives and a kid who probably isn't mine anyway, but who absolutely hates me. Blown boxcars and bodies all over the tracks."

This is the human side of Jack. It doesn't come out very often. He has a thousand pals and not a single friend other than me and maybe Connie. I tell you, think twice before you go for the brass ring, because life isn't necessarily pleasant should you actually get it. If you don't believe me, ask Elvis, Marilyn or pale-skinned Jocko.

"Jack, what are you trying to say?"

His voice sounds less world-worn and sarcastic than usual, and somehow hopeful. This is yet another side of Jack, the road less traveled.

"I wish…I just wish I'd been less flip about everything, maybe things would have turned out differently between us. Do you see that?"

"Yes, I do," I say, holding my breath as Steve's Porsche rockets us along. .

"Women are all about lasting relationships. I know this. I read it somewhere."

"That's true, Jack-ster."

"You're the most lasting relationship I've ever had with a woman."

"So this loose thing we have is a relationship?" This is encouraging, and also puzzling. Maybe he is asking me to forgive his wandering ways. Maybe he figures if we made a new start, something might come of it. With Jack, I can never be sure.

"I'm sorry I'm the way I am," he says. "I want to do something but I don't want to screw it up. I know I care, but I...." His voice trails off to nothing.

He is distracted, never a good thing when he's behind the wheel, and what happens next leads me to believe I was partially to blame, as well. Jack is looking over at me, trying to say something he thinks was important, and he isn't doing a very good job of it. His hands are off the wheel and waving and he is saying something about that's not what he means, but a big green-and-white Sparkletts water truck moves in our way, slow-tooling along right there in the lane in front of us.

"Fucking road hog!" Jack grabs the wheel, downshifts and hits the gas. That's the wild boy's way with everything—Power through the slide!

Steve's sportster coughs in protest, but the throaty engine roars and the tight assed little car dutifully swings wide into the center lane. Unfortunately, there's a blue Chevy Nova with Arkansas plates in our way, parked right in the middle of Sunset Boulevard with the emergency lights on. A tall geek with a pronounced goiter and a colorful map is standing on the road, one arm outstretched and pointing. He's showing his wife and the two little girls standing next to him a home that his map probably claims was once owned by Cary Grant, Clark Gable or maybe Bing Crosby.

"Thoughtful," I say. "He put his blinkers on."

"Phony star maps," Jack replies, hitting the gas again in his cunning but not very wise attempt to get a little ahead and cut off the water truck.

Trouble is, the Sparkletts water guy doesn't see the geek, the wife and their kids or my Porsche. Jack lays on the horn but it's too late.

It happens in less than a second. The truck's bright green left front fender lifts us neatly on our backs and sends us spinning past the Midwestern family and across the opposing lanes of the boulevard. We miss the Arkansas folks by a few feet while cars flash by from the other direction. Still upside down, we whirl-a-gig off the road and come to rest in the middle of a spacious green lawn next to a life-size cast iron darkie intent on tying up our horses.

I stare blankly at the iron black man in his brightly painted livery garb and think stupid thoughts about Holmby Hills answer to political correctness…It ain't prejudice if it's art. I am uncomfortable hanging upside down by my seat belt, and I'm hoping to hell this accident hasn't somehow put my boob job out of whack. My head hurts. Somewhere a clock is ticking and I smell gas.

"Jack, you okay?" I manage to gasp. There is no answer.

Then I remember Wild Jack believes seat belts are a government plot to take away one or the other of his rights, probably freedom of motion. There is a smear of blood on the cracked glass over the steering wheel, mute testimony that he may be right about that one.

CHAPTER 3

It was four days after our little road incident before I started to feel like my old self again.

It was a Thursday morning, almost time for my working session to straighten out Jack's checkbook, his fan mail and to do my weekly sort out on his tax receipts. Maybe I'd have a chance to slip in a few bad words about his crazy gardener. And after all that, I had plans that would involve borrowing one of Jack's cars, as Steve's Porsche would still be in the shop for another week.

I was on the patio in front of my pool house, about finished with my thirteen—the U.S. Army's daily dozen warm-up exercises straight out of my dad's old WWII basic training manual, and my own personal 13th, slinging a dozen baseballs through the old rubber tire hanging from a low branch on the Jacaranda tree to the left of my bungalow.

In the early summer when my aim's a little off, I'll go out of the strike zone, hit rubber and be punished with a shower of blue flowers. But that doesn't happen very often. Yes, I'm good with finances, and I have a semi-famous ass. But there's this one other thing I'm more proud of than anything—it's a useless skill in this man's modern world, and maybe it's even a silly habit, but I can really sling a baseball. The speed-gun over at the batting cages says I can still fire that pill over 85 miles per hour, and I also feature a wicked curve ball to go along with my figure. The Larch-ster and I have made a pile, betting a hundred bucks, anybody who can catch Speed-ball Clair, three in the strike zone. Easy money! If my fast ball doesn't whiz past them, the big, slow curve takes them out. Women haven't had a hardball league since the 1950's, and it's just too damn bad. I'm pretty sure it's one of the reasons we take out our frustrations on men.

I threw eleven in the zone before my mind wandered off and I started wondering where Jack had been going with his relationship conversation before he upended Steve's Porsche. I hit a rimmer that bounced back, so I had to fling an extra six throws, and then get my broom and plastic scoop bucket and sweep up. Jacarandas may be impressive with their cloud of vibrant blue flowers, but they are an almighty mess when they're blooming…just like Jack-the-boy-wonder, himself, I might add. As I finished, I noticed crazy old Ong Vung staring at me. He made a motion like he was drawing a line on the ground. I got the idea. He was on Jack's side and he could clip whatever he wanted. But the look on his face said Piss off, round-eyed bitch. I nodded a dare in his direction like I might come over and squash him like a flea, and in another moment he was gone.

My arm felt good. I daydreamed I was starting for the Dodgers this afternoon. I did a few stretches on the deck on Jack's side of the pool. Damn, they should let women in the game. A few innings, even. From my vantage point I could see Eddie Barth was watching me out the window while he sat at his little desk in the guest ghost nook. Jack was nearby, one-finger pecking at the computer that sat on the big unpolished chunk of black slate he used for a desk. The computer was at the center of a mess of open books, scripts and handwritten chunks of dialogue on yellow notepads. He had the most powerful personal home computer known to man, and there he was, Wild Jack Larch, entering his burly-man literary notions one letter at a time with his stubby forefingers.

Even from across the way, I could see the big white patch covering the stitches on his forehead, and the startling purple-and-black bruises around his eyes that made him look like a dazed raccoon. Jack favored big Ray-Ban aviator sunglasses, so, to me, he didn't look that much different. The two of them had already been to Starbucks, the ones for the road now cooling and forgotten on their desks.

The minor crack-up had only added to Jack's legend. His PR agency had been on the job. The spin was, he sacrificed Steve's priceless Porsche on purpose, actually saved a poor, ignorant Okie family that had no business standing on the California people's asphalt while they gawked at the homes of the rich & famous. From all appearances, Jack's flacks had done a terrific job; even the baristas down at 'Bucks knew he had heroically wheeled his way through certain disaster to save the day, just like Dunk Stingray.

After his little smack-up, you'd think Jack would have allowed somebody else to motor him about, at least for a couple of weeks, but no chance on that one. He couldn't even wait for my Porsche to get out of the shop. On the way back from the hospital he stopped in at Beverly Hills Classic Cars and bought a 1956 coral pink Ford Thunderbird with less than 100,000 miles on it, or so the if-fy speedometer said. It bottomed out on bad springs and handled like a hairy little road-monster, but Jack drove away from the dealership like the Little Old Lady From Pasadena, that is, like Jack-the-batster out of hell.

This morning, back in the safety of Jack's study, the Goy Ghost sits in his nook and does nothing. I wondered if he is still quivering inside from his coffee run. Jack tracks the monitor in front of him with the little finger on his left hand, muttering to himself.

Eddie had been watching as I did my daily dozen and flung the pills through the tire. Eddie was still a big fan of mine but it was too late for him; we'd been lovers for a week or two until he fell for first one and then the other and then simultaneously both of my Gal Pals associates. That was another minor key Hollywood revelation. Eddie, who was married and looked solid as a spokesman for a national bank was a hummingbird in the flowery field of romance. After I decided not to kill him, we'd declared a truce, and over time realized we became allies…I guess you could call us comrades and survivors in the Jack Larch Wars.

I had on my orange halter top and a pair of tight white-and-orange striped shorts, and I posed for them next to the big granite rock waterfall before skipping in like a schoolgirl.

"You're a Vargas pin-up girl from the 1940's!" Eddie shouted his approval. He knew Jack didn't mind him saying that, convinced as the Larch-ster was that his ghost was Hollywood Lite.

Appropriate Eddie should bring up Vargas, I was thinking. In the Vargas hey-day back in 1942, Dunk Stingray would have been in his prime— 26 or maybe 36, and in his hot joy of full manhood. I sashayed on over.

"Hi, guys."

"I love the retro look, Clair," Eddie said
Jack didn't say anything.
"Jack."
"Yes, Clair?" he asked, his voice flinty and determined.
Jack can be a pisser when he's trying to concentrate on his work.
"Where's my latte?"
"Uhh, Eddie here forgot." Jack had one of his pairs of
heavy steel Chinese exercise balls in his hand. They give off a soft
musical chime as he performs awkward maneuvers to move them
around, first in one hand and then in the other. There are times
when Jack is very big on finding his inner harmony. I think he's
just trying to hold off tunnel carpal syndrome.

"You both forgot," I said. "Anyway, I don't care—it's
shopping day!" I was feeling good. I had flung 11 of 12 through
the tire, I had places to go and things to do. Nails, facial, purses on
sale at Neiman Marcus.

Jack went back to his monitor, muttering to himself. "Then
Dunk says, 'I'm feeling the first flush of victory, here...' Naah,
'First flush of victory.' Did I write that? Flush is for toilets.
Jesus, Hemingway would crap his pants."

Jack never forgets that his idol, Ernest Hemingway, once
said The first draft of everything is shit. Jack always claimed he
knew how a story ended when he typed down the first word...but
after that, the real work began. With Jack, as apparently things
literati had been with Ernest, no novel or screenplay is ever
finished until the final, final, final deadline. That's when Jack's
publisher comes around screaming law suit, and Connie has to
come over and physically tear the manuscript out of his hands.
Even after that, going over the galleys is another rite of passage,
full of storm, thunder and a brilliant spectrum of delays.

Eddie took over on Jack's still-warm latte and handed me
his own. The big modern floor-to-ceiling slab glass windows were
open and the flesh-colored hollyhocks, purple foxgloves and
brilliant, velvety lavender and yellow petunias were rioting in a
full flush of colors in the faux English Garden. I was thinking,
See, 'flush' actually works for flowers. I said faux English Garden
because nothing was seeded, the plants were individually set in
place in a rare act of reluctant cooperation by my Hispanic illegal
under the guidance of Jack's cone head, who was not about to

actually put his hands in dirt. From where Jack sat, he could hear the waterfall tumbling into our black-bottomed pool. He said it gave him ideas.

"Victory makes me feel like sex," he muttered to his inner muse.

"No," Eddie shook his head. "Come on, Jack-ster. Dunk offed a couple of flaky Bulgarian wanna-bees, for God's sake. It's not like he won the Grand Assassin's Cup. I say just cut the whole scene. You don't need it. When you see him in the restaurant in Buenos Aries, you know he's made it back."

Jack gave Eddie a savage glare, but he took the literary bullet without flinching. Jack looked calm, but I knew the inner Larch was mulling dark thoughts about his adaptation partner. The Goy Ghost is a goddamn nobody, he was thinking. The jester can say anything he wants—I'm still the king!

I hung onto the paper cup containing Jack's lukewarm Grande Latte and took the steps two at a time up to his writer's inner sanctum. The mess in his bedroom made me pause. It looked like he'd brought back two or three girls from wherever he'd been clubbing on the weekend. I could almost see them, one on each side, lovingly holding his hands while he narrated how he'd destroyed his half-million dollar Porsche, once owned by Steve McQueen himself, to save a poor Okie and his family. I shook my head, trying to shake the unwelcome images from my mind. To work, Clair—to work!

His small study desk was the usual mess. I paid his bills, gathered his checks for deposit and read his letters, which were mostly fan mail except for one. This one must have slipped behind the others, because it was dated right after New Years day, the first week in January. It was sad, in a way, because it was from the widow of an old army buddy, informing Jack that his friend had died. See there, how little I knew about the Jack-ster! He'd had another actual friend beside me, and I hadn't even known it. I stacked the open letters in a pile with the silver letter opener on top of them. Jack would come up later in the day, put the letter opener on the shelf where it belonged and sweep the letters into the waste can without reading them.

Hey, I was done! I jumped to my feet and snapped off the green shade reading lamp on his desk. Then I bounded down the stairs, headed for the door. Free at last! I could practically taste the orange Jamba Juice I was going to have for breakfast. I paused on the way out.

"Can I drive your new bird?"

"You can drive my bird any time," Eddie chuckled, but I pursed my lips at him. That wiped the quick grin off his face. Eddie'd had his shot with me, and he'd blown it.

I gave my voice that school-girlish, pleading tone, and push my full red lips into a sexy pout, "Please, Jack. Please, please, please, please…?"

It was a good act, but Jack was definitely not in the mood.

"No, Clair-Bear," he growled at me. "Christ, my new car's a classic."

I tossed my honey-blonde curls.

"Jack, don't be such a bastard. It's not new and it's not a *classic.*"

"Marilyn Monroe owned that car, and she hardly ever drove it. It was her *personal* car."

"Jack, a couple days ago you put my car on life support."

There wasn't much he could say to that. He sighed, "If you have to go out, take the Jag."

I looked over at Eddie. We'd developed our own language. He did a little sideways tilt of his head and a brief squint of his face combined with a shrug that meant Let it pass.

"No bird for you, Clair," Jack said again for effect.

I gave Eddie another look, this one that said I was thinking I'd like to tell Jack where to stuff his bird. But I pulled myself back from the edge, the way I generally did with the Larch-ster. The cream-yellow Jag was a sweet little number in its own right (Jack ran around telling everybody it was once owned by one of the stars on General Hospital), and, after all, I needed a ride, and the Jag was light-years better than a taxi.

"Oh, all right," I told him, giving my voice just enough push so he could figure I was not amused. I put on a show, flouncing through the study like I'd gotten a mad on. My real aim was to make my getaway before Jack had time to change his mind, but then I remembered the letter from his dead friend's widow. I paused, framed in the doorway that led from the study to the great room, a huge dining hall with a giant fireplace and a long, heavy table that could seat twenty-six people if they owned the right film credits or maybe had been nominated for an Oscar.

"You got a letter from Miami," I told him.

"The town sent me a letter?"

I've already told you; Jack can be a real bastard. I bit my lip, struggling to keep my temper. "No, Jack. The girl."

"It's Mi-a Mi-i. Mia My." He repeated the name for emphasis, then paused, thinking about it. "Jesus, now you read my mail?"

"I've read your mail for years, remember? You let it pile up. Checks from publishers, threats from crazy people—everything."

"Yeah, yeah. What did Mia My say?"

Jack wasn't really listening. His mind was miles and continents away. He was in the southern hemisphere, marching along with Dunk Stingray as the heroic fellow sauntered out of the barren Andes foothills after dispatching three Bulgarian assassins.

"Her husband died," I told him.

I have no idea how those three words will affect Jack. I was just passing on the news from a letter he obviously hadn't cared enough about to open, even though it had been sitting on the cluttered oak secretary desk in his bedroom for months. He was in another of his foul moods, I had his permission to use the Jag, and all I wanted now was to get out of the study before some other bad thing happened. But I wasn't fast enough.

Jack stood up with a sudden jerking motion and shouted without turning around to face me. He was half-crouched over and his sudden piercing cry was that of a man with a big spear or stage-four cancer in his guts. The harshness in his voice startled Eddie, and it was more than enough to freeze me in my tracks.

"What?! NO!! It can't be!! How?" Jack screamed his anguish, talking more to God or the devil than anyone in the room. *"How could this happen?!"*

As I've said, I'd been around Jack for quite a while, competing with the fast young crowd that wants to hang with 'the new Hemingway,' as he likes to be called. In that moment I'm sure I looked every bit my nearly thirty-six years…and more. My eyes darted from Jack to Eddie. I was feeling uncertain, and even afraid—not of Jack , but for him.

"Some rich kid lost control of his daddy's SUV," I told him. "From what Mi-a Mi-i wrote, I think he saved her when he pushed her out of the way."

Jack sagged back in his chair.

"Yeah," he said to himself, talking in a low, defeated voice, "That's something he would do."

I was staring at Jack, shaking my head, the fun sucked out of my day. Eddie looked out the window and didn't say anything. I walked back across the huge open area and sat next to Jack in the leopard print chair I use when I have to over-the-shoulder proofread for him, and after a while I gently ran one hand through his unruly stand up hair.

"Jack, I honestly didn't know," I told him. "You never write him."

"I send Christmas cards," he grumbled. He glared at me as if everything was my fault, "Go do your shopping."

I knew him well enough to let the thoughtless, abrasive side of his personality slide on by. It was part of survival in The House of Jack. I didn't move. I could hear the antique windup clock ticking in another room as the silence lengthened between the three of us.

"What the hell, Jackie-poo," I said after a while. "I've got more purses than I know what to do with."

"Joe was blind as a bat, you know," Jack said. "Lenses thicker than mine. Course, I didn't wear glasses in those days. But Joe Bates did. He didn't really even belong in a war zone."

"Nobody belongs in a war zone, Jack," I told him.

"Don't give me that liberal, politically correct peacenik-commie-bullshit crap," he responded, his voice like hot iron.

"Maybe I should go," Eddie said.

"No," I told him. "Jack needs you now, Eddie. We need you."

Jack said nothing. For all his action/adventure stories, he'd never been a sharing sort of guy about the real war he'd once experienced. It would be weeks before I knew the entire bittersweet story of his old Vietnam buddy Joe Bates and the achingly lovely Mia My Nguyen. For the moment, Jack Larch stared silently out the window. He studied the tan-brown California hills that perked like young breasts behind my guest house, and then he actually made a beginning.

"It was 1964," he said finally, in a voice that lacked his usual storytelling fervor. Jack's voice was so quiet I could barely hear him and I didn't think he'd continue, but then he went on. "We'd assassinated the Vietnamese president a few years before."

"Jack, we don't kill presidents."

Jack gave me a strained, sorrowful look. Eddie held up a quiet, restraining hand in my direction.

"She's trying, Jack," Eddie said, interceding for me with the erratic Larch-ster, now struggling with some deep emotional knot beyond anything either of us had ever seen in him.

I thought I understood the chemistry. I was trying but I was just a woman and I'd gotten it wrong.

"Okay, Jack," I said, throwing up my hands. "I'm sorry. I'll be quiet."

It was a thin apology, but Jack accepted it with a nod and struggled to gather his thoughts. I bit my lip and held my peace.

"His name was Ngo Dinh Diem," he said after a while. Jack's voice was now so quiet Eddie and I had to strain to hear him. "What we don't realize at the time, with the South Vietnamese strongman gone, the whole country is about to melt down into one big dung-heap."

Bees, dragonflies and a green jewel of a hummingbird dart and flash over the deep blue foxgloves and the pink hollyhocks outside Jack's open floor-to-ceiling glass windows, and, as Eddie and I listen to the sadness in Jack's voice, their soft buzzing sounds magnify and become more and more intense until they are the muffled roar you hear on the inside of a passenger jet airplane…

CHAPTER 4

"It's late June 1964," Jack tells us, "and Joe and I have crawled—mind you, with a good deal of trepidation—up the gangplank into a converted cargo plane. Fuck trepidation—scared shit-less would be a better description. We take off from Travis Air Force Base near Oakland, and shoot west over the Pacific. I say converted cargo plane; that flying cow was an early Boeing 707 cargo plane, and the U.S. Army had made it into a troop carrier by bolting rows of old bench stadium seats to the floor, actual wood-and-metal rows with fold-up wooden seats on them. There were no windows except for the six little roundies on the emergency exit doors. Talk about cheesy! They had jerry-rigged lines of dim little 40 watt light bulbs overhead—hell, you could see where they stapled the exposed wires to the micro-board ceiling, and we weren't getting anything in the way of fresh air.

We stop overnight in Hawaii, supposedly for repairs. You know how that one goes; the fly-boys want a sweet night humping the civilian stewardesses while looking out on Oahu Beach or wherever. Meanwhile, we're supposedly on standby and restricted to temp barracks on base. I couldn't stand it, I went downtown. Technically I guess I would have been AWOL, but nobody caught me…No harm, no foul.

Next morning we take off on a long haul to Guam, and then a shorter hop to Clark Air Force Base in the Philippines. We deplane for two hours in the hot tropical sun, mai tais and grins from the G.I.s stationed there—you know, glad it's you and not me, sucker—and then back on the plane, next stop, Vietnam.

So it's a few hours later and we're inside our dark inner tube, cruising above a thick cloud cover that's like a more or less permanent grey shroud over Southeast Asia. Our air jockey throttles back and the whole damn aircraft shudders a bit as it slows, hesitating for a moment like it's thinking this might not be such a good idea, and then it plunges us into whatever fate is waiting down there.

I remember like it was yesterday; Joe Bates and I are arguing about this letter he'd gotten some weeks before. The guy is really annoying me. He's turning it over and over in his hands. It's this pastel blue envelope, one of those fancy little square jobs, and it's addressed in this neat little feminine hand, "A" for penmanship.

Me, I'm the original Mister Merciless. 'Last chance to open your goddamn Dear Joe letter,' I tell him. 'Last chance. Get it over with, sap-head.'

'I'd rather not,' Joe says back at me. He sets the letter down on his lap, takes off his thick glasses and starts wiping them on an old white cotton handkerchief he carries around with him like a goddamn baby blanket.

'Well then, Specialist 4th Class Joseph Bates, put the goddamn thing away. I'm trying to write down a few thoughts of my own over here. You know, last reflections as we dip into the mud and the blood, that sort of thing.'"

Jack looked up at Eddie and me, shaking his head as if it all might have been a dream, "You see, I was in it for the full ride—12 months in Vietnam—but Joe only had three or four months left as a soldier; he shouldn't have been there at all. It was one of those military screw-ups; back then they tried not to assign short-timers to Vietnam, it cost too much to fly them in and orient them, and then in a few months they'd have to send them right back State-side. But it had happened and Joe never complained about stuff like that, so there we are, packed like sardines in the dark and claustrophobic tube of a converted 707.

We take that last, decisive dip and sink into the clouds. I get these butterflies in my gut. I know we're going in because the soldiers lucky enough to be sitting next to the exit door windows, which are the only goddamn windows in our compartment, sing out every time anything happens.

'We're in the soup!' some dopey PFC yells out.

'Yep, nothing but fog on this side,' a warrant officer yells from across the aisle. I mean, what a bunch of lame brains, like you could have fog on only one side.

'I look over and Joe is finally, finally, finally putting his letter away, stuffing it in a worn copy of Joseph Conrad's novella

"Youth" that he'd been carrying around with him.

'Thank God,' I sigh. But in the next moment he's changed his mind, out comes the blue envelope again, and now Joe is examining the front as if it might contain some hidden cryptographic message that he'd missed.

I couldn't stand it. I yell at him, 'For God's sake, Joe! Jesus, holy fucking Christ, will you please open your stupid, stinking letter?!'

So Joe gives me a big, dramatic sigh and starts to open his precious letter, but at that moment the plane tilts on its side like a carnival ride. Everybody flashes worried glances around, and our angle of descent increases from uncomfortable to frightening.

'What's going on here?' A Colonel barks out behind us..

'Planes coming in to Tan Son Nhut have been taking fire from the tree-line, sir,' a staff sergeant says, 'So our pilots set them down as fast as they can.'

I look over and Joe's face has gone white, but it has nothing to do with the angle of our airplane. His hands go limp and one page of blue stationary and a photo of a girl and a guy flutter to the floor. Even in the dim light, I can see the guy in the picture isn't Joe.

That's it for me. I'm disgusted. No more odes to the muse today. I jam my spiral notepad in a fatigues shirt pocket that is already stuffed with pencils and scraps of paper.

'As if I was going to get any work done here…' I grumble. But I shut my flapper when I see Joe has his head down with one hand over his face. Joe is trying to hide the fact that he's bawling like a baby. I reach down, pick up the letter and take a closer look at the photo. It was what I figured. The guy in the snapshot is a bearded hippie wearing a headband designed like a U.S. flag, with the peace sign replacing the field of stars. *Joe's replacement part*, I think to myself.

The pilot's voice comes crackling over the makeshift intercom, 'Okay, ladies and germs, we're going in…'

I'm thinking we're going to get through it okay but we have this huffy staff sergeant who has been acting like he is in charge of our little section of the airplane since we'd left Hawaii. Now this guy frowns, taking a hard look over at Joe. I know what he's thinking. *We don't like no cryin' in this man's army. Crying is for faggots and girls.*

'What the hell's wrong with that soldier?' he asks me.

Even back then I knew trouble when I saw it, and I guess I knew how to snuff it as well as any enlisted man. I shrug and point to Joe's letter. 'Bad news from home, sir. Some scum-sucking peacenik ran over Specialist Bates's dog.'

'Ohh…' The sergeant thought about it for a moment. 'Goddamn country's going to hell in a bucket.'

'Amen to that, sir,' I tell him.

The jet engines are whining and the three-ring circus continues. The Colonel is waving his hands in a swooping arc, I guess more to get the sergeant's attention than to indicate our angle of descent.

'Isn't this a little extreme, sergeant?' he asks in a pointed way, as if it's the non-com's fault.

'No sir, not really. One bullet from an old M-1 rifle can take out an engine. Our pilot will do his best so that doesn't happen.'

Joe Bates is still hunched over nearly sideways in his seat, only now he starts talking at me through his fingers. 'One minute ago I knew what I was going to be doing for the rest of my life.'

'Joe, that's so much crap I can hardly stand it. Admit it; you knew she was breaking up with you two weeks ago. That's why you didn't open the letter.'

'Whatever happened to true love?' he wails

'Well, safe to say, this isn't it.

Joe frowns and snatches his letter and the photo back from me. And our plane breaks under the cloud cover and drops toward the runway like a spent rock."

That was decades ago. It's today and Eddie and I are in the big writing room in Holmby Hills, listening to Jack. He goes silent behind his big desk, just looking out the window at the flowers and the bees. I'm not sure he's done talking or not. I figured it doesn't matter. The Larch-man is a storyteller, and now that he's started, sooner or later the entire world will know the whole Story of Joe.

Turns out, I was right. Also turns out, I got lots more than I bargained for.

CHAPTER 5

It was a week later, and things had gone back to something like normal. Jack and his ghost writer were off somewhere at one of the film studios 'pitching the Dunk,' as Jack liked to say. I was splashing backstrokes in the pool, eyes closed and skin soaking in the warm, early morning sun. Twelve lazy strokes, then turn and kick, going back the other way.

Ong Vung was clipping dangerously close to my bushes, so I yelled at him and he scuttled back to Jack's side. He gave me his evil one eye look from under his cone hat, but he disappeared around the corner of Jack's house, heading for the front, and I went back to my laps. I paused at one end to take a breather and was floating there with my eyes closed when a shadow crossed between me and the sunlight.

"You are Jack's daughter?" a voice asked. I squinted through one open eye and saw she was Oriental, petite and beautiful. She had to be nearly sixty, but with her high cheekbones and delicately formed features, she would have been beautiful at any age.

"No," I said, standing up in the waist-deep water. "Jack doesn't have a daughter. I live over there." I pointed to my house. I was staring at her; it was rude, I know, but I couldn't help myself.

"I know who you are," I said.

"Jack has told you I was coming?" She spoke English with a French overtone, and a spice of Southeast Asia tossed in. She was wearing a light beige Ann Klein two piece suit, and it looked perfect on her.

"No. But he has spoken of you. I would shake your hand, but—"

I started to draw back but she squatted poolside and extended her own hand to take mine.

"Mia My Nguyen-Bates," she said. "You must be the one who holds Jack together."

"Clair Moore. I was sorry to hear of your loss." Her hand was small, but warm and firm. Mia My was a little person by modern American standards, probably just over five feet, and perfectly proportioned. She gave me an intense look, not at all guarded, but, for the life of me, I had no idea what it meant.

"Thank you," she said, breaking her gaze to cast her look around the garden. "It is nice here. I like flowers…"

"Jack's doing a meeting at Universal. He'll be back after lunch, which means about two, probably."

"That's okay," she said. I could see she was at odd sorts, probably wondering how she was going to spend her day until Jack got back. It was another case of Larch-ster thoughtlessness. Jack, all emotion over the loss of his old pal Joe, had probably tossed her some vague sort of invitation, never thinking she'd take him up on it.

"You can hang out here, if you want. Jack's maid will make us some cold sandwiches."

"Jack has a maid now?" When she heard that one, her eyes seemed to hold an amused secret.

"Jack has everything," I said. "Money, power, fame, a day-housekeeper… and still the same old fire in his belly."

"Friends?" she asked. "He has friends?"

That brought me up short. "Not so much."

"That is not good."

I wouldn't have shared confidences about Jack with just anyone, but there was something about Mia My that opened my cold heart, if only a little bit. "He has lots of show biz pals, but… I'm starting to get the feeling your husband might have been the only true friend he ever had."

"Good time Charlies." She nodded gravely. "That is too bad for him."

I hoisted my way out of the pool, slipped into some go-aheads, and threw a towel around my shoulders.

"Let's sit over there," I said, pointing to the redwood table with a dark blue sun umbrella outside Jack's study. "I'll get Maria to fix us something."

By the time I'd returned, Mia My had a neat stack of three tan suitcases next to her, probably rolled in from the front.

"I paid the taxi man," she said. "I hope I didn't over-tip him. I never know what is the right amount in America. In France, 15%, that is the rule. Here, anything is never enough.."

"Are you going to stay with Jack?"

"No," she said. "He informs me I am to stay with you."

I shook my head and we shared a slow smile.

"Full of surprises, that Jack," I said.

"If it is a problem, I stay at a hotel."

"No problem at all. I have a guest room, plenty of space."

Maria brought us tacos and chips with guacamole dip, and tall, frosty glasses of iced tea with lime slices. Mia My ate in a way that reminded me of another age and time, a time when graciousness and manners were not scoffed at and meals were for pleasant conversation and getting together, as well as for eating. I liked her from the moment I laid eyes on her.

"How did you meet Jack?" I asked. I didn't feel I was prying; it was just something to keep the conversation going.

"I'll trade you that if you tell me about the baseballs."

"You first."

"No, you."

Mia My picked up one of the balls that had rolled under table. She walked over to my makeshift mound and flipped the ball at the rubber tire. It was a girlish little lob, but it did hit rubber, bouncing back about half way to the mound.

"Not bad, I said."

"Yes, for a girl." We exchanged a knowing glance.

I walked over and picked up the ball. "You have to rear back and then use your body like a sling shot. Like this." I did a little windup and whistled the ball through the tire.

Mia My gave me an appraising look, "You are an accomplished pitcher of baseballs."

"When I was in high school in Texas. We had a small school, and I was better than the boys, so they let me. I actually tried out minor league pro, one time. Not one girl in a million can say that."

"What happened?"

"It's a sad story. You sure you want to hear it?"

By this time we were walking back to the table. My new friend had a natural way of getting people to talk about themselves.

"Not one girl in a million…" she prompted.

"Well, I was young and foolish then, and my mom and dad were gone. I was on my own and when this guy called to say he'd read about me in the local paper and did I want to try out with the Modesto Nuts, I said yes."

"And did you?"

"Well, they sent me air fare and told me to show up on a Sunday afternoon, which seemed a little odd, but I hopped a plane from Texas to Modesto, California. I have an address, and when I show up, it's the stadium. This guy who contacted me turns out to be a Public Relations guy, and he says because it's minor leagues I can go right out there and pitch."

"So good to be true."

"Exactly. They've set up a small room for me to change, but I don't see my uniform. I poke my head out the curtains they've rigged for me, and the PR guy's assistant says, 'Oh, it's right over there.' He points to this stringy little bikini hanging on a hook by the wall. 'You expect me to wear *that*?' 'Hey, it's the team colors,' he says.

"I'm so steamed I can hardly stand it. It's not a real trial— I'm some sort of publicity stunt. I go out there, and the real game hasn't even started yet. The ump is standing there, munching a bag of Cheetos. They're laughing and not making any secret about it. The big speculation is, how much of my crack they're going to see when I kick my leg."

"Kick your leg?"

I went through the pitching motion so Mia My could get the idea.

"So you are a night club act for sport fans."

"Exactly. But before I can think what to do, the umpire says 'Plaaaaay Ball!,' the catcher lobs me a baseball like I'm in third grade and some chump steps up to home plate with a bat in his hands. I throw that pill so fast it zips right past the catcher's mitt and hits him in the mask.

"Hey, tone it down, babes," he warns me. The batter has been too busy looking at my boobs, which, admittedly are sticking out of my skimpy little bikini. But the ump tosses me a new baseball and the batter steps in and I whiz a fastball right past him. 'Strike two!' the umpire says with a happy flourish.

Well, this doesn't set well with the hitter, who happens to be the Nuts' number one slugger. He fancies himself something of a *heavy hitter,* maybe like Mickey Mantle or Ted Williams, so I whistle another one up there, and he swings too late. 'Strike two!' the umpire says. 'Wait a minute,' I say. 'That already was strike two.' 'He gets as many strike twos as he wants,' the ump tells me.

I see how it is. It's not a real game and they're just going to make fun of me. There's a ball bag lying there, so I pick it up and trudge back to the mound.

'Nice ass, Babe,' the ump says to my back.

The batter gets back in the box. 'Lay it on me, lay it on me, lay it on me,' he chants.

He can hear the fans jeering. "Can't you hit a girl?" So he crowds the plate.

This gives him a better chance to hit, and so I brush him back with a close one. Maybe a little too close, because it sends him sprawling back in the dust.

He gets up and dusts himself off. 'You better not try that again!'

He crowds in again, so this time I bean him on the head. Too bad, he's not even bothered with his batting helmet, so he's sitting on the ground with a concussion and is going to be on the injured list for a week.

"Hey!" the umpire yells at me, like it's all my fault.

I've got another ball out of the bag, and since the catcher is already set up, I sucker him with a big fat slow curve, in the strike zone but a little high. It misses his mitt entirely, but catches the ump in the side of the head.

As he's taken off his mask, he goes over like tipping a cow and now I'm hitting two for two. The ump picks up a bat and starts out to the mound like he's going to brain me, but I take another ball from the bag and stare at him, and he thinks twice about it. That's all the break I need and I beat it for the dugout with the fans cheering and booing and hooting like crazy. And that was my big league baseball career. I could do a movie, "Six Pitches in a Bikini."

"That is funny…and sad," Mia My says.

We're back at the table near the pool and I can see from the wistful look on her face she's thinking back over the years. Jack's dumped his old buddy's widow on me without any warning, but *surprise,* I end up liking her.

"Hey, you don't have to talk about anything," I tell her. "We're just a couple girls hanging out by the old swimming hole."

"I don't mind. I want to talk about it. I think it's better if I do."

"Maybe it is…" I tell her. I've had my own shrink sessions. "Sometimes talking does help."

"It starts with a coincidence," Mia My says. "It is the sort of happening many women will assure themselves is fated or predetermined. You see, Clair, the same day that Jack and Joe landed in Saigon happened to be my 22nd birthday."

"You met Joe the day he came to Vietnam?

"No." Mia My shook her head "That is not what I mean. I met Joe a few days later. But that day he landed was a big day for Mia My Nguyen, too, because it was the day my mother, Ba Nguyen, declared me a hopeless old maid for the third year in a row."

"No, a mother wouldn't do that," I protested.

"Oh yes, my mother would," Mia My smiled. "On my 22nd, she huffed and pouted and sighed all day long, and then she replaced my birthday party with a mourning ceremony."

"No!"

"Oh, yes! There were only three of us for the festivities. I, of course, was the featured guest, the object of mourning. Then there was my mother, wearing a very simple dress, but sexy. Mama loved sexy. Tight around here." Mia My cupped under her breasts and lifted a little. "And my dear Auntie Kai made three. Auntie Kai was in true my mother's husband's aunt, which made her my great aunt. We had two servants waiting table, and it was very full with many food stuffs often prepared for funerals and state gatherings.

"Doesn't sound too happy," I said.

"Oh, so very grim, and all on purpose. Mama wore a dress of black chiffon, and her eye liner was smudged as if she had been crying. We sat down and Mama started right in on me.

'I myself was married when I was 17,' she said.

'And we all know how well that went,' Auntie Kai shot back at her. My father was exiled in Europe, not by the government but as the result of a falling out with Mama and Auntie Kai.

'That's not the point,' my mother replied. 'The point is children, the next generation. Life must be served.'

'Well, I guess you did your job,' Auntie Kai replied. She gave me a fleeting smile and patted a small wrapped gift she'd brought to the table. I knew it was also Auntie Kai who had bribed the servants to run out and brave the afternoon showers and Mama's glares to buy a bright orange balloon and tie it to the back of my chair. In spite of the balloon, which still bravely bobbed up and down though it had lost much of its gas, the rest of the dinner was a sober affair with many references to long-dead ancestors who had given selflessly to preserve the Nguyen dynasty. I nearly could not stand it.

'It's not my fault he died!' I finally blurted out right in the middle of the soup. 'He was a very old man!'

'With shriveled testicles,' Auntie cackled, agreeing with me. 'Hard to see him fathering anybody, much less the next generation.'

"Who died?" I asked. I was a little lost at what was happening in my guest's story.

"I'm sorry," Mia My said. "It's an old business for me, and I get ahead of myself. You see, not one week before Joe landed at Tan Son Nhut airport with our friend Jack, Mama handed me over in marriage to a horny old Frenchman named LeCroix. He was a very rich fellow in the bakery business."

"So you were married?"

Mia My nodded with a soft smile. And then the smile faded and she shrugged, remembering how it was. "It was horrible, every young girl's nightmare. We were married by an old priest, an old wrinkle face with the white hair, a priest nearly as old as my husband, and after being married to me for five or six minutes, my new husband died."

"Five minutes!?"

"Yes, he fell down on the cold tiles of the cathedral, dead as a stone. We were still in the church, standing at the foot of the altar where we were posing for the wedding portrait, a picture of the old goat and his beautiful young bride. Anyway, that marriage death had only been one week before, and here Mama was berating me at my birthday party, and honestly, I'd done my best. I probably shouldn't have said anything, but I was mad and it just came blurting out. 'He was older than dirt!' I shouted.

'He wasn't that old,' Mama said, spitting the words out. My mother is a tooth off the original fang, you know what that means?"

"I can figure it out, sort of, but I don't exactly know."

"In Vietnam, we have the tiger lady, Su Tu Hao Gam—the tiger ladies of Hao Gam. You don't mess with a tiger lady."

"Are you a tiger lady?"

"Some a little bit, maybe," Mia My smiled, waggling her hand back and forth in a so-so gesture. "But no, I tell you true, Mama was ten times bad, far worse than me. It was not my fault—you see, old man LeCroix was truly one very old man. His departure for eternity was not my doing. How am I to be blamed he chose that moment to slip away to his little piece of heaven or hell?" I told Mama that, and Auntie Kai tried to hold back a chuckle but it came out like a happy little snort. 'Chet roi!' she said. 'Dead already!' LeCroix collapsed under the weight of his marriage vows!"

Mia My nodded, the drama of LeCroix's passing still amusing to her after all the years, "I tell you, Clair, it is true. One moment the man is standing there like an ancient crab, all red-faced and proud with his bony arm around my shoulder. Then he gives a gasping shout, clutches his chest and sinks to the floor without another word."

"Wow! What happened then?"

"Oh, such a mess! Yelling and running up and down the aisles, as if that would help. His children are shaking their fists and screaming that I'd poisoned him and his grandkids are crying and looking confused. The priest is spilling the oils of the last sacrament here and there while some army medic who happened to be in the congregation tries pounding LeCroix's chest."

"But you were legally married to a man who owned a bakery."

"Twenty-three bakeries and 200 bread trucks," she corrected me. "But not to last. His heirs were quick to annul the nuptials."

"Sad," I said. I was starting to like this plucky lady who'd had such adventures in a far corner of the world.

"Yes, double-sad," Mia My smiled, "Mama had to content herself with her old ranking as the number three or four landholder in South Vietnam."

"But when did you meet Joe?"

"Oh, forgive an old woman." She had been marching around and animatedly waving her arms as she retold the story of her wedding. Now she sat back down and took a sip of her drink. She looked at me with a puzzled smile, as if I might be boring her.

I prompted her, "You were at your birthday party and your Mama is leaning on you to get married and have babies."

"Yes…" Mia My seemed lost in her memories, thousands of miles and millions of light-years away from me, just as Jack had been a few days before. But then a smile touched her lips, "I was so mad at Mama I wouldn't shut up and respect my elders. 'Since you're in the mood,' I shouted at her, 'let's parade out the entire line of losers! How about the noble Major Tran. Let's hear it for Tran-the-Stupid.'

'He was not stupid!'

"Mama's voice was going up," Mia My said.. "She could really shriek. On her top end, she could boil water and peel old paint right off of walls. But she had insulted me and I was twenty-two and it was my birthday and nothing was going to stop me on that night.

"Who was Tran-the-Stupid?"

"He was the other man who dared ask my hand in holy matrimony. I could hardly hold myself from laughing in Mama's face. 'He blew himself up with his own grenade,' I told her. 'That's hardly intellectually advanced.'

'Mama pounded both fists on the table like an outraged French nobleman, 'Since the age of sixteen you have fought off every arrangement we have tried to make in your behalf!'

'I should have the say in my own life!'

'I give up on you,' she said. 'I am not meant to have grandchildren.'

'Be honest. You don't want grandchildren, dear,' Auntie Kai interjected.

'Then what?' my mother shrieked. I checked around the room. No paint was peeling yet, but it might at any moment.

'You want another plantation and two hundred and fifty trucks to deliver fresh LeCroix French bread all over the country every morning.'

'Three hundred trucks!' Mama thundered. 'And I'm finished with this!' And with that last bit of fury, she threw down her linen napkin and left the table."

"Wow, again. Your mother was a bitch."

"Tiger lady," Mia My agreed with one small nod of her head.

"So then you went downtown and met Joe?"

"No, nothing so simple, Clair. Be patient with me. I will tell it all to you."

By then, Mia My was working on another glass of tea. It was nearly one thirty, and no sign of Jack. Neither of us seemed to have anywhere we had to be, so I nodded and she continued in her softly accented voice.

"Once the cook is sure Mama was gone, she brings us out a small lemon cake and a pot of tea.. 'Cake by LeCroix,' she says with a mischievous smile. 'They make the best.'

'Yes,' Auntie Kai adds with a giggle, 'but eat fast, because they don't last. Open your present, child.'

She has given me a golden ring, made in the image of a dragon."

There by the pool in Holmby Hills, Mia My held her right hand out to me and I saw a heavy, boldly carved ring. "Twenty-four carat, Vietnam red-gold," she said. It is worn smooth in spots, and it glows with a reddish light that is somewhere close to magic.

"Twenty-four carat?"

"Very soft. I have pictures, every three or four years I take it in and have it re-molded. At the time, I thought it was too much of a gift. I told Auntie Kai, 'I can't take this.'

'A lover gave it to me, a long, long, long time ago,' Auntie said, and as she remembered, a mischievous grin lit her beloved old face.

'Shouldn't you keep it as a forever treasure, Auntie?'

'I will be keeping it, through you.'

"I slid the ring on my finger, and as I did so, I remembered my dream, the dream I'd had the night before. I decided to tell

Auntie Kai. You could tell her things like that, and she always understood.

'The other night I had a silly dream,' I said.

Auntie Kai's face grew serious. 'I love dreams. And there are no silly ones.' Auntie Kai also loved a nip in her drink. She neatly poured a measure of brandy from an ornately carved jade flask into her tea cup, and added a few drops to my own. 'A taste of the dragon,' she said. 'Now, about your dream. Tell me, dear child.'

'Well…it is a strange one…I was on my way home from L'ecole Francais and I was walking past the Hoi Viet-My and I met a young warrior-prince with a flaming lance. He rode a fierce white horse and he was incredibly handsome. He looked at me and smiled, and he said 'One day you will be mine!'

'*Tot nhet!* That is a very, very good dream,' Auntie Kai said.

'But the Vietnamese-American School isn't anywhere near L'ecole Francais. '

'Silly girl. In dreams that doesn't matter.'

'I know this is crazy, Auntie, but the warrior-prince was an American.'

'A *Nguoi My!* That will give your mother a heart attack.'"

"Why would your new friend being an American make any difference?" I asked.

Mia My nodded, acknowledging that it shouldn't matter. "Well, Clair" she said, "you have to know what it meant in that time and place to be an all French oriented family. My grandfathers on both sides were Frenchmen. *Nguoi Phap.* We were French Catholics in the land of Buddha, the Tao and the Animists, and everything we knew about Western Civilization came a la Francaise, and now the *Nguoi Phap* had retreated back to their homeland in Europe and we had the barbaric Americans and everybody we knew resented them taking over, and…"

"Yeah, I think I get it," I said. "How did your Auntie feel about it?"

"Auntie Kai was her own woman. I remember she pondered what I had said for all of two or three seconds and then said rapid fire, in our native tongue, 'This is your time and your life. Your Mama can go to her destiny any time. As she herself has said, she's already done her duty.'   She stood and raised her tea cup in a salute to me and to the orange balloon flying bravely at my side, 'Here's to the young American warrior-prince. May he find good fortune and warm love in your arms!'"

    And for what was not to be the last time, there were tears in Mia My's eyes. "And you know, Clair," she said, "That's just exactly what happened. Maybe not the white horse, but my Joe didn't need one. Everything else came to the real, just as in my dream…"

CHAPTER 6

Jack came thundering up our shared driveway at about dusk, and from the weight of the bags of Chinese carry outs he pulled out of his new pink bird's trunk, Mia My's arrival was no surprise. He lit my citrus oil lamps to keep away the mosquitoes and we gathered around my bubbled glass outdoor table to dine on garlic chicken, mu shu pork, honey-walnut shrimp and beef-and-broccoli-in-brown-sauce. Jack, who never ate Chinese, and had used nothing but a knife and fork since I'd known him, easily slipped a pair of chop sticks in his hand, reverting to his days in South Vietnam like he was putting on a pair of old slippers. Mia My did the same, but I didn't want to make a spectacle of myself so I retreated to my kitchen for a knife and fork.

Jack couldn't seem to get enough food or information. He launched into a string of questions about each of Joe and Mia My's children. Upon being assured they were all well; in college, working out in the world, happily married and so on, he settled back and studied Mia My. "Did Auntie Kai ever get used to the States?"

"No…she still lives in France."

"How old now?"

"Ninety-six. She talks of going back to Saigon, but we tell her the life there is too hard."

"*Bac Ho* City," Jack gently reminded her. He turned to me, "Bac Ho is Uncle Ho, short for their revered leader."

"I know that, Jack," I said.

"*Thanh pho, Ho Chi Minh.*" Mia My mused over that one with a slight shake of her head, "I never believed I'd see the day."

I felt like a stranger in my own home, and like I was an outsider to Jack, as well…to Jack, the good old Larch-ster, the one steady and close friend I've put up with—and, yes, enjoyed—for quite some time now. Okay, I felt jealous, but come on, that's just me. I was about to get up and leave them to their old memories when Mia My placed her hand on my wrist.

"Your dear Clair here has told me you've been talking about the old days."

"A little bit," he admitted. The way he said it, I wondered if he regretted sharing even that little bit with me.

"How much do you remember?"

"I remember it all," he said. He didn't look annoyed, he looked worried. That calmed me down. In my mind I started talking to myself, the way I used to when I was on the mound, three men on base and nobody out. *None of this was about me. Jack had his problems. Who knew? Maybe I could help.* I know that sounds foolish, but the one realization I'd had since the crash interrupted the only serious conversation Jack and I had ever had was that I cared what happened now. Happy-go-lucky Clair was no more, at least for the foreseeable future. My game was on the line here.

Mia My hadn't taken her hand from my arm. She seemed to read Jack's expression as she reached out with her other hand and placed it on his. "We all were young and foolish, Jack," she said. "Tell your Clair what it was like. She needs to know."

"Why?" he asked in a voice that seemed constricted with emotion.

"There is no one else here for you, Jack. Only Clair and me. And Clair needs to know because you need to tell it to her."

That seemed to give Jack plenty to think about. He sat back, staring to the southwest over his rooftop at the low bowl filled with interlaced strings of street lights that spread away to the black line where the ocean began.

"Well…early 1964…I was telling you about Joe's letter…"

I could see he was only half-convinced this wasn't a bad idea. But then the storyteller in him took hold and he was off and running again, yanked away to that time forty years ago when all their worlds were young and full of fear and hope and promise.

"The cargo jet carrying Joe and me lands hard at Tan Son Nhut. It taxis off the runway and it brakes so fast and unexpectedly that it snaps our heads back. These days, a ride like that would be the stuff of law suits. Tan Son Nhut was more than an airport, it was a big military base on the Western edge of Saigon. The

Americans shared space there with the South Vietnamese.

We're mighty edgy after our corkscrew dive and bone-jarring landing. Everybody was feeling a little scared, wondering what would happen next. From inside, we hear a metal wheel staircase slam against the side of the plane, and the door behind the pilot's compartment pops open and there's a push-and-shove, all us soldiers eager to get out that door at the same time. Everybody is dazed and blinking in the light of the gloomy, overcast day, and maybe we're staggering about a little bit, to boot. It's mid-afternoon delta weather, heavy with moisture, and with that indescribable thick and rich smell of jungle—all mixed with the rank odor of spent jet fuel and motor oil. After the first rush to get off the plane, the rest of us come out in two's and threes, making our uncertain way down the metal stairway.

I remember Joe and I gingerly stepping out together; we're hunched over like frightened little turtles."

"No grand Dunk Stingray entrance?"

Jack grinned at me and made a deprecating sound with his lips.

"Clair, we're like frightened rabbits. Our eyes are flicking in every direction, looking for snipers. Of course, we don't see any. There isn't much of anything to see other than a few rusty tin Quonset huts and a general clutter of one-story structures of unpainted wood to one side of the long empty runway. The air is heavy and there's no wind; a yellow-and-red striped Republic of Vietnam flag hangs limp alongside the stars & stripes in front of a whitewashed cinder block building. At that moment I'm not feeling so good. I am terribly aware of the long sweep of low delta lands that stretches away into nothing on the other side of the wide concrete runways. I'm thinking *What have I gotten myself into?*

'It's okay, nugs,' our trusty staff sergeant pipes up. He's been through this before, and he knows what we are thinking. 'Nobody's shooting at us. The tree-line's about a mile over that way.' He gives a careless wave across the runway.

Joe squints through his thick glasses in the general direction where the non-com is pointing and then he scrambles down the metal stairs, taking them in a rush to the ground. I wasn't all that reassured, but I followed him.

Our feet hit solid concrete and we are in Southeast Asia. And this is the honest-to-God's truth, the next moment we are greeted by three teenage Vietnamese schoolgirls, little girls, looking all pink and cream and violet in their pastel colored, slit skirt *ao gai* dresses and long white silk pants.

'Wew-come to Vietnam!' they babble like a litany, and they offer us lotus flower buds. Joe scowls and starts to walk past, but I grab his arm.

'Joe, come on, be a sport—they're welcoming us to their homeland.' I give the girls a little bow, *'Chao, co. Cam ong, co.'* Hello, young miss. Thank you, young miss.

'Oh, you speak Vietnam!' The tentative smiles widen on their fresh young faces. *'Chao, Ong My!'* Hello, Mister Americans! And with that, they hand us each a flower.

Joe shakes his head, but I take both of the pale pink buds. I'm struck by the gesture. By this time a lot of the U.S press has already been duped by the commie propaganda. I'd read so much crap about how they hate us and we have no business being there that I'm glad somebody in Vietnam wants to see us. I feel I have to apologize for Joe, so I tell the little girls he is allergic to flowers.

'Al-err-zic?' A puzzled look comes over their faces, and you know, with his big heart, that gets to Joe and he softens a little.

'Never mind,' Joe interrupts my attempt to explain. He gives the prettiest one a little half bow and says his own, *'Chao, Co.'*

'The girl smiles back at him and, I swear, her teeth are spectacularly bad. She smiles and in a wink this attractive young maiden is transformed into something else by that mouth full of rotten, splintered and missing teeth. Joe tries to hide his surprise, but he literally has to take a step backwards. He gives me a look that says everything, then pulls himself into his stern military look, gives her a crisp salute and walks on.

We walk on until we spot a pimple-faced E-4 pushing through the crowded area and holding up a sign that reads 3RD RADIO RESEARCH UNIT. We don't know it yet but this is Toady, a back-stabbing prick of an orderly room ferret who will be a plague on our lives.

'3rd RRU. 3rd RRU,' he says. 'Anybody for the 3rd?'

Joe turns and sticks his hand in the air like a schoolboy, 'Over here!'

'You don't actually have to raise your hand, Joe,' I tell him. Seeing how much this bothers him, I will from that time on stick my own hand up whenever the opportunity presents itself…unless, of course, it's to volunteer for anything.

'Shut up, dick-head.' Joe tells me.

'You're sooo Regular Army, G.I.!' I keep after him. I was really on Joe in those days, no relief for the boy, you know? 'R.A., R.A.! Rah, Rah! R.A. Rat's Ass, man. I half-think you'll re-up and go lifer, thirty years and all the bennies. Joe Bates, lifer extraordinaire.'

'Jack, when you run on like that, I begin to question your sanity,' he tells me. That makes me smile inside. I'm starting to think maybe he is recovering from the sneak punch his nasty Dear Joe letter gave him.

'I'll bet you fifty bucks you find a prettier girl here than Busty, or whatever the hell her name was.'

A shadow crosses Bates's face. 'You know her name.'

'Yeah, yeah. Betty. Come on, man—she didn't see the greatness. She's not good enough for you.'

'You called me Rat's Ass, you prick,' Joe says, but I've got him smiling, too. He reaches out and finger-flicks my stovepipe hat, sending it flying. The Colonel who'd made such a fuss on the plane frowns at our horse-play, but I give him my professional innocent look and he doesn't make an issue out of it..

I retrieve my hat and run to catch up to Joe, 'Wait up, you dope!'

'You ever see such a bunch of teeth on a broad?' Joe asks me.

'On a fish, maybe,' I tell him. 'That was like a scene in a horror movie.'

'Yeah. Titled "Wew-come To Vietnam."'

We rattle on about this and that as we stand in line waiting to be processed in-country. Chatting away as if nothing much matters, we manage to push back the fear and near-panic we'd felt getting off the plane. *It's alright. Everything's going to be alright.*

I'll admit it, we had this vague sort of generic fear, and I suppose it was normal enough because of all the warnings the army pounded into us, but the fact was, when we stepped off our plane and stood on the lowland soil of the Republic of South Vietnam, it was already a war zone. They weren't adding combat pay to our meager salaries for nothing. We'd been warned, but for all that we weren't what you might call appropriately aware of our situation. Vietnam, after all, had been continually at war for decades, for centuries, for a millennium if you counted their wars with the Chinese. These people knew war like we knew hot cars and drive-in movies. Looking back, I think we were two hicks from this idealistic place called America, who enlisted to fight JFK's brushfire wars. Joe and I did it for JFK. You can say Eisenhower let us smell the swamp and the jungle, but our sainted martyr, Saint Jack, himself pushed us right into the mud."

"John F. Kennedy did not get us into Vietnam!"

"I already fought the war, Clarity," Jack said softly. "I don't want to have to fight it again with you.

It was over forty years later and Mia My and Jack were both looking at me like I was crazy. Me, Clair Margowski, who had seen the footage of teenage girls marching through Plano, Texas with signs that read, Girls Don't Kiss Boys Who Play With War Toys.

Mia My sat there, saying nothing. I couldn't stand it. I got up and went to the wet bar to pour myself a brandy. I was thinking they could have their fucking war all to themselves. You could see how screwed up I was. But I got my drink and saw they were still outside, sitting there like they were waiting for me. So I brought the bottle and a couple extra glasses and went back out and Jack started talking as if I hadn't interrupted him to argue about something stupid that I couldn't even half remember.

"So Joe and I stood in line for a few hours," Jack said, pouring himself and Mia My a drink. "We sign a bunch of papers saying we are adults who know what we're doing in a war zone and that we've had our malaria and black plague shots. Then we march outside and climb up on the back of an olive colored, open air deuce-and-a-half truck with a white star on the sides of the doors of the cab. We sit on wooden bench seats. After fifteen minutes bouncing along potholed streets, our deuce-and-a-half skids to a stop at a guard gate that has a large semi-circular sign over it proclaiming it's the 3rd Radio Research Unit. We're still on the Tan Son Nhut base, which is a fairly massive layout, what with the runways and various military companies and support groups all housed there.

'Oh, look how covert we are,' I mumble, looking at the big sign that tells everybody we're 'radio research,' which is military shorthand for everybody in the known universe that we're a covert operation. 'It's okay, Joe, so long as the Viet Cong can't read English.'

'Pretty bleak,' Joe says. For a moment I think he's agreeing about the sign, but he's staring glumly past the gates at our future home. 'No air conditioning.'

I look over his shoulder. The barracks are open air, with teak slats to keep out the rain and screens to discourage the bugs. Everybody's been telling us the Air Force dudes have cinder block barracks with air conditioning. What a bummer this is!

It's the end of the day work shift, and a stream of Vietnamese men and women walk past our idling truck. The women are wearing black silk pajamas, white silk blouses and conical hats. Some of the men have on cheap work shirts and Western style pants, but many are dressed pajama style. An M.P. is directing traffic in and out the gate, while a 2nd white arm band stands at ease, squinting at the exiting flow of Vietnamese workers. The first M.P. gestures to a cute young teenage girl carrying a heavy plastic bag. I'm thinking we must be big stuff to rate our own M.P.s I nudge Bates, trying to get him out of his Betty-funk, 'Pal Joey, look at that sweet young thing.'

'I want to inspect her teeth,' Joe says, still pouting over the splintered-toothed lotus-girl.

'Hey! You!! *Co Gai!!*' the M.P. shouts, pointing an accusing finger at the girl. 'Yeah, you—you little slut!'

The girl stops as if her body has been frozen by a death ray.

Joe and I look at each other. We're not used to seeing people treated like shit. 'Even the Chicago cops are better,' he says.

An old guy, some native worker, yells a high-sung, sharp warning in Vietnamese, but the M.P. ignores him.

'Let me see in the bag, Sweetheart.'

The girl shakes her head, refusing to open the bag. 'No,' she says in broken English, 'it only laundry, I clean for G.I.' Her protest becomes a tugging match and the bag breaks in a scatter of dirty laundry laced with stainless steel knives forks and spoons stolen from the mess hall.

'Oh, noooo,' the laundry girl wails. She tries to make a break for it, but she can't weigh 90 pounds soaking wet and the M.P. has her by the back of her silk blouse. The buttons in front pop off and the thin fabric of the blouse tears away from her upper body. She cups her hands over her budding breasts and runs away wearing nothing but her black silk pajama bottoms and her rubber go-aheads. And, of course, her conical straw hat. Vietnamese peasant girls won't go anywhere without their hats. Vietnamese skin tans deeply in the sunlight, and young *co gais* frown on darker skin, it is a sign of a lower class person forced to work the rice paddies, definitely a poorer choice for a marriage partner.

The second M.P. shakes his head in disgust as the half-naked girl darts away. He waves our deuce-and-a-half on through. 'Take a good look, Nugs,' he tells us. 'Welcome to Zipland. They got no conscience, no morals, and no balls.' Our truck starts up. The older worker comes back to help collect the knives and forks, but the first M.P. kicks him and sends him sprawling. The old man does an athletic little tuck and roll and comes up spitting fury, but he backs off when the American reverses his rifle and makes ready to rap him in the head with the butt of his M-14..

'Hey, newbies,' the M.P. yells up at us, 'get a good look at the hairy little monkeys we're dying for over here. We're fighting a war for monkey people, and they got nothing better to do than steal us blind.'"

I looked over at Mia My, but she was unperturbed by the racial slurs. She nodded and smiled, "We could always buy good, sturdy stainless steel American knives, forks and spoons on the black market," she said. "The merchants laid it out on blankets, and about once a month the fat army cooks would show up and buy back what they needed."

"I don't think that's funny," I said. "That's just stealing, plain and simple."

"What should he do?" Mia My asked me, pointing at Jack as a symbol of the American presence that had swarmed her country in the mid-1960's. "Shoot them all as an example?"

CHAPTER 7

Jack and Eddie the Goy Ghost seemed to feel they had some shot at selling their Dunk project to their new *best buds* from Universal, so they left early the next morning for round 2 at Jerry's Famous Deli in Sherman Oaks in the Valley, a show biz feed bag strategically located between the studio and Beverly Hills. Mia My was settled into my guest room. I had hoped for a word of explanation from Jack before he and Eddie made their escape, but the Larch-ster wasn't in a giving mood on that score, though last night he'd been talking a mile-a-minute about his old war stories.

By the time I got up for my daily thirteen and my obligatory laps, my house-guest was nowhere to be found. Her bed was made up, the room meticulous, but her suitcases were still in the corner and her toiletries were lined up in the bathroom, so I figured she was around somewhere.

I strapped on the classic yellow polka-dot bikini Jack bought me for a gag and found Joe's widow sitting by the pool, reading my copy of the L.A. Times.

"I hope you do not mind?" she asked, before I had time to notice she'd copped the business section. I wasn't upset or anything; after all, it wasn't as if she could read the print off of it.

"No. Anything good?"

"Stocks down. Taxes up." That impressed me. The lady spoke my language.

"Biz as usual," I nodded.

I did my thirteen and then stood at one end of the pool, procrastinating before taking the dive. Our pool isn't heated, and the first plunge is always a shocker.

"I can beat you," Mia My said.

That was news to me, and I brightened right up.

"No way," I said.

"So, you think I am an old lady," Mia My smiled. "Two laps." She got up and stood next to me at poolside. I looked down at this slim little sprite in her one piece bathing suit. She intoned, "Ready…set…" And, I swear, she dove in. It was neck and neck all the way, but she did beat me by a few inches.

"I win!" she laughed.

"You cheated! You never said go!"

She was still smiling. "No, I never said we had to go on the word 'Go'. You never wait for 'Go,'" she said.

"Is that a Vietnamese rule?"

"No, French colonialists."

She had me there. I grinned, tossed her a towel and headed for Jack's kitchen.

"Come on," I said. "Breakfast."

Maria was Jack's casual maid and sometimes cook. She had already made coffee. I gave her some money and she drove her battered Toyota to the village for breakfast burritos.

Mia My and I sat at the breakfast nook looking out over the garden, sipping Café Americaine, as she called it, hot milk with a dollop of regular coffee poured in on top.

"You never did tell me how you met Joe," I prompted.

"Well, yes," she said, sitting very straight and alert in her chair, for all her years somehow managing to look like a small schoolgirl in her damp suit with the big white towel around her shoulders. I found myself begging father time that I might look like that in another three decades.

Mia My's expression clouded, and I could see she was thinking back over the years. "It is maybe a day or two after my birthday party. Early in the morning, I take a *xe hoi* taxi from Mama's house—this house was on Louis Pasteur Street, a nice street, big French colonial houses surrounded with gardens and lawns, and those circled by high walls topped with broken glass to keep robbers and bad people away—I take a taxi to perhaps one mile downtown to the Edan Arcade. This is a big building for that time, enclosed with lots of shops inside. You should think of it as a prehistoric mall, you know, what malls might look like before your time."

"We didn't have malls when I was a kid."

"See how advanced the Vietnamese were," Mia My smiled. "They had paper money starting in the 14th century. Some professors of great intellect think we invented it."

"Yeah, right," I scoffed, returning her smile. I can't help myself; I like this lady and am already scheming how to make her my friend. Mia My must be very much like her great aunt Kai. Her pleasant way is infectious and I find myself less edgy than my usual on-guard manner in The House of Jack. Mia My has some sort of calming magic, an inner peace that must be infectious.

"Ong Phong was there to bushwhack me," she said.

"Bushwhack?"

"You know. Surprise. Ambush."

"Who was Ong Phong? And what are you doing at Edan Arcade?"

"At that time, Mama had a dress shop there. She does much business in the back rooms with her land rentals and counting her money, but in the front she sells dresses to all the fancy ladies of Vietnam. They know her in Saigon, yes, but they also fly in from Hue, from Da Nang, from Cape Saint Jacques. Each weekday morning, and sometimes Samdi, I must go there first thing. It is my job, to open the dress shop and wait for the rich ladies and their daughters."

"Okay, so then who is Ong Phong?"

"*Ong* means 'mister'. Only Ong Phong is not a mister, he is a Saigon Cowboy and a very bad person, a young man not in balance."

"Ohh…" I said. I was starting to see her meeting up with Joe wasn't going to be a simple We were waiting in line for the Space Mountain ride at Disneyland.

"Yes, a very bad person," she said. "This is so early, the shops are still closed. The Arcade is nearly deserted. Even the Milk Bar where Phong is sitting there joking with some of his pals, that place wouldn't be serving sodas and milk shakes for another half hour yet. But Mister Phong, he does not care about that."

I found her way of talking interesting. Usually her English was flawless, except for that touch of French accent that, me coming from Plano, resonated as somehow exotic. Sometimes in the heat of what she was saying she would slip her words around into what was probably proper Vietnamese sentence structure.

Don't be surprised I know these things. I did apply myself in school.

"What did Phong want?" I asked.

"Oh, he wants me," Mia My said. "This is before the very bad times when the Communists took everything from us. In the 1960's, Mama is very rich, even after Papa gave so much to gambling and his bad habits with the ladies, even without the 300 Dupuis Bakery vans, I would be a very good catch for a rascal like Phong."

"He was a rascal?" I asked. Interesting, but I couldn't take her seriously. There's something light-hearted about a rascal. But Mia My was frowning at me. The woman had some sort of sixth sense I wished I had. She saw right away that I didn't understand.

"Phong uses his table at the Milk Bar for his unofficial office. He is in the business of selling fake I.D. papers. He has many artist friends, very good with printing machines and ink. Since the war is going more and more badly, his business is very good, and this makes him bold towards me."

"So you're heading to work and there's this Phong guy…"

"Yes, small time gangster, Saigon Cowboy and his pack of rats. He sees I am coming and the Arcade is empty and he thinks this is very good luck for him. He jumps up from his table, leaving his fellow cowboy-rats."

"I overhear him say to them, 'I be right back,' and they know I will not give Phong the time of day so they laugh and scoff at him and say 'Yes, you will.'"

"Phong is a phony-of-baloney. He makes his hair stiff with wax and combs it in a big sweep in front. He thinks he is a lover like The King of Rock and Roll."

"How did you know he was going to hit on you?" I asked.

"Oh. Phong has been after me for years. But it is only with his new-found money in the fake passport business that he becomes bold. And a bold Phong is a very ugly person."

"Yes," I agreed. "I can see how he might be."

Mia My nodded. "I do ignore him and walk on past, but the mall is nearly deserted. That is my serious problem now. He gathers his courage and comes after me. He grabs my arm. 'Where you going, Lover-Girl?' he asks with a cruel twist on his lips. He is pulling at my arm, so I have to turn to face him. 'None of your business, you perverted little pussy-face,' I tell him. I jerk out of his grip, but he jumps around to stand in my way, and gives me a very ugly face.

'Half-breed prick-tease,' he hisses at me. He doesn't know English or French, but the Vietnamese believe they are *The One Pure Race,* and there are a thousand ways to say 'bastard'.

So I shove him. I make a quick move, and since Phong weighs less than a hundred pounds, I put him down on his butt on the floor. I tell him, 'From now on, watch your tongue or I'll cut it out. 'And your tiny little dickie-poo, too, if I can find it.'

Lucky for him, we were far enough away from his pals to be out of earshot. He jumps to his feet and dusts off his pants, and he yells after me something crazy like, 'Okay, it's a date, then!' That gives him his alibi and he swaggers back to his table. I overhear his bragging boast. 'We're going to meet this weekend and I'm going to fuck her silly,' he tells them. There is a ripple of uneasy laughter. Phong is an unstable person, and everybody knows he is dangerous, but none of his pals think he has any chance at all with me."

Maria came back from the fast food joint and I made her take a break from dusting or whatever and have a bite with us. We were sitting around the kitchen table wolfing down breakfast burritos when the big front door opened and slammed shut again. Somebody knocked a vase off a stand in the hallway, ran upstairs and banged around in the study and then scrambled back down again, screaming, "Well, for Christ's sake, where the hell is the old fart?"

Ordinary times in The House of Jack. It was Paul, Jack's disowned son, his only known offspring in a life littered with wrecked personal relationships

"Come in here and sit down, Paul," I yelled at him. Mia My gave me an approving look. "We all have our Phongs," I told her.

Jack's been married three times, and he has managed to lose three falls out of three. About Paul: Jack says he was born bad. I don't know the truth of that, but Paul's been in deeper and deeper trouble since the sixth grade. Not that it's entirely Jack's fault. Paul was barely a toddler when his mother, wanna-be film star Dorothy Chalice, whisked him away with the divorce, and Paul generally only shows up when he needs bail money or air fare for a quick trip out of town.

Paul sat down and made a grab for what was left of my quesadilla. I was too quick for him, and so he swiped a half a burrito from Mia My's plate. She didn't seem to mind. I guessed she didn't eat very much, or maybe she realized the trouble that was Jack's son..

"Who the hell are you?" Paul asked, glaring at Mia My with his half-crazed don't fuck with me or I'll kill you look. Paul was from the kingdom of wannabees like his mother, but he was an overweight bully and a failed metro sexual; even though he polished his nails, they somehow managed to look dirty under the carefully rounded edges. He had a deep salon tan, but he'd left his sunglasses on during the process and the wide circular white patches around his eyes made him look like an alien from some backwash planet like suburban Arcturia.

"This is your father's friend. Her name is Mia My.".

"Oh, Christ, another pan-handler," Paul said, eyeing her more closely as he chewed his newly-acquired burrito. He ate like he hadn't eaten in a week. "Don't you people ever quit?"

"This is Jack's son,". I said, trying to hold off an argument. But I was too late. Jack had entered at this unfortunate moment, trailed by Eddie, and they'd overheard Paul's remark.

"He's not my son," Jack said in a stern voice.

"Jack…" I began, still trying to be the gal in the middle.

Jack waved me off with a fierce look. "No son of mine talks to Joe's wife like that."

"Whatever," Paul said, sounding weary and bored. "Look, Pops, I need a thou, like right now."

"Good. Go see your mother."

Jack may be a fool with money, but he'd always gotten tight pre-nups.

"Mom's in the mountains."

Jack's number two ex was an aging ski bum, a wannabee in every sense—wannabee star, wannabee jet setter, a loud, annoying person. She was never in town, actually a very good thing, but she still believed she owned Jack. I've always thought there was a screw loose in Dorothy that maybe accounted for Paul's outright bad behavior, but nobody ever asked me.

Paul's voice sharpened. "Dad, I'm in trouble!"

Jack's brows furrowed. He took a deep breath, steadied himself, and then said in a low voice, "Where do you want to go?"

He didn't want to know about the trouble. He just wanted Paul gone, if only for whatever duration of peace he could buy before his son came back with the next nasty problem.

"Mexico," Paul said

Jack looked at me. "Get him tickets."

"And cash. I need some spending dough, need it bad."

"Five hundred dollars, on the other end." Jack said. He knew Paul's habits. If his son was given any significant money now he'd never make it to the airport.

"See to it," Jack told me. He slumped into the nearest kitchen chair and gave Mia My a resigned look across the table.

Paul followed close behind me as I took the stairs two at a time up to Jack's inner sanctum, hurrying so Paul wouldn't do his usual grab for my butt.. I speed-dialed Mexicana and got him a one way to Puerto Vallarta.

He shook his head and frowned. "Round trip," he demanded.

Paul's eyes, like his mother's, were disturbing—one was grey and the other hazel. Dorothy covered hers, affecting the Liz Taylor look with deep purple contacts, but Paul never bothered. I think he thought it gave him an advantage over the rest of humanity, which to him consists of little more than animals he can prey on.

"No, Paul," I told him firmly. 'Call us when you want to come back."

I knew he'd just cash in the ticket, blow the money and then call from the other end when he wanted to come back..

"Well, then give me two hundred now."

"No, Paul. Five hundred on the other end." I booked him in Jack's usual hotel. "Money will be at the front desk."

"Jesus, how am I going to get to the airport?"

I tossed him two twenties and slammed the strongbox drawer closed. Paul missed a grab on my sweet ass on the way down the stairs, but he laughed his nasty laugh again, and that had me thinking Paul must be a lot like Ong Phong, maybe there was a whole rash of ugly men out there. It was a real possibility; I'd certainly met my share. Paul was out the door and roaring away in some car with loud pipes before I realized he didn't need a taxi. He'd just made a couple of six packs of beer for his ride to the airport, and I'd been had again.

CHAPTER 8

Jack was still simmering from his bump-in with Paul.

"What happened at Jerry's Famous Deli?"

"Pricks didn't show."

"So much for show biz buddies forever."

"Damn straight." Jack's frown deepened. "Anyway, I'd appreciate it if you'd stop introducing Paul as my son."

"Jack, he *is* your son."

"Is not."

"Hey, if you want to disown him, that's your business."

"And what's my business is your business."

"Hey, don't try to pick a fight with me. My business is to try to keep your finances out of other people's hands."

Jack sighed and threw up his hands. "It's more than that, Clair, and you know it. You keep me grounded in some sort of reality that isn't self-destructive."

"And why does she do that, Jack?" Mia My asked, her quiet voice smoothing the ruffled conversation like oil on troubled water.

Jack wouldn't—or couldn't—find an answer to that, and a moody silence spread around the room.

"Wild Jack," I said. "Come on back down to earth. Mia My has just been telling me how she met Joe. She was just going into the Arcade Edan—"

"One of the few air conditioned public places in Saigon," Jack was quick to interrupt me. "The wealthy of Saigon are living in luxury and there we are sweltering in these open air barracks by the airport."

"Aww, you poor G.I.," Mia My teased him, not at all afraid to ruffle his feathers. I was beginning to really like her. Maybe I'd found a new ally in The Jack Wars. Her ploy worked, too. Jack settled down and started in on the old days again, and I gratefully told myself go with the flow. Anything to get us into the next inning after the nasty free-for-all with Paul.

"I remember our first day on the job," Jack said, settling in his favorite chair behind his big black slab of a desk with the last half-cup of black coffee left over from breakfast. "Joe and I are going to work, driven by this madman…an army lifer named Sergeant 'Red Dog' Moore. Red Dog is jeeping like a bat out of hell through the potholed streets, honking the natives out of the way and personally escorting his two newest recruits from our barracks at the 3rd Radio Research Unit to the White Shack. I guess he doesn't want us to get lost, or kidnapped, or something."

Jack saw my expression of disbelief, "Don't laugh, Clair. At that time, the VC was paying up to five hundred bucks for U.S. soldiers, dead or alive."

"That was so," Mia My agreed, suddenly serious and nodding her head.

"So what's the White House?" I asked.

"White Shack," Jack corrected me. "It's where we did our work."

"What's Red Dog like?" I asked. "Seems like a funny name."

Jack had drifted back in his memories and was once again in that long ago time, remembering the way it was, "Well, it fit his personality, and his looks, too. Red Dog was heavy set, but not fat. His pink skin went red after a few minutes in the tropical sun, but it never took on much of a tan. His scalp was sunburned through the short blond hair of his crew cut, and he wore heavy gold rings on both hands, and a watch bracelet made of thick links of gold, and a heavy neck chain of pure gold, which at that time was going for $35 U.S. dollars an ounce. When we first met I thought he was one of the original Ugly Americans, though later I came to believe he wasn't half bad. At least he had the welfare of his troopers as a top priority. Anyway, Red Dog drove like a demon. He yelled and spun the steering wheel, all the while slamming the heel of his hand against the little round horn in the center of the jeep's steering wheel.

"Now get this: it's mid-morning and it's already a hundred and ten in the shade and Joe Bates is actually wearing starched fatigues. He's up front with Red Dog while I'm lounging around in back. Vietnamese on foot are cursing us and jumping back as our jeep slams through the pot-holes. There are no sidewalks, so everybody shares the road. I'm thinking riding with Red Dog is fun, in a cruel way, sort of like watching a kid step on ants."

"Jack, it wasn't fun," I chided him.

"Sure, it was," he said. "And, instructional, too. Think about it, Clair. Here's Red Dog, yelling at the top of his lungs over the whine of the jeep engine. But it's all just a show, an act. He calms down for a moment and grins at us. 'Gentlemen,' he says, 'gold is your best friend! You can use it to buy a whore, pick up a bottle of Algerian red—or, most important—bribe your way back out when you get lost in the leech-sucking bush. Next payday, you both go downtown and get yourself a couple rings, at least.'

'Right, Sarge,' I tell him, even though I'm thinking I'll be a damn fool before I'm going to spend my meager and hard-earned army pay on stupid jewelry. But I can see Joe is taking this way too seriously.

'Where do we buy it?' he asks.

I give Joe the look of a thousand daggers, because now we are going to have to hear about buying jewelry, but just then Red Dog slams on the brakes and the jeep skids to a stop in front of the White Shack.

I'm looking over at the building and not liking the marines lounging in front with their little automatic shooters, but Joe is still thinking about the gold.

'How do I know they won't cheat me?' Joe asks.

'What, the gold merchants?' Red Dog laughs. 'Everybody cheats you in Vietnam. That's how they make a living. Get used to it.'

'Used to it? How?'

'They steal ten percent, it's okay. Fifteen is too much.'

While Joe is struggling with this concept, I notice that the windows of the building are safe behind heavy iron grillwork, and they are painted white as well, so nobody can look in. A guard with a machine gun is eyeing us from his post in front of a heavy dark green door.

'What is this place?' I ask..

"Red Dog eases his big frame out of the jeep and heads for the door, motioning us to follow him. 'The White Shack,' he says, waving his hand by way of introduction.

'Badges,' the guard mumbles.

'You got your security badges?' Red Dog asks

'Always,' Joe says. He's wearing his around his neck, under his clean white t-shirt under his newly starched fatigues blouse. He flips it out to let the guard have a squint. These badges, they're green, with TOP SECRET written across the top. His has a picture of Joe Bates wearing his 1st class army greens. Joe's thumbprints are on the back, in case anybody ever thinks he isn't who he is.

I fish around, but me, I've misplaced my stupid badge, serious business in this crazy-spy world. Red Dog shifts his weight from foot to foot and whistles "A Hard Day's Night," while I'm digging through all the notes and scraps of writing in my pockets.

'Either of you do crypto?' Red Dog asks.

'Low level,' Joe snaps right back at him. 'Dirty Mary taught me at the Palace.'

"Joe was referring to the Puzzle Palace," Jack said, looking at me. "That's the big NSA crypto headquarters back at Fort Meade, 20 miles or so north of Washington D.C. It's still there, Clair. You can google it if you want.'

I didn't say anything, and Jack continued with his story, "Red Dog nods and a big smile creases his ugly puss. 'Dirty Mary!' he says. 'That old bird still alive?'

'Lucky Strikes Greens goes to war,' Joe says, quoting Mary. You couldn't buy greens any more—it was a ad slogan from the early 1940's, one of those sayings that used to pop out of the old lady's mouth.

"Dirty Mary was a legend at the Puzzle Palace. She'd been a secretary in World War II when the Black Chamber had decoded *EAST WIND RAIN,* the Japanese signal to attack Pearl Harbor. 'Only we had no way to get the news to Hawaii,' she would chuckle happily in her gravely voice while she told that story. The chuckle usually became a coughing fit and somebody would have to slap her on the back before she settled down again. She had a talent for slipping alphabets and numbers around, and she stuck around as the Cold War began, teaching the new generations of military cryptographers from under a cloud of blue smoke from her cherished Lucky Strikes, which she smoked non-stop through her shift. That's where Joe learned to smoke."

"He quit after he met me," Mia My interjected.

"I'd quit, too, if you were after me to stop."

"Clair could make you quit, if she wanted."

That stopped Jack for a moment. He gave me an uncertain look, side-tracked for a moment, and went back to his story.

"Anyway, Red Dog tells Joe and me that Dirty Mary taught him to unscramble codes, too, and then he proceeds to put Joe in charge of everything over me. Naturally, even distracted as I am looking for my badge, that doesn't set too good with me.

'Hey, wait a minute,' I protest. 'I'm the same rank he is.'

'Not any more. Thou art only a Spec. 4.' Red Dog places a hand on Joe's shoulder and says, 'I hereby dub thee Specialist 5th Class.'

'Like that's fair,' I mutter..

Red Dog points at Joe.

'Now on, you work for him,' he says.

'Oh, shit,' I say, digging deeper in the scraps of paper in my pockets, still fishing around for my badge. 'Shit, shit, shit.'

'Ahh, Christ, come on.' Red Dog takes me by the scruff of the neck and starts to walk us in past the guard.

'Hey, Red Dog, you don't just—'

'Soldier, that's "Sergeant Red Dog, Sir!" I don't have all day to piss around. I'm vouching for this man.' And with that, he propels me through the green door into the world of electronic spies and dark secrets."

"Oh, Jack…" I scoff at the idea Jack is involved in anything as melodramatic as he's saying. *It's Dunk Stingray stuff.* I can't imagine this unlikely little block house building he's described could have anything important to do with a war effort. And if it did, I figured Jack, with his wild imagination, was as out of place as Dunk in a real war operation.

"No, Clair, this is ain't no shit," he says. "The White Shack was a key branch of our covert operations in South Vietnam. Joe and I were members of ASA with Top Secret codeword clearances, all the bells and whistles of modern spy-dom. The Army Security Agency. Army Intelligence. The walls in there were covered with topo maps, all of them heavy with colored pins showing coordinates, bearings and triangulations. On one wall some motivated dork with bad art skills has put up a crude poster of a G.I. leaning over to whisper in a smiling bargirl's ear. In the background, a ship is sinking beneath roughly sketched blue waves. The hand-drawn headline reads, 'Loose Lips Sink Ships!'

"You really did that?"

He nods at me, "Dunk Stingray, eat your heart out. Anyway, we are half way down the hall when I finally uncover my badge, hidden among some scribbled scraps of paper in one of my pockets.

'Jesus! About time,' Red Dog laughs. 'I thought we were going to have to shoot you.' He jerks a thumb with one hand, indicating the maps on the wall behind him, 'We intercept, we get the coordinates, we call in the B-52s and we bomb the shit out of their little hide-y holes.'

'He points again, this time a little more carefully, to the doorway of a nearby office, and his voice lowers as he speaks, 'Colonel Ogilvy, head of special operations, the so-called SPEC OPs unit…be careful…there's a reason they call him The White Snake.'

At that moment, two men wearing civilian clothes come to the doorway of the Colonel's office.

'Wendell and Leo,' Red Dog says, his voice dropping to just above a whisper. "The White Snake's Spook Operatives…not nice people. Again, I warn you: be very careful.'

I'm sure Joe is going to blurt out something like Why should we be careful? or What is a Spook Op?, but before I can get my hand over his mouth we are interrupted from the other direction.

'Take a look at this! ' a young corporal says, running up to shove a black-and-white 8 x 10 photo blow-up into Red Dog's hand.

'Doober,' Red Dog says, introducing the guy all around. 'This is Corporal Doober, short-timer. Meet Jack and Joe, your replacements.'

'So good I get two, huh?' Doober grins.

Doober is a light-skinned black man. He wears glasses almost as thick as Joe's and has a grin that splits his face from ear to ear. He points to the photograph, which is of a plane that looks like the U.S. Army version of a big Piper Cub, a fixed wing aircraft with the wing over the fuselage.

'We were up over Tay Ninh province,' he says. He smiles again and jabs excitedly at the photo. 'Beaver took a hole the size of your fist—right there, you can see it!—in the left wing.'

Red Dog squints at the picture, 'I'm pretty sure they can patch that.'

'Paper tape and clear varnish,' Doober says. 'Already done, sir.'

'Were you up for this one?'

'Yep! Another Purple Heart for the Beaver. I got nothing.'

'Hey, better the Beaver than your butt. I don't think we could patch you with paper tape and varnish.'

'You got that right, Sarge. Anyways, it don't matter. Two weeks and three days, I'm out of here!'

'Way to go, short-timer!'

Doober buzzes off to show his picture around and Red Dog points to a nearby cluster of desks.

'This here be the crypto/translation area, men.' He picks up a pile of papers, 'Intercepts, waiting to be decoded and translated, just waiting your delicate touch.'

'That looks like a lot,' I say.

I'm not happy about it. You see, I don't translate too good, and I'm even worse at code-breaking.

'Naah, it's all low level stuff. Use your Batman decoder ring.'

Joe, being the usual Joe Word-Nerd that he is, sits right down at the nearest desk, takes the top page and starts noodling.

'Yeah, you're right,' he says after an incredibly short time. 'Vowels stacked at the end. Primitive.' Joe does a series of fast calculations and scribbles replacement letters below the original lines.

'I've got my Hoa's…' I say. I get out the bright red Hoa's Viet-English dictionary I'd stuffed in my fatigues pants as a last minute inspiration when we'd left the barracks, but it's Joe's show and he waves me away.

'Don't need it,' he says. 'Look: Saw-two-planes-of - Invader-Gangster-Americans-yesterday. Send-more-bullets.'

'Number One, G.I.,' Red Dog says, slapping him on the back. 'You're the genuine artifact.' Then he points to me, 'You rotate out on the plane with Doober.'

At that moment, I'm sure the color is draining right out of my face.

'What?! And get shot at?' I yelp.

Red Dog chuckles and nods in agreement. 'Something like that,' he says.

Joe is no help at all. He says, 'Jack, I thought you wanted to see the action—you know, to help you write your stories.'

I'm looking around the room, noticing for the first time the icy air conditioning. It feels like the fingers of death are running up and down my neck. 'Yeah,' I say, 'but I didn't mean be the duck in the shooting gallery.'"

CHAPTER 9

It was dusk in Southern California and Wild Jack, Mia My and I were sitting under the heavy old redwood pergola on my side of the pool, lounging around my thick, bubbly glass table while we ate Papa John's pizza. We hadn't seen any mosquitoes lately, but I had the torches going, just in case. Since his stint in the tropics, Jack is deadly afraid of every bug known to man, but particularly mosquitoes.

I was feeling better than I had in a while about Jack. I know I sound confused. A few weeks ago, I was seriously thinking of bailing on the old shit—and Southern California, as well. I thought maybe I'd cut my emotional losses and start over, maybe talk my Gal Pals into buying some income rentals in the Bahamas or Baja. But doesn't life do crazy things! I get just this one little spark of hope that something meaningful could develop between us, you know, in that mili-second just before the old fartster upends Steve's Porsche and ends up looking like Rocky Raccoon. And now the three of us are sitting here talking about the storied days of Jack's fabled youth, and I'm more interested than you might imagine. I've got this born-again feeling. Maybe it's because of Mia My. I don't know what might come of any of this, but the way she talks and acts around us, she's got me believing Jack and I together are the way things are meant to be. God, I wish Jack had a hundred friends like her!

Eddie had taken off for parts unknown, which meant Jack had his pages in for the day and all was right with the world. Jack wolfed his way through his first slice of Tuscany Six-Cheese and started in remembering his time in 'The Nam.' Since Mia My showed up, it's been just about all he talks about. Jack has one of those highly compartmentalized minds. It can be Dunk Stingray all day long, but after the sun goes down he can turn that one off and click on The Jack & Joe Show. Mia My didn't mind. She encouraged him; after all, these were her memories, too.

Jack sipped his Ba Muoi Ba beer. He'd had one of the studio drivers bring him a case from Little Saigon in orange county, to help bring back the memories. He rolled the swig around in his mouth and frowned, "It's not the real thing, you know. The formaldehyde taste is gone."

"Formaldehyde is for pickling brains," I told him. I meant in jars for biology class displays, but Jack took it another way.

"That's just what it does, Clair" he said. "First time we *di-di* to downtown Saigon, I got myself properly pickled. You know, if you wanted to go off base, you had to sign out in the orderly room, but it was not very orderly. Imagine—Joe and I get there and there's a regular line of G.I.s in civvies waiting. They've set out an ammo box filled with condoms right next to the sign out book."

"Ick! How romantic," I said. I grabbed the last piece of pepperoni before he could get to it.

"Tell it like it is," he said, eyeing the pepperoni like he might make his own grab for it. That was another one of Jack's mantra, Tell it like it is. This from the writer whose macho protagonist has screwed 10,000 women and survived a million bullets, bombs, grenades, swords, daggers and assorted ice picks and other sharp objects..

"Well, the little rubber raincoats were free," Jack said. "So I took some, 'cause in Saigon it's always raining. We were in line right behind Doober, that black kid who had showed us the picture of the Beaver with the hole in the wing. Joe was dressed neat, like always, probably wearing one of his striped polo shirts and a pair of slacks. He had this small, leather-cased camera slung around his shoulder on a thin leather strap."

Mia My nodded, a sad smile playing on her face. "Yes, a Bolsley 35mm. He had that camera always."

"How about you, Jack," I asked. "What were you wearing?" It was hard to imagine my crusty old pal as a young man.

"Probably the Marlin Brando look, Levis and a white t-shirt with the rolled up sleeves…with a pack of Lucky Strikes bulging in one of the sleeves. I remember how impatient I was. It felt like we were going to be in that line forever. But right about then, as we're shuffling and kicking our feet and grumping about stuff,

Colonel Williamson, the Commanding Officer of the 3rd RRU, sweeps into the room. He's wearing a natty seersucker sports coat and a boater straw hat. Some fool whistles, but the CO likes to think he is a regular guy, so he just grins and clears his throat for attention.

'Ahem. Any of you men want to share a cab ride downtown?' he asks.

There's this embarrassing pause. The men in the line are all trying to look preoccupied. See, nobody wants to go with Williamson. Toady raises his voice, 'Anybody here want to hook a ride with the Colonel? Move to the head of the line. I'll get you out of here right now.'

Bates looks at me. 'Why not?', he asks."

Joe moves forward without waiting for an answer, but Doober holds me back. 'Williamson stops at the PX for some Hershey Bars', he tells me, 'and the Zip post office to pick up some stamps for his kids, and then he comes right back here. Hardly a good time, Old Sport, if you know what I mean...'

When I hear that, I give Joe the old finger-roll wave. 'See ya later, alligator,' I tell him."

Jack gave me that knowing professorial look I resent so much. I know I carry a lot of baggage, but I can't help myself. I think it's left over from a sports doctor I dated for a few months before he dumped me for a gay relationship with a back up center for the Bears.

"You see how fate works," Clair," Jack tells me. "Here's my buddy Joe Bates who never acts on his impulses, who never takes a random shot at anything, and there he goes, off on a lark with the Colonel."

"You're making a big thing out of nothing, Larch-ster," I told him. But I have made a mistake, and now Jack is going to pontificate.

"That one decision," Jack said, waving his arms dramatically in the air, "will change his life forever and shape his destiny for all time."

I wanted to tell him he was so full of drama queen crap that he was about to burst, but I looked over and saw Mia My was nodding in serious and silent agreement, and I had the sudden feeling this woman, who hasn't seen Jack in a decade or more, knows him far better than I ever would. I have another jealous flash, the good old Clair reaction to anything threatening…but this feeling ebbs away and I'm left with an overwhelming feeling of sadness. I can't tell you why I felt like that; I've always tried not to live in my emotions, life's too short and there's too much to do, but there it was. Jack had this hold on me, and I would do anything to break free, but I didn't know how. It wasn't the age difference, unless you think of it in reverse; Jack was like a little kid, and I didn't think he would ever grow up. But maybe I'm the little kid, too, the little girl lost who can't find my way home. Confusing, but a lot of mixed up truth in there.

I came out of my funk with a start. Mia My, too, seemed intent on setting me straight. For some reason, that was okay. I don't know why I could discount just about anything the Larch-ster told me, but coming from her, it was like gospel. "Joe and I talked about this day many times. This day, for me: I am walking along busy Le Loi Boulevard when that nasty Phong, spots me. He comes up close before I see him and he grabs my arm. He is with one of his punk cowboy friends, and he says to me, 'This has gone on long enough.' He has a hard and mean look on his face. He speaks to his friend, 'Can I use your apartment for a few hours?' This friend, probably in his sixth year at Saigon University thanks to one of Phong's fake identification cards, says, 'Of course.'

Phong is holding me by one hand, and he cups a cigarette in his other, acting like he is some big-time French bravado-man. He is not a very big person, and so I pull away from him. But Phong does not give up so easily. He throws down his cigarette, mashes it with his heel like he is maybe Humphrey Bogart and then he starts after me at a fast clip, walking so he doesn't make a scene. I walk away from him even faster, and I cut across the street just before a White Mouse handling traffic switches directions, and I'm already a half block away when Phong finally can cross the busy intersection.

But I tell you, Phong is crazy for me—and he is just plain crazy, as well. Now he runs after me, and he is pushing people and knocking them over, and when he catches up to me the second time, he takes my arm again, just as if he is my boyfriend for real.

'I was calling out to you, Mia My' he says with a love-sweet but sarcastic tone in his voice. 'Didn't you hear me?'

'Hello, Phong," I say to him, just as calm as apple pie. I know he hates it when I treat him like a little beetle.

'How nice to see you today,' he says. I pull my arm away, but he takes it again, and this time he holds it so firm that I will have to make a scene to pull away.

'I have an idea,' he says. 'Come to my apartment. We'll talk about things.'

'You have an apartment?'

'Yes, over by the university.'

'Do your parents know?'

'My parents have nothing to do with it.'

'Nor do I. No, thank you. We have nothing to talk about.'

I try to pull away from him, but he has me firmly by the wrist.

'I think you're coming with me,' he says as if he owns me."

We are decades and half a world away, but remembering the confrontation with Phong has affected her. Mia My shakes her head, looking down at the half empty bottle of Ba Muoi Ba on the table in front of her. "But he overestimates his own strength…or maybe he underestimates mine. I jerk my arm from his and head for two *Quoc Khanh* military policemen who are standing nearby.

'I'll get you, you rich bitch!' Phong yells as loud as he dares, but he can't go after me with the Q.K.s so close. You see, to survive and not be recruited into the army, he has to stay unnoticed, and he can't do that if he makes any sort of a scene, much less a scene with me. I know he has false papers, and I will be the first to point him out.   He looks around. I can see he is one step back in his plans. He is wondering if I will actually turn him in, and he is also trying to figure out which way it would be best to run if I do. He doesn't see me slip into a narrow side street. It is maybe a foolish thing for me to do. He could have gotten two or three of his pals and taken me when I came out at the other end. And if that had happened, none of what was to follow would have occurred. Joe Bates would never have met Mia My Nguyen. I would probably have been gang-raped and perhaps even murdered. But Phong has turned away and so missed his chance to change the way my small corner of the world was to become."

Jack nodded and cracked open another beer. I took the bottle from him, and so he cracked open another one for himself and picked up the story where Mia My left off. "A lot happened that afternoon in old *thang pho* Saigon," he said. "Joe told me all about it. He and the Colonel caught a cyclo-bus from the 3rd RRU to the main gate in front of Tan Son Nhut, and a taxi took them the rest of the way downtown.

The Colonel wasn't exactly a chicken-shit, like the men said. He was just a cautious, middle-aged married guy who wanted to get through his tour and get on home to his wife and kids. His idea of soaking up the local color was a drive in one of those pedi-cyclos, and in short-order he and Joe were riding along, each in their single person open carriages, pumped by muscular-legged native drivers. These cyclo-things are a cross between a two-wheeled carriage and a tricycle, and Joe is happy as a clam, snapping photos as they glide along. The Colonel is shouting back at him, pointing out all the dangerous stuff to watch out for.

'The cigarette sellers,' the Colonel shouts, 'they'll cheat you blind.' He points to a colorful stand featuring tobacco and candy and shielded from the weather by two large red and yellow striped umbrellas. 'The fruit and vegetable sellers...' He indicates the ladies squatting behind baskets of green, red and yellow bananas, bright golden jackfruit, soft spine husked *trom trom trop,* Asian pears and dozens of fruits, green vegetables and tubers that Joe could only guess at, 'Don't eat any of that. You'll be sicker than a dog. They shit on their vegetables for fertilizer.' He points out a café as they glide by, 'Open air café...never EVER go in those places...too easy for VC sympathizers to lob a grenade in there.'

They glide up to a group of young men dressed in flashy clothes, shiny Hong Kong silk suits and fresh new Levis and motorcycle boots. It's the bad boy look made popular by American movie stars. 'Saigon Cowboys,' the Colonel shouts back at Joe. 'Keep your hands folded—they'll rip your watch right off your wrist!'

The Colonel crosses his arms by way of example, but this amuses the cowboys, who have been alerted to his arrival by his loud comments. 'Hey!' he shouts as one of them tries to snatch his boater. He is successful in rescuing his hat, and then his cyclo is past the gang. As Joe's cyclo approaches, he snaps a picture of the cowboys. One tries to snag his camera, but the leather strap is tough and the Vietnamese is a lightweight. Joe reels him in and hits him with a quick punch to the face. Joe always had a good punch, and the cowboy falls back, holding his bleeding nose. ';*Nguoi My Sao!*' he curses. Ugly American! '*Nguoi Nam Sao!*' Joe yells back. Ugly Vietnamese! Joe may have been prim and proper compared to me, but he took no shit from anybody. And then their cyclo is past the cowboys and out of reach.

'No, no, no—not this way!' the Colonel shouts. 'Don't go this way!' But his cyclo has already turned off Le Loi onto a smaller side street.

'What's wrong, Sir?' Joe shouts.

'This way faster, boss-chief,' the Colonel's cyclo-boy reassures them. 'Shortie- cut. We get to *Nha Buu-Dien* chop-chop plenty fast.'

The Colonel sees the street is too crowded and narrow to turn around, but he isn't happy at the choice. 'It's not safe, packed in like this,' he yells back at Joe. 'People can reach out and touch you. Anybody could have a knife or a gun.'

That may have been true enough, but I'm sure the impact of that message escapes Joe entirely. He's enchanted by the rich and colorful parade of exotic street life flowing past, the same as I was on my first days on the Saigon streets. He told me later that he thought he was going to run out of film, but he didn't care. He was in the strange and mysterious Orient, in Saigon, the fabled pearl of the Orient.

What happens next is the stuff of legends. Once they are well along the side street, the Colonel's driver pulls to a stop. He hops off the bike and talks as he's backing away, waving his hands to reassure the Americans.

'You wait one minute. Okay-dokay? *Toi muon thuoc la. Basto Bleu. Toi de vay mot chuc nua.*'

The Colonel, obviously not happy with this delay, calls back to Joe, 'What did he say?'

'He said he needs some French cigarettes, Sir. He'll be right back. That's what *mot chuc nua* means, just a moment more.'

Joe's driver, who has gotten down from his own cyclo and has been fiddling with the handlebars, now begins to back away.

'Hey, where you going?' Joe asks.

Joe's driver turns and slips away in the crowds on the sidewalk. Joe and the Colonel aren't stupid. They give each other a quick glance and scramble out of their cyclos. Joe is held up when his camera strap catches on something, but he jerks it away. They sprint flat-out, but they get no more than ten paces separation from the cyclos when the Colonel's explodes in an ugly orange-and-black ball of flame!"

"That never happened!" I said, but even I wasn't so certain. Jack was that convincing as a storyteller. He had to be, to make some of the stuff Dunk Stingray pulled off seem believable.

"Clair, you don't know anything," Jack said, rubbing his eyes with one hand. He was looking old and weary. I had the sudden odd thought that I maybe I should be kinder to him. But I shut it down as a momentary weakness. A stupid thing to be thinking. Jack and I had a Hollywood relationship, loose and free, and that was the way he wanted it, the way we wanted it. And yet, I did feel at a loss, like I was missing something. You know how it is when you have a sudden realization that you may be wrong about a lot of things?

"Yes, Clair," Mia My said. "It did happen. I was there."

"What happened next isn't pretty," Jack nodded. "The Colonel is tumbled head-over-heels by the blast. Joe himself is lifted through the air for about ten feet and he smashes full-force into a tobacco stand. He falls through a canvas awning, with cartons and packs of cigarettes around his head. And as he struggles to his feet, the second blast from his own cyclo knocks him right back down again.

The way Joe described it to me, the scene was chaotic, surreal, and bloody. At least a dozen people were dead, and dozens more wounded. That was the deal; kill fifty of your countrymen to get one or two Americans. Terrorists never cared about the personal body count, Clair, that was the acceptable sacrifice for their noble cause."

Jack saying it like that just pisses me off all over again, but I bite my lip and let it pass. That was my magnificent gesture. I don't think the Larch-man even noticed, but Mia My did. She placed her hand on my arm and made a soft shushing noise, like she was talking to a little girl. The tough Rah-Rah girl, the tough and independent Gal Pal part of me should have been resentful, but

I felt calm and comforted. *I was family. I belonged in the story. Everything was going to be okay.*

"The Colonel may have dressed like a dandy, but Joe always said Williamson knew what to do in a crisis. Scratched and bleeding the way he is, that officer still has the presence of mind to clamp his hands around the lower leg of a man whose foot is lying next to him, connected by a thin ribbon of tendons. 'Specialist!' he shouts at Joe, 'That woman, over there!'

Joe is stunned and half-blind from blood running from a gash in his forehead. There's an acrid smell of explosives in the air, and his ordered world has come apart like a jigsaw puzzle. Joe looks around. He's in a daze, he wonders what his commanding officer wants him to do. The Colonel nods his head in the direction of a middle-aged peasant woman, a plump *Ba,* with blood spurting from her arm. Joe gets the idea. He rushes to her side and tries to stop the bleeding much as the Colonel is doing, but the woman is panicked, and her own red blood is spurting everywhere. She slaps Joe hard in the face and tries to push him away. 'Be still—I've go to hold the artery!' Joe yells, but he's got the sinking feeling he's going to lose this one."

Jack took a swig of his beer, grinned at me and dipped his head in a little bow to Mia My, sitting across the table from him. "And that's when this lady shows up, appearing out of nowhere like an angel of mercy. There's screaming and blood everywhere, and in the middle of it all Joe has a glimpse of a miracle—it's this beautiful Eurasian girl dressed in Western style, you know, a skirt and blouse instead of that slit skirt *ao gai* get up. The girl shouts at the bleeding old lady in French, and there is something about the tone of her voice that stuns the older woman into silence. *'Arête!'*

This angel pushes the woman down on her back and holds her. Joe manages to get his belt around the bloody arm and to pull it tight. The blood is still pumping out, but slower now. Mia My has bright red blood spattered all over her white blouse and summer skirt. 'Hold here for a moment, very tight!' Joe tells her, handing her the belt. 'Oui. D'accord. Yes,' she says.

Joe takes one of his shoelaces and laces it next to the belt. After that, the blood is no longer spurting out of the woman's arm. And then medics from Saigon General are there, pushing Joe and Mia My back as they take over. White Mice and Q.K.s are everywhere, and they're all bloody, too."

Mia My smiles and nods, "That is how we met the first time. I am standing next to Joe Bates. We are both excited with our victory of saving the woman. I look up at him. 'I was down there," I tell him. I don't say anything about Ong Phong. I gesture, pointing in the direction from which I have come, and I somehow have slipped into my dream, from now on, I am living it. I know this is my American warrior. I speak in English with my French accent, only it was a heavier accent in those days, 'I was about one half block away,' I tell him.

'You did very well,' Joe says. 'We did what we could.'

'You're hurt.' I see he has a bleeding cut on his forehead. 'You have a wound.'

'Not much,' he says, daubing at it with the old, dirty handkerchief he uses to clean his glasses."

Jack steps in with his double-team act, neatly picking up the conversation, "That was Joe, you know. On the one hand, he was this dapper, careful guy with his life-plan supposedly all laid out in front of him, but he'd read lots of old romance books; in his dreams he was the guy who would take a spear in the guts and comment how big they were making them these days, before he fell over. Here is this pretty girl, this vision—his vision of Oriental beauty—and she has come real and is right there, smiling at him. Joe may be stunned, but he's no fool. He goes for a hand-shake. She looks at it for a moment, and then puts her blood-stained hand in his..

'Joseph Bates,' he says. 'Just plain Joe.'

'Mia My Nguyen,' she tells him. 'Nothing plain about me.'"

And Jack grins at me in triumph, "Clair, I can tell you for certain that was the exact moment in space and time when Joe Bates left the comfortable old world of his past life behind. He traded his head in for his heart, and after that, his feet never touched the ground again, not for years—not ever! And I have to say, *Nam Viet* in the mid-1960's was not the time or place for a G.I. in Joe's position to be running around propelled by Stupid Cupid. Later on, Joe told me he felt it right away, he couldn't have been imagining it. Even in that awful moment with people wailing and screaming for Buddha and Jesus to come save them, and blood splattered everywhere, it seemed like there was this special chemistry between Joe and Mia My. And so there it was, the two of them standing holding hands in the middle of all that horror. Here's how Joe described it to me: He's holding her hand, and after a beat, her smile grows broader. 'Let go of my hand,' she says.

'No, you let go of my hand.'

'No. You first.'

'Then I'll never let go,' Joe says.

Up until he said that, they'd been half-teasing each other. But now she isn't smiling any more, and Joe thinks he sees something else, some dawning recognition in her look. He's not sure, but whatever it is, he's got the intuition that it's something very good. At that moment, he isn't going to let go of her hand even if the Viet Cong terrorists detonate a hundred *ep plastique* bombs. But life…you know, Clair, life is never that simple."

"I know, Jack," I told him in my ordinary pissy way. "Life is complicated."

Jack's eyes didn't meet mine. That made me wonder if he was guilty about his life and the things he'd done. That would be something new, The Larch-ster showing an ounce of remorse. But then I got the feeling it wasn't guilt, but more like a sad, defeated sort of envy, and that made me sorry I'd been so quick to pop off at him. Jack was talking about something he'd personally never experienced, and maybe he was even wondering why. That was my boy, he had nearly achieved the Age of Sainted Old Farthood, and he still didn't have a clue about the inner workings of love. I wanted to say I was sorry, but then he started up again in that low, remembering voice of his, talking about how Joe met his princess. The moment when he might have taken something for himself was lost, and he was off again, living somebody else's story.

"They just barely had that joyful brief thrill of recognition, and then their special moment was interrupted by something I could argue was worse than explosives—it was the shrill voice of Ba Nguyen, her mother.

'Mia My! Mon Dieu! Mia My!' Of course, proper French trained girls don't hold hands with peasants or lowly American troopers, and Mia My drops Joe's hand like it's a hot rock. Ba

Nguyen moves in like a Panzer tank. She parts the water, she strides through the bazaar crowd as if they are a field of wheat. And she's got an old woman in tow, the friendly presence that Joe will come to know as Auntie Kai. But that's all in the future. Joe's just standing there in shock from the explosives and enjoying the promise he senses with Mia My's warm, trusting hand in his own, and then here comes the terrible Mama Nguyen. He doesn't have a second to think as Ba Nguyen's voice rises into a tirade, 'I tell you over and over many times, you silly, ignorant, foolish child-daughter—*jamais, jamais, jamais* take this street!' Mama Nguyen waves her arms to the deity and gestures at Mia My's bloody dress, *'C'alors*—look, the mess you've made of yourself!' Her attention shifts to Joe, and her frown deepens. 'And *who* is this?'

Mia My is so flustered she shifts to a patois of French and Vietnamese, *'Mama, toi khong biet. Un Americaine.'* Mama, I don't know. An American. It's one of those confusing moments. Auntie Kai moves in close and gives Mia My a smile and a little hug, but her calming gesture is interrupted by Ba Nguyen. 'Come, come, and come, foolish people— we are out of here!' And without any hesitation, she takes her daughter by the arm and begins to march her away."

It had become dark now and the California air was chill. Jack was swatting at an imaginary mosquito he thought was buzzing around his head, but he wasn't quite finished yet. "That should have been the end of it, right there—but it wasn't. I tell you, Clair, you be careful with even the casual things in life, the things you do without thinking. The next thing my old friend Joe did would change the direction of his life forever."

I knew my role. "And what was that, Jack?" I asked.

"Joe raised his camera and snapped their picture as they were leaving the scene. There was only enough film left for one last shot, and he caught Mia My and her mother looking back at him, the daughter apologetic, and the mother glaring. Just the one shot and they were gone, down the street and out of his view."

"And taking a picture changed his life," I said, my voice heavy with my own special brand of big-time Clair Moore cynicism.

"Oh, yeah," the Larch-ster said. "Only he doesn't know it, yet. Here he is, still dazed from the explosion, and he's met a beautiful angel, only she's disappeared and he's alone again. Joe looks around. I guess he's trying to gather his thoughts. So much has happened in the space of a few minutes! He sees Colonel Williamson is talking with a White Mouse cop and a Q.K. The Colonel looks dazed and rumpled, and Joe knows that he himself doesn't look any better. 'They're long gone,' the Colonel is saying. 'That's the way it always is.'

'Who, Sir?' Joe asks.

'The cyclo-boys who tried to murder us.' Williamson shakes his head, thinking about their near miss, 'They'll blow you up for 5,000 piasters.'

'That's really sick, Sir," Joe says.

'Not you,' the Colonel corrects him. 'You're only worth five hundred.'

Joe has been rewinding his Bolsley, more out of habit than any idea of what he's doing. But now an idea comes to him. He pops the 35mm cartridge out of the back of the camera and hands it to the Colonel.

'I think I caught them on film, sir,' he says. 'Maybe they don't get away this time.'"

CHAPTER 10

The Larch-ster got up and cleaned the table, which meant he took the empty pizza boxes and the paper plates and made his way to toward my blue recycling garbage can.

"What was all that business with Jack's son?" Mia My asked me.

"Well, you know everything better than I do," my evil side snapped at her.

There was a long pause. "I am on your team, Clair," she said. You may not see it, but I am on your side, and I'm telling you something around here doesn't fit. There is something very wrong in this place, some old evil or sickness."

"It's probably me. I don't fit," I grumped.

"No. Not you, Clair."

"Most of the time I think I should just pack my duffle and hit the road."

"And go where? Desert the one you love?"

"It's not love!"

"What then?"

I looked off into the distance, staring at nothing while I hoped the question would go away, but Mia My still watched me, waiting patiently for an answer. I finally realized it didn't make much sense, me playing some sort of surly Lone Ranger with Jack's long time friend "I'm sorry," I apologized. "Survival in The House of Jack makes me a little crazy. Maybe I do love him. I honestly can't think straight any more."

"About Paul...?"

"Paul is a major thorn in Jack's side. He has been, ever since I've been in the picture, and certainly a lot longer, before that."

"No," she said. "I am not being clear. I mean, why does Paul so openly disrespect you?"

"Oh, that." I shrugged. "His mother taught him I am the evil person in Jack's life. I'm the Larch-ster's whore, the spider-lady trying to get her fangs into his fortune.'

Mia My shook her head. "Don't they know how many times you have saved Jack's fortune?"

"They have no idea…" I said. I paused and gave her a more appraising look "How do you know about that?"

"I do read his Christmas cards, Clair. Jack has told me things. You're *his* angel, you know."

I scoffed, "His little sister, more like. We tried to *l'amour* it up a bit, once or twice."

"Only once, actually," Mia My said, looking directly at me. "And you'd both had too much to drink. You don't give up on real love after only one half-heart stab at it."

I wanted to ask her a thousand questions about what Jack might have told her, but we were interrupted by the return of the grumpy Larch-ster himself. Jack's an early riser, up with the dawn to pay his dues to the muse, and that means he also tends to nod off long before the witching hour of midnight. But he came striding back to our table on those bandy legs of his, chest out and triumphantly carrying some glasses and a bottle of Spanish brandy that was his favorite. "Thought I was out for the night, didn't you?" He grinned at me and uncorked the brandy. He poured us each a finger and a few for himself and started in where he had left off.

"After another half hour of waiting for the M.P.s to release them, Joe and the Colonel walk out of the narrow street to Le Loi where they flag down a little blue-and-cream Renault *xe hoi* taxi that rockets them through the streets and back to the main gate outside Tan Son Nhut, without any further excitement.

Now, the fenced off compound where the 3rd Radio Research Unit is located has a mess hall, showers and latrines, and an Enlisted Men's Club. That night, Joe can't seem to calm down. He walks from his bunk area in his barracks over to the EMC, where he finds a deserted table and tries to read his Joseph Conrad book. He hasn't smoked since he picked up the habit from Dirty Old Mary back at the Puzzle Palace, but now he pulls out a pack of Lucky Strikes with the familiar red bulls eye on the front, and he lights up. His brain is working in a funny way, probably on overload. He's thinking, *Lucky Strikes Red goes to war, too.*

You see, at heart, Joe's always been a romantic. Like Conrad's hero in the book he's reading, he sees he's in a similar situation…although much of what has happened to Joe Bates never happened in "Youth", which now seems quaint and old fashioned to him. He shakes his head and sets the book down for good. He is never going to finish reading it. It's his life that's running now, and his reality has overtaken the fiction.

I'd been joking about his 'blue letter,' that nefarious piece of crap his old girlfriend had sent to take her vengeance for what she saw as his desertion. Joe slides the letter out of the familiar envelope and tries to re-read it. But that, too, seems to belong to a distant past. What kind of person sends her old boyfriend a picture of her new one? He feels whatever has happened before in his life is over. He fingers the three-inch Band-Aid on his forehead and then butt-lights another Lucky from the first one that he's only half finished. That was another Dirty Mary trick; she'd always have four or five going. She said the best decoding took place when there was a cloud of blue smoke around her head.

'Hey…!' the sergeant who was tending bar calls to him from half way across the room. 'Get you anything, Son?'

'Ahh…I don't know.'

'Scotch is good,' the sergeant suggests. There is a friendly tone in his voice. It was harder for a lingie—any specialist, really—to break into that unofficial club that exists at every military unit in the world, but word has gotten around and Joe senses he's passed some unofficial right of passage. He's been accepted here. He's a brother.

'Ahh. Right. Okay. Scotch,' Joe says.

He puts the blue letter back in the matching blue envelope with the photo of the hippy freak who has stolen his girlfriend. He gives it a little push across the table. It goes about half way. He pushes it again, and it hangs on the very edge. He flicks it with his finger, and it's gone.

The sergeant brings Joe a double. He shakes his head when Joe tries to pay.

'Those guys picked it up,' he says, indicating a table in the Non-Commissioned Officer's section, the NCO's Corner.

Red Dog, sitting at a table with three or four other sergeants, grins and waves him off. Bates is surprised to see his own hands are shaking. He wraps them around the scotch. He manages to get the glass to his lips and he takes a sip. The taste is bittersweet, the way only scotch can be.

'Welcome to Vietnam, Son,' the sergeant says as he moves away to serve another table."

Joe ties one on that night, but that's an exception, an interval. He's felt the force of the enemy, and now he's even more motivated to do his job. Red Dog tells him he can take a few days off, but he shows up at the White Shack the next morning, and every day after that. By the end of the week he is still sporting three black stitches on his forehead, but the big band-aide patch is gone.

Early one afternoon Joe is at his desk, plowing steadily through his stack of coverts when I come storming in with Red Dog right on my tail. Red Dog goes through his little stack of messages and stops in front of Joe's desk.

'How's the head?' he asks.

'No problem. It'll be okay.'

'Williamson's putting you in for a Purple Heart,' Red Dog tells him.

'It's just a scratch,' Joe says

"I flop down at my own desk and comment on the weather, 'Bumpy up there today.'

'About usual,' Red Dog says.

I lean back and put my feet up. I'm in my usual foul mood. I ask Joe, 'Break the code that'll win the war yet?'

'Not yet,' Joe says.

'Life sucks,' I tell him. 'It's not fair, you know.'

'How's that, Jack?'

'I risk getting my butt shot off every day. But here you— you go into town one time, save innocent lives, get a Purple Heart and win the love of a beautiful woman!'

Red Dog, who has been listening to me rattle on non-stop through our entire ride at a 2,000 feet altitude, raises his eyebrows and says automatically, 'Shut up, Jack.'

Joe shakes his head in denial. 'You don't get it, pal,' he says. 'I'm not in the mood for love these days.'

'That's what you think,' I tell him. 'Love is a freight train, and when it comes along, you're just a—.'

'Yeah, I got it, already,' Joe interrupts me. He's heard that old line from me a million times before and so he finishes my sentence '—you're just a bug on the tracks,'.

'I'm right, you know,' I tell him. But Joe's not listening."

CHAPTER 11

Back in the present in Holmby Hills, Jack, who'd had a second and a third snifter of Spanish brandy, fell asleep sitting at my outdoor glass table. One moment he was talking about Joe getting a Purple Heart, and the next he was snoring on the bubbled glass.

I started to get up from the table, but Mia My interrupted me. "You already know in your heart that you're not Jack's whore," she said. "Don't let your enemies stop you from being his woman."

"Jack's old," I snapped at her. "Really old."

"Is there some rule about that? If he's the one who truly loves you?" I was still trying to think that one through when she spoke again, "Come on," she said. "We can get him back to his place."

We were tipsy ourselves, and it was touch-and-go getting Jack up and half-walking and half carrying him around the pool and up the stairs to his bedroom. We managed to get his pants and shoes off, and by then he'd burrowed under the covers.

"No need to worry about the Larch-man," I told her. "He may seem three sheets to the wind, but when that old alarm goes off in his head at six tomorrow morning, he'll be up and pecking away at the Dunk Stingray wars."

She lifted the covers from his head and gently kissed his cheek. "He has come a long way alone," she said.

I felt a sudden warm blush of affection for him, and tussled his stiff main of grey-black hair with my own hand. "I guess so," I said. I'd been so busy worrying about my own troubles, maybe I didn't think enough about his.

Mia My and I drifted back to my place. I slipped into my favorite blue silk pajamas with the light yellow jasmine print, and when I came back down to the kitchen, she was bustling around, dwarfed in a big cotton robe I'd loaned her. She set a steaming cup on the kitchen table in front of me, and added a dollop of

Jack's brandy.

"Hot chocolate the Auntie Kai way," she said. She brought her own cup and sat across the table from me.

"I think I was not ready to meet my Joe when I met him," she said. "When I look back now, I see Mama had broken me not once, but twice."

"No, look at you. Your spirit wasn't broken," I protested.

She waved my comment off with a slight sideways movement of her hand and gave out a gentle laugh, "Well, pretty badly bent, then," she said. "And not once, but twice. First, Mama set me up with this stupid military man, eldest son in a very wealthy family, but three days before I am to give my hand in holy matrimony he trips on his own grenade and blows himself up. And then there was vile old LeCroix..."

"The baker-man," I smile.

"Yes. The ancient man-of-dough. Looking back, I know now how lucky I was that both of them were unavailable for sharing the joys of my bedroom."

"Fate, maybe," I agreed with her. She gave me an intense look.

"Yes. Most certainly, fate. How else to explain all the difficult times, the impossible moments. Dangerous times, Clair. Not like today in the U.S. of America."

"You think this is calm?" I asked.

She gave me that look again. It wasn't a harsh look, just an appraising one, and I had the crazy notion that I was feeling the spirit of Auntie Kai somehow present in my kitchen.

"No," Mia My said. "I see you are in your own dangerous time."

That made me uncomfortable, so I asked her to tell me about her mother.

"Mama was a cunning and relentless woman. She would do anything to marry me off to the right man. It wasn't that she hated me. She didn't think like that. To her, I was the slow child, and she was only doing her duty. When I was only 16, she was already having her fainting spells and her medical emergencies. You would note these were very uncommon in a strong woman still in her mid-thirties, but to a young daughter they can be very effective. It was lucky for me no suitable fellow popped up then, or I would have been a gonner.

When Mr. Stupid Grenade Man showed up with all his braids and metals on his chest, Mama had been hammering me for weeks with visions of her never to be a grandma, and me living out lonely days in a nunnery. So when, to my complete surprise, my soldier-boy proposed, the first word to pop out of my mouth was *Yes*. As for LeCroix, everybody in town knew he was dying from at least four separate illnesses. I said *Yes* to that one because I was sure he would die in the months it would take Mama to prepare for the wedding. But she tricked me again. She moved a team of seamstresses into the dress shop. It took weeks rather than months, and all too soon I found myself walking down the aisle with this rickety old man."

"Saved again by the mighty hand of God," I mused.

Mia My grinned, "It surely took no more the flick of His mighty little finger. You say your Wild Jack has age—that man was really old."

"So you meet this handsome young American soldier…" I prompted her.

"Yes, and Mama pulls me away from my dream, just like always…That really did me in. I remember I went straight to my room, threw away my bloody stained clothes, got into a nightgown and went to bed. I was feeling very sad. My bedroom was on the second floor. It was decorated in princess pink and looked out over the rose gardens my grandfather had planted."

"Sounds like a pretty room."

"Yes. But after LeCroix died, Mama sent a painter with a can of dark green paint to do it over. *A good color for old maids,* she told me. But I had a fit of my own, and that night at dinner I told Mama I was leaving for Paris to live with my father. You can imagine the explosion from the old tiger lady! I thought it was my defeat, but Auntie Kai made a truce for me. Mama would give me space to be my own person, and I would turn in my 1st Class Air France ticket."

"And did you do it?" I asked.

"Well, yes…but I made sure Mama knew I had money stored away. I could get at least to Thailand or Hong Kong if I had to, and I knew Papa would wire me more from there."

"You made peace with your mother."

"A fragile peace. I told you how she was at my birthday party. I had no girlfriends—they all were married, or had fled to Europe. You see how it was for me, Clair—a very lonely time with much uncertainty and fear. Mama has already broken my spirit twice, and I no longer am sure how strong I can be. Even that brief, wonderful moment with the handsome American of my dreams was broken up by Mama practically before it even properly started…after meeting Joe that first time, there was another time later, I was in my room, lying on my bed, probably feeling sorry for myself and Mama came storming in."

'Idle hands are the devil's workshop,' she says to me.

"I give her my best tired and bored attitude. 'Just a few moments of peace, Mama. That's all I ask.'

'Oh yes, don't we all. Peace in our time. Maybe your problem is we raised you too European. You should turn into a Buddha-girl, join those silly monks. Barbeque yourself. That's the way to find peace." The tiger lady is standing in the doorway to my room and she is wearing a pale blue *ao gai*. It is one of the few times I had seen her in native dress since her grandmother's funeral. Every few years, particularly after an emotional strain, she would go native for a few weeks until her craving for Channel #5, French cooking and designer clothing brought her back to her senses.

'What are you talking about, Mama?' I ask her. And she throws a book across the room! It lands on my stomach, knocking a little wind out of me. Mama doesn't seem to notice, or maybe she doesn't care what happens to me any more.

'Read this. Perhaps you will learn a little humility!' I look at the cover. It is a cheap reprint of an ancient book from Vietnamese culture, Kim Van Kieu. It is a lurid novel—or at least a long story—the romantic, wild and unbelievable adventures of a young girl. Kim is sold into prostitution and escapes one nasty situation after another. I had read it in high school. I sit up and stare across the room at my mother.

'You intend that I should read this?' I ask her.

'Yes, you should.'

'But you've never read it yourself, have you?'

'Why do you ask?' she answers my question with that one of her own, and her voice gets a sharp, snappy edge on it.

'You can never answer a question directly, can you?' I say, trying to provoke her even more.

'Alright, then,' my mother shoots back at me. 'I wasn't raised in the hand of plenty like you. I never had the time.'

'Why are you wearing that dress?'

'If it's any of your business, I'm apologizing to my ancestors.'

'For joining the Dragon Lady's Military Brigade?'

'No.'

'For stealing Papa's money?'

'It was my money!'

'Earned for your affair with our dearly departed president?'

'I never—' She blurts out that much and then she stop. For a moment I think she is going to have a stroke and die. But *su tu Hao Gam* never die, or if they do, they only come back as something meaner. Still, I got my spear in her that time, and in another second she was gone from my room."

Clair shook her head, "You accused your crazy mother of having an affair with the president of Vietnam? Lucky she didn't kill you."

"It was only a lucky guess," Mia My said. "Actually, a rumor, but it happened to be true. Mama was very beautiful, and she always had her way with men. Many important men sought her favors, but she always made them pay dearly for her companionship."

"After your Papa left for France, right?"

Mia My gave a slight, amused shrug of her slim shoulders. "Only Buddha knows," she said. "Anyway, here I am alone in my room with this musty smelling old book with pages that are yellow with age. I wonder if Mama has picked it up at the old market. I turn the first few pages and I find an ancient pressed flower. It is a dried clover flower, with a lucky four leaf, all of it very fragile, like my own dreams. Mama, without knowing, has given me a used book, and a version that was complete with an English translation.

In our house, we speak only French and Vietnamese, but I had taken a year of English at the *Hoi Viet-My*. I began pacing back and forth in my pink room, reading out loud in my halting English

> Kim Van Kieu, this
> perfect work to which one
> refers as one does to a drama of
> Shakespeare, a tragedy of
> Racine, a funeral oration of
> Bossuet, to the poems of Henry
> Wadsworth Longfellow or
> Robert Frost, is regarded as the
> most beautiful jewel of the
> Vietnamese language in
> painting the most tender
> sentiments of the human soul.

I yawn and lie back down on my bed. At this rate I will be asleep in no time. I turn past the introduction to the beginning of the great epic. I ignore the opening verses in my native tongue. My attention moves to the English translation and I whisper to myself:

> Within the span of a
> hundred years of human existence,
> what a bitter struggle is waged
> between genius and destiny! How
> many harrowing events have
> occurred while mulberries cover
> the conquered sea! Rich in beauty,
> unlucky in life! Strange indeed,
> but little wonder, since casting
> hatred upon rosy cheeks is a habit
> of the Blue Sky."

"Hey, that's heavy stuff," I said. "And you memorized it!"
"You bet, Clair," Mia My grinned. "Kim Van Kieu is like heavy perfume. But at that moment, my mind kept going back to one line, and I found myself repeating it over and over, 'Rich in beauty, unlucky in life.' That was Kim's destiny. I had this

shuddering thought like a dagger of fear in my heart. Was that also going to be my own?

I sat up. I was fully awake now, thinking back over all the times that I and my schoolmates had read and wondered at the perils of this famous prostitute, sold by her needy parents into the hands of cruel villains, clever sex deviates and corrupt old men.

The one thing about Kim Van Kieu, I realized, was that the girl never gave up. Even after Kim gave herself over to the corrupt and the vile, she had kept her spirit. She never sold herself for money or power, as had my own mother. Kim Van Kieu's soul was and always would be free. I remember very clearly, Clair, it was as if a light dawned for me. In my own life, I hadn't actually given up. I had simply bent like the graceful willow, as had Kim Van Kieu.

'Thank you, Mamma,' I said. I remember I said it in a fierce whisper. I didn't have to read any more. I leaned out of my open window as far as I could and threw the book into the back yard. I was happy to see the frayed binding gave way and the ancient pages came apart and went fluttering down like soft rain onto grandfather's garden."

CHAPTER 12

It was about half past eight the next morning in the Larch-ster's big modern reinforced concrete and slab glass house in Holmby Hills. Eddie was taking the day off to get his teeth brightened, but Jack was pounding away at Dunk Stingray, who had somehow gotten himself stuck on top of a sandstone mesa surrounded by vertical walls from which it would be impossible for any ordinary man to escape.

Mia My was reading the financials and I was frying Jack's favorite breakfast of bacon-and-eggs. For the moment, we were at peace, and then there was a furious knock on the front door. Before anybody could say anything, Maria had opened it and let in Dorothy, who sailed right past her, screaming as she stormed into Jack's study. Frizzy-haired Dorothy Chalice, Jack's Number Two ex-wife, wanna-be movie star, dedicated ski bum and mother of Paul, and the one who still gave the Larch-ster the most trouble in his personal life.

"You thoughtless bastard!" she screamed, pounding at his neck and shoulders with her fists. "How could you let him go to Mexico?"

"Dorothy, stop it. Paul's a grown man." Jack growled, covering up by hunching over, pulling in his neck and protecting the loose manuscript papers on his desk as best he could.

"He's a dope fiend, Jack, and it's your fault, letting him grow up without a father!"

"You left me, Dorothy, remember? You were distressed that you couldn't take me to the cleaners!" It was an old argument, and they automatically continued it every time they met.

"God-damn-pre-nup!"

"You signed the papers."

"No, no, no. I remember very clearly! You got me drunk, Jack!"

"It was broad daylight, in Connie's office!"

"You're agent would say anything for you!"

"And her secretary!"

"Same thing, Jack!"

"And the notary."

"I didn't know what I was signing!"

"Dorothy, stop hitting him!" I yelled at her.

She turned on me like a viper and things went completely out of control. "*You!* you greedy, money-grubbing bitch!" she yelled.

I thought the madness would go on until somebody called the cops, the way it usually did in The House of Jack—but then there was another voice in the room, the topper over everybody. It was sharp, imperious, in command, and totally unexpected.

"*Top!*" Mia My said. Not 'Be quiet' or even 'Stop.' *Top!* Jack didn't look surprised, but the rest of us in the room looked like we'd been hit by Mr. Freeze's ice-ray gun. That was my first hint of what a tiger lady could do.

"Who are you?" Dorothy said, seeing our tiger lady for the first time and talking in a suddenly subdued voice. I don't think she'd even noticed Mia My before.

"I am the widow of Jack's best friend," Mia My replied in a deceptively soft way.

"Pfttt! Jack doesn't have any friends," Dorothy said, regaining some of her composure.. "He has hanger-ons, hookers and lover-girls, like Missy Hot-Pants here."

Mia My stood. She said nothing, but there was this presence about her. At that moment she was the tallest person in the room. I felt she was about to spring across the room and do…well, I didn't know what, probably claw Dorothy to death. I know that sounds silly, but that's the way it seemed to me at that moment.

And I don't believe I was imagining things. Dorothy saw it too. She actually stepped back a foot or two.

"Wooh, now Honey," she said. "Don't go getting' yourself tangled in a bad mess from which you cannot extract yourself."

Dorothy was a trailer trash girl who fell back on lofty phraseology in her moments of uncertainty.

"Jack has more good friend than you know," Mia My answered. Her voice was soft as a knife going through butter. Dorothy didn't even think of interrupting her. "Jack has me for his friend. He has my family. He has Clair here, too, a good, good very close friend. He is a very lucky man, lucky with friends."

Dorothy finally found her voice, "Well, that's just a lot of crap—"

Mia My raised her voice a little, and it wasn't just a butter knife, I could sense steel and coiled springs and claws, a dangerous armory of hidden reserves. "When Jack married you, he did get a pre-nup," she said, cutting to the heart of the matter. "It is valid in a United States of America court of law."

"What? How do you? Why, how dare you—"

"He showed it to me, years ago, after you hurt him."

"I never hurt him!" Dorothy shrieked.

"You left him and took away the baby! You no longer have any rights here! Jack should put the dog on you!"

Dorothy blew out a breath and looked around the room for support. "My Paulie is Jack's only heir," she huffed.

"I don't know Paulie," Jack said. "And I don't like the way he turned out. You took him away from me before he was out of diapers," He frowned and shook his head. "And that's that. He's no son of mine."

"He is! He *is!*" Dorothy insisted.

But now the pack of us, led by Mia My, was advancing on her and she was backing out of the room. "You've got to live up to your responsibilities, Jack! In this life you don't get to do whatever you want! We'll see after you're dead and gone who your heir is! And with these kind of people looking after you that isn't going to be too long!"

She looked from Mai My to me and back again, glaring her suspicions that we somehow had gotten our hooks into the fabulous fortune she was convinced Dunk Stingray had earned Jack Larch over the years.

"You better get out of here, or I'm going to bean you," I said, picking up one of the steel balls lying around on Jack's desk.

This didn't seem to phase the crazy Dorothy, but then Mia My made the slightest movement, the dangerous feline coming out of her cage. It was barely a twitch, a hitch of one shoulder…but it was enough. Dorothy turned on her high heels and practically ran for the front door. Another moment and the wicked witch was gone, slamming the front door on her way out.

We watched as she jumped in her dented and grimy Cadillac SUV, put it in reverse and spun the wheels on Jack's gravel drive. Ong Vung, who looked like he was sleeping with the hedge clippers in his hands, had to jump out of the way as she spun the steering wheel and roared past him down the drive.

"She will destroy you, Jack," Mia My said.

"Don't be silly," Jack said.

"I have my family. I cannot always be here."

"She's crazy, but I can handle her." Jack retreated from the front alcove. "That your Macy's bag?" he asked me, indicating a big shiny red shopping bag with a white star on the side.

"Not me, Jack. I don't shop at Macy's. Did you know when they bought Marshall Fields in Chicago they changed the name to Macy's?"

Jack gave me a strange look of bemused appreciation. "No respect for tradition, huh?" By this time we had retreated to the breakfast table. "Where are my fried eggs?" he asked. I figured he was through thinking about his troubles with Wild Paul and Crazy Dorothy, at least for the moment. "Scuse me for a moment. Gotta take a leak."

"Why isn't this vile woman gone from Jack's life?" Mia My asked me.

"Beats me," I said.

Jack was back. That had to have been the fastest whiz in the world, but I didn't think much about it at the time. But later, when I passed through the hallway, I noticed the Macy's bag was gone.

"She hates Clair," Jack mumbled, unhappy that his eggs weren't on the table and this thing couldn't just be swept under the rug.

"She'll do anything to get Jack back under her thumb," I said. "A couple of months ago, she tried to have him institutionalized. She came over and started throwing things, and then accused him of beating her up. The time before, she set the living room on fire. I had to put it out with a garden hose.

"When the two of you work together, you are very strong," Mia My said.

"Dorothy is Jack's ex. Technically, she's none of my business," I said.

"That is where you are wrong. There is no *technically* in the business of love. Everything is real or it is not. You must stop denying what the two of you mean to each other."

I didn't know what to think of that. I wanted to tell Buddha-lady that she was being a butt-in-ski…but I was beginning to think she was right about a lot of things, and she might be right about this one, as well. So I held my peace and retreated to the stove. There'd already been too much yelling and carrying on for one morning. I had left the burner on and Jack's fried eggs were crisped beyond acceptability. I tossed them in the garbage can and cracked in a new pair. In a few minutes, new fat was popping in the pan. I served them sunny side up with the brown edges all around, along with three or four pieces of thick-sliced pepper-and-hickory bacon that I had in the warmer. The Larch-ster didn't say anything, and so for the moment all was peaceful, at least as calm as it ever got in The House of Jack.

The Goy Ghost called and said he wouldn't be available until after lunch, so after Jack gulped down his eggs, he settled back with a second cup of coffee and started in on the old times again. It was as if he had switched off on the new Stingray adaptation and now was writing the story about his olden days with Joe. Jack was like that; he almost never revised anything, not even on the computer. He wrote it in his brain and then it came spilling out the way he wanted. His only reservations came when he compared himself to his giants—Hemingway, Faulkner, F. Scott Fitzgerald and Joseph Conrad. Once he started to doubt himself, which usually came after he finished the draft that was supposed to go to press, revision mania would set in.

"The barracks at the 3rd Radio Research Unit, he said, "that had to be the closest thing to camping out in the tropics, I guess just short of living in a canvas tent. We had these screened in open walls with louvered slats of old teak wood that were slanted to keep out all but the heaviest gusts of rain. And there were old black fans spinning from beams strung at regular intervals across the open ceilings.

"Each one of us was assigned a bunk, upper or lower, and we each had a wooden footlocker and a wall locker. Our beds were rigged with individual mosquito nets. The bugs of Nam are vicious. That's why I hate bugs, even today. After a week, Bates and I went downtown and bought a 2nd layer of netting on the black market.

"So I'm lying in my bunk and Doober looks down at me from his bunk, which was over Bates and across from mine. I'm sitting on my footlocker, making notes in a small journal, and I'm bored and itchy to do something. Just then I see Joe coming in the screen door at our end of the barracks.

'Hey, dude, here come the Purple Heart man,' I say to Doober. 'Hi, there, Bates,' I'm still jealous of his exploits but I'm over being totally pissed; I'm kind of flat-lined, tired of hearing about the exploits of Nug Wonder-man.

'Hey, you missed chow,' Doober says.

'I'm still catching up,' Joe says. He's talking about his precious little crypto translations over at the White Shack.

'R.A.' I mutter under my breath.

'What's that, man?' Doober asks.

'*Regular Army.* Never mind.' I set down my notebook so I can concentrate on attacking Joe. I give him my innocent sideways glance. 'Soo, about this beautiful girl…you gonna date her, slugger?'

'Get off it, Jack. How did you hear about her, anyway?' Joe is properly annoyed, and I find this satisfying.

'Everybody heard,' Doober chimes in. 'Colonel Williamson—'

'—said she had a face like an angel,' I interrupt him. It's my Plague Joe Show, and I don't want any outsider ruining it.

'I got your angel right here,' Doober jokes. He's a good natured fellow, nothing much gets to him. He's been reading a cock book he picked up in the street. He tosses it over to Bates, and Joe takes a serious look at the cover for a moment. The title is "Little Angel Go Fuck," the first in a series of similar classics that were flooding the Orient at that time; "Little Angel Go Fuck Hong Kong," "Little Angel Go Fuck Singapore," and so on.

Bates gives Doober a little grimace and delicately two-fingers the book back as if it was covered with half-dried jazz.

'Hey, just joking, guy…' Doober says.

'I'll never see her again,' Joe says with a glum look on his face.

'You got her name, didn't you?' I ask him.

'Sure, but…Saigon is a big city.'

'Not too big for the freight train of love, you pussy-weight,' I say.

I look at Joe, but his expression says he isn't buying it.

'Maybe it's better, anyway,' Doober says.

I throw one of my balled-up paper scraps at Doober. 'Why's that, oh wise short-timer?

'The White Snake got a real hard on for grunts who fall for Zip bitches.'

'That's his job, asshole.' I say.

'Well, nug, be advised—he takes it real serious.'

Joe's had enough of us. He strips naked and picks up his towel and soap. He takes a long time studying his feet before he slides them in his rubber go-aheads.

'Goddamn, I think I got athlete's foot," he says. 'And it doesn't matter, one way or the other, what The White Snake thinks about Vietnamese women—because there is no freight train of love.'

He pushes open the screen door and heads for the showers, leaving us shaking our heads behind him. And that's how it goes for a while," Jack says.

The Larch-ster's troubles with his son Paul are forgotten for the moment. Wild Jack's on full tilt, he's Jack the story guy, steaming full speed ahead.

"That was a very rainy year, 1964. The sun comes up, the clouds thicken over and by noon the rains are pelting down across the wet and steamy delta lands, pouring down on the old and moldy French city of Saigon. The days go by, and Joe and I settle into our routine. Every single week day, and even Saturdays, Joe wakes up at dawn, cleans up his area, and throws on his cleanest fatigues. He downs some reconstituted eggs and maybe a leg of fried chicken in the mess hall, and then he trudges down the runway to the White Shack where he churns his way through his stack of intercepts.

Before he leaves, he reaches through my now triple-layer mosquito nets and grabs my ear or musses my hair. Me, my morning preparations are a bit more careless than Joe's. I throw on whatever I can find and stagger down the runway to the apron next to the White Shack where our two Beavers are parked. Like as not, I'm wearing yesterday's fatigues jacket, and if I'm lucky, I'll find a Babe Ruth or a Butterfingers bar in one of the pockets, enough sugar to keep me awake until Red Dog and one of the pilots show up, which they eventually do, if they're not there before me. It's a loose arrangement; we're not on a really tight schedule. Just show up, that's all. Don't keep anybody waiting too long. Finally, when we've got two teams, we fire up the old clatter-boxes and take off, one after the other. After a few hours of bouncing around in the air, we land somewhere like Long Xuyen or Can Tho in the delta or Nha Trang up the coast for lunch and a refuel, and then we take off again.

This was wild times for me, nothing bad about it except a little scary being up there in one of the Beavers. My nights are full of hazy happiness as I get tanked on Ba Muoi Ba beers and go cruising around the bars and nightclubs all over Saigon."

"Were you on dope, Jack?" I asked him.

"He gave me a serious look, as if I wouldn't believe him. "No, Clair, I wasn't. Sure, it was everywhere, heavy grass and those little waxy opium balls…and sure I tried everything a time or two—but this was *my* war, I had to experience the dope part, but I wasn't going to miss the rest of it.

"*You're* war," I repeated after him without any of the skepticism I might have had a few weeks before. This was the inner Jack I was seeing, what made Jack tick, and—I don't know why—I liked it more than I would have believed. Jack wasn't entirely a Hollywood phony, there was some sand in the old boy's bottom after all.

"Hell, yes," he said. "Hemingway had his war. Crane had his war. Christ, Heller and even that fruity old Greek Xenophon had their wars. I went to see it, Clair. I had to see it!"

Jack fell silent for a moment, then started up again, "I remember it was about three in the afternoon, a week or two after

Joe's run-in with the cyclo-boy explosion. Joe was in his other world, noodling a translation and paying no attention to the clatter of the telex machine down the hall or the radio blaring *Sherrieeee Babieeee* through the damp and icy chill of our workroom. I couldn't stand it. I'm trying to get some impressions of a bargirl I'd been with the night before down on paper and Bates is annoying the hell out of me by muttering his goddamn translations to himself.

'Gangster-stepped on-stepped on-stepped on…' he says.

He stops like a needle that's stuck on an old phonograph record, saying the same thing over and over again, and then he automatically reaches for his Hoa's. He leafs through it until he finds the word.

'…stepped on-punji stake.' He carefully closes Hoa's, and then signs the message with his initials and puts it in his out-box. 'Huh,' he says, 'When you're in the bush, you have to watch where you're stepping, Jack…'

'Talking to yourself again, huh, Lingie?' I say, throwing out a jab to see if anybody's alive in there. I put my head down on my desk, motionless and oblivious to the rest of the world. 'Lord, Lord, Lord, that formaldehyde beer…' I say to the cool surface of the wood on which I'm resting my head..

'That's an old wive's tale,' Joe says.. *Ba Muoi Ba* doesn't have any—'

'Go away, Bates,' I moan. Suddenly, I'm not feeling all that well. Maybe it was some of that *trom trom trop* I picked up off a street vender to see if Williamson's warnings were right. I lurch to my feet, put one hand over my mouth and head for the bathroom.

Red Dog comes out of Colonel Ogilvy's office in time to see me slam the door to the john behind me.

'What's wrong with him?' he asks Joe.

'He says Ba Muoi Ba has formaldehyde in it.'

'I thought it did," Red Dog says. 'But I thought it just tingles your brains a little. Drinking too much of it is what makes you sick.' He sits on the edge of Joe's desk.

'The White Snake wants to see you, Joe.' Red Dog looks over toward Ogilvy's open doorway and lowers his voice a notch. 'Be careful.'

'Careful of what?'

But Red Dog won't say any more. He just shakes his head. Then he heaves himself off the desk and walks away toward the telex room. Of course, Joe and I had occasionally glanced in Colonel Ogilvy's office while passing by, you know, just out of curiosity, but neither of us has ever been in there before. The way Joe described his first look, the walls were covered with maps of the city, the suburbs and the outlying provinces. I mean, we had maps, but Ogilvy had maps on maps on maps, no room for a picture of mom or the pet dog on his walls.

Windows painted out in white, of course. It was a fairly large room with space for the Colonel's desk and a small, round table with three chairs. On the bookcase behind him was a large picture of Ogilvy himself standing next to a smiling President John F. Kennedy. The picture was inscribed with the old Irish blessing, "May the wind always be at our backs!" and signed by Kennedy himself.

So, when Joe walks in, two men in civilian clothes are sitting at the table, busily looking at open files in front of them. Red Dog has already pointed them out to us; they are the spook operatives who work for the Colonel. They don't bother to look up when Joe enters, but Joe's no fool, he can tell they are more interested in him than in the paperwork in front of them.

Colonel Ogilvy himself is this tall, scary man with a straight military bearing. His face is so thin you think you're looking at a skull, and there's a thin smile painted on his lips that never reaches his light blue eyes. 'Specialist Bates,' he says, returning Joe's salute. He points to the scatter of black-and-white 10 X 12 photo blowups on his desk. 'You took these, I believe?'

'Yes, sir,' Joe answers.

'You take good pictures, Specialist. See anybody you recognize?'

Bates takes a moment to orient himself, as the Colonel doesn't bother to turn the photos around to face him. After a moment Joe points to one that shows one of the pedi-cyclo drivers.

'Here's one of the guys who tried to kill us, sir,' he says. 'This was Colonel Williamson's driver.'

'Good. That's what Williamson said, too. ARVN security picked him up this morning. Anybody else?'

Joe points to another picture. 'This was my ride.'

'Excellent. We got him too.'

The Colonel picks up the two photos and hands them to Joe, 'You absolutely, positively, 100% sure?'

'Yes, sir! We were with them for 15 minutes or more. A man turns out to try and kill me, I remember.'

'Excellent,' the Colonel repeats. His lips turn into a thin line that shows more grimace than smile. Joe, who hasn't had experience in these sort of matters, thinks he's home free. Nothing to worry about here.

'What's going to happen to them, sir?' he asks.

To The White Snake, Joe must look like the innocent that he is, a young recruit who has no experience with anything more violent than Friday night high school football. The Colonel shrugs and looks over at his two operatives.

'Maybe it will lead to something...' he says with a vague gesture, letting his voice trail off into that grey area where many things are uncertain.

Joe turns around and sees Leo, one of the spook ops, grinning behind his back. He is in the act of making a quick, slashing motion with one-finger across his own neck. Ogilvy shakes his head and looks down at the photos. He clears his throat and shuffles the pictures, finds the one he wants and hands it to Joe. It's the last picture on the roll, the one Joe snapped of Mia My as her mother pulled her away through the crowd.

'Do you know these people, Specialist?'

Joe isn't sure why, but he knows his face is red as a beet. He hesitates, then realizes the Colonel is measuring him, quietly waiting for an answer.

'That's the girl who helped me before the ambulances came, Sir. Her name is Mia My. We saved a lady who was bleeding badly and—'

'And that's her mother,' the Colonel interrupted, stabbing at the picture with his forefinger. 'You don't know them personally, then?'

'No, sir. We just met by accident. Is something wrong, Sir?'

'They're French-Vietnamese, Specialist Bates...They don't like us...and we don't particularly care for them, either.'

'Her mother certainly didn't like me,' Joe blurts out.

'How about the girl? Do you have anything going with her?'

'No, Sir! We just met, Sir. By accident, like I said.'

"Colonel Ogilvy frowns and stares at Joe, sizing him up with his cold look. He reaches over and taps Joe's security badge on top where the words TOP SECRET are very much in evidence for all the world to see.

'Watch your step, boy. You seem to be a good army man, and you could have a good future here.'

Joe doesn't know what might happen next, but in that moment Red Dog interrupts from the doorway.

'Colonel, I need my translator before we go up again.'

"The White Snake clears his throat and spins around to face Red Dog.

'Right. We were just finished, Sergeant.'

As Joe Bates leaves, the Colonel sinks heavily into his chair, He seems lost in his thoughts. Both Leo and Wendell give up on their files and turn to face him.

'I think he's lying, Colonel,' Leo volunteers.

'That's stupid, Leo,' Wendell says. 'He's just a dumb linguist. What would he have to lie about?'

The White Snake's gaze wanders to the photo of Jack Kennedy. Ogilvy probably is thinking of earlier times when, as a matter of course, his opinion had been requested by certain members of a youthful team the President had pulled together, a hot young team of insiders that the jealous were already calling "The Best and the Brightest.".

'Okay, we kill them all—what then?' he murmurs out loud.

Wendell, thinking the Colonel is talking to them, shrugs, 'Sir, it's not that way. I think we just have to kill enough of them until they get the idea they can't win.'

The White Snake clears his head with a characteristic gesture, a little, unconscious shudder, a sort of half-tic of the muscles around his sunken eyes and sallow cheeks that takes place when he clears his mind to concentrate on what he calls *the here and now..* He gives his operatives a flickering bleak look, but he says nothing. JFK smiles enigmatically from his little corner of the desk. The White Snake knows in his heart this is all he can expect from his own dead President.

Back at his desk, Joe uncertainly leafs through the new batch of covert interceptions that Red Dog has brought in from the diddy-boppers, the guys who listen to the tapes and transcribe the Morse Code, still undecyphered, but typed double-spaced the way Joe likes to work on them.

'You okay?' Red Dog asks him.

'Yeah, I guess so…' Joe says.

'You don't tangle with The White Snake. You don't even want to know him.'

'Yeah, right,' I hear this because I've returned to my desk from the bathroom. I groan with my head back down on the desk. 'But, problem is, he's kind of our boss.'

'He was one of the guys in charge—or at least, he was the fall guy—when Ngo Dinh Diem went down.' Red Dog says in a low whisper.

'But what…?' I start to ask, interested in spite of the roiling anguish sweeping through my guts.

Red Dog interrupts me, looking over his shoulder to be sure he wouldn't be overheard, and impatiently waving his hands, 'You don't really want to know. The coup didn't go down as planned. Kennedy's boys never meant they should kill the poor schlump.'

'But…?' I start another stupid question. See, this is all new and important—this is the real business of the war, right next to the bone, and I sense it's somehow dangerous stuff, too, but I've got this terrible hangover and I'm still trying to catch up.

Meanwhile, Red Dog sees we don't get it, so he's still trying to explain, 'Ogilvy's big mistake was he should have gone himself, but he stayed back at the Farm and sent some idiots over. Misunderstandings happened. The operatives managed to blame the locals, they were simply overenthusiastic, or so the story went. The CIA did their best to clean up the mess with the press and everybody, but after that The White Snake lost his star.'

'He was a general?' Joe asks. His mouth is hanging open as he looks from Red Dog to the Colonel's open office door and back again.

Red Dog nods, speaking in a hasty whisper.

'Yeah, and on his way up, too. But after that mess, Kennedy says, It's your war now, go fix it. Of course, that was silly, suggesting a one man quick fix to an unsolvable problem, a little like Don Quixote tilting windmills that have grenades taped to them.. They sent Ogilvy over here to punish him.'

'Talking about me?' Colonel Ogilvy is standing behind them in his doorway. I'm thinking the man must have superhuman vibes.. His lips are pinched in that characteristic thin line and his face is creamy white as the chalk he uses in his briefings.

'Not really, Colonel,' Red Dog lies, hoping that The White Snake hasn't overheard enough to connect the dots.

I see the shit is about to hit the fan. 'We're talking about Ho Chi Minh being an admirer of Abraham Lincoln,' I say, managing to sit up in my chair.

'You don't look too well, Specialist.' Ogilvy says to me.

"That's all the opening I need to try to change the subject. 'I feel like I'm gonna die, sir. I want to die.'

Red Dog follows my lead with a shake of his head, 'Jack, go to the infirmary. It may be catching.'

Colonel Ogilvy frowns, 'Who'll go up with you this afternoon?'

'I'll do it, sir,' Joe volunteers.

'You sure, Specialist?' The Colonel asks.

I get it right away, and I don't like it. See, apparently, I'm expendable, but Joe's a whiz at decoding and translating. Him, they might miss for a few weeks until they could ship out a new replacement from the Puzzle Palace. Me, they won't miss for five seconds, just long enough to clean out my foot locker and sell my mosquito nets to the highest bidder.

'Yes, sir!' Joe says in his best army voice.

'All right, then. Settled.' The Colonel spins on his heel and goes back inside his office.

'You sure, Joe?' Red Dog asks, even though we all know it's already a done deal. 'You've never been up before.'

'You never show that kind of worry about me,' I grumble. 'You just don't want to lose your goddamn, precious crypto-boy-wonder.'

That damn Red Dog grins at me and nods his head, as much as admitting it. 'There's something to that,' he says.

I don't know where Joe has gotten his new reckless attitude, but he flips his thumb in my direction. 'This moron can do it,' he says. 'How tough can it be?'"

CHAPTER 13

"I'd already been up over the delta dozens of times," Jack said. "I knew what it was like. But Joe's experience was going to be quite different from any of mine. He filled me in when they got back. He'd never forget it, and because he was my friend, neither would I.

"You have to try to imagine it: When we go up, we're inside a cramped compartment in this olive colored Beaver with its aluminum-and-fabric wings. It sits at one end of the airport runway, waiting its turn. It's just over 30 feet long with a wingspan only 48 feet. That means it's dwarfed by most everything that takes off from Tan Son Nhut. It's really like an antique, already an old fashioned toy plane for that day and age.

"Think about it: You're cramped in this compartment with your floor-to-ceiling stacks of direction-finding electronic gear, and you rock from side to side as a dark blue U.S. Navy Phantom jet directly in front of you howls and then takes off, disappearing away from you like an arrow shot from a bow, still accelerating and already rocketing toward the horizon at over three times the speed you'll ever go in the Beaver. For ten seconds, the cramped quarters inside your sturdy little recon plane are filled with deafening thunder. Then, as the sound rolls off into the bright blue sky, you're again aware of the engine clatter from the Beaver's radial piston engine, four hundred and fifty horsepower to pull you up into the still and heavy air of early afternoon. At times like this, it doesn't seem like nearly enough.

"Lieutenant Chivers, our pilot, has over the past months employed his sense of humor by awarding Purple Hearts to the plane itself for the many times it has taken nicks and punctures in the course of duty. He's painted heart after heart in rows under his side door. The rows have grown to three of nine each, and a freshly painted lavender heart in the fourth row attests to the latest puncture, the hole in one wing that Doober recently showed around and pointed out was the size of a fist.

Lieutenant Chivers sits up front. He's propped open a small door that leads to the rear compartment and he's flipping through a worn copy of Playboy while he waits for clearance to take off. A silvery flying boxcar lands on the runway in front of us, looking like a Silver Stream camper that has sprouted wings. After a few minutes, an olive colored Caribou rattles in. The interior of the Beaver is unbearably hot and stuffy.

Red Dog and my temporary replacement Joe Bates sit on small wooden seats behind the pilot. Everywhere Joe turns, he faces black trays of electronic recording and direction-finding equipment. Surrounded the way he is, he can't actually see out from where he's sitting. He wipes the sweat running down his thick eyeglasses with his handkerchief. He hunches forward in his seat to where he can see a small angle out of the pilot's front window, just enough to assure he is going to get very sick from the ride. Red Dog, who has ten years experience doing this all over Southeast Asia, has provided him with a half-dozen brown paper bags. 'Don't barf on the gear,' the sergeant says, handing Joe a headset and donning one of his own. He spends the next few minutes giving Joe tips on how to tune and dial, how to fish for hot signals across the entire band of radio frequencies. He shows where little arrows hand-drawn on tape indicate frequencies of interest. He stops mid-sentence and adjusts the heavy-looking army .45 that is riding awkwardly on his hip.

'You didn't bring any gold,' Red Dog says, the accusatory tone clear in his voice.

To Joe, this remark comes out of some other, unknown world. He doesn't take it very seriously. 'Nope," he shrugs. 'No gold. Didn't bring any Wrigley's Spearmint, either.'

'Look, I wasn't kidding, Bates. You always carry gold. I got a pound of it right here…and more here…and here.' Red Dog fingers the heavy necklace glittering over his t-shirt in his open fatigues blouse, then holds up the shiny watchband on his left wrist and wiggles his golden-ringed fingers. 'That way, we go down, you can buy your way back out of the bush.'

'If we go down in the Mekong, you'll sink like a rock,' Joe says.

Red Dog gives him a quick stare. 'You know, I never thought of that.' There is a pause while he mulls it over. 'I'd hate to, but I could always strip it off. Anyway, I'm a pretty good swimmer. I think I'll be okay.'

'Hope we don't have to find out.'

'Yeah. Me, either, son."

The clatter of their single Pratt and Whitney R-985 radial engine increases to a roar and their Beaver starts down the runway. With the heat and lack of lift they are nearly off the end of the asphalt before their sturdy little plane lumbers into the heavy, moisture laden atmosphere. As they make a slow turn and struggle for altitude, Joe leans forward through the door to the pilot's compartment and manages a glimpse out the side window to see the second Beaver, a tiny toy plane hundreds of feet below, just starting to lift off from the runway behind them.

The two Beavers labor through a series of upward spirals and meet at 2600 feet. Lieutenant Chivers wags his wings and banks in a sweeping turn to head in a south-westerly direction, aiming for the flat rice paddies southwest of the Mekong River. The second Beaver takes a parallel course a few miles to the west, and they began trolling for intercepts.

Joe Bates finds, much to his surprise, that he doesn't get airsick at all. He dons his headsets and is soon lost in the buzzing audio world of the ditty-boppers, the guys who regularly intercept Morse Code and write it down lightning fast. A second surprise, the air is cool enough to be damp and chilly, pleasant at first, but, as he doesn't have a flight jacket, he's feeling increasingly uncomfortable. Red Dog gives him a big beach towel embossed with a Chianti label, and he gratefully wraps it around his shoulders. 'Compliments of the downtown Pizzeria," Red Dog says.

Joe realizes he's great at de-crypting coded messages, but he doesn't know Morse Code well enough to transcribe it on the fly. He is winging it, just hoping he can pick up some scrap of code and point it out to Red Dog. I told him that was all I did. Still, after a half hour, Joe has nothing but static in his ears. He gives up fiddling with the dials and takes the headphones off.

'It's getting colder up here!' he yells at Red Dog.

'Clouds moving in,' Red Dog shouts back, pointing through the sliver of open cockpit door to the billowy dark grey bottomed clouds in the near distance.

'I wasn't getting anything.' Joe admits.

'Usually don't around here. Maybe we can go over by the Cambodian border. Those bastards over there never shut up.'

Red Dog yells up front to the pilot and Chivers chatters into his mike and then turns 90 degrees, heading west-north-west, and the other Beaver turns as if on a string and parallels them, still keeping several miles distance between them. It is this triangulation, the reference of the same radio signal from differing locations of the two planes that gives them their bead on the target. With a little luck, they can pinpoint a sender within 50 yards.

The weather continues to get worse until giant cumulus clouds billow in the near background, framing the Beavers like two lonely sentinels flitting along at the base of giant, snowy mountains. Red Dog motions that Joe can stand and lean forward through the doors. Chivers obligingly banks to the left and then the right, giving Joe a view of the sweep of waterlogged rice paddies below, interrupted by an occasional village hamlet, and now as they approach the border, giving way to savannah, light forest and a hint of rolling hills to the north. One lone peak stands out in the distance.

'*Nui Ba Den,*' Red Dog yells over the engine sound. 'Black Lady Peak.'

'Don't we have a station up there?' Joe asks.

'Sometimes…'

'It's going to rain,' Chivers yells from the pilot's seat.

'Good for the crops,' Red Dog replies. 'How about one more pass?' He motions to Joe. They put their headphones on and go back to their dials. Joe's dials are to his left side. He leans back, watching the yellow lit dial near his head as he ignores the notepad balanced on his legs. He listens to the mad *screeeeee* sounds. Layers of electronic nonsense pour into his ears. There is a scrap of music and he hears part of the station break I.D. for VTVN, Radio Saigon, in clear Vietnamese.

And then, in the next moment, there is a sudden, sharp, interruptive noise, a *snap!* not unlike a bamboo cane hitting a desk, and Joe's notepad flies up off his knees and strikes the aluminum roof of the plane. Joe is stunned. He panics, looking around at the suddenly claustrophobic audio equipment surrounding him as his notepad flops back down and falls off his lap onto the floor. Joe sees a bullet hole in the center of the notepad! Above the churning rattle of the piston engine, he hears air whistling through a hole in the ceiling, and another in the floor between his legs. He grabs at his crotch and is horrified to see blood all over his hand, his own warm, bright red blood dripping from his pants!

Red Dog yells, 'We took one, Lieutenant!' Then he sees the blood. He shakes Joe's shoulder, 'Bates! Drop your pants!'

Joe stands hunched over in the narrow compartment and unbuckles his brass belt. His olive fatigue pants fall down around his ankles. There is an angry red blood line creasing the inside of his left thigh, a few inches below his balls.

'H-how b-b-bad is it?' he manages to stutter

Red Dog rips open a first aid kit, twists the top off a bottle of iodine and splashes it all over Joe's thigh.

'Not bad,' he says. 'Not deep. Just a graze wound.' He hands the antiseptic bottle and a wad of gauze to Joe.

'Can you handle it?'

Joe says he can.

'Rub it in real good,' Red Dog tells him. 'Pour it on. The assholes dip their bullets in their own shit.'

Encouraged by that remark, Joe empties the bottle until there is more iodine than blood on him.

Red Dog claps him on the shoulder and worms his way through the door to the empty seat next to the pilot.

'I think I see the bastard!' Chivers yells. 'Nowhere to hide down there! Is your guy okay?'

'Yeah, he's fine,' Red Dog says. 'Let's go get that son-of-a-bitch!'

Red Dog works his .45 out of its stiff leather holster and clicks off the safety.

'Hey, I thought only officers got .45's,' the Lieutenant says.

'It was my dad's,' Red Dog says. 'Blew holes in Japs, Gooks and now Zips.'

Chivers puts the Beaver in a turning dive that brings it in low over an area of rice paddies intersected by the winding branch of a river.

'You're going to shoot him with that?' Bates asks. He's made his way to the doorway, where, pants still down, he's trying to see as much of what's going on as he can.

'I'll piss on him if I have to!' Red Dog yells.

Joe has a momentary glimpse of a man on the ground. The guy wears black pajamas and he's running hard, arms pumping like his life depends on it, which it does. He's like a little toy-man and the rifle slung over his shoulder looks like a harmless stick.

Red Dog drops open the window on his side of the plane and the rush of wind in the cabin makes talking impossible. He squints along the barrel of his big automatic pistol and fires five shots in rapid secession, *blam, blam, blam, blam, blam!* There isn't time for more. In a flash they are past their target, and Chivers puts them into a banking turn.

By the time they come back, the man is gone.

'You get him, Red Dog?' Chivers asks.

'Crap. They just disappear. I don't think so. Winged him, maybe.'

CHAPTER 14

Jack finished telling the story about how Joe nearly got his balls shot off. After breakfast, the Dorothy incident and his bout of story telling, he took a shower, dressed for work in pastel slacks and a polo shirt and drove off in Marilyn Monroe's bird. He said he was going to straighten out Connie about the evergreen qualities of Dunk Stingray. The was late by the time he returned, not very happy with his agent's refusal to see the obvious.

"Obstinate bitch," was the way he put it.

"What about dinner, Jack?" I reminded him. "You have a guest."

"Ahh, jeez!" He slapped his hand against his forehead in the traditional Hollywood studio exec's gesture that meant How could I be so stupid?

"I took the liberty of ordering carryouts from Dans."

"You get my double salami and cheese on the king-size? With the pickle?"

"They all come with a pickle, Jack. And yes, I did."

Dan's Subs made the best submarine sandwiches in Southern California, and it wasn't much later before the delivery service showed up with our feast. Then we were once again sitting under my pergola and he was in the full flush of his story telling. Jack on a roll is the ultimate pitchman; you just can't turn away from the guy, can't turn him off, can't shut him out, and can't shut him down. Maybe that's the charm of the bastard. Maybe that's why I still hung around my little pool house in Holmby Hills when I should have headed back to Plano, Texas, to find one of my high school sweethearts who maybe had divorced but still worked out and had most of his hair. And maybe I loved the bastard. Mia My thought so. Jack himself, well, easy to see he didn't have a clue.

Anyway, the night air was up from Baja, warm and balmy. Mia My was looking fresh as a spring flower in her yellow jammers with the daisies all over them, and I was doing okay in my lavender muu muu. Jack, of course, had on his favorite poolside outfit, a wildly colorful Hawaiian shirt and a pair of hiking shorts. He was barefoot, as usual. He slapped a few imaginary bugs he thought might be flying around his head and plunged on with the adventures of two young bucks in The Nam, his own true-life adventures at last revealed…the Adventures of Young Wild Jack and his side-kick Joe Bates.

"Hai Ba Trung", He said, "translates literally 'Two Ladies Trung'. The Trung sisters, famous ladies in Vietnamese history for defeating, for a few years, the hated Chinese invaders. These gals were immortalized in bronze by Madame Nhu, sister-in-law of the dead South Vietnamese president, in a statue placed in the circle at the end of Hai Ba Trung Street, just before it ran into the river, a statue ridiculed by most citizens of the city because it was cast in Madame Nhu's own likeness. Saigon being the decaying *Pearl of the Orient* that it was, the several blocks up from the river were devoted to honky-tonk bars, night clubs and tailor shops dedicated to trade with foreign soldiers. In recent times past—you know, the decades before World War II, and then the 1950's after the Japs were kicked out—these troopers looking for a good time had been French soldiers of fortune, the hardened members of the French Foreign Legion. Now it was us Americans, and we were despised and sought after for our money and our soft hearted approach to life."

"Yeah, soft hearted," I said. "That's you, all right, Jack."

"Give the guy a break," Mia My said. She was smiling, but her words stung me a little. I figured maybe she didn't know that much about our relationship, after all. I started to say something but she shook her head. "Let him tell his story."

That's all the opening Jack needed, and he started right back in, "It's the night after Joe missed having his dick shot off by an inch or two, and I'm happily escorting him along Hai Ba Trung Street past the New York Bar, the Cherry Bar, the Happy Bar, the Tuyet Lan Bar and other establishments of equal distinction. Of course, we've stopped in here and there for refreshments, but we're still fairly steady on our feet, though to be honest, Joe is walking with somewhat of a 'hitch in his git-along.' That's because the raw edges of the wound on his thighs are rubbing against the gauze patches taped there.

'Okay, G.I.,' I tell him. 'Here we are in the very heart of Oriental decadence. Let's see if we can forget our troubles for a while.'

'I don't have any troubles,' Joe protests. You see how it is; for my best pal I pick a world champion of denial.

'Your back home girl dumps you for a hippy-loser?' I suggest a possible source of unhappiness.

'I never think about her any more,' he says.

'So then you find a new girl here in Saigon and lose her in the blink of an eye...'

'I don't think about her, either!'

'You nearly get your Johnson blown off.'

'Well, there is that,' he says, hitching his pants to a more comfortable position.

A Vietnamese kid who looks to be about twelve years old pushes in front of us and blocks our way, 'Hey, you two G.I. happy-boys—you like good fucky-fuck? Over there!' He points to a gaunt young girl leaning suggestively against a metal grid light post.

Joe groans, 'She can't be over 13.'

I don't like it any more than Joe does.. I rear back like I'm going to swat the kid with a round-house punch, 'Get back to grade school, you twerpy little fuck-head pimp!' I yell at him. The kid ducks and runs away, only to be replaced by an even younger girl with an innocent look on her sweet face and a handful of tattered vintage French porno postcards.

'Naughty French postcard,' she lisps. 'Velly, velly sex-y, for you only, G.I.'

'*Khong. Khong.*' Joe shakes his head, no. The girl presses close, trying to push the cards into his hand. He looks around for me, but my attention is drawn to the flow of traffic, and the jam of cars and cyclos slowly parading by.

'Joe...' I say, taking the poor guy by the shoulder and pointing to a black Mercedes sedan driving by. We both have a quick glimpse of a pretty girl in the back seat. 'Is that her?'

'Mia My!' Bates calls out, I'm sure he does this before he even knows what he's doing. The guy's hopelessly in love, her name is bursting from his throat and that's the only way he knows he's shouting. He forgets all about the pain in his thighs. In another second, he's running after the black car, stopping traffic and nearly getting run over by a cyclo-cart. *Xe hoi taxis* and angry bike peddlers shout and curse him as he goes, *'Nguoi My Xao!'* Watch out, you crazy Ugly American!

'Joe, wait!' I try to yell some sense into him, but Joe isn't listening. 'Jesus H. Christ,' I mutter to myself, looking around and trying to estimate the trouble we're in. And then I find myself cutting between a curbed jeep and across two lanes of traffic, trying to catch up to the poor, miserable love-sotted bastard.

"Traffic is stop-and-go, but it isn't slow enough that Joe on foot is going to catch a moving car. After two blocks of near disaster while he's darting in and out of traffic, he stops. The black Mercedes is pulling further and further ahead; he has to admit it's hopeless. Ten seconds later, I pull up at his side.

'Never…catch up…to her…' Joe pants.

'Hah!' I trumpet. 'And you said you didn't want anything to do with her!'

Joe tries to sort out his thoughts while he catches his breath. 'I…I just wanted to talk to her.'

'More denial! No, no, no, no, G.I. The freight train of love has struck! Come on, Joe, admit it!'

By now we've turned down a side street, somewhat off the beaten path. The street is poorly lit, and we're walking down the narrow center of it. It's a bad neighborhood. There's piss running in the gutters and garbage cans loom out at us from the sidewalks.

'One chance in a million that we'd ever meet again, and she catches me buying dirty postcards from some street-pervert.'

'You don't know that, Joe,' I tell him. 'Maybe she didn't even see you. But the important thing is, *you saw her!* Come on— this thing is fated!'

'What, fated love!?' he hoots. 'Jack, you are so full of bullshit…' His voice trails off and he sinks into his Betty-funk.

'Man, you're going to meet her again. The Larch-man knows these things.' I gesture to a neon sign, "Hong Kong Bar," that flickers behind grimy windows. 'She works around here, somewhere. And she wasn't just cruising. Her Mama was in the back seat with her.'

But Joe isn't listening to me. 'What's wrong with me?' he wails. 'Why can't I find true love?'

'You mean the girl back home?'

'I don't know what I mean,' he says.

'Joe, we're in a war zone. People are getting blown up every day. That's what they're paying us that extra twenty-five bucks a month, you know, combat zone pay.'

'So?'

'So, you can't blame your Betty for not waiting.'

He has to think about that one for a moment. Finally, he decides, 'No, I guess I can't.'

'You never even gave her a ring, did you?' I ask him.

'Well…no,' Joe says in a small, uncertain voice. I think he's listening to me now.

'That's because you were doing the right thing,' I tell him. 'You know we don't have time for chumps who knock up their girlfriends and then go off and get killed in a war.'

'I guess…'

'You ever think now might not be the right time for true romance?' I ask him.

'What about the freight train of love?'

I have to admit he's got me there. I pantomime with my hands, the train coming fast is my left hand, smacking the bug sitting on my right. 'Well, now—that is something else!'

'The freight train of love beats out true love?'

'Joe, it's the same thing.'

'I think you're confused, Jack,' he says.

'No, G.I.,' I tell him, speaking in bargirl patois, 'You number one confused lover-boy-man.'

Joe grins, 'You buy for me hairspray, I love you so too much I drive you fuck-crazy, G.I.'

The Hong Kong Bar's gritty interior perfectly fulfills the promise of the grimy neon sign outside. The green neon 'r' in 'Bar' is nearly black, giving the impression that it says 'Hong Kong Ba', in Vietnamese "Hong Kong Married Lady." But, after an hour and a half, Joe and I aren't translating much, and the lady is starting to show her soiled underwear. There's a line of empty *Ba Muoi Ba* beer bottles in front of me, matched by Joe's empty scotch tumblers.

'How come you can drink as much scotch as I can beer?' I ask him..

'Because I'm damn good at holding my liquor…and because they water it down so much.'

'So what do we know?' I ask the mirror behind the bar. 'We know Joe's girlfriend works somewhere downtown.'

'Or lives downtown…'

The happy note for me is that Joe has accepted the notion that this exotic stranger is his girl. 'Right. We just have to figure out where.'

'I think I'm going to forget her,' he says.

"See, Joe's confused at this point. With him, it's two steps forward and one back. But I know he's going to pull through. I give him an unbelieving look. 'Yeah, like you could.'

'Serious. Maybe I'm better off that way.'

'In your dreams, Mister Lonely G.I..'

"By this time the Hong Kong Bar has emptied out. There are only a few patrons left, and they look like they might be okay sleeping the night away on the floor. I notice two bargirls, the last two in the joint. You know the old song, "The girls all look prettier at closing time." Well, these two don't look half bad to us. They've been sipping Saigon Whiskey at a corner table and whispering girly talk to themselves. They giggle at some secret joke and then come over to our table.

'Hey, G.I.s, you buy for us just one more tiny Saigon Whiskey?'

'What are your names?' I ask them.

'My name Tuy. And this Lan.'

'Well, Joe,' I say, ' here's your chance to forget the past, make a brave new start on the field of love.'

"Lan shows us the tip of a butterfly tattoo on the curve at the top of one of her breasts. 'You like see my tattoo?'

"A day or two later, Joe told me that bit of blue and yellow butterfly wing was the last image from that night that he remembered with any clarity as things began to spin more and more out of control. 'Once,' he told me in the slurred way guys like us talk when we've been drinking, 'Once, I'd had a life-plan, tucked safe and close as if it was in my back pocket. But at that moment everything I ever wanted has been denied and lost, and I can't for the life of me remember what my grand plan might have been.'"

CHAPTER 15

The night air in Holmby Hills had finally cooled as the onshore breeze floated in from the ocean. Jack brought out his favorite smoky old Duke D'Alba Spanish brandy and was sharing with Mia My and me.

I had an odd feeling and thought I saw weird Ong Vung hiding in the bushes to one side of Jack's house. Just one brief flash of motion and then he was gone. If he was there at all.

"You see anything over there?"

"Maybe something," Mia My said.

"We get a lot of deer, coming down from the hills," Jack said. "I was telling you about our adventure in the Hong Kong Bar." He smiled ruefully, shaking his head as he remembered waking the morning after he and Joe had met their two new girl friends in the Hong Kong Bar, "I tell you, Clair," he said, "You might think it's the same thing everywhere, but the morning after can be terribly agonizing in South Vietnam, even for a young man whose body is used to plenty of alcoholic abuse. That next morning, Joe slowly opens one eye and then the other. He sees the room is slowly spinning from left to right. His mouth is dry and cottony, and his head throbs with a splitting headache. Somewhere in the room a girl is talking. He doesn't recognize the voice. He doesn't think he knows her.

'Yessss…' the voice says. You buy for me one big can hairspray…'Toni' brand…yes?'

You see, the previous night's joking about preying mantis bargirls has become our new reality. There's a second girl in the room, and she chimes in, 'Oh, yes, me, too! The 'Toni' brand. Toni do it right!'

Joe sits up and squints around the room. He finds his glasses and hooks one end over his left ear, managing to get them on right side up. Of course, it's Lan and Tuy, the girls we picked up in the bar. We're in a small room with no furniture other than two mattresses on the floor and one battered-looking set of dresser drawers. Tuy and Lan are nearly naked. They're sitting in their panties, facing me like attentive little puppies, and I'm taking orders like a short-order cook, writing their wants and needs down on one of my paper scraps. Their orders are for the stuff most favored by the bargirls of Saigon, lipstick and perfumes and ladies things available exclusively at the well-meaning and centrally located downtown P.X.

'Oh, no…' Joe says with a frown and a shake of his head. I can see he's feeling rotten and disgusted with himself.

'Oh, my sweet Joey-pie,' Lan says. 'You want take more picture of my tattoo?'

She cups her naked breast and moves it up and down, making the butterfly seem to fly. But I have to say one thing for our boy Joey, he did know how to recover. Later that day, after we made our promises and took our leave of our new sweethearts, the boy takes advantage of Red Dog's generous offer to have his photos printed using the set up they have at the White Shack. He insists on souping his own negs, but once the regular photo specialist gets a glimpse of Lan's tattoo, Joe's photos become a major subject of interest. In the days that follow, Joe does his best to pour himself into the mound of translations on his desk, but I'm afraid I'm not much help. You see, I'd confiscated one of the breast shots, and colored in the tattoo with red and blue pens they used to mark the triangulations.

'You even stay in focus when you're drunk,' I tell him. 'That's a great talent, Joe.'

'That was the single dumbest thing I've ever done."

Wendell calls from Colonel Ogilvy's office door. 'Bates. Colonel wants to see you.'

'Oh boy.' Joe sighs and looks over at me. 'Word sure travels fast.'

But Ogilvy hasn't seen the nude pictures of our latest escapade. He glares at Joe from a seated position behind his desk and ignores the salute.

'Specialist, you came here under false pretenses,' he snarls. His eyes glitter and his voice is cold and harsh.

'I don't know what you mean, Sir.' Joe fudges for time, trying to figure out what he's done wrong now.

'We don't take anyone under a year,' Ogilvy says. 'If we did, we'd just be training them and then we'd have to go fetch somebody else and train them. This paper I'm holding right here in my hand says you've only got a couple months left and you're out of this man's army.'

'That's not my fault, sir. My time left in the army is clear in my record, and those are my orders. I was only obeying my orders, Sir.'

The White Snake stares at Joe and then waves him quiet. 'Okay. Maybe you didn't know. Maybe somebody screwed up in records.' His voice takes on a softer tone. 'Look, Specialist, we need linguists and from what I see you're a pretty good one. You've got an opportunity here, soldier. You decode like lightning, and you seem to care about the war effort.'

'Yes, Sir. I do.'

'So here's the deal. Here's the Spec. 5 stripes that Red Dog promised you.' He starts to hand them across the desk, but at the last minute, he pulls them back and sets them out of reach on the desk between them.

'But, here's a better deal,' The White Snake says in that hissing way of his.

He pushes a sergeant's golden chevrons across the table. 'If you re-up, we'll make you a *real* sergeant.'

'You mean hard stripes?' Joe asks. Hard stripes of any rank are a mixed blessing to a guy who has enlisted rather than being drafted. It means you get more money and respect from the lifers, but it also means you are seriously Regular Army. As I'm always telling him, the RA stands for Rat's Ass.

'Right,' the White Snakes says. You'll be a full Regular Army sergeant, son. And...' Here the Snake pulls another chevron from the top drawer on his desk. This one has the three stripes on top, and an additional curved one on the bottom.'You keep your nose clean and in six months, we guarantee a rocker. You'll be E-6 by next February.'

If The White Snake had thought to ask me, and if I'd been inclined to tell him straight up, I would have warned him he was moving at too speedy a clip. Joe didn't respond well to pressure. The way to catch a fish like him was to throw the bait out there and let him savor it for a few days. But the Colonel hasn't asked me—

not that I would have told him, anyway—and he is moving way too fast to have any chance at success. A frown crosses Joe's face. He's stalling for time, trying to let it all sink in.

'I can't say I haven't thought about re-upping,' he says. His frown grows deeper and lines appeared on his forehead. 'How long would I have to re-up for?'

The Colonel, who isn't used to debating issues with his men, frowns in turn. 'Right now,' he says, 'I believe it's four years.'

Joe Bates stares at The White Snake, not knowing what to say. Since the Colonel has run out of talk and is clearly waiting for a decision, Joe decides to put him off.

'This is kind of sudden. Let me think about it.'

Something cold happens in the Colonel's eyes and he tosses Joe his E-5 soft stripes.

'Don't take too long,' he says.

As Joe leaves, The White Snake is glaring at Jack Kennedy, who enigmatically smiles back from his photo. Joe stumbles out of the Colonel's office, shaking his head. Red Dog is standing by his work station, waiting for him.

'That guy's crazy,' Joe says, flipping a thumb in Ogilvy's direction.

'Told you so,' Red Dog said. He holds up Lan's photo. 'Wow. Nice tattoo.'

Sergeant Hinkelby, who runs the ditty-bopper section, stops by. 'Lunchtime, troopers,' he says. He takes the photo out of Red Dog's hand. 'Hey, nice tits.' Joe snatches it from him.

'Don't be that way, Specialist,' Hinkelby chides him in a good natured way. 'God made women round and cuddly so they would be appreciated.'

'So now you're doing God's work, Sarge?' I ask him.

That seems to amuse Hinkelby. 'Never thought of it that way, but yeah, I guess I am.' He claps Red Dog on the back. 'I'm jeeping over to the airport restaurant. Wanna come?'

'Judy Joy's landing in-country this week,' Red Dog says, raising one eyebrow.

'Yes, she is,' Hinkelby amiably agrees. 'Supposed to be today.'

I lean back in my chair and put my feet on my desk. 'Okay, I'll bite; who's Judy Joy?'

'You're damn right, you'd bite. Judy Joy is Miss April 1964 Centerfold, you dumb screw-head nug.' Hinkelby grins at Red Dog, 'You in, buddy?'

'For Miss April 1964? Does the Pope wear a tall hat?'

'Why yes, I believe he does,' Hinkelby says in a lordly, good-humored manner.

The two sergeants leave our small section in a jovial mood. As they walk down the long hallway to the dark green door at the front of the White Shack, he and Red Dog are singing "Love is a many-splendid thing" in their really amateurish *basso profundo* voices.

After that, time goes by slowly for us in the White Shack. Joe and I figure we'll work through lunch and knock off a half hour early to go downtown. I remember I was looking at a black lacquered eggshell painting of a naked girl that I'd bought from a sidewalk peddler on Le Loi Street, marveling at how they'd got the nipples right, using egg shells like they do. Of course, the Vietnamese are obsessed with sex; they would get it perfect if anybody could. I'm multi-tasking; that is, I'm also throwing a rubber ball at a calculated angle against the floor. The ball bounces from the floor and against a map of the Central Region that's taped to the wall and then returns to my hand, like magic for stupids. I'm making it more of a challenge by trying to hit the city of Hue, but it's not that easy. Joe, of course, is working on his translations.

'Think they'll really see Judy Joy?' I ask him.

'I think I got it,' Joe replies. He doesn't even bother to look up from the encoded message on the desk in front of him. 'They ran the consonants backwards with the vowels a-e-i-o-u stuck together in front.'

'Joe, who gives a willie-wangle? Ping or Ving or Ding or Minh needs more bullets.'

Joe continues with his translation, but after a moment, he sits back with a sigh of frustration.

'What?' I ask him.

'Tranh needs more bullets,' he says. I can't tell if Joe is more disgusted with me or his message. He reaches for his pack of Lucky Strikes.

'You already have three burning in your ashtray,' I tell him.

'Shut up, Jack,' he says, talking over my head just like Red Dog does. Joe shakes out a new unfiltered and lights it from one of those smoking in his ashtray. This is sad behavior. I feel I've got to do something. 'Hey,' I say as if I'd just come up with a brilliant new idea. 'Let's go see the girls tonight.'

Of course Joe knows which girls I mean. He frowns at me, 'We manage to sneak out on them with our wallets mostly intact and you want to go back there?'

'Sure. We can stop at the PX first and buy some stuff to make our peace.' I throw high, hitting above the DMZ, and then I miss catching the ball and have to crawl under my desk to retrieve it.

'Even if I could, I'm not going to,' Joe says. 'Not ever. That wasn't my idea of how to be with a woman.'

I poke my head above the top of my desk, and roll my eyes, 'Oh for God's sake, Joseph Bates—' And in that moment whatever I was going to say is interrupted by an abrupt sound, a flat, hollow *Pam!* It's the distinctive sound of an explosion in the middle distance. Joe and I stare at each other, thinking the same thoughts.

'What the holy hell…?' I ask nobody in particular.

'Do you think…?' Joe asks. We're both remembering Red Dog and Hinkelby have gone over to the airport restaurant, which is in the direction of the explosion.

'Naaw…probably not…' But we both jump to our feet and walk to the guard station in the front of the White Shack. The guards usually knew first what's up. And, what's more, they carry machine guns. Far from home, half way around the world in uncertain circumstances, there is some sense of security in small details like that."

CHAPTER 16

It was way past Hollywood bad boy Jack Larch's bedtime. He was an early riser, he liked to think of himself as dedicated to the muse. That meant he always hoped to get his pages in before sunrise, before that damn phone started ringing and Tinseltown came calling. But there was an explosion forty years or so ago at an airport located just outside a city then called Saigon, and if you knew anything at all about the twin lives of Jack Larch and Dunk Stingray, explosions have always been a very big deal. Jack was like a little kid. In the time I'd known him, he always had this fascination with fireworks, with anything that went *boom*. And he had researched the hell out of explosives If you wanted to know how to build your own bomb, just ask the Larch-ster. You wouldn't even have to get him on the phone, just pick up a couple of Stingray pulpers. Jack actually did build a few his own with some explosives he bought from a pal of his in the prop department at Paramount. He detonated them out on the Mojave desert, and I was surprised Homeland Security didn't show up to water-board him or something. All this to say, although it was getting on late in the evening in Holmby Hills, Jack wasn't going to stop telling his tale, not right at the moment when he was in the middle of something big that has gone boom on the delta.

"That very night," he said, "Joe and I head out to the Tan Son Nhut Main Gate, talk our way past the gate guards and pile into a battered cream-and-blue *xe hoi* taxi."

"What do you mean, 'talk your way past the guards,' Jack?" I asked him. I was thinking he had too much Dunk Stingray coming out of his ears. "Nobody just talks their way past some guards."

"It was total army bullshit," Jack agreed. "If you were E-5 hard-stripe or above, you could leave the base, even on Orange Alert. I'm only E-4, and Joe's a newly ordained E-5 soft striper." Jack grinned at us, and I see a shade of the young devil in him; in that moment, he did look like a reckless schoolboy. "We would show them our Top Secret security badges. That always did the trick.

"Anyway, we manage to slip out the gate, and this taxi driver rockets us toward Saigon General with the usual carefree way of driving those guys had. I'm always in demand because I've got O-Neg blood, and since the call's gone out, it's another reason we got off base so easy that night. By this time, we know the basic scuttlebutt about the explosion. I know more about it than Joe, me being a far superior gatherer of this type of information. 'Some Viet Cong sympathizer slipped in the night before and put a big package wrapped in tan butcher block paper over one of the concrete beams,' I tell him. 'You know the layout of that restaurant. Easy to put a package up there and people might not notice.'

This airport restaurant, located in a brand new terminal, is being hailed at that time as something of a design marvel, what the local writers were calling 'Bamboo Modern.' They are touting it as a symbol of the 'new, up-to-date Vietnam.' I tell Joe, 'They're saying Hinkelby didn't have a scratch on him. See, he thought Judy Joy was coming in at the other end of the terminal. His ears are ringing, though.'

'How bad is Red Dog?' Joe asks.

'Nobody knows. I guess we'll see for ourselves.'

Down at Saigon General, we have the customary pint and a half sucked out of us on the first floor. Then we wring a room number out of the admitting nurse and slip up to the third floor without asking, you know, to have a look for ourselves. Red Dog is in a bed at the end of a long line of cots. He looks terrible. He has a heavy bandage around his head and his left arm is in a plaster cast. There are hundreds of fresh scabs on just the part of his upper body that we can see, bloody spots from where the doctors had removed chunks and bits of cement from his chest and arms.

'Hi, Sarge, how ya doing?' I say, never at a loss for words.

'You people aren't supposed to be here,' a hospital orderly snipes at us.

'Special clearance,' I say, flashing my magic green Top Secret badge.

'What's going to happen to him?' Joe asks the orderly in a gruff way.

The 'Voice-of-Top Secret' has the hoped for results, and suddenly the orderly turns friendly. 'As soon as he stabilizes, we'll ship him out to Clark in the Philippines, Sir.' The orderly frowns, remembering he also has responsibilities to the patient, 'Just a few minutes for you guys, okay?'

'Maybe we better go…' Joe says.

But at that moment, Red Dog opens his eyes and grabs Joe's arm. 'No. No. No,' he says in the hoarse, croaking voice of a guy who's half in and half out of sedation. Red Dog's eyes are crossed and his slurred whisper is hard to understand, but something is really bothering him. 'Specialist. Bates. Joe. Listen to me!'

Joe's eyes widen like he's been galvanized with a hot wire up his butt. 'Okay, Sarge. I'm right here. What is it?'

'Cherry bar,' Red Dog says. 'Cherrr-eeeee Bar! Get word to Tuyet Lan. Tuyet Lan. She's my honey-bunch. Tell her I'll be back for her. Tell her…not-to-move. Important. Not to give up the apartment.'

'Okay, Sarge,' Joe reassures him, repeating his request. 'Tuyet Lan. Cherry Bar. Don't move from the apartment. We got it; we'll tell her.'

Red Dog looks like the drugs are taking him away. Still, he shakes himself, forcing himself awake. 'My honey-bunch. Not to give up the apartment…my honey-bunch…my gold bars…' And with that, he drifts off into his narcotic slumber and begins to snore.

I look over at Joe. 'Hmmm. Gold bars,' I say. 'We better go see the honey-bunch.

'Forget it, Jack,' Joe tells me. 'This kind of stuff doesn't happen in real life.'

'Hey, pal—nothing about Vietnam is real life. Or haven't you noticed?'

We leave Red Dog's room, practically running as we head down the hall. As luck would have it, it's a slow night and our cabby is still waiting for another fare, so in no time we're shooting the other way across town, heading for the Cherry Bar. As our little ferret of a taxi darts in and out of traffic, my mind is going high speed, turning over the possibilities. 'This looks pretty darn good," I tell Joe. 'You know how Red Dog is always wearing gold. He's got a fetish.'

Joe gets an alarmed look on his face. 'Don't let that imagination of yours run wild.'

I do my Long John Silver impression. 'Har, shiver me timbers, matey! Gooooold!' The cabbie turns around and looks at me like I'm nuts. They do that, you know, take their eyes completely off the road ahead to give you the evil eye in the back seat.

'We're not going to take his gold. He's our guy, Jack,' Joe tells me.

'No, of course not, Joe. But we have to make sure honey-bunch doesn't get it.'

Joe doesn't completely trust me with this one. 'Come on, Jack, be serious. We have to be careful. We don't know what we're walking into.'

'Hey, okay. You take the lead, *mon capitain*.'

The *xe hoi* taxi screeches to a halt in front of the Cherry Bar. As usual, I plead poverty and let Joe pay the fare. The two of us brush past the usual assorted street trash plying the sex and dope trade, and we hurry into the lush maroon leather, subdued lighting and soft whispering laughter of the Cherry Bar."

CHAPTER 17

"So what was the Cherry Bar like, Jack?" I ask. Mia My and I have both perked up. All these bombs and people blowing up are interesting, in the standard Dunk Stingray sort of way, but we sense Jack is about to get to get some meat on the bones of his story, which for both of us women is about people, about men and women and how they relate to each other and what happens in their lives, and really, about the youthful lives of these two guys, Jack and Joe themselves.

"It was a nice place," Jack says. Then he thinks about it. "Well, nice for the sort of place that it was."

I'm looking like I want more details, so he says, "Imitation crystal and fake gold on big chandeliers they probably stole from some French mansion. The room isn't too big, not too small, just right to have a bar along one side, and about a dozen tables scattered around. The walls are entirely maroon, trimmed in brown, some Vietnamese interior decorator's idea of what it might be like living inside a cherry dipped in chocolate.

"The tables are filled, you know, the fellows buying Saigon Whiskey for the girls, the ladies sitting close but not too close, the illusion of intimacy, talking their chop-socky English, clapping their hands in their fake gestures of delight, maybe touching this or that G.I.'s arm for a light moment, Oh, you just too funny, Mister Amelican!' It's really crowded, and my heart sinks. Not much chance we're going to find Tuyet Lan in here. For one thing, her name is common trash, certainly not her real name. The name Tuyet Lan means 'Snow White,' one of the most common names chosen by bargirls and ladies of the night throughout the land, sort of like trailer trash girls come up with names like Roxi, Jo Ellen and Maybelline.

There must be two dozen girls in the Cherry Bar, and they're moving from table to table, from prospect to prospect as fast as their skin-tight brocaded silk dresses will allow. They're all wearing the Western look hairdo that's in fashion, the dramatic beehive and the cute dip-and-curl, and not a hair out of place, courtesy of Toni and the understanding PX sergeants.

I generally get what I want in crowded places. I squeeze into a table as a pair of Sea-Bees stagger to their feet and head for the door. Joe slides in across from me and two bargirls automatically detach themselves from their beaus and drift over to make sure we pay our short-term rent for the table.

'Hi, G.I. Joes, you buy for us two small Saigon Whiskey, we talk-talk, okay?' We have sat down; our act of sitting is an implied contract, and the girl who moves next to Joe is already waving to the bar before he can get his first sentence out. '*Khong. Khong phai.*' He tries to sputter in Vietnamese that he doesn't want to buy her a drink.

'Ohhhh, you speak Vietnam! I like special talk-talk with you!' Her hand continues to wave to attract the bartender's attention. I reach up, take hold of her wrist and pull her arm down to her side.

'He's trying to talk to you, sweetheart."

The girl glares at me, but Joe uses the interruption to speak up.

'We're looking for Tuyet Lan.'

'I Tuyet Lan.' the girl says without a moment's hesitation. We might have half way believed her, but the same exact words pop out of the second bargirl's mouth at exactly the same moment.

'Two Tuyet Lans,' I say. 'Joseph, an authentic miracle: It's snowing Tuyet Lans.'

'No, seriously,' Joe tells the girl, giving her his Mister Serious look. 'We've got to find the real Tuyet Lan.'

'That me,' the first girl repeats. 'I real Tuyet Lan.'

'No, me,' the second girl says.

I'm finding this damn tiring so I stand up on my chair and yell at the top of my lungs. 'Will the real goddamn Tuyet Lan please stand up before I get really mad?!'

'I thought I was taking the lead,' Joe says.

All I can do is give him the Vietnamese one shoulder shrug. A girl comes near and scans us with the bargirl once-over. She has been standing in the corner talking to an older American who is wearing civilian clothes.

'I am Tuyet Lan,' she says in a quiet voice. She's very pretty, but awfully young. *Two young and innocent for an old fart like Red Dog,* I'm thinking.

Joe asks her, 'Do you know Sergeant Moore?' The girl looks blankly from Joe to me and back again. She shakes her head no.

'Red Dog,' I insist. 'Sergeant Red Dog Moore.'

'Red Dog sweet face,' the girl says. 'Yes. I know him.'

'There's been an accident…' Joe says

Tuyet Lan pouts. It's difficult to read her emotions, but I can see right away that the bad news isn't turning her into a ball of tears. 'Is Red Dog dead?' she asks.

'No. But he'll be out of town for a while.'

Tuyet Lan shrugs and starts to turn away. Joe looks over at me and gestures to the door. He's thinking we've done our duty and now it's time to pull a fast adios. I give him the old wink, and I quietly but firmly take Tuyet Lan by the arm. 'Red Dog says we should share the gold bars 50-50.'

'What?' The girl turns and stares at us. Her dark eyes have gone wide under her heavy eyeliner and thick, artificial lashes. 'What that you say to me?'

'Oh, no,' Joe throws up both his hands, just the way I expected he might. He blurts out, 'I don't think you should tell her—'

'Nonsense, Joe. This is Red Dog's honey-bunch. We can trust her.' I lean close to the girl and half-whisper, 'The gold bars. There's a lot of them. He told us we should split them with you, half-half.'

'What? Where?'

'Hidden in the apartment. He told us where.'

'Come!' she says in a whisper charged with excitement, 'We go NOW!'

The bar Madame, a shop-worn 40-year old Ba who has been watching us closely from behind the bar, shrieks at Tuyet Lan in shrill Vietnamese.

'*Tuyet Lan! Khong phai! Em a dai. Viet! Het roi!*' Get over here right now!

Tuyet Lan looks like a young teenager, but she's probably seen more death and disaster in her few years than Joe and I combined with a squad of troopers. She yells back in a voice that matches the bar manager's,

'*Di-Lai, Ba Sao,*' which roughly translates as Go screw yourself, ugly old lady!

By this time Tuyet Lan has me by the arm and is half-pulling me out of the room in her eagerness to get after the treasure.

'You coming, Joe?' I yell back at him.

'No thanks,' he says. 'I don't want any part of it.'

'I'm leaving, pushing my way through the crowd and in that moment the whiskeys come.

'You pay two Saigon Whiskeys, right now,' the bargirl who'd first said she was Tuyet Lan demands.

That's about all I hear, and then Tuyet Lan and I are out the door. Joe fills me in later on what happened after that. No way Joe was going to pay her for two glasses of weak tea. He and I always had this running battle, who was the cheapest G.I. in Saigon."

"You're cheaper, Jack," I told him. You win that one, hands down."

Mia My nodded in agreement. "Joe told me before you became the Stingray man and got foolish with your money, you were the cheapest man in the world," she said.

"Well, in Hollywood, anyway," I said to Mia My. "Maybe not in the whole world, you know, counting everybody. I don't think Jack's as cheap as Ebenezer Scrooge."

"Or Scrooge McDuck," Mia My chimed in.

"Are you ladies interested in this story at all," Jack grumped, "or are you just going to rag on me?"

"Tell the story, Jack," I said sweetly.

"Yes, you tell it, Mister Cheap-boy Storyman," Mia My repeated.

"So Joe's still at the Cherry Bar, bargaining over drinks. He offers to pay for one, but orders a real scotch for himself. The girl brings the drinks and he pays, and she says, 'Okay, G.I. now I sit by you short time and we talky-talk."

'No, that's not going to happen,' Joe tells her. 'You brought me my scotch, I paid you for your stupid Saigon Whiskey.

Now get lost and leave me alone. I've had enough bargirls to last me a lifetime.'

'Nguoi My Sao.' she says. Ugly American.

'You got that right, sweetheart…well, almost right,' Joe tells her. 'Sour would be more like it.'"

CHAPTER 18

"Joe knocks off his drink and bolts from the bar. An hour and a half later, he's wandering up Le Loi Street. He still has a few hours left until the 11 o'clock curfew, and the streets are crowded with soldiers, civilians, and newly-arrived peasants in from the countryside, everybody gawking at their first view of the big city. Joe is experimenting with a fairly high speed Ektachrome; by keeping the lens open, he's found he can get an artistic effect with the color film, lots of blurred street lights and glittery, stuttering neon.

He walks into the nearest brightly lit archway, and here's where fate strikes again, it happens to be the entrance to the Arcade Edan. A bunch of newspaper kids have the evening editions of the local newspapers spread out in front of the Edan Theater. "Boujour Tristesse" is playing and one of the newspaper kids is crippled and supporting herself with the help of a home-made crutch and a beautiful smile. Joe makes sure he gets that picture. He buys a roll of peanuts from a little peanut girl for 2 piasters, and snaps her picture in return.

Wandering down the interior main courtyard of the arcade, he pauses in front of the Maison Blanch, a fancy dress shop that features a manikin dressed in a lacy white wedding dress. A middle-aged lady selling a basket of *trom trom trop*, the delicious grape-like fruit, hails him from her squatting position on the sidewalk outside the dress shop.

'*Anh! Anh! Anh muon vu?*' Friend, friend! Do you want a bride?

She gives him a hearty grin and then spits a thick wad of bright orange spittle on the sidewalk next to her. '*Khong,*' Joe replies, trying to think of Vietnamese words to phrase what he was thinking, that all women were trouble. 'May I take your picture?'

The middle-aged *Ba's* grin widens. She's not sure what he's asking. She cackles happily, patting the tummy of the woman squatting next to her, who looks to be about eight and a half months pregnant. 'This one comes already with nice baby,' she says in Vietnamese.

'No, not her. Just you. Your picture.' Joe likes the idea of the dreamy French manikin in her filmy white lace wedding dress floating like a cloud over the earthy presence of this betel-nut juice spitting street seller.

'Okay, for you 50 P,' the lady says.

'Ten P,'

'Thirty. Thirty P.'

'*Khong phai. Hi Muoi Piaster. Het roi.*' He'd gone up to twenty; his final offer.

The Peddler *Ba's* face breaks into an even wider smile.

'You speak Vietnam,' she says. 'Good, good! For you, 25 P.'

'Okay. Deal.'

Joe fishes out a grimy blue twenty and a somewhat newer rainbow-colored five and hands them over. The woman gives him her best black-toothed grin, bright orange saliva around her gums, and he snaps his shot.

'*Cam ong, Ba,*' he says, thanking her.

'*Anh, Anh, Anh...!*' The woman stands quickly and tries to engage him in more conversation, but she's too late. Joe's attention is caught by something he sees in the dress shop. There is a young girl behind a counter. She's looking down at her lap while she hand-stitches the hem of a dress. He stares at the girl, the street *Ba* and his camera both forgotten. Impossibly, in a city of over a million people, he's found Mia My!

And she looks up! She sees him, recognizing him immediately! She smiles at him, and, just like that, the freight train runs him over for the first, last, and only time, and my buddy Joe Bates is hopelessly in love.

Walking on air or as if in a dream, Joe opens the door to the dress shop and walks in. He enters the extreme hostile territory of the store, which caters to *haut* fashion and the high society of Saigon, The Pearl of the Orient. Two customers, a stuffy mother and her daughter, are discussing a wedding dress with the woman Joe recognizes instantly as Ba Nguyen. Joe is oblivious to everything else in the world but the girl. He walks between Ba Nguyen and her customers, stopping their conversation for a moment. Mia My watches as he approaches.

Ba Nguyen has been momentarily distracted by the details of her conversation, which is about changes to the wedding dress in the window, the one that had first attracted Joe's attention. But the ever-vigilant *Ba* sees Joe's direction quickly enough and moves to intercept him.

'*Monsieur!* Sir! May I help you?'

She is one truly formidable obstacle, but Joe is a man possessed by *l'amour*, and he will not be stopped by anything or anybody. 'Yes,' he says, arching his eyebrows, '…ahh, I'm looking for…ahh, an *ao gai* for my…ahh, sister.'

Ba Nguyen sniffs her disdain. And worse, she is suspicious. She can't quite place him, but thinks she has seen this young man somewhere before. From his looks and his casual civilian clothing she guesses he is an American soldier, and that is enough for her. '*Peut etre* a tourist shop *apres les* bars of Hai Ba Trung Street,' she tells him. '*Ici, a la Maison Blanch seulment haute couture pour les damsels distinctive.*'

'What you have here will do very well for my sister,' Joe tells her. 'She is a very discriminating person, with a college degree in English.'"

Nearly a half century later, sitting outside under an evening sky in Southern California, Mia My smiles faintly and nods her head, remembering the treasured moment. The Larch-man is a champion storyteller, but this memory is hard-wired into her, and she effortlessly takes over telling her part of the tale. "I see Joe is in such trouble with Mama," she says. And everything he says, he just digs himself in deeper. Mama frowns. She glares at Joe. She knows little English and is tangling her French and Vietnamese. She starts to take on the role of tiger lady.

'*Khong phai, jeun fils*—' But here she gets interrupted, and I do think it was fate, because once you let the tiger out of Mama, it's too late. But in that moment before she can become the legend, her customer, that Vietnamese mother, sharply interrupts her, speaking in rapid fire Vietnamese. '*Top!* Now wait!' the customer says, and with her rising tone of voice I see we can soon have a tiger fight, 'We are here first. Who is this young foreign person to barge in when we are accounting for a big sale in your store?'

With this, the Vietnamese daughter bursts into tears. '*Mamma, Mamma, toi khong biet.* Let's just call the whole thing off.'

'Now look what you've done!' Ba Nguyen roars at Joe in Vietnamese. '*Di! Di! Mao len!* You must go at once! You are clearly out of place here!'

My poor Joe! Mama will crush him. She will strike him with her fists if she has to, and make him run away in defeat. I know I have to do something. I must come to his aid, just as I did that first time we met in the bloody side street. I stand and put down my sewing assignment.

'Mamma,' I tell her, speaking in French, '*S'il tu plait.* You make sure we do not lose this sale with this important customer. I will handle this rude intruder.'

Before Mama can say another word, I take Joe by the arm and escort him to the door. I see Mama wants to disagree in the worst way, but she has her hands full because the customer has started making additional demands about the *tres importante* changes she wants with the dress. She speaks in stumbling French, which only upsets her daughter more.

'*Mamma!*' the girl cries, *khong noi tieng Phap! Toi khong biet noi tieng Phap!*' Mother, don't speak French! You know I don't understand French!

I see my own mother, very frustrated, glaring after me. I give her my big fake glittery-diamond smile as I escort the rude young American out the door. 'Come now,' I say to Joe as we pass her, 'You'll be more comfortable outside this shop of ladies things.'

Joe smiles. He looks like he's in a daze. I don't think he really hears a word I'm saying. But I have him by the arm and that is all that seems to matter to him. Once we are standing outside the shop, he does find his voice pretty quickly.

'Do you work here all the time?'

'It is my mother's shop' I tell him. I shrug to let him know it is a minor detail of my life that is not important to me.

'She speaks French.'

'*Certainement! Tous les Nguyen parlez Francaise.* My father's father was French. And my mother's mother. We were here before you *Americaines.* '

Mama peers out the window at me, but she can't get away from her customers. I give her a little finger-roll wave, happy to see she is stuck inside with her responsibilities.

'Can we...?' Joe is fumbling for words. I think he wants to ask me out on a date, but he doesn't know how. Here he is, a half a world away from his safe home in America, in an ancient land with a complex and sophisticated culture. But my Joe is not to be denied. He starts again, 'I mean, can I...I mean, would you walk a little way with me?'

'What would be the point of that?' I see the look of discouragement start on his face. I'm not used to men having so little guile, to men who approach me in such a way that we might be friends. I raise my eyebrows, a question to see if he will explain himself.

'To see if we could like each other a little bit,' he says.

'With Americans there is no 'little bit,' I tell him. 'With you, it's all or nothing. Don't say otherwise; I saw the movie."

'W-what movie?' he stammers.

'Ok-la-homa." I start to sing for him, "Where the wind come sweeping on the plain."

'Well, walk with me, anyway.'

I take another look over my shoulder. I am so pleased to be bathing in Mama's fury. I keep up my happy girlish singing, "Where the waving weed can sure smell sweetly – I can't remember the rest – La la la la la la la la la la la la!" By this time I can see Mama is nearly beside herself. She has started towards the door once, twice, three times, but each time her customer calls her back. I wave to her, telling her she is not to worry.

'*Cinc minute!*' I pantomime, holding up five fingers on one hand as I walk away with Joe towards the Arcade Milk Bar, which is kitty-corner and a few shops down, across the enclosed walkway from the dress shop"

CHAPTER 19

Mia My went on telling her part in the story, "The Milk Bar for the Edan is inside the arcade so it is protected from the sun and the rain, but it is constructed to look like the tables and chairs are outside, as if it is a charming French sidewalk café. When Joe and I get there, the usual crowd of five or six flashy Saigon Cowboys and their girlfriends have pulled two tables together. They are smoking and drinking their expressos and their cold teas. Joe orders us two Thai Teas with ice cubes and we sit at a table as far away from the others as we can get.

'You have no sister back home, do you?' I ask.

'No.' He smiles, admitting his little fib to Mama. 'But if I did, she would have looked good in one of your mother's dresses.'

Our conversation is interrupted by a cat-call from one of the teens. 'Mia My, what are you doing?'

I know who it is, but I pretend not to hear the sing-song insistence of Ong Phong's Vietnamese. I concentrate all my attention on Joe. 'And where do you come from in America?' He tells me he is from a small town near Chicago. 'Ohhhh,' I tease him, 'you are a gangster-man.' His face goes red and he denies it. 'And what do you do in Chicago, Mister Gangster-man?'

'Well, after I get out of the service, my uncle wants me to run his business.'

'And what does he do?'

'He has trucks to distribute soda-pop and…other things.'

'I have seen the movies,' I tell him. 'It is *exactemont* like Al Capone!'

'No, no, no…let me explain—'

And this is when that mean voice interrupts again from another table. It is evil Phong. Maybe you remember Phong, who has failed many times in his efforts to seduce me?

'*Hai! Mia My di do dai?*' What are you up to, Mia My? He asks in his rude way, as if he possesses me.

'*Di, di mao len, Phong!*' Go away fast, Phong! It's none of your business.

'*Nguoi My sao!*'

But my Joe knows Vietnamese, and he speaks right up to protect me. '*Ca le, Nguoi Nam sao lam. Ca le, sao nhet!*' Joe says. Perhaps the Vietnamese is uglier. Perhaps the ugliest.

Phong's face grows dark with anger, and he glares at Joe. It is a surprise to me that my new American friend speaks Vietnamese.

'*Un petit peu,*' he says, showing off a little.

'And French!' I say, properly impressed.

'Only a little,' he says. But he's looking over my shoulder. He sees my old enemy Phong has gotten up and is coming over to our table. I turn around and see him, too. But Phong only gets half way to us when the angry look on his face changes to one of fear. He quickly dives under our table. There is a big checkered tablecloth on our small round table, but it barely reaches down enough to hide him. And he needs good hiding, because in that moment a big squad of maybe ten ARVN soldiers with white Q.K. bands over the long sleeves on their arms rush into our area from someplace of hiding. They swarm all over the Milk Bar where we are sitting. They have rifles and are very pushy and rude. And in another moment a Quoc Khanh sergeant swaggers into the Milk Bar. He is a short guy and very plump. His eyes flick around like those of a hungry little pig. He's looking at all the kids at the other tables. He demands to see identification from everybody.

I guess it is funny, in a way. Joe is the only man in the place who does not have to worry, and he is also the first out with his I.D. card. He shows his drivers license, which is from the state of Illinois. The Quoc Khanh is French trained. By the snarl on his face and the tone of his voice it is easy to see he doesn't like Americans. '*Nguoi My,*' he says in a bully-boy voice, looking for a reason to add Joe to his collection bag.

'It's not a crime,' Joe says in a mild voice.

The QC sergeant slams Joe's wallet back on our table and moves on to the next. I can feel Phong's hand, trying to feel up my leg. I give him a kick. His hand retreats. I am one second from turning him in, and he knows it.

The sergeant is flipping through wallets at the next table. *'Muoi sao, Muoi sao, Muoi Sao'*, he cries out to Buddha. Sixteen, Sixteen, Sixteen—Is everybody here sixteen?

The truth is, everybody here is over sixteen, and he knows it. But he has to prove it or he can't haul them away.

A corporal indicates one of the flashy Saigon Cowboys with a jab of his rifle. He gestures to his leader, *'Ong, ong, ong!'* The sergeant takes a closer look at the Cowboy's papers. He smiles and grabs the Cowboy by the face with one hand. His smile broadens and he squeezes the face. *'Hai Muoi Sao!* He's 26 if he's a day!'

The Cowboy's sunglasses fall off his face. He shakes his head violently, but he can't shake out of that grasping hand. He does his best to deny it. *'Khong! Khong! Muoi sao! Muoi sao!* No! No! Sixteen! Sixteen!'

'Khong phai!' the sergeant laughs. If we believe this paper, you'll die of old age before you reach seventeen!

The sergeant is about to hand the papers back to the Cowboy. These loafers are all of age to be drafted in the army, but they come from wealthy and powerful families. The sergeant must be careful. Still, he tries one last trick; he rubs his thumb hard over the ink on the 16. The ink smears, and the 1 of 16 disappears to reveal a 2 underneath, a 2 belonging to 26. 'Hah!' the sergeant calls out in a happy voice. 'A miracle of aging! You just became 26!' He shoves the smeared papers in the Cowboy's face.

A slutty-looking girl jumps up from the same table. She sobs and screams, *'Khong! Khong!* You can't take him! You must not! I'm pregnant!' The sergeant puts his hand on the top of her head and roughly pushes her back in her chair. 'You should have thought of that before you rolled over for him,' he says.

There is no law in South Vietnam that men who are soon to be fathers can escape the military. Because this fellow has been caught with bad papers, he will be drafted for the automatic three plus three plus three—nine years before he will be discharged. The Cowboy goes limp and slumps to the white tile floor. The sergeant jerks his thumb and two of his men hitch their rifles one one shoulder and drag him away by his feet, clunking his head against a stiff iron chair leg as they go..

'They always take somebody,' I tell Joe. I can see he is not used to such rough ways. He looks at me, wondering if he should protest. 'But they can't just—' I hold a finger to my lips. 'They are all food for the army. They are all way over 16. Phong here is nearly thirty—aren't you, Phong?' I knock on the table, 'You can come out now, little coward boy.' He does crawl out then, looking around to make sure no soldiers remain. He glares at Joe, but there is something about my Joe that stops him. Joe is a solid man, a real man. He weighs at least seventy pounds more than Phong. And still more, he smiles at Phong. I can't tell if he realizes what a snake Phong is or not. But I know Joe is not afraid of him.

'*Nguoi My Sao,*' Phong says as he slinks away.

To Joe it is as if Phong isn't even there. 'What's this about?' he asks me.

I shrug it off. 'They are all rich-daddy boys. Their parents buy fake papers for them to keep them from the military. Come, we must go back or Mama will send the White Mice cops to find us.'

'We walk back toward the shop. Our hands brush, and it seems like the most natural thing in the world, in the next moment we are holding hands. Joe asks me, 'Can I…can I see you again?'

'Mama hates Americans,' I tell him.

'But…but…'

We have reached the shop. I turn to face him and we are in shadows under an awning. I see he wants to kiss me, and I am thinking fiercely that I want the same as well.

'I'm always here, working in the shop. Where would I go?'

We lean forward and our lips are so very close and in that very moment Mama bursts out of the front door of our shop. We are so lucky; I don't think she has seen us. We pull apart from each other like two frightened crickets, and in the next moment she does spot us.

'Mia My! There you are! I need you inside, right now!' And so I give him a sad smile and my shrug, done the French way, and I'm hoping he knows we will meet again."

CHAPTER 20

Mia My finished telling us about her first little date with Joe…actually, finished telling me, Larch-ster the boy-wonder having drifted off to sleep with his head on the cool bubble glass of my outdoor table.

"Let's just leave him here," I suggested.

She gave me a look of disapproval. "Sometimes, I think you don't know what you have here," she said.

"What?" I shot back, my guard suddenly up. I didn't need Jack's pal's widow telling me how to run my life.

"He is your Jack," she said.

"Jack runs around with every available bitch in town."

"But he cares for none of them," Mia My said.

"He only tolerates me because I'm the girl next door."

Mia My shook her head, but she was done talking with me. She went to Jack's side, placed one of his arms around her shoulder and started to lift him. She was a little person, but stronger than I would have thought, and in another moment she had him tottering on his feet.

I figured, Oh, what the hell! And I went over and took the other arm. Mia My and I had both had a few, and Jack was a lot further into the bottle, and as we wove past the pool on the way to his place, I actually stepped where there was nothing but air, and in the next moment I was falling into the warm water and pulling them both in with me. We were at the shallow end, but still, it was a madcap moment with Jack sputtering and flailing around.

"What happened? What happened?" he cried, slapping at the water with his arms..

Mia My smiled at me and then took Jack's arm and placed it around her shoulder again. "You fell into the pool, Jack. Clair and I jumped in to rescue you. Now you owe us big-time, Mister Hollywood Writer-man. We saved your life!"

"Nobody saves my life!" Jack yelled, but now he was laughing and splashing water on Mia My.

"Oh, then, maybe we have to drown you, to take away your bad attitude," she said, diving for his legs.

"Ha! Not a chance!" he laughed. But just then I tackled him, too.

"Oh, no! *Et tu,* Clair?!" he shouted.

"Your Shakespeare isn't going to save you this time," I told him, and we were all laughing and wrestling and having a good time until Jack's neighbor across the way put on his backyard spotlights and yelled he was going to call the cops unless we all shut up, and Jack yelled if that guy didn't shut up he was going to get some M-80 firecrackers, and somewhere here and there dogs started barking. About then we thought we heard a siren in the distance, so we all headed for the house, still soaked and laughing, though now getting a little chilly in the night air..

So that was how it came to be that we were heroines, even though Jack couldn't remember any of the details. We just stuck to our story, and he bought in on it. That night, he got us some of his big bath towels and we sat around the kitchen while he made us hot chocolate for a reward.

"Where were we?" he asked. Wild Jack the relentless storyteller had his second wind. "Oh, yeah, I remember. Well, a couple days after Bates has his first date and nearly goes kissy-face with missy here, Joe and I are over in our section in the White Shack when Sergeant Hinkelby drops by. Hinkelby, who isn't really a bad sort except when he's drunk, has taken over Red Dog's duties. Joe asks him if anybody's heard anything about our old boss. Hinkelby scratches his head, his fingers working his thin blond crew cut like there might be lots of dandruff there, 'I don't think he's coming back soon.' He's about to move on when he stops, 'Rumor is, he was serious about a girl at the Cherry Bar.' My head pulls back in the neck of my fatigues shirt like a frightened turtle's. I'm not interested in talking with anybody at the 3rd RRU about Red Dog's girl, who is now a little bit sort of *my* girl. But Joe points a finger at me and says, 'You have to ask Jack about that.' Right there, I could kill the guy.

'There's pretty girls everywhere,' I say, glaring at Joe to shut his fat trap.

Hinkelby isn't the brightest bulb in the pack, and he takes it for granted that Joe is talking generically, that I'm a tramp-girl expert, or something. After all this is the army, and social lives are structured by rank. Joe and I are low-lifes on the social totem pole. Since E-6 hard-stripers don't pal around with E-5 or E-4 soft-stripers, Hinkelby assumes we don't know anything about Red Dog's private life. And, of course, we wouldn't have, but under the influence of morphine he'd blabbed to us about his honey-pie and the gold bars.

'Hey, dinking around with hookers and whores is cool, as far as it goes,' Hinkelby says, 'but the word on the street is that Red Dog wanted to marry her.'

"Well, that squeezes the blood right out of my face. You see, after Joe left me and had his fated meeting with Mia My, Tuyet Lan and I wandered over to her place, and, things being what they were, you know, her being all torn up with grief and me trying to console her, well, we'd gotten somewhat involved.

"But this time it's just my paranoid, suspicious nature that has me worried. Hinkelby actually has something else on his mind. 'Shacking up is one thing,' he says. 'But I heard Red Dog wanted to marry her.' I'm already white as a sheet, and if I could go any whiter, I'm sure those words would be doing it.

"But Joe unintentionally takes the heat off me. He's thinking along the same lines as Hinkelby. 'That's crazy,' Joe says. 'He'd lose his clearance.'

"Hinkelby nods in agreement. 'Yep,' he says. 'End up driving trucks out in the boonies.'

"All of us who work in the White Shack have Top Secret clearances. When you lose your clearance, there are punishments to let everybody else know how foolish you've been. We all know pounding rocks at Leavenworth prison would be just a pipe dream that would never happen—driving truck convoy through Central Vietnam would happen, and that could get you seriously dead. The army loved to make statements like that, A fricking bullet in his brains, all because he fell for some helmet-haired dink bargirl.

'And for what?' Hinkelby asks. "Any man who goes native for serious is crazy. Come on—fish sauce and rice for the rest of your life? Spitting that orange betel juice on your Mama's couch? Can you imagine?'

"Hinkelby starts to move off for a second time, and then remembers something else. 'Hey, Bates,' he says. 'The White Snake wants to hiss at you.'

"Now I see it's Joe's turn in the fright-kettle. I know all about his meeting with his new girl, and we're both wondering if maybe The White Snake knows about it, too. Joe stands and slowly walks toward the open door of the Colonel's office. I get up and go over to the water cooler to hear as much of it as I can.

"Joe is no sooner in the door when Ogilvy slams a pile of photo blowups on his desk.

'Specialist Bates,' he says in an angry voice. 'I heard you broke up with your girl back home!'

'Well, yes, sort of, Sir...'

'What do you mean, sort of?'

'Well, Sir...actually, she broke up with me.'

"The Colonel slams down a pile of black-and-white photos on the desk. Joe can see they are his photos, the ones he took the night he and I picked up the two girls in the Hong Kong Bar. 'What is going on here, Bates?', he yells. Ogilvy shuffles the photos, placing the one with Lan's tattooed breast on the top. He taps the photo.

'Nothing serious, Colonel. Just a wild night on the town. I confess, I did have a little too much to drink.'

The Colonel's voice becomes one step less cold. "I don't know why, Specialist...maybe I'm crazy. Maybe I'm going soft-headed. Do you think I'm going soft-headed, soldier?'

'N-no, Sir. Red Dog said I could use the dark room—'

"Ogilvy cuts him off, but his voice is down another notch. Now he's talking matter-of-factly, with a shade of personal feeling. 'I'm going to take you at your word, Specialist Bates. I believe you. You see, you're a young man, and the emotions run high around here. Nothing wrong with boffing a pretty girl every now and then, so long as it isn't serious. You say it isn't serious...it isn't serious, is it?'

'No, Sir,' Joe repeats. "Not serious at all."

'Okay, so that's settled. I don't care about this any more,' Ogilvy says, giving Lan's tattooed breast a last brush as if he might be fondling it. But then his voice rises to its original cold inflection. He takes a second set of photos out from under the first and slams them on the desk in front of Joe.

'But I do care oh so very much about this!'

Joe is sure Ogilvy is some sort of god of surveillance, he's sure the Colonel has already snapped shots of him meeting Mia My. The shots are grainy black-and-whites, and he picks the top one up to have a closer look—praise Buddha, praise Jesus, praise the dearly departed souls of all the saints—it's not a shot of him and Mia My! Instead, he sees the snap is one of Red Dog and some girl…wait, he knows that girl. He looks at the rest of the pictures. They are grainy, out of focus and poorly lit, but he's sure. The girl is Tuyet Lan.

Ogilvy snarls at Joe, 'Your boss, who thinks he's so smart with his language skills and his knowledge of the native ways—your boss comes within an inch of marrying this whore!'

'A-a-are you sure, Sir?' Joe stammers.

'You're telling me you knew nothing about this sordid affair?' Ogilvy shouts.

'I only heard rumors—after the explosion, Sir.' Joe tries to embellish, always a mistake. He says, 'The men were talking about it.'

Ogilvy is on him like a hawk. 'What men?' he asks. 'Who told you?'

Joe thinks fast, seeing the trap the Colonel has sprung. If he mentions names, the circle widens, and nothing good can come of it. He decides on the only course of action he can think of. He tells the truth. 'Red Dog did, Sir.' He says. 'After we gave blood, we went up to his room to see him.'

'You went to Saigon General?' Ogilvy knows that will be easy enough to check on. Bates will either have a valid alibi or he'll be in the brig.

'Yes, Sir,' Joe says. "We gave our pint and a half.'

'I've heard enough. Get out of here,' Ogilvy says. His voice is cold as ice. He doesn't trust anybody, but he's decided he's got as much as he's going to get out of Joe Bates.

Joe leaves the office, but when I lean over with my paper water cup, I can actually see a reflection of the Colonel in the glass covering the crude Loose Lips Sink Ships poster. Ogilvy's got a sour look on his puss and he's staring at his favorite photo, the one of himself with President John F. Kennedy in the good old times

before now, now when they both are dead,....JFK dead for real, and
The White Snake in every other way."

CHAPTER 21

At last Wild Jack's storytelling was slowing down. Mia My and I convinced him to get out of his damp Hawaiian attire and head for the sack. He found a matched pair of sweats that looked to be nearly 20 years old and headed upstairs for his bedroom, still grumpy that two girls had to rescue him from his own swimming pool.

We two ladies left for my guest house in high spirits, giggling like schoolgirls that we had put one over on him. It was too late to sleep. I could see I had this love-hate relationship going with the lady from Saigon. I was jealous that she knew so much more about Jack than I, and yet she seemed open and willing to talk about those early days that had meant so much to their friendship. We got into warm sweats ourselves, and settled in on my soft leather couch in the living room.

"So when was the next time you saw Joe?" I asked.

"Oh, not two days later!", she smiled. "He was waiting for me at the Arcade, sitting in the Milk Bar."

"What about the Saigon Cowboys?"

"Joe was never afraid of them. They are at their corner tables, very quiet, except for the one the Quoc Khanh had taken away for the army. That one was gone for good. Joe is sitting there at the table with two Thai Teas, waiting for me. I come up to him and he tells me I look beautiful, which I do, because I have spent much time hoping he would show up. He jumps to his feet when he sees me coming.

'Mia My!' he says. "I hoped you'd show up.' He was always so serious, my Joe, so I have to tease him a little bit.

'And why would I not *show up*?' I ask him. 'I have to open the shop this morning.' But I sit down so he sees I am only joking, and he hands me his photographs. They are all very good. I show him the one I like the best, a photograph he has taken of the crippled newspaper boys and girls selling papers in front of the cinema theater. He picks another one. It is a snapshot he has taken in front of the dress shop. I don't understand. I think he photographed the dress in the window to please me.

'Oh, that dress is nothing,' I say.

He points to the middle-aged Ba, the lines of her hard life and early old age all over her, and then to the graceful European manikin floating in the window. 'It's the contrast,' he says. 'Between the two cultures, East and West, rich and poor…between the dreams and the realities.'

I smile then, and I tell him of one of my little girl dreams. 'When I get married, I'll have a dress twenty times prettier than that one, with a long train of silk behind. Mama will make it for me. She has promised to do so. I'll walk down the aisle at the Saigon Cathedral with the man of my dreams and everyone will look at me.'

'That will be beautiful,' Joe says.

'Yes, it will,' I say. I don't tell him I've already walked that walk before, and with disastrous results.

'Because you're beautiful,' he says.

We have somehow finished our iced tea glasses, and I must rush to open the store or Mama will surely catch us together. That day, I smile all the hours, even when I prick my finger on a needle and get a tiny drop of blood on a silk gown and Mama yells at me. I feel so very happy. Even in Saigon, in the middle of a war that has gone on forever, there are times when the world can seem a wonderful and even magic place.

CHAPTER 22

If Wild Jack, the aging wonder-scribe, had been up late drinking Spanish brandy and fallen in the swimming pool the night before, it wasn't so you'd notice it. By the time Mia My and I wandered into his kitchen looking for a late breakfast, the morning was bubbling with the usual confusion. Jack's frail old gardener was peeping out from under his conical hat to nibble the poolside acacia trees with a long electric clipper he could hardly hang onto, and the Larch-ster himself and Eddie were yelling at each other about God-only-knew-what. Eddie paused briefly to admire my Dallas Cowboys cheerleader outfit, which still fit me like a glove. Jack ignored me as usual, taking the moment to shout at his half-senile old gardener, "Ong Vung, get away from the pool with that damn thing! You're going to electrocute yourself!" The gardener gave him a sour look, snapped the thick orange cord out of an outside wall plug and disappeared, scuttling around the side of the house.

Mia My was looking at the gardener with a puzzled look on her face.

"What is it," I asked.

"Nothing. He just reminds me of someone…but I don't remember who.'"

Jack interrupted, calling for her support. "We've got this great stuff, the Buddhist riots, and Eddie wants to cut it all out!"

This had me confused. Jack and Eddie were supposed to be working on adapting Stingray in Bagdad.

"Jack," Eddie complained, "We're already getting long, long, long. The screenplay's going to be longer than the book—if you ever write it!"

The Larch-ster got that stubborn look on his face that told me Eddie wasn't going to get anywhere..

"Tell him how important the Buddhist riots are, Mia My. Tell him!" Jack implored.

Mia My yawned and headed for the refrigerator, looking for some eggs or ham to cook, or maybe some left over carryouts she could zap in the microwave.

I found the new direction disconcerting but not entirely strange. It just added to the normal dislocations that existed everywhere in The House of Jack, something like an impossible reality, an Escher lithograph turned 3-D and come to life.

"Oh Great Storyteller Man," I said. "Aren't you getting your tales confused? Now Dunk Stingray has to fight off Buddhist riots?"

Jack looked at me like I was an idiot. "Clair-the-Fair, where you been? Eddie and I switched off Dunk a couple days ago. We're doing Joe's story."

This was too much, too fast, even for me.

"Where's Maria?" I asked. "I need breakfast."

"Her day off." Jack shook his head impatiently. I could see he was on a roll and my wants and needs were not nearly as important as his famous bug on the railroad tracks of life, or whatever that was all about.

"For God's sake, Mia My," he said, waving the arm with the dagger-in-the-heart tattoo on it in a wide and impatient sweep from her to Eddie, "explain to The Ghost here how important the Buddhist riots are."

Mia My had apparently given up on breakfast. She looked up from the L.A Times crossword puzzle she'd started and gave Eddie a nod of agreement. "You should keep that part of the story, Eddie," she said.

And that left me really feeling out in the cold. Jack decides to boot Dunk and write about his glory time in *The Nam,* and I'm the last one to hear about it. He's probably been out on the front lawn since sunup, riding Toro the grass mower with seedy old Ong Vung and asking him to refresh his memory about the restaurants and bars in jolly old Saigon. But I did a fast recovery. Turn on a dime, that's life in The House of Jack! After all, Jack doesn't talk over his work with anybody until he's got it locked down on paper…anybody except now Mia My. I had to fight a little to back down the tiny tsunami of envy that swept over me. Damn it! As if I didn't have enough to worry about, with every young Hollywood hooker trying to get into his pants.

Jack, his point of view validated, gave up on Eddie for the moment and came over to the granite divider between the kitchen and the living area, the place where he pecked out his pages to sate his muse. He eyed the Amazon mask on the wall, the one Dunk Stingray had used to pop out from the back end of a van to startle the English bank robbers in Stingray In Picadilly. He picked up his Chinese exercise balls in one hand and poured himself a cup of coffee with the other. The metal balls gave their softly content little chime noises. I saw by the level in the pot it was now three day coffee. I pried the warm cup from his reluctant grasp, poured the moldy old stuff out, and started to make a new pot. This was an old argument between us. Jack was used to my behavior; he gave me the usual grumpy look, but he didn't say anything. In ten minutes he would have another cup, fresh-brewed, and so he'd happy, charging off on his new story, The Adventures of Joe. .

"You make a cute couple," Mia My said.

I shook my head, still sour about being left out of the change in literary direction.

"The point, the point, the point!", Jack said, suddenly enervated and having set down his Chinese bongers, now waving both hands as he lurched around the room. If I haven't mentioned it before, Jack had bad knees, and he didn't march around when he weaved his stories, he more or less lurched from place to place on his bandy legs, each time seeming one step away from bumping into walls or some table or chair.

"Look, here's how Joe and I got personally involved in the riot thing. When a person says the word "riot," it's abstract, really, like a conversation out of the blue about crap you see in newspapers and on TV news, but almost nobody ever experiences a riot first hand. It was no different for us, that is, before it happened. It's mid-morning, another day of our tour in the green wetlands of Southeast Asia. Joe and I are over at the White Shack. Joe is translating—no big surprise—while I'm reading a Hemingway novel, maybe For Whom The Bell Tolls. I usually love Hemingway; so clear, so crisp, just the right words and no more…but for some reason at this moment Ernie pisses me off and I fling the book across the room. This being the tropics, the moisture plays hell with book bindings, and the thing comes apart in a shower of pages that drift to the floor.

'Crap!' I say. 'crap, crap, crap!'

Bates gives me a wild look. I guess I startled him. 'What?' he asks.

'How come fricking Hemingway gets away with run on sentences?'

'What do you care?' Joe asks. 'Hemingway is dead.'

'I guess...' He has me on that one.

Joe points to the work on the desk in front of him. 'This is interesting. Four weird copy blocks.'

'How are they weird, Joe?' I ask. 'It's just covert crap: Ping needs more bullets.'

'No, this is different,' Joe says. 'Get this.' He reads from the page in front of him. 'All units and friends must promote instability in the puppet government. The Phan Hui Quat puppets of the Invader-Gangster Americans will fall soon.'

'Sounds like trouble for the Catholics,' I say. I don't know why that pops out. Maybe something at language school, that course where we learned that 90% of the land in Vietnam was owned by 10% of the people, and they were mostly Westernized Vietnamese who had become Catholics under French rule.

Joe gives me a startled look. 'How you figure that?' he asks.

'The whole country's going under,' I tell him. 'And it's our fault. Getting rid of President Diem was the single dumbest thing JFK ever did. Diem was Catholic, but he was a strongman. Quat is also Catholic, but everybody knows he's weak. The VC can't wait to pull him down. And they're going to dupe the Buddhists into helping them do it.'

'You can't know that, Jack,' Joe tells me. But he's not certain. He's got this frown all over his face.

'I bet you ten bucks right now we have another Buddhist riot within the week. That's the way they do it.'

Joe's frown deepens. He's thinking about other things. 'Mia My's family is Catholic,' he says."

"Well, Clarity Supreme, I've already told you my goal is to experience my own war. You know if there's anything like a riot or a rumble I've just got to be there. After all, I've gone to a lot of trouble to see a war. Early that afternoon, we get off work, change into our civvies and head for the orderly room to sign out. I remember it like it was yesterday. Bates was wearing a red-and-white striped polo shirt, and he had his new camera bag, a pea green Air Vietnam bag he'd picked up at the old market.

"The sign out orderly is, as usual, pimply faced Toady. He gives us one look and slams the sign out book shut. 'You guys think twice about signing out,' he says. 'We're up to orange and there's talk of street riots.'

'Word sure gets around,' I say, looking at Joe and ignoring Toady. 'Top Secret doesn't mean shit anymore.'

'We already thought twice about it,' Joe says, pulling the book out from under Toady's hands. Toady can't stop us. He doesn't have any authority, and we're not on actual lock-down at the base until Code Red.

'Yeah,' I say. 'He did and I did. That's twice.'

'Smart ass lingies,' Toady says. But Joe and I don't care, we've already scratched our names and are out the door.

"I'd been having the twitch for a real American hamburger, not those stringy buffalo burgers we can get at the stands on the base, so our *xe hoi* taxi rockets us to the downtown USO. I'm surprised; it looks much different from the last time we saw it, just a week before. The exterior has been heavily sandbagged, and there are G.I.s stationed outside with M-14 rifles on the ready. You'd think we'd be used to this, because of the guards with machine guns outside the White Shack…but those are special, those are marines guarding our Top Secret secrets. These guys are ordinary grunts with standard army issue rifles.

Joe is ever one to state the obvious. 'Wooh!' he says. 'Guards and sandbags. All this trouble, we better get French fries, too.'

'Yeah, make it worthwhile.' I'm giving the G.I.s the once-over. 'Maybe somebody else read your covert memo,' I tell Joe. 'Word's getting out.'

'When even Toady knows, that's pretty pathetic,' he agrees.

"I walk right up to the G.I.s. like we're buddies from back home. I have this need to know everything. Curiosity hasn't killed me so far. 'You guys new in town?' I ask.

One of the soldiers eyes me like I might be a terrorist Buddhist monk in disguise. 'Yeah,' he says, deciding I'm probably safe. 'First week.'

Joe's been eyeing their rifles, which don't have any clips. 'Where are your bullets?' he asks. The soldier looks unhappy, his expression saying more than he dares with words. He furtively shows us a clip in the pocket of his fatigue jacket.

'Yeah, right,' I say. 'We're just military advisers. You wouldn't want to actually shoot anybody.'

The timing couldn't be better. A small Fiat speeds by and somebody flings a Molotov cocktail at us. The guy who flings the little glass bomb is in the back seat. He yells out the open window. *'De lai, dai quoc xam luac My!* Go fuck yourselves, invader-gangster Americans!' The bottle falls short of the sandbags, but it hits the street and ignites with a whoosh. I pull Joe behind the sandbags. Joe never, ever had any sense for his own safety…

Anyway, I yell at him, 'Get in here, you idiot!' Good thing, too, because the bottle rolls for a few feet and then explodes with a sharp crack and a shower of glass fragments. One of the G.I.s has glass shrapnel in his arm, and another holds his bleeding face. I can't be sure, but I remember thinking he was going to lose an eye. Our ears are still ringing from the blast when Bates shakes off my grip on his arm and starts to walk away.

'Joe, where are you going?' I'm looking at him like he's a crazy man. I point to the entrance of the USO. 'What about our hamburgers?' He shakes his head, pointing down the street.

'I have to make sure Mia My is alright,' he says. 'It's just a few blocks away.'

'I'll come with,' I offer.

'No,' he says. 'I have to talk to her.'

"So I go alone into the USO, and it's a little strange. Everybody is emotionally wired, high strung like they might come apart at any moment. But I see the café in the USO is still serving. I'm not going to miss an opportunity like that. It's a Joe Heller Catch-22 moment; I have a burger with fries and a chocolate shake…meanwhile, my buddy Joe is running down Nguyen Hue Street as if he's Superman and bombs and bullets will have no effect on him.

"He stops to take a photo of a burning cyclo-bus that's been pushed over on its side. The wide boulevard is deserted and littered with debris. A looter sees him and yells in Vietnamese, 'Hey, what you doing here, filthy invader-gangster American?' Joe sees the fellow has his hands full of radios and watches. 'No, what are *you* doing, filthy Viet Cong thief?' he says. He takes the guy's picture and trots on.

"He's close to the Edan Arcade now. He runs toward the main entrance, and as he does so, a stream of rioters pours out of a nearby side street. It is a mixed batch of young people in street clothes and Buddhist robes, mixed with a few older men who look like they may be more experienced at the art of riots and street violence. This group heads for the Arcade as well. Angry cries ring out in the air. 'Kill the Americans! Down with the hated European Imperialist Pigs! Kill the rotten Romanists!" It's a foot race, but Bates is closer, and in good shape, too. He easily beats them to the entrance and pushes his way through piles of garbage blocking the door and makes his way inside.

"The crippled kids are at their regular post, manning their newspaper station outside the cinema. They gape at him as he rushes by. He yells at them, 'Get to cover! Get to cover! *Di! Di! Mao len!* Do it! Go! Very fast!' They scatter as fast as they can, grabbing up their papers and scuttling pretty good for kids on crutches and canes, and Joe runs on down the wide interior corridor, heading for the Maison Blanch."

Jack grinned at me, "Better than Dunk Stingray, right Clair?" Actually, that's what I was thinking, but I didn't want to give him the satisfaction. I looked over at Mia My. "Where were you at this time?'

She gave me a calm little smile, and I got the feeling she believed fate or karma or something like that had a hand in all of this. "Oh, I was at the dress shop," she said. "Mama insisted we go to protect our shop."

"Your mother sent you into the middle of the riots because of a few lousy dresses?"

"You don't know Mama," Mia My said.

Eddie, the Goy Ghost, had been feverishly leafing through pages, making notes and trying to catch up. "Yeah—here! He glared at Jack. "You stuck the dress shop scenes back in!"

"Eddie, they are very, very important!" Jack insisted.

"Well," Mia My added, "They were certainly important to Mama and me. But we have the radio tuned to VTVN, Radio Saigon, and the announcer is giving us the blow-by-blow. There are burning automobiles on Le Loi Street. There is a mob scene over by the Old Marketplace, and Catholics have been robbed and beaten nearly to death by the river ferry. Auntie Kai and I—and even Mama—are starting to have second thoughts, maybe we shouldn't have left our home, when my Joe comes bursting in the door!

"Mama sees him, and of course, her face goes stern and cold and her lips get thin with that look just before the tigress strikes. But Joe doesn't have time for the tigress, and he doesn't seem to care that she might claw him to death.

'They're coming!' he shouts. Rioters! They'll be here in a minute!'

"Mama hates not being in control. She shouts back at him, 'Young man, this isn't funny—'

"He ignores her as I poke my head out from behind a curtain in back. 'Mia My! They are already in the Arcade! They'll be here in a minute!'

"I run to the front door, and see them pouring in, a bunch of ugly people in a rage, swinging sticks and throwing rocks. At that moment, I realize we have to close the grill. We have this folding iron grill that pulls down to protect the plate glass window and the door in front. Mama yells to Auntie Kai, 'Get the expensive cloth bolts out of the window and in back!'

"Mama and Joe and I struggle to pull down the grill, but we are in too big of a hurry, and it only comes half way down before it sticks. Joe starts to go outside.

'No!' I try to warn him. But he doesn't listen to me. He knows it is the only way; from outside maybe he can get enough pressure to pull it the rest of the way down. He goes out there and gives it one hard yank and it snaps free and comes all the way down into place with a big metal clank. Joe has saved us, but we are safe inside and he is on the outside. He reaches through the grill and squeezes my hand.

'I'll be okay,' he says.

"Mama is screaming my name. Even in this dangerous moment, she can see there is something between me and Joe, and yet she has to try to control my life. Still, I have no choice. Joe tells me to go, and so I retreat inside and slam the inner door behind me.

"Outside, there is only a dark and narrow doorway next to the grill. It is shuttered and locked, and he can't escape that way. But the hallway is unlit and he hides there, thinking he might not be seen."

Eddie looked up from the mess of papers on his little desk. "What in holy hell have you done here, Jack?" He held up three pages stuck together with a bright yellow paper clip with a pale green Post-It note slapped on top. "This doesn't fit. We've got Bates at the Arcade, and *Bam!* We cut to young Wild Jack at some nightclub?! Where the crap is your logic for this cut-away?"

"That nightclub was the beginning of the end for me," Jack says. "Or maybe the end of the beginning. That's where I met Myette."

"Myette?! Who is Myette?" I ask. I figured I might as well get my question in. Jack was going to tell us anyway.

Jack gave me a wry smile. "You should know, my pretty Clair. Here, today, we have woman's lib. Women are always bitching about their new frontiers—lady reporters getting into the men's showers, not for sex, but to interview them while they're scrubbing their balls. Women bitching about getting into Men's Clubs…hell, they closed down the men-only club on the top floor of the Animation Building over at Disney. Women bitching about snagging their nylons when they butt their way through the glass ceiling—"

"Get to the point, Larch-ster," I interrupted him. "We all know how nefarious modern women are. Who the hell is Myette?"

"The point is, Clair-Bear, not counting the tiger ladies, women in Vietnam didn't used to be the way women here are today. They had very few opportunities in life outside of marrying, hopefully to some rich man. In fact, one of the few ways a woman could become a success on her own was to be a night club singer. Most every young girl wanted that, worse than she wanted anything, you know, become a famous night club singer, and then get married. American soldiers weren't exactly welcome in the night clubs, but I'd started going and kind of liked it, so it became a habit of mine.

"So, after Joe so unceremoniously dumps me to run over to the Arcade Edan, I tank up on my hamburger at the USO and drift over to the Van Canh Vietnamese nightclub on Calmette Street. It's still there, you know—I googled it—but today it looks like it's mostly a restaurant, while back then…well, it was something special, a place where you could hear music so beautiful it still haunts me. Anyway, I sit down and order a Ba Muoi Ba, and that's when I spot Myette for the first time. She's on this raised stage at one end of a big room, and she's in one spotlight, slim and graceful in a filmy *ao gai,* all white with pale pink orchids. She's singing a slow waltz love song and the live band behind her struggles to keep up. There's a shivery, pure quality to her voice, and when she sings *Em yeu Anh* the people crowded around the tables in the darkened room go wild, clapping and cheering. Hey, no way I'm going to walk away from a special moment like this. I'm half-a-world away from UCLA and the Fellowship in Graduate English that I gave up to be here. In fact, I'm the only American in the place. Myette sings every third or fourth song, and as the afternoon wears into evening, I'm steadily adding to the line up of empty beer bottles on the table in front of me. What's more, I have my own little peanut girl feeding me a steady diet of peanuts. I have everything I need, and the Buddhist riots are very far away.

Unfortunately, the world is not a peaceful place, and there's a half-dozen rowdy Saigon Cowboys sitting at a table in back, and they decide having an American in the audience is an affront to their dinky dicks or something. They start yelling stupid stuff like I'm defiling their women and they want to cut off my imperialist invader-gangster prick and bash my head in."

"Okay," I looked over at Mia My. "So Wild Jack was getting his rocks off in some nightclub while Saigon burned.

Mia My smiled at me, shaking her head, "You should not be so hard on poor Jack. I think it is true. Meeting Myette messed him up plenty, and for a long time."

"But I want to know about Joe and you."

"Well, we are not in very good shape at that moment. These riot people fill the central corridor of the Arcade, and they are screaming in Vietnamese, things like, 'Down with all French pigs! Down with the hated European colonialists! Kill the American gangsters!'

"And maybe I am safe for a little bit, but my Joe is out there…snapping his pictures. There is much violence, and we can hear it all and see much of it through slits in the grill protecting us.. Windows in the neighbor shops are smashed and the rioters get a fire hose and spray water in the Air France offices. They throw rocks in the windows of the jewelry shop. Some of our neighbors rush out to defend their shops, but nobody can stop this mad crowd. They have clubs made of wood with nails in them, and big rocks. Some injured merchants lie bleeding on the ground and try to crawl away, or they stagger around screaming in their shock and pain, their bodies all bloody. There are flames, too—the rioters are throwing fire bombs. And Joe captures it all with his little Bolsley 35 millimeter camera.

"Joe could be like that, lost in the moment of taking his pictures. He only comes back to his senses when a fire bomb smashes against the iron grill of our place, exploding and washing a ball of flame against the Maison Blanch. There are flames everywhere at Joe's feet, but he has nowhere to run. He kicks the broken half of the bottom of the bottle back into the swarm of rioters and stomps on the flames before they can catch on the inner wooden frame and start the fabrics burning in our dress shop.

"And in that moment, there is a furious young Buddhist novice in brown robes who jumps out of the crowd. He glares at Joe and swings a wooden 2x4 club. Joe snaps his picture as the novice screams *'Nguoi My Xao!'* But it isn't a Buddhist monk. And what is more, Joe recognizes him. It is Phong, the Saigon Cowboy from the Milk Bar, come to do vengeance against me. Joe yells at him, 'Phong! Are you still not seventeen?'

"Phong is full of fearful rage at being recognized. He swings his club at Joe with all his fury. But Joe has learned good boxing somewhere in his life, and he steps inside the killing blow and pokes Phong in the face with his fist. He smacks him hard, breaking his nose. Phong grabs at his bloody nose and falls backward in his surprise. The crowd rushes around and in another moment Phong is gone.”

"So I’ve got this right, Jack?” Eddie asked. “Joe’s a hero again, and you’re getting drunk in a bar somewhere?”

"Night club,” Jack corrected him. “I didn’t know things had gotten so bad at the Arcade. And if you’d seen the way Myette looked that night, you’d have hung around, too…well, a regular guy would have. I couldn’t help myself. I had to meet this incredible Oriental lady songbird. I scribbled out a little note and handed it to one of the waitresses to pass on to Myette. I said some romantic nonsense, something like, ‘She sings so beautifully I want to die of happiness and cry in sorrow at the same time.’ The Cowboys see me passing the note and they start yelling stuff like, ‘If Myette answers you, we’ll cut off your balls.’ Myette is about to go on with another song, and everybody in the audience sees as she reads my note.

"Meanwhile, the unruly guys at that other table are starting to act up. ‘My knife is longer than your knife,’ one of the Saigon Cowboy punks brags, and he pulls out a big switchblade.

‘Oooooo, you rebel-with-no-cause,’ another says.

‘You very James Dean, you!’ the third beams his approval.

"These guys have been doing their own drinking, and the first Cowboy takes a little swipe at his pals with the knife. The others jerk back from him; nobody wants to be cut in a game of joking around. I’ve had my eyes on the Cowboys…after all, I’m not a newcomer to Saigon any more, and I know bad shit happens when you’re not watching out. I’m getting a little concerned that they’ve got a knife and seem amused about the idea of using it on me. So I’m not paying attention, and I’m surprised to hear a voice over my shoulder. ‘Hello, G.I., she says. ‘So you think I sing like an angel?’

"So that’s how it was on that fated day,” Jack said. “I met somebody I thought sang like an angel, and Joe earned a dinner with Ba Nguyen.”

Mia My smiled. “Yes. After the White Mice came and chased away the rioters we had a big mess to clean up, and Joe stayed to help us. And after that, Mama felt it would be bad manners not to invite him to dinner. I didn’t want that to happen.

I thought he would have one taste of the tiger lady and run away and be lost to me forever.

"The way it came to be would have been funny if you didn't know how crazy Mama could be. She made him sit at the distant end of the long black table in our dining room. That table had big marble squares inset in dark wood, and looked more like a tomb than a table! Anyway, there is Joe, way down at the far end, then many empty chairs in the middle between us, and on the other end Mama sits with Auntie Kai on one side of her and me on the other.

Ong Han, our faithful servant with the one blind eye stands at attention at Mama's side. The chef stays in the kitchen, and we have a younger man bring the food. It is short notice, so we only have three or four courses, a very big sin for a family of traditions *a la Francaise*.

'It is the best we can do,' Mama assures Joe in her stiffly formal voice. 'On such short notice.

'Oh, no," Joe replies. *'Cam on, Ba.'* I have already seen how brave Joe is to help rescue our dress shop, but with Mama, he also shows no fear. I think it annoys her a little. He is very respectful, and speaks in Vietnamese or in his very bad French, but she likes the men around her to also be a little afraid.

Mama clears her throat. I know she will hate the next thing she knows she must say. She speaks in formal Vietnamese, and knowing my mother, I am aware that she is hoping he doesn't understand her. She says, 'If you had not been so brave, we would have lost our shop. We are deeply grateful.'

'I am glad to have the opportunity to be of assistance,' he replies, also in Vietnamese.

'I told you he was nice, Mama,' I say. This has the desired effect of bringing a faint heat of anger to her cheeks. Auntie Kai has an amused expression on her face, but she cocks her head slightly, a little warning to me not to go too far. Mama ignores me, still speaking to Joe, 'We do not like Americans…all those Baptists and hillbillies. We have our own mountain people here— monkey people in their loin cloths who never take baths.' She is talking about the Montagnards, the people of an ancient culture we lowlanders have driven to the mountains the way you did here with your Apaches and Navajos.

'My mother hates hillbillies, as well,' Joe says. 'We are Catholics for many generations.' I am a little surprised at this, but I swear, Mama's mouth drops open. 'Yes,' Joe continues, laying it on a little thick, 'The Diocese of Joliet, Illinois. St. Liborius Parish. I was an altar boy, and a very good one, I might add. I won a Saint Christopher medal for it. *Ad deum qui lay tificat, Juvum tutum meum.'*

"Mama recovers as best she can and gives Joe a grave nod. 'That is very good, young man,' she says.

'And where is…Mr. Nguyen?' Joe asks.

"Mama's face reddens a little and she purses her lips. Papa's name is disqualified from discussions around the table, but she can't find a delicate way to extricate her way from the question. 'Mr. Nguyen travels constantly,' she says. 'He is currently in Paris, for the business.'

"Auntie Kai breaks out in a big smile. *'Madame et Monsieur Nguyen… disengagement…'* she says.

'Mama and Papa are separated,' I repeat, just in case Joe hasn't gotten the point.

'Oh,' Joe says, realizing that he has stepped into the cow pie.

"Mama could have left it alone, but she has never been able to do so in the past. 'My husband is a fornicator!' she bursts out.

"I can see that is more than Joe wants to know. He grimaces at me, and I shrug in the European way. 'Many things in life are sad and this is just one of them,' I say."

At that moment, Jack stepped in to do his tag-team narration. "Meanwhile, over at the Van Canh nightclub, I was actually getting it on a little bit with Myette. It's late and she's finished singing for the night. We're sitting at my table, talking about this and that over glasses of iced tea.

'So you come from Hue?' I ask her. "How did a beautiful singer like you end up here?'

"She has a terrific voice, a touch husky and that is very rare in a Vietnamese woman's voice. She laughs and places a hand on my arm, and I feel a thrill from my head to my toes. 'Well,' she says, 'first we went to Nha Trang, a lovely old French city , where I sang in the Perfumarie Nightclub.'

"In that moment, I hear a loud voice behind me, 'I have your happy treat for you, Mister Amelican *Nguoi Xao!*' There's a thump on my upper arm and a burning feeling. I look down and one of the Saigon Cowboys has jammed his knife in my arm. It's stuck there, buried to the hilt. It's one of those moments when the world stands still. I'm thinking, This can't be happening to me, but goddamn, look right there, there's a goddamn knife stuck right through my arm!

'Holy shit!' I say. I'm stunned. I can't believe it. But then I see that Myette has a bit of the tiger in her, and it's a good thing for me that she does. She leaps up with a furious scream, *'Dien cai dao!* Crazyhead!' She whirls like a dervish, and I find the slit skirt *ao gai* leaves plenty of freedom for movement as she knees the Cowboy in the groin.

"He doubles over, but he's not out of the fight. *'Chet roi!'* he screams. You just signed your death warrant, bitch!'

"But he has no idea the world of trouble he is in. The night club singers of that day and age might not have a union, but they are intensely loyal to each other. In another few seconds, the Saigon Cowboy and his punk friends are surrounded by girl singers and members of the band, all armed with bottles and bats and even a heavy set of marimba mallets. It's no contest, and the punk cowboys retreat between the tables, heading for the doors.

"The leader of the punks, the guy who stuck me with his knife, looks like he's unhappy the way things are turning out. He shakes his fist at us. *'Trung ta de vay!'*, he screams. We'll be back! But in another moment the Cowboys are out the door. I'm still sitting at the table, wondering if I should move my arm because the blade might cut a major artery or something. Blood is running in a little trickle and dripping from my elbow onto the floor.

'What we do now?' Myette asks me. I figure leaving it in is going to do more damage than pulling it out.

'Somebody has to take hold of the handle and yank it out,' I tell her.

'I'll do it,' she offers. That surprises me, but I say, 'Okay.' She grabs the knife with both hands and starts to pull, but it's stuck, and, worse, now the shock is worn off and it's starting to hurt like hell. Myette gives a loud cry like she's one of the Hai Ba

Trung sisters and gives it her all. The knife comes out, but the pain in my arm is enormous and I see there's blood everywhere. And that's when I lose my grip on things and sink to the floor..

"When I come too, I'm in an apartment somewhere. My arm is wrapped tightly in a compression bandage made from white sheeting soaked in my own blood. But that's not the worse thing. I think I'm seeing double. At least, I see two Myettes. I reach out with my good arm to touch the image closest to me. 'Myette,' I say. 'No,' the girl says. 'I am Yvette. He is Myette.'

"For just a moment I think I've died and gone to heaven. Then I gather my scattered wits. Yvette has said the words, 'He is Myette.' And they're both standing there looking at me, twin images with enigmatic smiles on their faces, waiting to see if I can catch up or not. And, loss of blood and high alcohol levels in what remains of the blood in my body not withstanding, I'm about to find out how complicated the sexual rites and mating practices of some of the ancient cultures of South-East Asia actually can be."

"Jack, you didn't!" I say. I'm thinking to myself, That must be where Jack came up with those racy scenes with the Romanian twins in Stingray in Slovinia.

Jack frowns, reviewing it once again in his writer's mind, the mind that has come up with so many fictional scenes that he wants to be sure what is real and what is not. "No, I didn't...I don't think..."

Eddie shakes his head. "Just how do you expect us to play this in the screenplay?" he asks in that complaining, ghost-writerly way of his.

CHAPTER 23

Mia My and I were sitting around the pool. I was pecking away at my laptop. Natural Gas looked like it was going up so I was shifting a few stocks around to see if I could get in on the up-tick. Mia My was lying on a lounge chair, talking to one of her sons on her cell phone as she watched the clouds drifting by. She was dressed in white silk today, a white silk Vietnamese dress, with white pants and a slit skirt, and she was talking rattle-bang on the phone, arguing with her son. She finally slammed the phone shut.

"I've never seen you upset before."

"This is serious business, Clair! My son has no brains! I must tell him to do everything!"

"Ohh…he's not a business guy?

"He thinks he is, but he is too focused, he never, never ever sees the big picture."

That was a new idea to me.

"I thought focus was good."

"Everybody can focus, Clair. The monkey and the rat both want the mango. But is the fruit filled with poison? Are there bad snakes nearby?"

"So he's in the food business?"

"No, commercial real estate."

That perked my interest a bit. I hit the pause button and gave her my full attention.

"So, what's the deal?"

"You know we at the top of the market right now, Clair."

I'd suspected something like that, but, you know, nobody wants to get out too soon.

"The bubble is big, bigger, close to burst, but he wants to buy. I tell him to sell. Sell, sell, sell!"

"Oh," I said, "I'm thinking of buying, myself. My two ex-Cowboy cheerleader pals and I own two big rental units, and we're looking at an even bigger one."

"Ohh," she said, giving me a tragic look and making the sign of the cross to bless herself.

"What are you doing, warding off evil?"

"Ward off bad luck for you," she said.

"Does it work?"

"For me, not lately."

"I'm sorry, I didn't mean…"

"No, it is okay. I must wear white for mourning ten more times. Then I can be less sad."

"And you'll get married again?"

"Never!" She gave me a fierce look. "But then I can stop crying all the time."

That was news to me. I hadn't seen her cry at all. But you never know about people; at least it seemed I never did….

"Where's Wild Jack?" I asked.

"He and Eddie-The-Ghost went for a hike on the back of your property. Here, see—they come back now."

She pointed to the faint trail that went up on a sharp curving ascent past the boulders behind my guest house and on up into the hills. The back end of my property was one of those odd parcels of undeveloped land the local government wanted to buy to add to the mountain trails, but it was an isolated patch as the big money tree huggers needed to buy up several connecting pieces of the puzzle on either side of my land before they made me an offer. I guessed, if Mia My was right with the sell-sell-sell, the people who owned the connecting pieces might be dumping their lots soon.

Jack and Eddie came clumping down the mountain and flopped into chairs around my glass outdoor table. Jack was wearing his hiking gear. My spirits lifted when I saw him, and he grinned back at me. He had on short tan pants, a tan hiking shirt, a big floppy hat, lightweight leather gloves and hiking boots. Eddie was in his ordinary Dockers, a red-and-white striped rugby shirt and his street shoes, so I could pretty well guess whose idea it had been to take a brief expedition *up into the hills.* Still, Jack was the one who was red-faced and flushed, so I guess it had been a little hotter than he'd planned on. I went in for a six-pack of bottled iced tea.

"Gaad, peach flavor," Jack grumped, but he gulped it down anyway and reached for a second bottle.

"Where'd you guys go, to the High Sierras?"

"All the way to the cyclone fence," Eddie said.

"What were you doing up there?"

Eddie started to say something else, but Jack impatiently cut him off.

"To see what we could see," he said..

"Why are you wearing gloves, Jack?"

"What is this, an interrogation? I didn't want to skin my hands if I fell."

He pulled off his light leather gloves and stuffed them in one of his wide cargo pockets, wiggling his precious writer's fingers as if he used them all to type.

Actually, I knew the place they had to have stopped. It was where my property ended. They couldn't go any further because the gate was locked, and I'd misplaced the key, if I'd ever had one. There was a steep ravine—a cliff, really—that dropped off on the other side of my fence, so there wouldn't be any incentive for the aging boy scout explorer and his moderately overweight ghost pal to go any further, even if they'd been in the mood.

"Well, it's hot and muggy out. You could have picked a better day."

Jack mopped his sweaty forehead with one arm, leaving a dark stain on his long-sleeved shirt. "Have a little charity, Clairity. Sometimes your day picks you," he said. "Where'd we leave off our story?

"Joe was having dinner with Mama Nguyen," I said. "Ad you're about to engage in complicated Oriental sex with Mimi and Vivi.".

"Mymette and Yvette," he said, his frown deepening in my direction. "*My*-met and *Eye*-vette."

"Oh, for God's sake, Jack, what's it matter after all these years?"

"You talk like an old married couple," Mia My smiled.

"Well, he's been married two or three times, depending on who is counting," I said. And he's also really old, so that counts for both of us."

Jack shook his head. Something I'd said had stung him, but I wasn't sure just what. He was an easy target; over the years so many things had popped out of my mouth unbidden, I wasn't sure which one had hit the mark this time. Of course, knowing the chameleon spirit that was Jack, I didn't think anybody could say it was entirely my fault. Still, I had that feeling again that I'd been having lately, the notion that I shouldn't always be popping off at him. Was this what love was all about, just being careful about each other's feelings? Where were the hearts and flowers? And when was the last time he'd been considerate about me?

"Saigon. The riots," the Larch-ster said, giving me a grim look and shaking his head as if he was gathering his thoughts. "I think I already told you, Joe uses the White Shack dark room to develop his photos. It's not a day or two later that The White Snake's office is adorned with a dozen or so photo blowups Joe took of the downtown riot. The White Snake is talking to Wendell and Leo, his two CIA ops, and he's not happy. We're right next door, doing our translating—at least Joe is, I'm back into The Sun Also Rises—and when Ogilvy shouts like that, we can hear every word.

'Specialist Bates shot these,' Ogilvy yells. 'A lousy, stinking Spec 4 enlisted man. A lingie, to boot! He got everything: Nguyen Hue Street. Le Loi Street. The Arcade. Where were you numb-nuts idiots when this was going on?'

Leo gulps and says, 'We were in the Cherry Bar, Sir.'

'So you cover the bars and you miss the Buddhist riot!'

Wendell clears his throat, 'It was an assignment, Sir. Perhaps you remember that's where we spotted Red Dog, Sir.'

Joe and I take that moment to wander to the doorway. After all, they're talking about his pictures. I take one look in and head back for my desk. But Joe speaks up, 'They're not real Buddhists, Sir. At least, not most of them.'

Leo is happy to have this interruption by someone he believes is insignificant and stupid. 'Christ, Specialist,' he yells. 'You can't tell a monk's robe when you see one? They're *bright orange,* for Christ's sake!'

Bates shakes his head like he's talking to a dunce. 'Real monks shave their heads. It's a strict rule. Most of these guys didn't even bother. And the ones that did…well, they have a tan-

line. You can see it there, on my pictures.' He points across the
room to one of his photos.

Wendell, who is a devious bastard, switches sides.
'Interesting,' he says. 'Buddha is in the details, as one might
remark…'

But Colonel Ogilvy is not amused. He wants a moment
alone with Bates. He shoos his guys out, which means they will be
hanging out in our small section, because they have no place of
their own. 'Bates, come in here,' the White Snakes says. 'I want
to talk to you.' Wendell gets up to leave. He doesn't really care.
But Leo gives Joe a black look as he leaves. Joe enters and sits
stiffly in the chair. He looks at the picture of Colonel Ogilvy with
his arm around JFK's shoulder. They are dressed in sweats and
smiling, like they've just been playing touch football or out sailing
on the Potomac.

'Relax,' Ogilvy says as soon as they are alone. He waves
one hand at the pictures covering the wall, indicating the blowups
of Bates's snapshots, 'You did good work. We turned the negs
over to the ARVNs and the White Mice. There are going to be
arrests all over town.' His smile turns nasty, 'A whole new wave
of recruits for the Army of the Republic of Vietnam.' But then the
grin disappears from his face. He stares at Joe for a moment and
then reaches into a desk drawer and retrieves another picture from
it. It is one of Joe's pictures taken before the riots, the one he took
just before finding Mia My in the dress shop. There's the Maison
Blanch with the wedding dress on the dreamy manikin in the
window and the earthy street seller Ba in the foreground, grinning
with her betel-nut blackened teeth. But this is a blow-up, and Joe
shoots in fine-grain black-and-white, so his photographs are
exceptionally sharp and show minor details that can't be seen in
the ordinary size photos. Through the window, in the background,
Ba Nguyen, Auntie Kai and Mia My are clearly visible. 'Again
we see these people,' The White Snake says, obviously looking for
some answers.

'I already told you, Sir. I met the daughter with Colonel
Williamson after the pedi-cyclo explosion.' The Colonel's glare
deepens, and Joe stumbles along, 'We're just casual
acquaintances…the mother is pretty starchy.'

'Nothing serious, right?'

'Oh, no, Sir. You can't get serious with a mean mom and a maiden aunt looking over your shoulder all the time. In fact, I can't even get to first base.'

'And you're already hitting home runs with your girl with the butterfly tattoo on her breast.'

'Yes, Sir. That's right, Sir,' Joe lies.

'Right. Keep it that way.' There's a pause while Joe wonders if he will crumble under the White Snakes intense look. 'Dismissed,' the Colonel finally says.

"Joe leaves, heading for the bathroom to throw some cool water on his face, but Leo is sitting on my desk, thumbing through a tattered copy of Playboy. From where we're sitting, we can both see Ogilvy's reflection in the glass of the Loose Lips poster. The White Snake takes another photo from his desk.

"Leo and I can both see it. 'That's a shot I took of Joey-boy and Missy Prissy Lovey-Dove at the Milk Bar," Leo says proudly. Ogilvy mutters something that might be, 'Looks like first base to me...'

"Leo grins at me, 'Bates ain't the only guy good with a camera.' He wanders back into the Colonel's office, and pretends surprise as he sees the photo blow-up of the Nguyens on the desk. 'Oh,' he says, pointing to Mama Nguyen. 'I know her. That was the president's squeeze, right?'

"The White Snake whirls around and for a moment it looks like his reflection in the glass is going to strike like a cobra and take poor Leo down like a hapless chicken. 'I goddamn know who she is, Leo!' he shouts."

"No rest for the wicked, you know," Jack said. "You have any more iced tea?"

Mia My has fielded another call from her son, and has moved to the other side of the pool so she can more comfortably yell at him.

"What's with her?" Jack asked.

"She's advising her son on his business. He wants to buy a sky-scraper or something, and she thinks it's a bad idea."

"He better listen."

"Like, she's a biz whiz?" My look clearly said I don't think so.

"She ever gives you that sort of advice, Clair, you better take it."

I gave him an unbelieving snort, "I'll do that, Jack."

"Do what you want," he said with a shrug. "You will, anyway."

Jack doesn't like to get involved in my business. I suppose I would think more of his opinions, but, as I've seen what a mess he's made of his own finances, I automatically turn off to whatever he says. Sometimes that really gets his goat. This time, it doesn't seem to matter.

I went to get him a can of diet Coke, and when I came back, he was zoned out, idly watching one of those small airplanes drag a banner over the hills that read BLOW-OUT COMPUTER SALE.

Mia My's voice has gone up another level, to something impossibly shrill. Jack grinned at me, "She's a great friend, but I'd hate to be her son."

"How the hell is that advertising supposed to work?"

"What?" Jack asked in return, looking like he was coming back to me from a long way away.

"The plane up there. No phone number. No address. There's a great sale somewhere, but anybody who sees that banner doesn't know what to do about it."

"We'd usually fly a little higher than that," Jack said. "Not much higher, maybe 2500 feet or so. It gets bumpy up there, particularly in the afternoon when the clouds start. And chilly, too. You'd be surprised. I mean, imagine, Clair…chilly in South Vietnam.

"See, I'm going up there with Hinkelby on a regular basis, now that Red Dog is out of the picture. Seems like we're up there all the time, and then there's this one time about a week after I got stabbed in the arm…Lieutenant Peabody is flying, and the door to his compartment is closed. He doesn't get along with Hinkelby the way he did with Red Dog, something about Hinkelby likes President Johnson and the Detroit Tigers, and the Lieutenant doesn't. We've been running the grid for a couple of hours, ever since lunch, actually, and rain is smacking against the outside of the plane. After a while, Hinkelby strips off his earphones and points at my bandaged arm. He shouts at me over the engine noise, 'What the hell happened to you, lingie?'

"I take off my headset and shake my head, 'I'm not getting anything.'

'I asked what happened to your arm.'

'I got knifed in a Vietnamese nightclub.'

"Hinkelby gives me a wise nod, He's about to give me some non-com's army wisdom. 'You should stick to the bars and the whorehouses. I never got knifed in the New York Bar or the Chez Rene."

"And at that moment, as if God Almighty or Buddha wants to get in a comment of his own, the engine on our Beaver stops, just all of a sudden, and for no reason I can see. After three hours of non-stop rattle-bang from that noisy radial engine, the silence gets our attention right away. Hinkleby opens the door to the front compartment. 'Lieutenant, what's happening?' he asks.

'I don't know,' Peabody tells him. 'I'm switching tanks.'

"Hinkelby crawls up front and pokes his head out of the open passenger side window. 'Hey!' he yells, 'The fuel line! We got petrol streaming out from the plane!'

"That shoots my concern way up into the red zone, and it's not just that I wouldn't have thought Hinkelby, who had quit high school and fudged a diploma to join the army, actually knew a word like "petrol." I suppose gliding might be fun in other circumstances, but whatever Peabody is trying isn't working, and we're taking a long glide down into the bush. You think of odd things at moments like that. I'm wondering why I haven't taken Red Dog's advice and stocked up on heavy gold neck chains.

"Hinkelby ducks back in our compartment and snatches the coordinates map from me. With the clouds and the rain streaking the windshield, I don't know how he can instantly snap to a clear idea of exactly where we're at, but apparently he can do just that. He pushes his head back up front into the pilot's compartment . 'We're nearly to the old Michelin rubber plantation,' he yells. 'There, just about dead ahead? Can you make it that far?'

'I guess we'll see,' Peabody yells back, their petty disagreements gone like they never were. He talks into his radio, 'Code Hyena Arthur Charley. This is Low And Slow with an emergency set down.'

"Hinkelby flops down in the seat next to me and starts fiddling with his .45 automatic. Seems like all the sergeants have army issue .45s they got from their dads or uncles. The agitated way he's fumbling to get the safety off isn't reassuring.

'The plantation's been deserted for years, but scuttlebutt is there might be a caretaker,' he says.

"We've been gliding for over a minute when I see out the side window up front that we're only about fifty feet up, coming in fast on an overgrown lawn in front of what looks like a deserted mossy old colonial mansion with no windows or doors.

'Oh, crap,' Peabody yells. '*Merde!* Shit, shit, *shit!*'

"Our problem is we're running out of lawn. We actually do touch down okay, but in twenty feet the stationary wheels on our Beaver hit a ditch. We bound in the air ten feet or so and come back nose down. We lose both wings in the crash and flip over, tilting upside down and skidding through a stand of bamboo to a shuddering stop.

"Hinkelby, Peabody and I are all flung around and turned upside down. I get it worse than the others when one of the heavy radio intercept units topples over and falls on my bad arm. After about twenty seconds of scrambling around, Peabody and Hinkelby crawl out of the plane on their own steam, but then they have to lift the radio stuff off me and pull me from the plane. I'm clutching my arm, which is bleeding again. It feels odd, like maybe it's broken.

'Wait, my pistol!' Hinkelby shouts. He crawls back in the plane and after a bit of scrambling around, hands out the army issue automatic, shoving it butt-first in my direction. I hear a voice over my shoulder, '*Nguoi My...*' and I spin around and nearly shoot a ten year old Vietnamese kid. Thank Almighty Jesus the safety was on or I would have shot him.

'Don't kill him!' Peabody yells as Hinkelby inches his way out of the upside down door of the Beaver. The kid, who probably didn't realize how close to eternity he'd come, points toward a tree-line about a mile and a half away. *'Viet Cong a day. Mot chuc nua. Nguoi My di! Di-di mao len!'*

'What's he say?' Hinkelby asks. He doesn't speak any Zip, and neither does Peabody.

'The VC are coming,' I tell them. 'We have to go very fast!'

'Where are they coming from? Which way do we go?'

"The kid I almost shot has a plan that just might save us. He motions we are to follow him. There's a battered Vespa scooter inside a garage in back of the old French house. Peabody drives the Vespa scooter, which is badly overloaded because Hinkelby is hanging on, seated behind him. I'm coming up behind both of them, riding a black Solex bike. That's a half-motorized little bike with a tiny motor up over the front wheel that helps propel the bike with a cheesy friction drive. It is so bad you have to pedal for extra speed. The kid points down a rutted gravel road, indicating we've got to go a couple kilometers. We look in the opposite direction, and sure enough, some guys in black pajamas are sprinting toward us. The kid frowns and melts into the countryside. He's about as eager to meet the VC as we are.

"That's all the encouragement I need. I'm steering with one arm and pedaling like crazy and I still can't keep up with the overloaded scooter, and the guys in the black pajamas are gaining on us, and this isn't at all the way I'd imagined The Adventures of Wild Jack in Southeast Asia.

'Peabody yells, 'I think I see it!' and he's right, in the distance there's a yellow-with-red stripes flag of the Republic of Vietnam hanging limp over a government checkpoint where our gravel road meets a two-lane blacktop, the road back to Saigon."

Back in Holmby Hills, Jack's narration went silent. By now, the plane dragging the ad banner had moved on out of sight. I looked over at Eddie for corroboration, but he just shrugged, he hadn't been there. I pruned up my face at Jack. "I don't think I believe you, Jack." You're adventures are starting to sound a lot like a low-budget exploiter."

"You shouldn't wrinkle your face up like that, Clair-Bear. You'll need botox before your time."

Actually, I'd had a light botox touch or two, but I guess he hadn't been paying attention.

Jack looked hurt that I didn't believe him. "You don't have to believe it, Clair, but that's the way it happened, me peddling a stupid little Solex bicycle to save my ass from the Viet Cong. Good thing, too. I wasn't going to get a Purple Heart for getting stabbed in a nightclub. But breaking my arm when the Beaver crashed…well, you can see they had to give me one for that."

"You have a Purple Heart?" At that moment Mia My returned from the cell phone shouting event she'd been having with her son. "Mia My, does this lying sack have a Purple Heart?"

Mia looked at me like I was crazy. "Of course. Why would he lie about that?"

That set me back a little. "I don't know…It's just a little...far-fetched."

She took Jack's arm with an easy familiarity that I envied. "Long ago," she said, "but not far away." She pushed up the short sleeve on his tan hiking shirt to reveal his tattoo. I hadn't noticed before, but there was a real scar, a line about an inch long, at the intersection where his tattoo blade entered his tattoo red heart. She lifted Jack's arm to show another scar. "There's where it came out on the other side."

Incredible! That made my head spin! Jack had shifted his big, ugly tattoo off center to hide the big ugly real scar where he'd been knifed by a Saigon punk cowboy. "Death Before Dishonor," indeed! And now I had to wonder how much else that he poured into his Stingray adventures might have some elements of truth to them. Jack's art was imitating his former life more than I would have imagined..

"That wasn't necessary," he growled at Mia My, pulling his arm away from her. I wanted to tell him that I was sorry, but he'd already gotten up from the table and was retreating around the pool toward the main house.

It's funny and maybe even odd how an emotional moment like that one can change other things that are—or at least seem to be—entirely disconnected. A few minutes later, my Dallas Cowboy Gal Pals Dina and Debbie showed up, bubbling all over about the new unit they were hot for us to buy. It was bigger than anything we'd done—almost two hundred units—and if we managed to pull it off, we'd be in hock to the bank for a decade.

I couldn't figure myself out. I'd had my reservations before, but now Mia My's conversation with her son was fresh in my mind.

"This is Jack's old war buddy's widow," I said.

Mia My was looking Oriental and out-of-fashion in her white slit skirt *ao gai* dress. She seemed involved with some strange needlework, and so the gals of Gal Pals, Inc were happy to say *"Hi"* in a polite way, and after that ignored her like she was part of the hired help.

Dina and Deb are power blondes, both divorced, early 40's, lots of wear on their butts but still looking for the action. I've always thought of them as friends, but actually, we're more like business acquaintances. I know they don't really respect my opinion. They listen because I'm a one third partner, and then they do what they want as often as they can get away with it.

"I'm a little nervous about this one," I said. I picked up a stray baseball and winged it through the rubber tire hanging from the Jacaranda tree.

"We know you are, little timid bird," Deb gave me a scoffing laugh, like I was odd-gal-pal-out, and that pissed me off even more.

"Bet you couldn't do that again, Dina said, nodding her head at the baseball, now nestled against the cliff face. "You've been dragging your heels for a week now. You always think it's too much money."

Dina pushed the contract in front of me. "We don't have time for this. Sign there," she said.

Mia My, sitting on the lounge behind them, gave me a negative shake of her head. It was so imperceptible that for a moment I thought I might have imagined it. But no, there it was again, just the slightest warning from someone who didn't want anything from me.

I don't know why, but that simple gesture filled me with a strange new confidence. Ever since Mom had run out on Dad and then Dad had run off with some floozy I'd always been Clair-Against-The-World. Dad had left me a worn coin purse with a five dollar bill and a slip of paper containing the number of social services.

After that, I'd learned to survive on my own, fought and slept around to get my way, sold sex to get my education, traded more sex to get A grades instead of B's, somehow lucked out to become a big-time Cowboy cheerleader with a fetching hip switch and a devilish smile. Pro cheerleaders aren't teammates, they are sexy cut-throats who will do anything for a featured over-the-shoulder butt shot on national TV.

It's hard to think like a teammate when you've never had a team, but that one gesture from Mia My resonated in me, and gave me a new confidence. I wasn't alone. I had an ally, somebody who believed in me. I mean, that was so odd and unfounded an emotion that I was momentarily stopped in my tracks.

"Sign it," Dina ordered in her usual pushy way.

"No," I said. "I want to think about it some more."

"Told you," she said to Debbie. "Well, Missy Clair, we came prepared for this." She took a second contract from her bag and placed it in front of me. I didn't have to read it. Any two partners could buy the third out.

"I'm not totally against the deal," I said. "I just think we should take a harder look at the numbers. They're asking a little much...actually $120,000 too much."

"We don't care," Dina said. "We have to go ahead now or the deal's off. And if you don't come in with us, you're out."

I could feel the anger building in me. I know I am too emotional, but we had been partners for a while, and we had made lots of money together. I was ready to reach for the contract and sign it and be done with them...but Mia My looked up from her Oriental needlepoint—I saw she was shaping a silk tiger—and she silently mouthed the words "The numbers.

I took a closer look at the paper in my hand and saw I was being played. I started counting to ten. I got up to six before I felt ready to speak. "We're worth more than this," I said. "You can buy me out, and I'll sign that right now, but the price will be determined by independent audit."

My partners frowned at me. They didn't like it, but they could either back down or buy me out at a fair price. I knew them pretty well. They weren't going to back down. `I hand-wrote my conditions on the contract, above the place where I had to sign. I went to my fax and made three copies, and we each signed all three and passed them around with a good deal of ill will.

Mia My looked up from her needlepoint,. "I'd like to take that bet," she said, smiling at Dina.

"What bet?" Dina said.

Mia My gestured at the rubber tire. "Clair gets three throws. Each time she hits bulls eye, you pay us one hundred dollars. Each time she misses, I pay each of you one hundred. Okay?"

"Deal, Oh, lady-from-the-Far East." Dina and Debbie slapped hands and then slapped Mia My's hand by way of sealing the deal.

I went over to the small raised pitcher's mound.

"That's too close," Debbie said.

"Ninety feet. Major baseball regulation," I said.

"Okay, go ahead, sling it, babe," Dina laughed.

That pissed me off so much I threw the first one high and wide. The ball actually whistled over the tree branch and hit half way up the hillside behind it.

Mia My took two hundreds from her purse and pushed them across my bubble glass table to my ex-Gal Pal partners.

"Cheesh," Dina said, "We should have bet a thou."

"You're on," Mia My said, "One thousand dollars a throw, two throws left."

"Hey, it's only money," Debbie grinned.

"Sucker born every minute," Dina said, making a ceremony out of slapping Mia My's hand.

I settled down and whistled the next two through the center, not even brushing the rubber. The Gal Pals stood there, looking at me with her mouth hanging open.

"It's okay," Mia My said. "We'll take a personal check."

While Dina grumped and grumbled as she wrote out a check, Debbie wandered off to hit on Eddie, who was finishing up with Jack in his glass-walled study, and the three of them left together for God only knows what close encounters of the third kind, maybe something The Ghost could write off as research for the ancient story of Jack, Myette and Yvette.

CHAPTER 24

I don't know if I've explained my theory that Jack is sometimes exactly like a dog. I don't mean a dog of a man. I mean, he has a marvelous canine mentality, the ability to forgive and forget some of the horrible things I've done to him. That Dog Whisperer guy on TV calls it *Living in the now.* Jack can be mad as hell at me one moment, and the next time I see him, he'll be himself again. It's not that he has forgotten what happened. I think it's more that he knows who I am, and he puts up with me. That's the thing about Jack; he accepts the way I am, his screwed up, messed up Clair-Bear, which is one of the few reasons I can think of why I haven't sold my house and moved on.

All that just to say by the next morning when Mia My and I gathered in his kitchen for scrambled eggs and turkey kielbasa, he started right in with his lurid Nam adventures as if I hadn't questioned his manhood and integrity-in-storytelling (with Jack it's the same thing) the day before.

"So because Joe and I have now both been dinged by Mars, the great god of war, we are invited to sit in the Non-Com Officers section of the Enlisted Men's Club with Hinkelby and Peabody.

'They trucked the Beaver out,' Lieutenant Peabody informs the general public.

'You guys didn't torch it?' The sergeant tending the bar sounds incredulous. The guy doesn't even have a security clearance, and he's concerned about the radio gear. Of course it's one of the things they drum into everybody. We fly a couple thousand feet up, low and slow all over the delta, and the VC would pay a million bucks to know exactly how we're always pasting them in their little hidey-holes.

"I think quick, to cover it up. No sense tarnishing our new images as heroes who escaped the jaws of death. 'I popped the incendiary, but it was a dud,' I tell him. The Sarge nods knowingly from behind the bar. We've had lots of trouble with the fire grenades. 'God damn equipment,' he says.

'Goddamn tropics,' I add with a wise nod of my own.

"Anyway, they sent out a flying crane and lots of flapping fire-power and the Beaver was back here on the apron across from the White Shack, sitting crumpled up on the tarmac practically before we were back from the plantation. They hustled the radios inside, and nothing was missing, so our butts were okay with the regulations. And we've got another Beaver flying down from Phu Bai.' Phu Bai is our station north of Hue, tucked a few miles south of the DMZ. You need two Beavers to get a triangulation, so that's important, otherwise we're out of business.

"Meantime, I get to show the cast on my arm all around, and everybody agrees, that's a Purple Heart for sure. I'm ecstatic, something's finally happened to me.

'It's my war after all,' I tell Joe.

'You're a certified idiot,' he says.

'Heard The White Snake offered you hard stripes,' Hinkelby says, looking at Joe.

"Joe doesn't like the fact that everybody knows. He's in the delicate position of having to tell other sergeants he doesn't want to become a lifer. 'That he did,' Joe agrees. 'All I have to do is re-up.'

'Three years?' Hinkelby wrinkles his nose and frowns, thinking it over.

'Nope. Four.'

"But Joe didn't have to be worried about Hinkelby's feelings. The sergeant shakes his head. 'Four years with The White Snake,' he says. 'I'd shoot myself first.'

Mia My had been outside, yelling at her son on the cell phone again. She came in with a satisfied expression on her face.

"See, Clair," she said, looking at me across the breakfast table, "We both sell. Sell, sell, sell."

Jack looked away, maybe watching the single cloud that has somehow managed to float across the clear blue sky over the beige hills behind my place. I got the feeling he couldn't care less whether either of us bought or sold anything. But then he surprised me.

"You took her advice?" he asked me, out of the blue.

"I was thinking of selling anyway," I said, giving him a sour look. I thought he was going to say something more, but he bit his lip and looked back at that stupid little cloud, which by now had half disappeared over the nearest low hilltop.

"After your airplane went down, that is about the time Joe and I started dating in the serious way," Mia My said. Jack nodded, only half way out of the new funk I'd put him in.

"Joe goes to mass with me on a Sunday morning and Mama can say nothing, because it is church, you know? And after mass, Mama is busy mingling with her society friends, and so Joe and I go strolling down Le Loi Street, holding hands and window shopping in the shops. Of course, Auntie Kai has been given chaperone duty by Mama, and she walks along ten or twelve paces behind us. Joe doesn't like this, and he keeps looking back at her. 'Gee, our first date,' he says. This way is our custom, but I can see he is disappointed.

He asks me, 'Did I make a mistake bringing up your father?'

'No,' I tell him. 'You would know sooner or later. Ten years ago, Papa gambled he could marry his young French secretary and take over the properties and businesses that Mama inherited from her father. In the company they formed, he had 49% and Mama had 49%, and he thought he could count on Auntie Kai's 2%.' 'So he miscalculated,' Joe says. I nod and give him a sad smile. 'Now he lives in Paris on whatever Mama doles out to him. Enough to live on, but not enough to marry a pretty French secretary.

"I call to Auntie Kai and point at the expensive wallets in a shop window. *Des Elephante, n'est pas*?' I ask her. Auntie dutifully turns to look in the window, and I surprise Joe with a kiss full on his lips. He whispers, 'Could you ever slip out on a real date with me?' I answer his question with a dare, 'Next week Mama goes to Paris on business. Are you man enough to meet me?'"

Jack nodded happily, his attention back on the story, "Joe took a big risk to do that. He went over to the orderly room to put in for R&R, you know, Rest & Recreation. It's like a pre-arranged vacation…you get a week or two off, and the army flies you to places like Thailand or Hong Kong. But Joe put in for downtown Saigon. Toady just about had a fit. He couldn't believe anybody would give up a chance to get out of the country for a few days. But Joe was firm about it; he insisted he wanted to go downtown to brush up on his language skills. Since there was no rule against it, Toady couldn't stop him. Actually, there was some precedent— from time to time, one of the guys would fall for some bargirl and take R&R—not out of the country, just to shack up at the Majestic or the Hotel Catinat for a couple of days.

But Toady can't keep quiet about it. He shows up at the White Shack at noon the next day. I'm there, just farting around, waiting to see if they have the new Beaver ready. Nobody likes Toady, and I'm no exception. I'm slouched at my desk, reading a book of Hemingway short stories, and the warty little guy's standing uncomfortably at attention outside Ogilvy's door while a marine with a machine gun stands beside him. That is the protocol; Toady doesn't have a security clearance so he can't be in the building without an armed guard standing over him.

'Toady,' I call out to him. 'First time in the White Shack?'

He bites his lip and nods his head yes.

'See the red cans?' I indicate the fire grenades set on each grey file cabinet around the room. He nods his head again, not looking very happy. The marine fights down a grin, knowing what's coming.

'You hear the Ooga sound,' I tell him, 'you get to the nearest can and pop it. 'We'll have ten seconds to fire the whole room.'

"I go back to reading my book for about thirty seconds and then hit the gas horn I've hidden under my desk. Toady surprises me; he's faster than I would have thought possible. Quick as a snapping turtle, he's got one of the grenades and is about to pull the pin.

'Put down that grenade!' Ogilvy roars from his office. 'God damn it, Specialist Larch…you stand at attention right here until I can get to you!' He points to a spot outside his door and motions Toady into his office.

'You told me to keep an eye on Specialist Bates, Sir,' Toady pipes up eagerly. The Colonel grunts that he did. 'Well,' Toady says, 'He wants to take R&R.'

'Where does he want to go?'

'Downtown Saigon, Sir. For a week.'

'Has he accumulated the time?'

'Yes, sir. He's got more than that.'

"From my position outside The White Snake's office I can see the Colonel is pacing back and forth like a caged lion. He glances at the picture of himself with JFK, and then resumes his pacing. 'You won't believe this,' he tells Toady, 'but I used to be a real military person.' Toady doesn't seem to know what to make of this. 'Yes, Sir,' he says. 'I mean, no, Sir.' The White Snake gives him a withering look, and he wisely shuts up.

'Give me the paper,' Ogilvy says. He reaches for the orders, snatching them from Toady's hands, and scrawls his name across the bottom. 'What?' Toady asks. 'You're letting him do it, Sir?' The Colonel silences him with a glare. The little clerk takes the paper and hustles out of the room. On the way out, Toady nearly runs me over, but in going around me he bumps into Leo, the Spook Op, who is hustling into The White Snake's office. 'Get out of my way, worm,' Leo snarls. But in his eagerness to talk to the Colonel, he's already forgotten Toady. 'They tied his hands and feet and put him in a cage full of hungry rats! Those ARVN spooks are un-fricking-incredible!'

I figure that the Colonel has better things to do than to punish me, and I start to slip away, heading down the hallway to walk across the apron so I can maybe see the new Beaver for myself. As I go, over my shoulder I hear Ogilvy talking to his spook. 'Forget the rat cages,' he tells Leo. He speaks in the soft, urgent tones that helped him get his nickname in the first place. 'Something else has come up,' he hisses."

Mia My smiled and smoothly took over the tag-team story telling from Jack. "That was the beginning of the rainy season," she said. "Joe knows he is in big love with me, and that means he's in big trouble with Mama and even bigger troubles with the army. He is forbidden by my mother and he is doubly forbidden by his commanding officer. And yet there he is, standing in the rain in the garden of roses that my grandfather planted so many years before. He is looking up at the windows, at the lighted one that he hopes is my room.

"I come down to meet him. It is dusk and I look pale and ghost-like in an *ao gai* I have selected, one of the lightest pale lavender. I hesitate for a moment at the side door to the garden. He turns and sees me, and I walk slowly towards him along the cobblestone footpath grandpapa laid by hand between the ancient rose bushes.

"Joe is wet with raindrops in his hair and soaking the shoulders of his jacket. A smile lights his face. 'Mia My! I was afraid you might not come!'

'I always keep a dare,' I tell him. Our lips brush lightly. The rain is warm, and we walk hand-in-hand through the garden. We stop to smell the lilac bush that Papa brought from Northern France when he was courting Mama. 'This flower garden was grandpapa's pride and joy. We try to keep it up, but help is hard to find, and I think it is going back to jungle soon.' There is a rumble, and then another. It is mortars, starting up in the nearby province to the west. The Viet Cong are getting more and more supplies from the north, and are beginning to put pressure on our fortified hamlets that were supposed to be safe havens for the peasants. 'The war is everywhere,' I tell him. 'I won't let it get us,' he promises. It is the fervent promise of a young lover, but there is something solid and strong in Joe that makes me believe him. And then we are kissing in the warm rain and I'm laughing because I spent hours on my hair, my dress, my face. I tell him this, and he just laughs. 'You are beautiful as you are,' he says. The rain is coming harder, and so I take him to a flower-covered bower. We hear none of the street sounds from here. The rain patters down on the leaves and we are speaking in hushed whispers. 'There's a perfume in the air, my Joe says. "Jasmine,' I tell him as I kiss his lips. 'It's the jasmine.'

'No,' he tells me, 'it's you, Mia My…it's you.'

"Now we are kissing with more passion and the rain is coming down harder, and we are silly, getting soaked kissing in the downpour from the heavens. Auntie Kai has her quarters in one wing, but I know we won't see her. I had thought to take Joe to Mama's big bedroom, but there is so much old anger, so much unhappiness and bad luck smoldering in the corners of that room that we go instead to my bedroom, the room of my dreaming days that looks out over the glory of our old rose garden that has not yet given itself over to the approach of the wild tropical overgrowth."

Jack looked up from some notes he was making at his desk while Mia My talked. Jack was about as good as Louis L'Amour at writing love scenes. As you probably know, Louis walks his heroes and heroines toward the bedroom, boots them in, and closes the door behind them. A Dunk Stingray love scene is something like a James Bond tryst. They last about as long as it takes the Stinger to climax, which is longer than the average lusty male, but shorter than most real women are hoping for.

Jack's mind has already raced past what he thinks of as the *mandatory love scene.* "The White Snake has these two spook ops, Wendell and Leo," he reminds us. "Wendell is a bit of a nut job. He loves Spirou, the Belgian comic book published in French that he picks up at Johnny's Book Store, the same place everybody changes their dollars for black market piasters. Wendell's favorite comic book character is Lucky Luke, the drool European impression of a laconic cowboy.

"Leo, on the other hand, is stupid and so committed to his mission that he's dangerous on every level. Leo calls Wendell an overeducated asshole, says it right to his face. And he hates the French, an entire people he looks on as a bunch of pompous idiots. These two losers have been trying to find Joe. They are in the park by the Saigon River, right where Hai Ba Trung Street ends in that famous statue of the Trung Sisters that Madame Nhu had built in her own image.

'Sex,' Wendell says, defending the French, 'They know about sex. And cooking.'

'They butt-hump,' Leo retorts derisively, 'And they eat snails…Oh, oh…ahh, look who's here…'

"Leo and Wendell have been on stakeout all over town, trying to find Joe and Mia My, and they've just gotten lucky. They spot the couple riding on a scooter. Joe is driving while Mia My rides in back, holding a cluster of balloons. Leo manages to fish his little 12 millimeter spy camera out of his pocket and snap a few before they round a corner and are out of sight.

'The zoo!' Leo says. 'I bet they're going to the zoo!'

"It's not a bad guess. The Saigon Zoo is a favorite date place. Wendell and Leo start out on a dog trot, heading in that direction. But the day is muggy and they don't get a half block before they hail a cab. It doesn't matter. Joe has stopped for ice cones along the way, and the spook ops actually get to the zoo first. They pay the small 20 p fee and are loitering as inconspicuously as two buffoons such as they can manage when Joe and Mia My show up."

Mia My smiles, remembering the Saigon Zoo. "That was such a beautiful day! Joe and I are so in love, we are walking on clouds, the war is very far away, and we don't see these Leo or Wendell people, we don't see anybody but each other. We have picked out our own little peanut girl, a little street-monkey of maybe eight years, and she is following us everywhere. Each time we come to a bear cage or the elephants, there she is, sticking a little cone of twisted paper with a few peanuts into Joe's face. Joe doesn't like this because he thinks he ought to buy his peanuts at his own pace, but we have made a deal. Every time we would find an animal that needed nuts, he must buy a cone of peanuts from the little girl and get a kiss reward from me. That seemed to work for everybody.

"Joe has been telling me about how his boss, the one they called The White Snake, likes him and wants him to extend his time in the army. So I ask him if he will do this. He laughs like he doesn't want to. He tells me, 'They think I am going to re-up. But the only reason I can see to give the army four more years is that I could spend them here with you.'

'They would promise you that?' I am so foolish; I know so little about what Joe does, or about how the army thinks about Vietnamese girls. Joe gives me a gloomy look. 'Well, no,' he says. 'Just the first year.' 'What would you like to do?' I ask him. 'What would make you happy?'

'If I could…I might want to run my uncle's company.'

'Your uncle the gangster?' I tease him.

'Oh, he's not really a gangster,' Joe says. He's become
serious. I can see things are troubling him. 'We're throwing
peanuts to the elephants while there's a war going on.'

'Maybe we've seen enough elephants and lions and bears
for now,' I tell him."

And at that moment the storytelling about Joe and Mia My
in a zoo in the 1960's was interrupted by a present day hammering
on the front door of Jack's house in Holmby Hills. "Open up! It's
the police!" a rough male voice shouted.

"What the hell," Jack growled, more annoyed than
surprised. "If that goddamn neighbor of mine…?"

"Jack, they're serious!" I ran to the front of the house, and
it wasn't just a few cops, it was an entire squad of SWAT people,
everybody dressed in their helmets and padded vests. And a K-9
team with two efficient-looking German shepherds. The dogs
sniffed and snooped around, spending lots of time at a chair near
the front hallway

The handlers pulled the reluctant dogs away and everybody
rushed through the house, not really turning things over or tearing
them apart—they knew better than that in this section of town.
One of the dogs led the way, charging upstairs while the other
raced out in back and went around behind the pool, barking at the
gate that led to the pathway up into the hills. The first assault
apparently having revealed nothing of significance, they gathered
in the kitchen, crowding around Jack, who hadn't moved from his
writer's chair behind his big dark grey slab of a desk.

"Who's in charge? What's the meaning of this?" Jack
lowered his brows and growled at the police. I had the impression
he was reading from one of the pages of a Dunk novel, some scene
where the enraged homeowner works up a righteous rage because
the Stinger has broken in on the right guy, but only after he'd
covered his ass. I knew Jack Larch; he was play-acting. Jack's
lived on the wild side and he's had his house tossed before, so he
certainly knew the moves.

That's when we got our next surprise; a police lieutenant
entered from the front, accompanied by Jack's ex-wife Dorothy.
Dorothy's eyes were flicking here and there and everywhere, her
disappointed expression saying she wasn't finding whatever she

was looking for. But the day was a banquet of surprises. Jack didn't even get to say anything to Dorothy before the entrance of her little group was followed by a pair of cops towing a reluctant Ong Vung, who was handcuffed and swearing up a storm in a Vietnamese hissy-fit, looking more like a ruffled stray cat than a gardener. It's the first time I'd ever seen him without his straw cone hat. The flesh of his face was warped and fire-scarred on one side, twisted like red putty into a frozen grimace. He was wearing a toupee, and it was sitting awry on his head from his tousle with the police. He had a glass eye, but his one real eye glared in anger and frustration, and he fell to the floor when he got too close to Dorothy, who took one smell of his body odor and angrily gave him a kick with the sharp toe of one of her high heels.. Ong Vung sprang to his feet like an old cat, and looked like he might make a dive at her in spite of his handcuffs. But Jack quieted him with one upraised hand.

"What's up, Dorothy?" he growled at his 2nd ex-wife. "Paul still in Mexico?"

"I know it was here," she said to the police lieutenant, ignoring Jack completely. "I saw it a few days ago. He sells it!"

The Lieutenant shook his head, spreading his empty hands, "Well…?"

"The pool house!" Dorothy shouted, looking at me in triumph. "They probably stash it out there with his whore!"

"Hey, watch your language," I said, raising one fist like a lady thug. "The only difference between a wife and a whore is a piece of paper."

"And between a wife and an ex-wife, another piece of paper," Jack said, his eyes twinkling at me in amusement.

By now the SWATS were combing through my rooms, but both dogs were barking and sniffing at the back gate. The police unlatched it and the SWAT people trotted on up the barren hillside after the dogs, leaving the police lieutenant and his two cops with us.

Jack growled at them in his customary Dunk way. "Take his handcuffs off, for God's sake, can't you see he's an old person?"

"An old person who practically bit my ear off!" One of the policemen pointed to his bloody ear.

"This isn't fucking Watts," Jack responded.

"We've got a warrant," the Lieutenant said, pulling papers from his pocket.

"Address for the main house," Jack said, scanning the warrant like he'd seen dozens of them, which he probably had. "Pool house is a different address. So is the coach house. Looks like a million dollar law suit for you, Mister Vung. You're going to be in the chips, my friend."

The Lieutenant's face turned a shade of red and he snatched the warrant back from Jack's hands, but he gestured to one of his men to release Ong Vung. While they were turning the key, Jack got off a quick snapshot with his cell phone. One click, one flash, one *briiiing* noise.

"Give me that phone," the Lieutenant snarled.

"Sure," Jack said, tossing it across.

The Lieutenant looked at the phone, at Jack, and back at the phone again.

"Who did you send that to?" he yelled.

"Half the internet," Jack said.

"Yeah," I smiled. "The half that watches YouTube."

The way Jack looked at me, the humorous light dancing in his eyes, I was starting to think Mia My was right, maybe Jack and I did have something special after all.

By this time, Ong Vung was rubbing his wrists and glaring at Dorothy. She might have pushed him over and there was the one nasty kick, but, after all, it was the cops who had handcuffed him. I took a closer look at Ong Vung. He was bent and crippled, probably something that had happened to him in the war. Yet, before anybody could stop him, the stiffened fingers of his one good hand darted toward Dorothy's mid-section, and she doubled over in pain and fell to the floor. While the cops moved to help her, Ong Vung slipped out the open slab window and darted around the side of the house. The police looked for him, but he was gone. And, by then, they had more on their minds than one crippled old gardener.

The SWAT team had reached the fence at the back of my property, and at the insistence of the dogs, cut through the fence and climbed down the nearly vertical wall to the bottom of the ravine. There they found a red Macy's shopping bag with a pound of marijuana and just enough coke to send Jack to prison for a long time…and a badly decomposed corpse that, after forensic inspection, proved to be the remains of Joan the cabaret singer. Joan had been Jack's third ex-wife, the one everyone decided had disappeared simply because she had decided that two weeks or so of marriage to Wild Jack was enough for a lifetime.

CHAPTER 25

The fallout from that grim discovery took quite some time. The original theory that Joan had fallen while hiking *the back forty* was replaced with deeper suspicions when the angle at which the bones were scattered indicated she may have been partially dismembered. Jack was taken away to the Beverly Hills police station for interrogation while the experts crawled down the rope ladder they rigged to my fence. They measured and peered and pondered factors like the rainy season, gravity and the effects of coyote hunger. The general opinion proved to be *nobody knew for sure,* and, once Jack's nasty lawyer arrived, they finally had to let Wild Jack go with the stern warning not to leave town.

Under questioning, Dorothy's story about Jack being a dope dealer started to fall apart. I remembered the Macy's bag with the red star on it had showed up right after her previous visit. As she'd been booked a time or two for using, the suspicion pendulum was swinging in favor of a frame-up on her part. It looked like a botched attempt to get back at her old ex, probably trying to get more money out of him or maybe simply wreck his life.

As for Joanie, although Jack had married her, she hadn't been in his life long enough to really know who she was.

"She was a moody person," I reminded him.

"Yeah. Jealous of you. Just like Dorothy."

"Right. It's my fault."

"For being too pretty," he nodded with the hint of a smile.

"But moody is a long way from suicidal."

"Sure, but she did drink a lot, and she snorted a little. Thinking back, we'd been having a disagreement or two."

"Shortest honeymoon on record."

"Tinseltown romance," he agreed. "She's disillusioned, she's just gotten hitched to a real bastard, she doesn't know what to do, she gets a little high, gets confused, goes for a walk not realizing there's this steep canyon behind your property."

"And falls over a waist-high fence in her way?"

"No, Clarity-the-chaste, she confused. She tries to climb over, catches her skirt on the top, and the rest is history."

"Certainly plausible," he says. They have found a shred of fabric clinging to the fence. It sounds to me like Jack may have been talking out loud to the police in the interrogation room. "At least, that's the way I would have written it."

I could see he was trying to shrug it off, but he'd back from his interrogation a lot more moody and depressed than he had left.

"Come on, Jack," Mia My frowned. "You are too old for a bad funk. It will kill you."

He tried to pass it off like a professional, squinting at us with his writer's attitude,. "It doesn't fit, it just doesn't make sense. Joanie wasn't a hiker, hell, she was after me to make over our bedroom on the main floor so she wouldn't have to climb one lousy flight of stairs."

We sat around for days, grilling Jack and going over it and over it. He was right—nothing did make sense. Joanie had been a torch singer with a so-so talent. Jack had picked her up one boozy night at the House of Blues. They'd driven south until dawn and were married in Tijuana, honeymooned the next day at The La Fonda, a seaside resort a dozen miles deeper into Baja, and then returned to Holmby Hills where it took less than a week of constant fighting to realize the mistake they'd made. The Mexican divorce, handled by one of Jack's slick professional friends, also took less than a week. Joanie asked if she could stay for a few days until a gig opened up for her in San Diege. Jack said yes, so long as he didn't have to see her. Of course, she used one of the guest bedrooms in my house. And then, about a week later, Joanie, who traveled light, had disappeared with her lone suitcase. That happened one evening when I was attending a play at the Almanson theater downtown and Jack was out drinking with his buddies.

None of it made much sense—no way Joanie would be hiking the brushy trail in the middle of the night up the hill to where they found her body, and they never did find the suitcase, though her clothing was scattered down the wash—but that was about all Jack remembered of her exit from his life. And he couldn't come up with anything more. It was just after that, he cleaned up his act enough so he wasn't falling down drunk and was able to once again turn out his pages, that old debt he always said he owed to his goddamn stupid muse.

But Wild Jack being addicted to writing as he was—he called it *dedicated to the muse*—his idle time wasn't going to last more than a day or two. This was Holmby Hills, and when the fog wasn't in, the sun always rose in the morning. And when that happened, chances are you would find Jack at his desk, a cup of three day old lukewarm coffee at his side.

On this particular morning, I'd already replaced his coffee with new brew, Maria had run out for some Sausage Eggs McMuffins from Mac's place, and Mia My and I were at the breakfast table. Mia My was wondering out loud if maybe she ought to be heading back to San Francisco to pick up the pieces of her life, and I was wondering to myself just what I was going to do now that I was flush with cash but not sure about the rest of my life.

"I've always thought of Saigon as a cosmopolitan playground," Jack said, the words dropping into the quiet pool of morning like a smooth stone in water.

"So we're back to the Story of Joe?" I asked.

"Shut up, Clair," he said, the way Red Dog had shut him up in the far away and long ago. "So much to do in Saigon, all the color and mystery of the Orient."

"That's Joseph Conrad talking again, Jack," I remind him.

But nothing and nobody ever could stop Jack from his storytelling. Dorothy's attempt to frame him for dope dealing couldn't. The death of Joanie couldn't. I certainly couldn't. The past was the present was the future—it was all the same to him, the world one big story that had to be told. I didn't want to even try to stop him. He told me once that storytelling was his way to wall off the pain, it was his way to stay relatively sane in a world that had no rational answers. I think he was right about that. Jack had a way of blocking out the things he didn't want to—that he couldn't—face in real life.

"Conrad certainly nailed it, Clarity-Wonderwoman. Nobody's done it better since." He paused, reflecting on the world as he'd known it decades before. The tragedy of Joanie's death was put away in a box, set on a shelf somewhere in his mind. It was waiting for the missing parts, the keys that would unlock it and give it some sense, if he was ever able to find them.

Still, in spite his denials, I could see recent events had worked an evil spell on him. The normally dapper Larch-ster hadn't shaved in days, and there were dark circles under his eyes. He looked at Mia My with a rueful smile, "I guess I'll always envy that week you had with Joe. Young, in love, in one of the most exciting places in the world…you didn't know Leo and Wendell were following you everywhere they could. The White Snake had pictures of some street seller trying to get Joe to buy an exotic bird of paradise. Here these guys are with the opportunity of a lifetime to drink in the spice and flavor of another culture and all they can come up with is a handful of antique dirty postcards and a copy of Little Angel Fucks Hong Kong, At that, they got into one of their silly arguments over Little Angel. It's true—I overhead them.

'I didn't think Little Angel ever got to Hong Kong,' Wendell says. 'Not in real life. How you think she got there?' Leo has his feet up on Ogilvy's desk. Naturally, the Colonel isn't anywhere around, he's taken three days off, probably gone to Tokyo, at least that's the rumor. 'Maybe she took the bus,' Leo says 'Why does everybody else have all the fun?'

'Gets boring, being us, doesn't it…'

But then Leo has an idea, 'Hey, remember our pal Joey's other girlfriend—the one with the tattoo on her ta-ta?'

'Yeah…so what?' Wendell says. 'Remember, the Colonel said not to interfere.'

'Hey, *me* interfere with true love?'

"The smile on Leo's face makes him look like the evil troll Santa kicked out of his workshop. So Joe's out there somewhere, I don't have much of a clue actually where, and I can't even warn him that *some bad shit is about to come down.*

"It comes to pass that, three days later, Joe is with Mia My, sitting at the Milk Bar. He leans forward to kiss his girl, and she warns him, 'Mama will be back this morning.' And in the next second their tender moment is interrupted by the furious scream of a wronged woman. Naturally, it's Lan, the tattooed girl Joe and I first met at the Hong Kong Bar.

"Lan screams at Joe, yelling at the top of her lungs, 'Dirty, rotten, no-good *Nguoi My* fuck-bastard! You number 10 crummy rotten cocksucker!' Mia My looks from Joe to Lan and back again. Lan ignores her and swings her heavy purse at Joe.

'You marry to me!' she screams. "You sleep with me, you take dirty picture—you marry to me!

"Mia My stands. She looks shocked, stunned by the events. She dusts her hands together and slowly backs away. Joe calls after her, but fate is not on his side. As if he isn't in enough trouble, at that moment Ba Nguyen and Auntie Kai arrive.

"The two older women rush to her side. "Mia My! What are you doing?' Mama Nguyen shouts, ready to pull her daughter away from this low class American soldier who has obviously created a scene. But Mia My pushes Mama away and marches off on her own. 'Nothing, Mama,' she says in a cold voice intended for somebody else. 'Nothing at all.'

'But that's Joe Bates,' Mama says. Perhaps her trip to Paris has illuminated her. Perhaps, now that it's too late, she's willing to give her daughter this one chance to marry beneath her.

"Auntie Kai, who has seen much in life, remains behind to watch the scene play out. She watches as Lan rains punches on Joe, who is still hunched over at the table, still trying to get up to go after Mia My. He grabs Lan, managing to grip her wrists to keep her from doing him serious physical harm. Even in this time of disaster, Joe is thinking. He realizes Lan is a bargirl, a pretty peasant girl recruited from somewhere in the delta. He's a smart guy; he knows Lan moves in the shady world of booze and affairs with G.I.s... there is almost no chance she could have found him by herself.

'Lan,' he says.

'I never want to see you again!' she screams.

"Joe shakes her a little harder to get her attention. 'Lan, how did you find me?'

'Amelican soldier-boy told me, you pig!'

"Lan's glance reveals Leo the Spook Op, grinning at Joe from across the broad aisle of the Arcade. Leo gives him a little finger-roll wave, taps his little spy camera to show he's got everything on film, and rushes away.

"Joe's beside himself. He lets go of her wrists and stands. 'Lan, we're not married!' he yells at her. 'We're not even engaged!'

'That true,' she screams. 'Still, you a evil bad Amelican pig!'

'How much did *Soldier-boy* Leo pay you to say that?'

"Joe's hit the mark. A sudden look of fear jumps into Lan's expression. She thinks Joe might call the White Mice cops, and in her experience they always take the side of the American soldiers over that of an ordinary, common bargirl. She has only one clear thought—now she's got to get away fast. Lan swings a vicious swipe at Joe with her heavy purse. She misses him but she sends Thai tea and Joe's precious Bolsley Jubilee camera flying."

Jack shook his shaggy iron grey mane of hair and then he changes the scene on us. "There are few things I remember that were as sorry-assed as those shows they put on over at the Enlisted Men's Club at the 3rd," he says. "They'd warm things up with a bad local band. You haven't heard anything until you have to suffer through a failed Vietnamese nightclub singer making her sodden way through Old Cape Cod. An hour or so of that and you're begging for a VC to torture you, no lie. And when the men were appropriately liquored up, they'd trot out a shop-worn round-eyed stripper, some poor blonde trying to bump-and-grind her lost way back to the States.

"You always went, of course," I commented.

"Right," he agreed.

"Part of the war," I prompted him. "The playful side of the mad god Mars."

"That's right, Clarity-Rarity," he answered without a hint of rancor in his voice. "I had to see it all, everything from Bob Hope to Blueberry Hill sung without any 'L' sounds."

"Very hard for Vietnamese people to speak the hard 'L' sound," Mia My commented mildly. "We don't have that sound in our language."

"Anyway, the following Saturday night I'm enduring the sights when Joe comes in, plops down on the folding chair next to me and orders a scotch. He lights up one of his rank Camels unfiltered and gives me a look that tells me he wants to talk. I'm working furiously on an idea, notes and scraps of paper all over the table, and I really don't want to be bothered.

'What are you drinking?' he asks.

'Serious writers don't drink, Bates.'

'Oh,' he says. 'Now we're a serious writer.'

That hurt, but I didn't want to get into it with him. 'Not when they're writing,' I say, keeping my voice level.

'Well, okay then,' Joe says.

'Take my word for it. Hemingway never wrote when he was drunk. It's impossible.'

'That was just for his image.'

'Damn straight.' I look up at Joe. Something's not right. I grab my scraps of paper and my pen and stuff everything in the jacket pocket of my fatigues. I give him the extended sigh that lets him know he's a real pain in the ass.

'So, what's up?' I ask

'I don't know what to do,' he wails. 'I can't get her out of my head.'

To me, it's the freight train of love, and it's all very simple. 'You have to go for it, Joe,' I tell him.

'What...? What do you mean?'

'You know what I mean. Why are you sitting here mooning? You throw on some civvies and get your ass downtown. See if she can resist the legendary Joe Bates charm!'"

Mia My nodded without a moment's hesitation, confirming that was how it had happened so many decades ago, as if it was just last week. "He came knocking on our door that very night. Auntie Kai came to my room to get me, but I refused to see him. Then his loud knocking made Mama realize he was there, and she threatened to call the White Mice. I cried all night; I was sure he was gone for good. Half of me said good riddance, because I thought he had cheated on me so badly. I wouldn't listen to Auntie, who swore she had heard differently.

"So the next morning we are seated at our normal pew up front at the cathedral and Joe is so bold he comes right up and sits next to me. Mama screws up her face in the fiercest glare, but she can do nothing but fume, after all, it is church—the big High Mass ceremony, no less—and she has her family name and reputation to consider. I ignore Joe for the longest time, maybe five minutes or more, but finally I feel a little sorry for him, and, after all, he had been very brave to come sit by me, and that's what Kim Van Kieu's shining knight would have done. So I point to a nearby alcove where candles burn in red cups to remember the dead.

'They killed him right over there,' I whisper.

'Who?' Joe asks me. He is grateful I have spoken to him, but he has no idea what I'm talking about.

'President Diem', I whisper back. 'He was…a very dear friend to Mama.'

'Who killed him?'

It is such a simple question, and yet the gulf between us is so great that I cannot find the words to tell him the truth. It makes me angry. 'You think it is so simple! You will fix everything *les method Americaine.* You ruin things and then you leave! This is why we do not trust you!' I'm whispering so loud that half the people in the cathedral can hear me. I get up and start to push past him.

He protests, 'But you can't blame me for that. None of that's my fault! Mia My, wait—!

But I am starting to walk away. I see the Spook Op named Leo watching us from across the way. I know him because Joe has pointed out that he is a bad man. Joe sees Leo as well, and he walks up to him.

Leo throws up his hands, a mock gesture to defend himself. He doesn't really think Joe will do him violence. 'Hey, we're in a church,' he says.

'Tell me about Diem's assassination,' Joe says.

'Oh, that.' Leo straightens his tie. 'It happened…right over there. He ended up right under the little red winkers. Leo points to the brass stand holding the rows of candles. It is clear to

Joe that Leo was here at the time of the assassination, or soon enough after to witness the body.

As Leo points out the exact spot, Joe looks in that direction and Leo grabs him by the throat and begins choking him. 'You're such a smart little lingie! You have no idea what you're messing with. Life is cheap here, boy! A guy like you goes missing real fast, nobody even notices!'

But Auntie Kai has noticed. She has moved nearby, and is lighting a candle right next to them.

'*Pour le President!*' she says in a quiet voice, and she stabs Leo in the back of the shoulder with a thin dagger that is sometimes worn in the hair by certain Vietnamese ladies.

'Christ! You're just looking for it, Lady!' Leo howls. He squirms around, but he can't reach the dagger. Instead, he groups for and pulls out a pistol from his shoulder holster.

A French priest with several altar boys in tow is walking by, heading for a mass service at one of the smaller altars in the alcoves surrounding the main devotional. He sees what is happening and yells, '*Non! Dons le maison de la sacre cour!*' Leo is a spider, and he only strikes in the quiet of darkness. The last thing he wants is a commotion, and now other worshipers are moving toward them. Leo sees there are too many witnesses. He puts his gun away and retreats, still trying to get at the dagger in the back of his shoulder. As he goes, he says, 'You're a dead man, Specialist Bates. Dead, you hear me?'"

"So you and Joe made up?" I asked her. She smiled and shook her head, "No, Clair. It is never so easy for the young and foolish," Mia My nodded to me and Jack. "It is like you and Jack."

"We're not like that," I protested.

"You're young, and he's foolish," she said. She saw Jack was going to grump about something so she added, "Foolish about things of the heart. Our Jack has been run over so many times by his own freight train of love, he is afraid to get back up on the tracks." That really set back the Larch-ster Boy-Wonder, but Mia My went back to her story as if she'd spoken absolute truth about poor Jack, and he had nothing more to add that could possibly matter one way or another.

"Anyway, Mama managed to drag me away from the church without seeing Joe, and a very long week went by after that. She made me stay home from work, too. I was confined to my room, a sort of house arrest. It was that Saturday when I finally saw him sitting alone at the Milk Bar in the Arcade. There were two empty Thai Teas, the proof that he'd been there a long time, and was about to give up on me. I came up behind him, quietly as I could.

'Hi, G.I. Joe,' I say to him.

"He jumps right to his feet, and I point to Auntie Kai, who is following me, about ten feet behind, like a good little Auntie, and not the needle sticking kind who can take out bad spook men.

'Auntie Kai tells me that, *au contraire* to all indication, you are a good man, Joe Bates. An exceptional one, in fact, and I must not let you go without speaking to you, or I will regret it for the rest of my lonely days in a nunnery.'

"Joe bows to Auntie and stutters out a greeting. She gives him a polite nod, but doesn't speak. It's my show. 'Don't say anything,' I tell Joe. 'You would only mess it up. I have decided to give you another chance, because Auntie Kai says I must. Tomorrow morning we take the food and clothing from the side entrance of the cathedral to St. Vincent's Orphanage. If some Americans wanted to help, they could bring a truck after the mass.'

'A truck!' Joe says. 'Of course, a truck!'

"I can see he has no idea how he's going to get his hands on one."

"So this is what happened," Jack said. "Bright and early the next morning I drive up to the motor pool the 3rd Radio Research Unit uses, and Joe's in the Pool Sergeant's little shack, arguing with the greasy old truck wrangler. I'm driving a battered motorbike I won in a poker game, and I've got a monkey on my back, a real monkey that I won in the same said poker game. Some guys turn over four aces and haul in a plantation by the river and the hand of a beautiful lady. Me, I win a beat up Honda 150 and a flea-bag monkey possessed by evil spirits. He's one mean son-of-a-bitch of a monkey, too, let me tell you. He bites something fierce and the only way I teach him respect is to drive like crazy. It puts fear of the lord in him, and because he's known me for a few hours, he knows I'm his lord and master.

I park my bike and walk in as the grease ball sergeant is saying, 'You don't have that kind of authorization, Specialist.'

'Come on, Sarge,' my pal Joe is arguing. 'It's for the kids.'

'You lingies could start your own orphanage with the girls you knock up.'

"I come splashing into the hut, and the sergeant lets up on Joe and starts yelling at me, 'Jack, get that stupid monkey out of here! I don't want him shitting on the floor! Ain't nothing smells bad as monkey crap.'

'You sound like a man who knows, Sarge,' I tell him.

'I need that truck,' Joe says.

"I hand Joe my monkey before the sergeant can swat him with a monkey wrench, *ha ha, no joke.* 'Take this fellow outside, Joe,' I tell him.

'Uck! He has fleas!' But Jack leaves, holding Mister Jives out at arm's length away from him.

`The minute Joe is gone, I start handing out my poker winnings, digging in all my pockets. It makes quite a big multi-colored pile. 'More,' the sergeant says. I reach in other pockets. The pile is getting quite large, but it's piasters, on the black market only 260 to the dollar. Joe has been fumbling with the door knob. It's hard to open a door when you're holding a mean monkey at a decent distance so he won't give you fleas. Joe sees I'm emptying my pockets. 'Not enough,' the sergeant says.

"I find a last wad of my poker winnings in one of my back pockets and add it to the pile. 'Still not enough,' the sergeant says. And that's when Joe, who has given up trying to get out the door, hands me back the monkey and lays five twenty dollar bills on top of the pile. The sergeant nods once and scoops up the big pile of money. 'Keys are in the truck,' he says. 'And no fricking monkeys! You hear me, Wild Jack? I find any monkey shit in that deuce-and-a-half, I'll ream your ass!'"

CHAPTER 26

"I'm full of misgivings, but Joe's my pal so I find myself driving a deuce-and-a-half as fast as I can on a nearly deserted raised two-lane blacktop, a road that runs straight as an arrow through the rice paddies. We're following Mia My's Mom's black 1950's Mercedes that is also going like a bat out of hell.

Nobody wants to linger out here. We don't have any experience at this, but we figure if we go fast enough, any VC interested enough won't have time to aim their mortars before we're past. Mortars are usually fired by three man teams, but the VC have learned to take the supports and the base plates off. They wrap a towel around the tube and aim it on the fly, jamming it into the ground and devil take the blow-by from the back end. Even at that, without the plate they fire wild, and it will take a lucky shot to blow us off the road.

I've re-named Mr. Jives, my flea-bitten monkey, *Evil Jack*, and I've got him chained to the top of the seat. The vile creature is peeling *trom trom trop*, throwing the spiny rinds on the floor, sucking the flesh and spitting the big inner seed out on the floor..

'You think this thing will bite me?' Joe asks.

'He'll bite anybody,' I say. 'The secret is, just keep stuffing food in him.'

'You think the girls are getting along?' I ask Joe.

"I've brought Tuyet Lan along, and she's riding in the Merc with Mia My. He gives me a questioning look and I shrug, 'It was her day off. Go figure; I thought she'd spend it doing her nails, but she wanted to come.'

"The Mercedes ahead of us slows and then turns off on a side road. Now we're bumping over gravel, and I'm even more worried. Joe and I are way out on the proverbial limb, just by being out here in the boonies. We're big bait for the VC with our

Top Secret Security Clearances. I can see us in some jail in Hanoi, with the North Vietnamese Reds calling on their pals, the Russians, to wire up our dicks to tell them about stuff like code-breaking and how we crack their secrets at the Puzzle Palace back home at Fort Meade.

"I look over at Joe. He's wiping his glasses on his t-shirt. I know that Joe will never talk. He'll die first. So they'll have to torture me to get to him. First, they'll break my legs, then probably shoot me in the kneecaps and work their way on up. I wonder if Joe will talk before or after they start squeezing my balls with a pliers.

'This isn't a secure area,' Joe says, as if he's noticed for the first time.

'Yeah, like anywhere is,' I tell him. Lately there's been a rash of bike bombings downtown, and even one or two on base at Tan Son Nhut. The VC must have gotten a big shipment of plastic explosives from their North Vietnamese supporters. You can't fight even a guerilla war with rocks and sticks, but the Viet Cong are getting plenty of help. *Ep plastique*, they call it. They stuff it in bike handles or the seats, or leave it in cute little packages in bars and restaurants.

'I mean,' Joe tries to clarify that he's talking about our clearances, 'we're not supposed to be out here...'

"I can't believe it. I yell at him, 'Joe, we're doing this for you!'

'I'm sorry I got you into this,' he says.

'You had no choice. It's that fricking freight train,' I tell him.

"After a few more miles, we follow the Mercedes across a small wooden bridge over some swampy sort of a creek and pull up next to the orphanage. I watch as Mia My and Tuyet Lan hop out of the black French car. Both girls are looking mighty fine— wearing jeans and with their hair let down. Tuyet Lan has on a bit more makeup than Mia My, but she's not wearing that helmet-like bee-hive hair on her head the way the girls down at the Cherry Bar usually do themselves up. I know I was somewhat of a lusty gutter-tramp in my youthful prime, but at that moment I was seeing her for the pretty girl she was, not just some bargirl who wanted to hit on me for another *Saigon Whiskey*.

"In no time, a whole gang of happy, laughing kids surround us, and, after the mandatory round of begging for candies, the nuns get them to help unload the truck. It's a lot of stuff, a whole truck full. There are boxes and boxes of food and clothing. The older kids carry them away to the orphanage buildings, with the nuns shouting and pointing out directions.

'So many kids,' I comment to Tuyet Lan.

"She gives me a neat, appraising look touched with more than a little scorn, as if I know nothing.

'In Vietnam, they outcasts,' she says. 'Half-breed baby. Nobody want them.'

'Why's that?'.

'You only think you have purity of hate with your black peoples problem. People of Vietnam, we hate everybody. We are same-same like poison snake, we bite very quick.'

'That can't be true,' Joe tries to protest.

'Huh,' Tuyet Lan laughs, bitter beyond her years. 'We hate curse-ed Chinese. We hate Cambodian—we call them *flat face.* We hate Montagnards from the hills—we call them *monkey people.* They wear loincloth and when they come to Saigon they shit anywhere on the sidewalk. We hate Thai people and Laos people. French people, we hate very much.

'But you're getting along with Mia My, and she's half-French,' Joe points out.

'A person, you can like,' Tuyet Lan says, a smile curling her lips, a smile saying that we educated and rich Americans can be *so simple-headed.* 'A people, you can hate.'

"I am amused and impressed at the same time; two Americans getting a lecture on cultural relationships from a bargirl who can't be more than seventeen and has probably only had a few years of rural education before she ran away to Saigon. Joe shakes his head, trying to take it in, but Tuyet Lan isn't finished with us, 'Mia My has a four-times curse. She rich, she part French, she Catholic, and she date American boy Joe here. *Everybody* hate Mia My.'

'Why would they not like that she's dating me?" Joe asks her. .

'Oh,' Tuyet Lan says. 'That one simple: We hate Americans most of everybody.'

"I can't stand it any more, and so I pipe in, 'Well, why the hell do you hate us? We're here to rescue you from the bad guys!'

'No, you *are* the bad guys.' She points out this or that child in the crowd milling around us. 'Look here—Black G.I. father, for sure. That one, white G.I. father she will never see.'

'Or maybe a Frenchy,' Bates suggests.

"Tuyet Lan shrugs. 'All same-same.'"

"It's a clear case of family values trumping both capitalism and communism. She may hate the Viet Cong for what they've done to her family and friends in her rural home, but at heart Tuyet Lan doesn't care who is in charge, just so long as the babies are fed.

"Unloading the truck takes longer than I'd hoped, and by then it was getting on in the afternoon and time for some tea. Two of the nuns serve, and the four of us—me, Joe, Mia My and Tuyet Lan form a polite little group.

"The Sister Superior seems to have taken a special liking to Tuyet Lan. 'You are all welcome to come back any time you can,' she says, her eyes appraising the young girl from the Cherry Bar. Maybe she's thinking she can convert her into a nun. Me…well, by this time my eyes are flicking over the area, looking for the black rumps of VC crawling through the fields toward us, dragging their satchels of *ep plastique* and maybe one or two grenades they've filched from dead G.I.s. I'm like the hero in an old Western flick, sitting where I can see anyone approaching. Mia My is talking about her mother's recent visit to Paris, and the polite chatter is going on and on. I can't stand it. I get up and start to pace back and forth. Finally, I say, 'Well, I think we better be going. We have to get back before dark.'

"Here's our problem: By day, the roads belong to the government. But once the sun goes down, the wild wolves come out to feast and roam about, and you better be tucked in your bed, because they're very, very hungry. Clair, you're probably thinking, *Well, hell, it's only tea time, 4:30 at the most.* That's because you haven't lived in the tropics, where they have the shortest sunsets in the world. One moment, the sun is sitting on the horizon and it's all bright sunlight. You look away and*!* it's darker than hell, with a fog coming in if you're lucky, with a full moon spotlighting you if you're not.

"Sister Lavernia smiles and nods, and stands to allow us to be on our way. Rumor is, their truce with the VC only extends until the sun goes down, and that only because the *nasty boys* will be coming for their cut of the supplies Mia My and the good Catholics of the cathedral have supplied to the very people who are trying to kill them, or at least drive them from the country. 'We mean it, Mister Jack,' the old nun tells me. You can come back any time.'

'*Yeah*, I'm thinking to myself—*like that's ever going to happen!*'"

CHAPTER 27

By now Jack was pacing the floor, almost like he'd caught some flicker of his impatience from that time in the 1960's when he was so eager to leave the orphanage and race back to Saigon. He chuckled and waved his hands, "Clair, even at that," he said, "it takes another ten minutes because we have to hug a lot of kids and toss around some more candy, but Joe and I are finally following the shiny black Merc, bumping our way over the bridge—which, thankfully, hasn't been mined while we've been drinking English tea from thin China cups with our pals, the nuns. Another ten minutes and we're back to the two-lane black top. I'm plenty relieved when we hit that asphalt and start speeding like two straight arrows back towards *thanh pho Sai Gon.*

"Of course, it's not that easy, and I'm not all that comfortable, because the road has been built through a lowland swamp, raised by conscripted peasants digging dirt from each side of the road. That means our little convoy is sky-lined about six feet above the rice paddies, which spread out and away from us like a green quilt in every direction.

"I'm feeling naked and unprotected, once again a little like my image of me as a rusty tin carnival duck in a shooting gallery. The rice paddies are squares or rectangles outlined with low ridges of dirt, old sod fences that hold the water in and delineate the areas owned by this village or that absentee landlord. The sod fences that ridge the individual paddies are themselves overgrown with potato plants, and it is in these that the peasants dig damp little cells to stand or sit in knee-deep water and hide from the Viet Cong, and the Viet Cong dig to hide from us. My very active imagination is working overtime. I see men in baggy black shirts and pants popping out of every hillock, pointing ancient but lethal M-1 rifles—taken from dead ARVN soldiers—and drilling us with bullets smeared in their own shit.

"We've changed partners. Now Bates is ahead of me, driving the Mercedes with Mia My at his side. We go along for a few miles when I hear a sharp *Pan!* Noise, and the big black sedan starts fishtailing in front of my truck. I slam on the brakes and hang in there, managing to stop before slamming into them. But the Mercedes is out of control. It swerves and slides to a stop, hung up on the undercarriage with the front wheels over the edge of the road.   One little nudge and it will go over the side, but at least I've missed running into them by a foot or two. Tuyet Lan and I come running up as Joe is helping Mia My out of the car."

"This actually happened?" I asked, looking at Mia My, who I still saw as my source of ultimate truth rather than Wild Jack the author of the many Dunk Stingray adventures.

"Of course," she said, smoothly taking over the narration. "I was there. Jack is yelling like a crazy man, 'Gunshot? Gunshot? Where? Where?' My Joe calms him down, shaking his head and pointing to one of the rear tires, which is shredded. 'Blow-out.' Joe goes over to take a closer look, then shakes his head. "Nope,' he says. Not a blow-out' He pulls a strip of wood from what is left of the tire. It is studded with nails.

'We have bad trouble, here,' Jack says. Joe has already opened the rear trunk and is fishing for the spare tire. But Jack has been looking around wildly, looking off in the distance, studying the potato plant ridges around the rice paddies, looking for the danger he knows is there.

Joe works furiously. He finds the spare, and is frantically working to take the bad tire off.

'Oh, oh,' Jack says. He slaps Joe on the shoulder. "Joey-boy, we can't wait, old sack.'

'What? What?' Joe asks, shaking Jack's hand off and too busy to be bothered.

'Jack, we can not wait. Here come the savages, and they aren't bearing peace-pipes. Come on—*come on!* Everybody in the truck!'

"We run for the big army truck, and Jack helps me and Tuyet Lan to climb up in back. Even at that time, Joe is still trying to put things together, 'But the car...' 'It is our oldest automobile,' I tell him. 'Mama has three more.'"

"That's right," Jack said, taking over the storytelling. "I have a bad, bad feeling about this. I tell the girls to lie on a pile of old sacks on the floor, and if we have to stop, they are to crawl under the sacks. I throw a few *trops* to Evil Jack so he doesn't attack me, and I gun the truck, getting us back up to speed

'We can't just leave it.' Joe is looking out the rear mirror on the passenger side, still complaining about the Mercedes. I guess it was his value system, learned from his parents who grew up in the Great Depression. But I don't have time for his problems. While he's looking backwards, I'm watching the road ahead, and what I see causes me to worry about our immediate future. The VC have rolled a line of forty-five gallon drums across the road and have stood them on end, building a hastily constructed barrier. Two of the guys I've been hoping not to meet are standing in front of the barrels. They're classic irregulars, dressed in their cone straw hats and wearing black silk pajamas and rubber go-aheads they probably got from some street merchant in Saigon. One has an M-1 rifle, and he looks like he might know how to use it.

'Top! Top, hai la chet! Stop or you're a dead man!' He points his rifle at us so we'll know he's serious.

"I wait as long as I can, trying to figure some way out of the trap, but there is none, so I slam on the brakes at the last minute.

"Joe is yelling at me as we skid to a stop, 'And they don't let us carry weapons!' He takes the entire bag of *trom trom trop* and throws it out the window, followed by Evil Jack. 'Go get it, monkey!' he yells. To this day, I've never been sure just why he did that. Maybe he figured Jack was some sort of *combat attack monkey*.

"Meanwhile, Tuyet Lan has unlaced one corner of the canvas that covers the truck bed so she can see what's happening up front.

'What are they doing?' Mia My asks.

'The monkey! The Americans think these men are joking!' Tuyet Lan has been frantically digging through her large handbag. She comes up with a small, silvery automatic pistol.

'What are you doing?' Mia My asks, suddenly taken out of her own element. 'If the authorities find you have a *pistola?!*'

"But Tuyet Lan has been transformed into a crazy woman. 'No more rape and murder by ignorant peasant men with the big idea and the small dick!' she shouts.

"And then things go from bad to worse. Joe and I see a small group of three or four armed men approaching at a fast dogtrot from the rear of the truck. They're about a hundred yards away, and closing fast. But I notice the two guys who have stopped us at the barricade are just young guys, and not looking all that professional about what they're doing. They seem distracted by the monkey, who is scrambling around at their feet as he goes for the fruit scattered around on the ground. The guy with the M-1 kicks at Evil Jack, but he isn't giving up on the *trom trom trop* scattered around.

'*De xe hoi cam-in-ion, de quoc xam luoc My, hai la chet!* Get out of the truck, invader-gangster Americans, or you're dead!' At that moment, three pistol shots ring out and one bullet catches the young guerilla with the rifle just off center in his forehead. The second irregular grabs the rifle and fires, starring the front window of the truck and narrowly missing me. More pistol shots ring out, and the second guerilla doubles over and then crumples to the ground.

'Oh, God…' Joe says.

"But there's no time for questions or remorse, Tuyet Lan is yelling at us like a crazy person, 'Shit! Fuck! Piss ! *Di! Di! Mao len!* Let's get out of here! Now! Go fast!'

"I drop the truck into low gear and run over the bodies with a few horrible thumps, and then push past the 45 gallon drums, which prove to be empty. Tuyet Lan tosses her pistol on the bodies as they move past. Later, she tells me *It was okay, G.I.,* she had no more bullets, anyway.

"As we move on out of there, a dark shape looms in the open window on Joe's side of the truck. Joe yells and throws up his arms to defend himself, but it turns out to be Evil Jack, who crawls in through the window and scrambles to his position on the seat back, grubbing around for the remaining *trop* that are scattered here and there. The oil drum barrels and the dead guys and Mia My's car are behind us. The late afternoon sun has dropped like a bright stone behind Thailand, straight west from us. Minute by minute it's growing darker now, and I can see the glow from the city lights reflected off the low fog moving in and up over the city from the Saigon estuary.

"We breeze through two city check-points and to the main gate outside Tan Son Nhut. Night business is booming at 100 P Alley, the area is the usual crazy mess. Joe helps the girls down from the back and Tuyet Lan makes a beeline for a taxi; she's late for work, you know? I yell after her , 'See you at the Cherry Bar,' but she's already gone, not even a wave from the cab. Joe looks badly shaken up. Mia My tries to apologize, 'I didn't think anything like this would happen...' But it's not the time or the place. One of the American M.P.s at the gate yells, ' Hey, young lovers, take it somewhere else. We got traffic through here!' That's all she needs; Mia My bolts out of there like a frightened bird.

"So Joe and I head on back to the motor pool to turn in the deuce-and-a-half, and, believe me, it takes all our worldly goods to buy our way out of that bullet through the windshield. Transistor radios, binoculars, watches, everything. 'It's just a goddamn window pane,' I grump to the Motor Pool Sarge.

'Two hundred dollars,' the Sarge says.

'All this, and next payday, another hundred,' I tell him.

'Okay, but you bring it or I'll break your ass.'

"The deal's been made, and Sarge suddenly turns into *Mister Nice Guy*. 'Hey, did you guys hear?' he asks. 'Red Dog's back!'

"That takes both Joe and me by surprise. The last time we saw him was at the hospital, and Red Dog had looked like he was out of the action for good. I would have given odds he would never pass military muster again, not in this life. *Early retirement at half pay*, is what I'd told Joe when we saw how banged up he was.

'Ahh...how's he look?' I ask. To be completely honest, I'm thinking about myself and Tuyet Lan and not at all about our pal Red Dog.

'He doesn't look happy,' Sarge says."

CHAPTER 28

"So the next day we're at our desks in the White Shack, doing our usual things—Joe is mulling whether or not *Phong needs more bullets*, and I'm half way through The Old Man And The Sea for the 3rd or 4th time—and we look up to see Red Dog himself, standing in Ogilvy's door. 'God DAMN it!' Red Dog yells. 'You know where *everybody* is in this stinking town!' He pauses, fishing for the words. His face is flushed and he himself is doing the one thing he warned us never to do—he's out of control in The White Snake's presence. Red Dog continues, he can't help himself, he's a man in love, 'You mean you *can't* find her or you *won't* find her?' But he doesn't wait for an answer. He turns on his heel without saluting and churns away.

"As he passes, I state the obvious, 'Sarge, you're back!' Joe looks up from his crypto chart and pipes up, 'Hey…what's happening?' Red dog yells, 'Tuyet Lan's gone! Vanished!' I'm hoping that's the end of it and he'll leave so I can sweat it out alone, but he flops down in a chair right next to me. His face and arms are still pockmarked with scabs and stitches, and I can't be sure, but it looks like he's picked up a lazy eye from the explosion. The right one focuses on me but the left one seems to be wandering around the room, searching for something to kill.

"Ogilvy comes to his door and looks like he's going after Red Dog. But when he sees the sergeant sitting with us, he gives us his dangerously charged expression, does a 180 and goes back into his office. After that, Joe eyes Red Dog skeptically, giving him the quick once-over, 'We thought they were sending you home with an honorable discharge.' Red Dog gives the desk in front of him a frustrated kick with his heel. 'I re-upped for four

fricking more years! I pulled every string I had to get back here—
and they tell me she's got a new lover!'

"When I hear this there's a lump in my throat that grows so
big I can hardly swallow. I manage to say, 'Who says?'

'The girls at the Cherry Bar.'

Joe gives me a quick glance and then eyes the sergeant,
'What are you going to do?'

'I'm going to find him,' Red Dog says. 'I'm going to find
him and I'm going to cut him up in little pieces.' He's taken out a
big pocket knife. The damn thing is big as a survival knife, eight
inch blade, at least, so big it practically won't fit in his fatigues
pocket. It's one of those fold-over knives, and he hits a button and
it swishes open and locks with a deadly click. He waves it around,
cutting up the imaginary bastard who dicked his princess. I'm sure
I have turned white as a ghost.

'Well, right…okay, then,' Bates says, handing Red Dog his
small stack of translations. But the sergeant shakes his head and
pushes them away. 'Give them to The White Snake,' he says,
'Ogilvy is your new boss.'

'We report directly to Ogilvy?' Bates asks. We all know
this can't be good.

"Red Dog points one stubby finger at Joe. 'Bates reports to
the Snake. You report to Bates. And I've been demoted to a lousy
hard-stripe E-5…no offense meant…' And with that, Tuyet Lan's
other lover staggers to his feet and wanders away, heading down
the long hallway for the front door.

"It takes Ogilvy an hour or two, but he finally calls Joe in
to his office. Joe sits on the other side of Ogilvy's desk, but the
Colonel ignores him. After twenty minutes of this, Joe clears his
throat and says, 'You asked to see me, Sir.'

'Right,' The White Snake says. He slides two grainy photo
blowups across his desk. They show the deuce-and-a-half with the
bullet starred window, and me, Joe, Tuyet Lan and Mia My. 'Now
I just want to know why you *Top Secret Security Clearance People*
can't keep it in your pants for even a few months over here?'

'Uh, we were taking clothes to an orphanage, Sir,' Bates
said.

'With full knowledge that you were breaking the basic
rules of your Top Secret clearance! With full knowledge that you

were in an unsecured area, with no support, no back up—and no permission!' The White Snake can not conceal his rage. He stands and begins pacing around the room. 'Carrying every secret of our mission in your stupid little brains, you choose to waltz around the countryside like a happy tourist?!'

'But we—' Joe tries to break in.

'If the VC catch you, they wire your testicles and turn on the juice until you sing like blubbering babies…which takes about thirty seconds, more or less.'

'But we—'

'And I already warned you that girlfriend of yours is the daughter of a known—a *notorious*—French sympathizer.'

'But I—she's not—'

'And the other girl in this picture, now let me see…oh, yes, I think I recognize our own distressed Sergeant Red Dog's missing sweetie-pie.'

The White Snake slumps back down into his chair, staring off into the distance, and there's a long silence. Joe finally says, 'May I go, Sir?'

'Go?' The Colonel considers, 'Sure. But don't go far, until I figure out what to do with you.' And with that, the officer waves him out of the room.

"As if that wasn't enough, something even more crazy and unexpected is about to happen. Joe is shaking like a bamboo stalk in a typhoon as he comes out of The White Snake's office. I gather him up and as we head for the door, he tells me how we've both been made with the photographs, probably more of Leo and Wendell's work. Okay, bad enough—but then, as we are leaving the White Shack and walking away from the guards, a peasant girl in grimy pajamas and the usual conical hat calls out to me. 'Zack—*Zack*!'

I wave the girl off. I don't recognize her, and Joe doesn't see her. Neither of us have time for beggars or cheap sex in the alley.

'I didn't think he was going to let me out of the office,' Joe says. 'I guess it sounds ridiculous, but I thought he was going to kill me right then and there.'

'He's The White Snake,' I tell Joe. 'He's just playing with us before he strikes.'

"The peasant girl calls out again, this time more insistently in a hoarse, low voice. 'Zack!' she whispers again and again. 'Zack!!' And that forces me to take a closer look. *Jesus Christ in heaven, it's Tuyet Lan!*

"Joe backs away, and for once I don't blame him. 'I'll leave you two love birds alone,' he says. He walks away, and I don't see him again until that night in the latrine.

"We're both shaving, or pretending to. My hands are so shaky that I'm doing a great job of nicking myself. I've been over at the club, and I know the deep crap we're in.

'Those people we shot—' I start.

'She shot,' Bates corrects me. 'She did the shooting.'

'Okay, okay, Joe—*She* shot. They were the sons of a provincial chief. And they are both dead, deader than stones.'

'Not Viet Cong?' Joe asks.

'Who knows?' I shrug. 'The story is, they were just a bunch of local kids farting around, holding up traffic for a little pin money.'

'I'm not buying that for a second,' Joe exclaims.

'Me, either,' I tell him. 'But The White Snake is.'

"So somehow between the latrine and throwing on our clothes in the barracks and on our way back over to the 3rd RRU's Enlisted Mens Club, I make up my mind. 'We've got to get her out of Saigon,' I say.

Joe gives me a wild-eyed look. 'What?'

'We've got to, Joe. She saved our lives.'

Bates looks at me, trying to find the heart of the matter. 'You love her?' he asks.

'Of course not,' I say. I shrug. 'I got miles to go before I can catch the train.'

Bates nods, eyeing me closely. I know he only half believes me.

'I think I've got an idea,' he says. We talk it over on our way to the club, and I decide it's totally wacko, but it just might work.

"As we expected, Red Dog is already half blotto, sitting alone at a table while he slugs his way through the beginnings of a hard liquor night. I hang back in the EM part of the club while Joe moves over to the NCO section. He slides into a chair next to the sergeant.

'I know where to find Tuyet Lan,' Joe tells him.

'So do I,' Red Dog says, giving him a look of bleary dejection.

'What?' .

'The White Snake told me everything,' the sergeant says. 'She's hiding, but they'll pick her up in a few days.' He eyes us both. 'I know everything, Bates. Everything.'

"Joe shakes his head, unwilling to give up. 'What did the Colonel tell you?'

'You know…that slick buddy of yours somehow got to her.' Red Dog's head sinks until he's face down on the table, crying or sleeping or both, it's hard to tell.

'The Colonel's lying,' Joe says. 'I want to tell you a different story .'

Red Dog doesn't bother to lift his head. 'Bates, I *saw* the pictures.'

'Pictures can mean anything, Sarge. We went to an *orphanage*, for God's sake! Who was it first warned me about The White Snake?' That gets Red Dog's attention, and a half hour later Joe has him in a *xe hoi* taxi, heading for Cho Lon, the Chinese section of town.   Red Dog is still three sheets to the wind, but he's curious, and half believing Joe, who is laying it on thick. 'She's waiting for you, Sarge,' Joe tells him. 'She loves you, God only knows why. Love is like a freight train…' he starts and Red Dog wearily joins him in the refrain, '… and we're just bugs on the tracks.'

Both men lapse into silence as the little cream-and-white taxi rockets them across town. But Joe Bates has other fish to fry, and after a while he asks Red Dog, 'Sarge, I have to ask you something…What did Colonel Ogilvy have to do with Diem's death.'

'That's classified,' Red Dog says automatically, without a moment's hesitation.

'Come on, Dog-man,' Joe pleads. 'Just give me the scuttlebutt version. It's not like I'm going to tell anybody…or like you have to protect The White Snake.'

Joe mentioning the Colonel decides Red Dog. He gives
Bates a sour look and a small nod of agreement and starts talking.
'Ogilvy was head of CIA OPS, Southeast Asia Section.
McNamara thought Diem wasn't pushing the war effort hard
enough. Kennedy told the military to put some more pressure on
Diem. Somehow—and nobody to this day is exactly sure or saying
just how—somehow Ogilvy's fuck up fellows got overly
enthusiastic about their mission.'

'Jesus,' Joe says.

'Yeah, the whole family.'

'Huh?' Joe isn't following.

Red Dog gives him a sad half-smile. 'Jesus, Mary and
Joseph.'

Before that taxi ride is over, Joe convinces Red Dog that I
never was involved with his girl, and for her part, Tuyet Lan
knows she's in big trouble, so she's ready to take Red Dog back.
Realizing he's got a fortune in gold bars hidden away somewhere
is a good secondary motivation, even if true love isn't exactly in
the picture. Joe leaves him with Tuyet Lan, and I'm feeling this
huge rush of relief, like I've brushed my hands of the entire mess.
But you know the problem…"

Jack has lapsed into silence. He starts suddenly, looking
around as if he wasn't quite sure where he was or how forty years
could have flown by so fast. My guess was that he was done for
the night. He got up and started to wander back to his own
quarters. As he was going, I heard him mutter, "Clair, I was
responsible. I had set that goddamn freight train in motion myself.
And nothing in this world was going to be able to stop it."

"No, Jack," Mia My said. "Do not be such a proud fool."

I've got to say, Mia My was fearless, the way she went
after him.

"What do you mean?" he said, stopping his exit and turning
half around to face her.

"Red Dog, he started his own train, just like Joe and me,
just like you and Clair."

"I'm afraid our train never got out of the station," I said.

"That is maybe not all his fault," Mia My said, burning me
with one of her tiger lady stares.

I looked back at Jack, to see what he had to say about that, but he was already limping around the pool, heading for his digs. She gave me one quick, imperious nod of her head and I saw in the fierce expression in her dark eyes the strong will inherited from her mother and from countless generations of tiger ladies before her. So I went after him, and, unbelievable as it sounds, Jack and I were together for the first night since his crazy short-term marriage to Joanie the blues singer, and this time, to tell the truth, it was some kind of wonderful, as the song says.

Half way through the night, I woke to find him looking at me.

"What, Jack?" I asked.

"You ever try to do the right thing, but it gets misinterpreted and what happens after that haunts you for the rest of your life?"

"You mean us, Jack?"

"God, no…not us, Clair. I screwed *us* up…but I don't mean that. You're the one, single-best thing that ever happened to me. I wish I'd met you years ago, before I got so terminally fucked up…" We made long, slow, sweet love then, and that left wondering at the wild swings of fortune and emotion in the sometimes screwed up but never boring House of Jack.

CHAPTER 29

The next morning when I rounded the pool and walked into Jack's kitchen, the first thing I heard was The Wild Man himself talking with Eddie.

"It was the dumbest thing, Eddie. It should never had happened."

I got that old familiar feeling, and snapped at him, "You talking about us?"

"I'm talking about Red Dog and Tuyet Lan," Jack said without skipping a beat. But I saw Eddie's eyes widen when the Larch-ster came over and kissed me on the cheek. *That's the thing about the Larch boy-wonder…you never knew what he was going to do.* Eddie may have been a ghost and they're supposed to be quiet about their clients' private lives, but I wondered how long it would be before the old rumors resurfaced about Wild Jack and his Clair-Bear

"What about Red Dog & the Cherry Bar Princess?" I asked, pouring myself a half-cup of barely acceptable two-day coffee.

Mia My wandered in with her own cup, and so I poured for her as well. She gave me a smile and an approving nod that I was pretty sure said more than *thanks for the coffee.* "Where are we at, Jack?" she asked.

"The White Snake has convinced the locals that Tuyet Lan had blood on her hands. So she can't hide in town, and she can't go back home, and she can't go to Nha Trang or Tay Ninh or anyplace. Vietnam isn't that big, and there's nowhere for a pretty bargirl to hide. So Red Dog convinces her to run away to Thailand with him. In a way, it's not a bad plan. Dangerous, but what isn't in that time and place? He dyes his hair and sticks on a corny fake moustache and gets dressed in a business suit. She cuts her hair short and trades in her fancy brocaded silk bargirl's outfit for a smart Western culture dress that Mia My loans her.

"The next day the two of them are waiting in the airport together while the flights are being broadcast over the intercom. *Flight 173 to Hong Kong…last call. Flight 23 to Bangkok…now boarding. Flight 127 to Pnom Penh, now boarding.* Tuyet Lan has heard the magic words, *23 is boarding.* She stands and looks at the gentleman in the crooked moustache and the stiff new suit. Red Dog shakes his head, no. 'Wait until the last minute, honey-bunch,' he says.

"He sinks lower in his seat because he's spotted Wendell and Leo at the entrance to the terminal. The two of them visually scan the place the way they've been taught, and then they move through the big room at a fast trot. I think they're expecting to see Red Dog in his tropical tan khakis, and so the Sergeant is passing muster. He actually hears Leo say, 'The Cherry Bar girls said Singapore.'

'Singapore Airlines, then,' Wendell points to the far end of the terminal. The voice drones again over the intercom, *'Flight 23 to Bangkok, last call…'*

'Okay, Honey-bunch,' Red Dog says, 'now we go.'

"Home free, right? Red Dog and Tuyet Lan hustle their buns to the gate, show their tickets and pass through the door leading outside to the tarmac. But once they are outside, they find themselves at the end of a line of civilians waiting to climb the portable metal stairway to board the DC-3 Thai Airlines passenger plane. The line isn't moving at all, not a good sign in any age. After a few nerve-wracking minutes, a Ford Falcon with a wailing siren and a winking blue light stuck on top races toward them across the tarmac, followed by an open deuce-and-a-half carrying a half-dozen ARVN soldiers. The shiny waxed Falcon, which is painted a special lavender purple, pulls to a halt next to the passengers, who do their Oriental best not to show their discomfort.

"The driver of the light purple Falcon hops out of the front seat and scurries to open the rear door for a dapper ARVN Major. That stands for *Army of the Republic of Vietnam*, if I haven't mentioned it before. This Zip Major has a lavender silk scarf tucked in his shirt. At first glance, he appears to walk with a graceful glide; on closer inspection, it looks like he has serious back problems, and his glide is more of a hitch in his stride that he's trying to smooth with the assistance of a cane topped with a golden handle in the shape of a coiled dragon snake.

"The ARVN Major takes a look up and down the line. He smiles briefly at a pretty airline stewardess. As is often the case, his teeth are bad, and his smile is somewhat fearful to behold. And clearly, nobody is smiling back. The Major approaches Red Dog and Tuyet Lan. He motions the two of them out of line with his cane, then indicates with a sweeping motion that the rest of the line can move forward and board the plane.

'*Papier, s'il vous plait,*' he says to Red Dog. Red Dog quickly takes his papers from his inside coat pocket and hands them across. The Major nods, but doesn't hand them back. He turns to Tuyet Lan, '*Papier Official, s'il vous plait,*' he says politely. It is obvious he doesn't think she has any, or, if she does, that they won't pass muster. After some fussing in her purse, Tuyet Lan hands across her passport. The Major frowns, comparing the photograph to her face. He reads, 'Mia My Nguyen. You are Mia My Nguyen?' Tuyet Lan replies that yes, she is.

'Ahh, one of our many Nguyens,' he says. *'Celle alors!'* He has dug with his thumb into the type, smearing ink on the page. 'Un-fortunately...' he begins, now speaking in French accented English.

"At this point, Red Dog moves closer to the Major. Standing next to the ARVN officer, he takes the massive gold chain from his own neck. 'I see the Major has a fine gold walking cane. Can you admire the workmanship in my own neck chain?' He slips it into the near pocket of the dapper man's uniform jacket.

'Ahh,' the Major replies. 'A fine piece...but we have a serious matter here.' Red Dog's gold wristwatch slides into the Major's pocket.

'Nothing is so serious,' Red Dog calmly says, 'that it cannot be talked out by two men of the world who see eye to eye.'

'Still...' the Major says, eyeing the heavy rings on the American's hands. Red Dog shrugs and nods in agreement. He places them in the Major's now-sagging pocket with the rest. *'Okay, that's all. Het, roi. Ca fini.'*

But the ARVN Major shakes his head, '*Non, Monsieur.*'
He taps Red Dog's briefcase with the tip of his cane. Red Dog
sighs and hands it over. The ARVN Major hefts the case. It is so
heavy he has difficulty lifting it. 'Very heavy,' he says. Red Dog
shrugs, resigned to the loss. The ARVN Major hands him back
their papers. He gives Red Dog a curt salute and turns on his heel.
In a moment, he has returned to his Falcon, and the car and the
deuce-and-a-half loaded with soldiers is speeding away.

'We can go?' Tuyet Lan asks him.

''Come on, before they close the door!' Red Dog grabs her
hand and pulls her up the metal stairs. But as they reach the top of
the metal stairs, there is a widening space between them and the
doorway. Tuyet Lan hesitates, and then it is too late—they are too
far away. They down to see The White Snake's two ops, Wendell
and Leo, happily pulling the metal stair with them at the top of it
away from the DC-3.

"Red Dog makes his decision. He's going to jump anyway.
Leo and Wendell see this, and give a last mighty tug, widening the
gap even further. Red Dog actually says, 'Oh, what the fuck!' and
jumps. It is a crazy, hopeless thing to do. Arms outstretched, his
fingers miss the lower edge of the doorway by inches, and his body
lands hard on the tarmac.

"Tuyet Lan is right there, she sees it all from the top of the
metal staircase. Leo raises his fist in the air, he's pumped with
victory and late to realize the disaster he has caused. 'Oops,' he
says. 'Red Dog, you missed your flight!' But Wendell, who is a
little brighter than Leo, looks down at Red Dog's quiet form. 'Oh,
shit,' Wendell says. One side of Red Dog's head seems misshaped
and flattened, and blood is flowing from his nose, from his ears
and from his slack and open mouth. He will never regain
consciousness, and will be dead by the next morning.

It's a very bad moment. The Thai Airlines stewardess
stands in the open doorway, looking down at them. Three or four
ARVN *Quoc Khanh* military police come running. One of them
tries hopelessly to give poor Red Dog mouth-to-mouth, while the
other two roughly grab Leo and Wendell. Leo takes his CIA status
very seriously, showing considerable tough-guy attitude. He
attempts to demonstrate some martial arts moves, and in the fuss
and bluster of the moment, Tuyet Lan makes her way back down

the metal stairs like she's going to rush over to comfort her fallen lover. But she edges past the mini-conflict and the still-warm body, and disappears through the gathering crowd."

CHAPTER 30

"So the next day Joe and I are attempting to maintain total invisibility at our desks in the White Shack. I'm in such a serious funk that I'm not even reading Hemingway. Wendell gives us a furtive glance as he rushes past, heading into The White Snake's office.

'This can't be good,' I tell Joe.

"In about thirty seconds, the Colonel appears in the doorway of his office. He stands there, weaving a little and licking his dry lips, looking around for someone to strike. His gaze settles on Joe. 'Specialist 5th Class Joseph Bates,' he says, the whispery menace clear in his voice, 'I understand you were the last person who talked to our dearly departed Red Dog.'

Bates shakes his head no. 'I tried to cheer him up, Sir' he says.

I raise my hand like a schoolboy, something I picked up from Joe. 'We all talked to him, Sir. He was over at the EMC last night.'

"The Colonel shakes his head, rejecting my statement. He's sure Joe is behind this entire failed escape plan. Ever since Leo and Wendell uncovered Joe was dating Mia My, The White Snake has been building a case against Joe in his head. His message is clear. *You're dead meat, Specialist Bates. I'm going to get you.* After a long, cold stare, he turns on his heel and slides back into his office. It's a good thing, too, because Joe is physically shaking with fear. I'm sure that in just one more moment he's going to pee his pants.

"That night, we go out behind the 3rd. There's a loose board in the high wooden fence surrounding our perimeter. Everybody knows it's there, probably even the Viet Cong. There's a low berm between the fence and the airfield, and we've rigged a poncho overhead to keep out the rain. Flares are dropping over the airport, and, out of sight in the distance, the mortars are shooting up and landing with the distinctive *poomph…crump, poomph…crump, poomph.,…crump* sound that they make. Way out there, a Browning is sawing away in long bursts. 'They better save their ammo,' I say to nobody in particular, 'or they'll be out by midnight.' Joe doesn't say anything. I'm drinking from a half empty bottle of Algerian red, and smoking some good hash I picked up from a *tuock la* lady on Nguyen Hue Street, a half block from the USO. 'You want a hit, Joe?' I ask. Joe shakes his head. 'What will The White Snake do to me?' he wails.

"I shrug one shoulder. The ghosts of Nam have gotten to me. I'm becoming a role-player; I'm a sophisticated survivor in an old French colony, I'm one of Hai Ba Truong's men, enjoying a moment of peace from the Chinese hordes. I even smoke my toke in the cupped hand way made popular by hopeless French Legionnaires shielding the glowing embers of their smokes from hilltop Montagnard sharpshooters. 'The White Snake's got no proof," I say. 'Let him hiss, Joe. Another month and you're out of here.'

'Sure, sure, sure…then what do I do about Mia My?'

'Maybe you just get on the big bird in the sky and fly back to the real world,' I suggest.

'No!' Joe shouts, loud enough to alert the guy patrolling on guard duty on the inside of the wooden fence.

'Hold it down, guys,' the poor guard says through a crack in the fence. 'I don't want to have to report you.' I hand the guy the toke through a knot-hole, and he takes a long drag before handing it back.

'I know she's the one for me, Jack,' Joe tells me. 'We were meant for each other. And if I leave here, it's done. With my clearance, they'll never let me back in the country, not even as a civilian!'

'Okay, okay. You love her, Bates,' I say.

Joe stands, bent over a little under the low-slung poncho. He's made a decision. 'I'm going to re-enlist!' he says.

'Woah there, fella! That's four years hard time!'

But Joe has made up his mind. 'I don't see any other choice,' he says.

So the next day he walks into The White Snake's office in full surrender, ready to sign on the dotted line and give up four years of his life. I'm hovering around outside the door, doing my best to stay up on what's going on. Leo and Wendell are in there,

probably enjoying the show. Bates is pleading his case, but now
the Colonel is shaking his head, rejecting the deal. 'B-but it's what
you wanted!' Joe stutters.   The White Snake sits behind his desk
in stony silence. 'But—God *damn* it, why not?' Joe blathers.

The Colonel, who knows a thing or two about punishment,
stares at Joe a long time before he answers. 'You had your chance
with me, soldier. I thought you might be interested in a real career
with this man's army, but you turned out to be one hell of a
flaming security risk, didn't you?'

Joe isn't normally an emotional guy, but he's quite outside
of himself, sickened with Red Dog's senseless death and
maddened with his frustration and despair over losing Mia My.. 'I
may have done a stupid thing or two,' he shouts, 'but nothing
compared to you…Sir!'

'Be careful, Boy…' The Colonel's voice is a warning
rattle deep in his throat.

But Bates rushes on, ignoring the warning, 'You people
aren't happy until you fiddle around and ruin everything!'

The Colonel eyes him with hooded lids, wondering how
much he knows, how much anybody knows about him. 'What do
you mean, Specialist?' he asks.

Joe jumps to his feet and points an accusing finger at Leo
and Wendell. 'Red Dog is dead and it's their fault!'

'Sergeant Moore was a deserter.' The White Snake spits
out the sentence like a curse.

Joe reaches in his fatigues jacket pocket, pulls out a paper,
unfolds it and waves it in front of their faces, 'Sergeant Red Dog
Moore signed out for R&R in Thailand! He had a right to get on
that plane! And he was coming back in five days!'

'What?' Ogilvy looks at Leo and Wendell, speechless at
this turn of events.

Joe probably should have shut up right there; he's made his
point and there is nothing to be gained by continuing. But he's
consumed with his anger. 'You're all screw-ups!' He shouts, as
loud as I've ever heard him. 'You interfere in people's lives and
you screw-up everything you do! Here's your deserter, Sir!' And
with that, he slams the R&R papers down on the desk and rushes
out of the office without saluting.

As he leaves, I hear Leo grumble, 'I'm gonna kill that bastard...'

'Oh, you kill everybody, Leo,' Wendell says, as if he doesn't have a care in the world.

I manage to scuttle back to my desk just in time as Joe slams into his own seat. 'A few weeks ago the Snake was practically begging me to take those stripes!' he says in a loud voice. I try to calm him down. 'Hey, you just saved four years of your life,' I tell him. And that was just about when the base sirens started up.

'*Troi, dut, nuoc, oi!,*' Joe exclaims. 'What the hell?'

In the next minute, a claxon horn goes off inside the White Shack. The sound is deafening, just a huge blast that whites out every other sound. . Hinkelby comes running down the hall. 'Okay, boys, he shouts, 'We've gone to red! Break out the incendiaries!'

He's running around the room like a man possessed. He digs in a file cabinet until he comes up with a box of red fire grenades. He rushes around the room, placing one of the powerful little red beasts on each file cabinet. As there are file cabinets everywhere, this is a lot of grenades. Joe and I stare at him like he's gone nuts. I raise my hand in the acceptable Joe Bates manner and speak up, 'Sarge, you pop more than two or three of those mothers in this room and you'll incinerate us all.'

'By the book, Jack!' Hinkelby tells me, 'By the book!'

Ogilvy pokes his head out of his office and sees what Hinkelby is doing. 'One or two per room, Sarge,' he says, and then stalks on down the hall. I give Hinkelby an I-told-you-so face, but Hinkelby doesn't see me or, if he does, he doesn't pay any attention.

'What's going on?' Joe asks. The White Snake pauses in mid-stride. He turns around as if looking for some killing weapon, but he says nothing. He turns away again, continuing down the hall.

'Military coup!' Hinkelby informs us in an excited tenor voice. 'The Zip generals are trying to topple Phan Hui Quat. Flyboy General Ky's got his planes up. General Minh's pulled in some of his ARVN units and occupied the base!'

'Tan Son Nhut?!' Joe says. 'What about the 3rd? RRU? '

The White Snake has paused again, half way down the hallway. He turns to face us again, and I see the lines on his face are deep with anger. He looks at us and spits out his words. I get the feeling he's having his own unguarded moment, revealing he is full of loathing for us, for the army, for his own stunted career, for everything about his life. 'You horny toads sit tight and let your pants cool down a little bit.' Just that, and then he continues on down the hall and makes his way out the heavy green door.

So with Code Red, we're confined to the base. Everybody's walking around on tippy-toe, not knowing whether to fire the grenades and make plane for Thailand or just sit tight and ride things out. Nobody knows who's in command. One thing's sure, the old president of the Republic, Phan Hui Quat, is out.

Joe and I head over to the EMC, and it's plenty crowded. We push around until Hinkelby makes room for us to squeeze in at his table.   Hinkelby's already a few Ba Muoi Ba's to the wind, and he's in an expansive mood. 'Red Dog's big dream was to open a fancy whore house in Bangkok,' he says. 'Gone to gold,' he says, raising his half empty beer bottle. 'Goodbye, good old Red Dog.' He pauses, trying to collect his half-addled thoughts. 'Another few minutes, I'll be gone, too.' He stands, now saluting me and Joe with his brown Ba Muoi Ba bottle.

'Where you going?' I ask, half thinking he's going to do something stupid like taking a header off the water tower.

'Hey, I am not staying *here*. E-5's and up can still take the Grey Snail if they live downtown.'

'Oh, like that's fair,' I grump at him.

Hinkelby looks at Joe, 'Well, at least *you're* E-5, aren't you?'

'You don't think the Snake has restricted me personally?'

'Only one way to find out,' Hinkelby says, wrinkling his nose as if that might clear his blurred vision.

It only takes Joe about five minutes to swap out of his civvies into his tropical dress uniform. He makes his way to the orderly room with me tagging along behind for support.

'Hey,' Toady barks as we walk in. 'I just mopped the floor.'

'Sorry,' Joe says. 'I didn't know.'

Toady pokes his head out of the door of the mop closet and sees who it is. 'Joseph Bates. Congratulations.'

'Yeah? For what?'

'Didn't you hear?' Toady asks. 'They're shipping you back to the P.I. in three days. First plane they could get. I stamped the orders myself, earlier today.'

Joe shakes his head, taking the news in. 'But…I have nearly a month yet…my papers…who signed off on me…Williamson?' Toady has returned to his desk, and is intent on putting back together the parts of a small electric fan. He doesn't bother to look up. 'Noooo, The White Snake, himself. *Chao, Ong Bates,* as you lingies say. Goodbye, old soak. You're going back to The World…that is, if the fat, stupid Zip generals let your plane take off.'

'Damn it,' Joe says. 'Damn it, damn it, damn it.'

'Yeah,' Toady yawns, 'it's like quicksand. Just when you think you're out, The Nam sucks you back in.'

The sign out book is in front of Joe, open to a new, nearly blank page. Joe pushes his thick glasses on his nose as if he's reading, turns back one page, finds a blank line between two scrawled signatures, signs out, and then turns the page back to the nearly blank one.

'Not many people signing out,' he says.

'Course not, Dopey," Toady snorts. "Payday's not 'til tomorrow. And it being Code Red don't help none.' He doesn't even bother to look up. He swears as a screw rolls away from him and falls off the desk onto the floor. 'Oh, crap,' he says as he squats down on his hands and knees looking for it.

Joe has signed out, but it's already late afternoon, and so he decides to spend the night at the 3rd. The next morning, he changes to his civvies and checks his secret stash, the thick wad of American currency he's accumulated by selling his PX allotment of cigarette and booze on the black market. He takes his camera and his small Air Vietnam flight bag and heads for the front entrance of the 3rd RRU. Things are a little touchy; now the sandbagged machinegun emplacement next to the entrance is fully manned and it looks like they've got a real string of bullets in the Browning.

As Joe tosses a friendly wave to the guys in the pit, one of them yells, 'Hey, lingie, come on over here!' Bates is eager to leave. He gives a glance down the road and then reluctantly walks over to the machinegun squad.

'Yeah? What?' he asks.

One of the troopers, a corporal, pulls a card from his fatigues shirt pocket. The card is from the Royal Bar. On the backside is a note written in a flowery female hand.

'Can you tell me what this says?' the corporal asks. 'I'll give you 20 p.'

'Here,' Bates says, reaching for the card, 'I'll do it for nothing.'

The troopers gather around. Joe sees the Grey Snail approaching in the distance, a grey-painted school bus with wire mesh bolted over the windows. He's going to have to make this fast. Joe reads, '*Em yeu Anh.*'

'Yeah, yeah, yeah—what's that stuff mean?' the trooper asks.

'*Em* is 'little sister.' *Anh* is 'big brother'. *Yeu* is 'love.''

The troopers all tease the corporal. The Grey Snail is getting closer.

'Yeah, yeah, go on,' the corporal prompts.

Joe translates in straight English, '*Em* cannot wait until the next time *Anh* comes to town to share our special warm and tender love, for *Em* adores *Anh* fully, completely and madly with all her heart. *Em* longs for the day when *Em* and *Anh* can once again be together in each other's arms. Until then, *Em* holds the bright promise of their love and the affectionate memory of the time of happiness and joy we spent together. All my love, *Hoa.*'

'That's her name—*Hoa!*' the trooper says.

'*Hoa* means 'flower',' Joe tells him. 'Lots of bargirls use it.'

The Grey Snail pulls to a stop in front of the 3rd. A weary handful of G.I.s begin to get off. Joe hands the card back to the trooper. 'Hey, thanks, dude,' the trooper says. You sure I can't give you something?'

'Naw, don't mention it.' Joe grins and waves again as he boards the bus.

'E-5 and above,' the driver drones. He closes the door and drives off as Joe takes a seat. Code Red is an uneasy time. Most don't want to take a chance going downtown, even if they can. Except for Joe and the driver, the bus is empty. But Joe isn't worried about anything. The train has come for him. And instead of being crushed on the tracks, he's hopped on board. Joe Bates is about to take the ride of his life.

CHAPTER 31

"Nguyen Hue street is a wide boulevard separated with a strip in the middle. It's also called *The Street of Flowers* because this center strip is occupied by dozens of flower stalls. Joe hires two pedi-cyclo drivers and goes from stall to stall, buying flowers. When these prove insufficient for his plans, he hires a gas driven pedi-cart, and soon all three are loaded down with colorful blooms. Joe isn't interested in just any particular flowers. He has piles of red and pink and white roses, but it's not like roses are the flowers of romance. Flowers themselves speak of love, and so Joe buys every type of flower and every color in the rainbow. He has small hand-sprays of sweet peas and violets, big stalks of happy sunflowers, bird of paradise, carnations, deep blue iris, medium blue bachelor buttons, light blue bluebells. He has giant lilies and tiny fragrant lilies-of-the-valley. And, of course, the orchids. Dozens and dozens of orchids.

"Some time later in the morning, Ba Nguyen is doing her usual bitching about her daughter as she walks with Auntie Kai through the Edan Arcade to the dress shop. 'She is becoming absolutely undependable. I can't tell her anything—what is this?' Joe Bates expression of love is piled in front of the door of the dress shop, a beautiful shower of every color and shape of flower that exists. Ba Nguyen, of course, does not approve. She tries to kick the flowers out of the way. 'Wrong delivery,' she yells. 'Idiots! This isn't a flower shop!' But Auntie Kai smiles and shakes her head, *'Khong phai...'* she says in that soft way of hers. Mia My comes trailing up behind them, and her eyes widen as she sees the flowers. By now Ba Nguyen has kicked her way through the huge bouquet, unlocked the door and entered the shop.

'Come,' she beckons her daughter. Don't make a fool of yourself! Come inside—*now!*'

"But Mia My lingers behind, looking at the flowers. Ba Nguyen is busy behind the counter, preparing for the day. 'Well, that's the end of that,' she grumbles.

'*Khong phai…*' Auntie Kai repeats. Ba Nguyen gives her a sharp look and then her eyes widen as her sharp gaze flicks across the arcade. Joe Bates is standing there, looking at Mia My. His eyes are peeping out over hundreds of roses, so many roses it seems impossible one man can carry them.

"Mia My sees Joe and his roses, and her hands fly to her face in surprise. She struggles with her emotions. And then a smile begins to break through like sunshine across her pretty face. While Ba Nguyen can do nothing but glare her anger, her daughter takes a hesitant step, then another, and then she is running to him. Joe drops the flowers and she is in his arms. And then, before Ba Nguyen can think to call the White Mice cops or some favors from the *Quoc Khanh*, Joe unexpectedly kneels on one knee and holds up a diamond ring. 'Mia My,' he says, '*Anh yeu em.*'

"Meanwhile, back at the ranch—that is, the White Shack—Ogilvy walks by and sees I'm working but Jack's nowhere around. At least, the Snake thinks I'm working because I've managed to light a little votive candle to my muse with a short story I've been writing under my pile of unread translations. 'I'm looking for Specialist Bates,' the Colonel hisses at me.

'Aren't we all, Sir?' I lie outrageously. 'He's the best, and I've got a few problems right here that I think he could solve.' I tap the pile of transmissions on my desk. They're dead issues, actually the same pile I found on my desk when I got there. I give a look like maybe I just thought of something. 'Maybe he went up in the Beaver with Hinkelby, Sir?'

'Hinkelby on a Saturday?' The Snake gives me that long, cold stare of his, measuring me with his fib-o-meter. I give him nothing back. I am a master of the military cover-up. After all, I am a spy and all, with a Top Secret clearance. *Jack knows deception.* Still, I don't get off scott-free. Ogilvy snorts, 'What are you smoking, Specialist?'

'Only the good stuff, Sir,' I reply, still giving him nothing.

'Yeah. That's what I heard,' he says, retreating back to his own office.

But the assholes don't give up. That evening, Leo and Wendell come storming into our barracks and start to trash Joe's area, which consists of his wall locker next to mine, his foot locker at the foot of our double bunk, and his bed, which is the double-decker above mine. As I'm trying to scribble down a few notes, this bothers me mightily.

'Looking for somebody?' I ask. Perry, my new pet parrot, is temporarily perched on one end of the metal mosquito netting. His full name is Perry-the-Pirate-Parrot, so named because he only has one eye and a crusty temperament. Usually, I camp him out under the poncho on the backside of the wooden fence surrounding the 3rd, but for the moment he's scoring seeds and spitting the shells on the floor while he keeps me company. He's a *writer's* parrot, you see.

'Where is he, Jack?' Leo starts in on me, using his interrogation mode. This makes Perry jumpy. He changes position on the metal perch, first one foot and then the other, and then swinging upside down.

'Where is he, Jack?' Perry squawks, blinking at Leo with his one good eye.

'You're not allowed to have a fucking parrot, dog-face,' Leo snarls, missing with a half-hearted swing at the bird. He's not really concentrating. He knows Joe isn't here, but he'd love to squeeze some information out of me.

"Wendell opens Joe's wall locker. A big, striped snake flops out. Wendell leaps backward and lets out a girlish cry of terror.

'Or a snake,' I tell him. 'We're not allowed that, either.'

'Not allowed!' Perry squawks. Not allowed!"

"Leo loses his temper and swings in earnest at Perry. But the green-and-blue feathered wonder is quick, and Leo misses by a mile.

'Shut up that fucking bird!' he screams.

'Not me,' I tell him. 'That's a pirate parrot. He's totally without merit, like me.'

"Leo takes the bait. He actually assumes one of his stupid karate stances. 'Yeah, well, I'm without merit, too,' he mutters, advancing on Perry. He looks silly, his hands out in the acceptable martial arts manner, ready to chop and slash, man against bird. He lets loose with a vicious backhand chop. Perry strikes with his big beak, almost like an afterthought, and Leo has a bloody gash in his hand.

'I'll kill him!' Leo roars, reaching in his jacket for his automatic.

'Killllll!' Perry screams like an unleashed marine, flapping his wings and launching himself in the full attack mode. A few pecks to the head and shoulders and the two operatives go tumbling backwards through the screen door at the end of our barracks.   Perry gives out an angry squawk and they run off, now in full retreat.

"By the next morning, still no Joe, and now The White Snake is running out of suspects to victimize. He's finally showed up in the 3rd RRU orderly room, the mountain coming to Mohammed, so to speak, where he's pounced on Toady who has fear on his skin like a coating of sweat.

'He signed out two days ago, Sir,' Toady stammers. He-he's not due back until tonight.'

'I never gave him approval to do that,' the Colonel hisses.

'Spec 5's and above...' Toady reminds him, his voice withering to nothing under The White Snake's cold stare. 'R-right, Sir. I guess you didn't, Sir...I-I-I didn't actually personally see him sign out, Sir. I can't be on duty 24 hours a day...or I would have reported it to you.'

"The Colonel slinks out and Toady slumps into a nearby chair behind the battered desk that the sergeants use for their endless pinochle games. He knows this isn't the end of it for him, and that there will be repercussions. Assuming they gather in Specialist Bates with a minimum of fanfare, there still will be some fang mark on his file, special remembrance from The White Snake.

"It's now three days since he signed out, and Joe still has a few hours left before he's due back at the 3rd. He's downtown, dining alone at the Catinat Hotel. No biggie, the 3rd is only a half hour away and he's got hours yet until the Saigon 10 o'clock curfew. He has just finished a big steak, certainly brokered to the hotel from some mess hall sergeant on the black market, and he's sipping the last of a glass of fine French wine. Wendell and Leo hustle in and sit down next to him.

'*Got* you, dog-face,' Leo exclaims in triumph.

'What do you mean, *got me?*' Joe starts to protest. 'I'm signed out. I'm not AWOL. You can't just-'

'You got that wrong, Bates. We can do pretty much anything we want.'

"For what seems like no particular reason, Bates makes a dash for the archway leading out to the street. It seems like an odd move for a smart fellow like Joe, but Leo and Wendell are tired of fooling around. Leo jumps to has feet and neatly tackles him. He snaps a pair of handcuffs on Joe and stands, dusting his hands in triumph.

'First string linebacker for Penn State!' he says.

"Joe's broken glasses hang from one ear. He's shaken by the crashing tackle, and his vision is blurred without his glasses. He unsteadily gets to his feet. Seeing he is off-balance, Leo gives him a little shove and he falls again, this time hitting his head on a table on the way down. When he doesn't get right back up, they each take a leg and drag him out to a waiting *xe hoi* taxi. By the time Joe wakes up, they're half way back to the White Shack. They're not even going to bother to take him back to his barracks at the 3rd to pick up his things.

"The Colonel takes no chances. They lock Joe up for the night in the narrow, windowless room at the back of the White Shack, officially a broom closet, but occasionally used to detain people with special knowledge of interest to Colonel Ogilvy. And the next morning, he's escorted by Leo and Wendell across the rain-slick tarmac to a waiting Pan Am 707. No doubt about it; Specialist 5th Class Joseph Bates' tour of duty in Vietnam is over. He's going back to The World.

"Joe is looking hang-dog and depressed as you might imagine, and the big shiner he got when he hit the table leaving the Catinat adds to his look of defeat. The plastic rims of his glasses are awkwardly repaired with black electrical tape, and one of the lenses is starred.

"The White Snake stands at parade rest, hands behind his back, a faint, cold smile lifting one corner of his thin lips. 'Who's the screw-up now, Specialist?' he asks. Joe shakes his head and refuses to look at the Colonel, the man who has broken his dreams and destroyed his life. He says nothing as he limps on past, heading for the metal staircase that leads up to the airplane.

"Leo and Wendell are standing at the base of the staircase. 'Don't fall off this one,' Leo gloats. 'You'll fall a little further than Red Dog.

"The portable stairs leading up to a 707 are higher than those used for DC-3s. Still, Joe says nothing. He ducks his head as if he's trying to hurry past the two ops. As he goes by, Leo tries to get in a last sneak punch to the side of his head. But Bates, ever the good boxer, steps inside and gives him a short right to the head. Joe connects, too, breaking Leo's nose and splattering blood all over his face. And then he continues up the staircase as if nothing has happened.

"Turns out, The White Snake has detained the plane. The entire 707 is waiting for Joe Bates. The door closes immediately after he's inside. The plane taxies through the light rain to the end of the runway and takes off.

"All over Tan Son Nhut airbase, thousands of G.I.s hear that sound and turn their heads to watch wistfully as the *golden ticket jet* rises effortlessly through the fog, on its way back to the land of the free and the home of the brave..

"Inside the 707, Joe sits alone, tense and expressionless. Grey clouds block the view outside his window. He's thinking about the ride down into the combination of heaven and hell that he'd taken just a few months before, and how much his life has changed. Grey clouds block the view outside his window. It's like Vietnam is clinging to him, refusing to let him go. *Will they call him back? Can they?* He doesn't think so, but The White Snake is devious and cunning. *Maybe he's got some trick up his sleeve. Maybe he will be brought up as a deserter, or worse, a traitor.* A stewardess comes by, offering orange juice. She's wearing a short skirted uniform and some sort of ridiculous pouf hat. Joe turns down the orange juice, but admires her legs as she walks away.

"The White Snake was happy. He figured he'd gotten everything he wanted. But what he hadn't counted on was our good pal Joe Bates, who was driven by a higher power—the power of love. Still climbing, the 707 breaks through the murky low clouds and a shaft of golden sunlight streaks in through the open window and lights Joe's face and the area around him.

"The golden yellow light seems to do wonders for Joe Bates. A slow smile spreads across his face and then grows broader. He's in the sunlight now; he's broken free. He makes a little gesture, pumping one fist and quietly whispers one word. 'Yes…!'"

CHAPTER 32

Well, even I can see Jack has really blown this one. Too much Dunk Stingray and not enough Nora Roberts. "What the hell,' I tell him. "This doesn't feel right. What's Joe got to celebrate? The Colonel got everything and he got nothing.."

"I never said that," Jack shook his iron grey head of hair, the familiar bittersweet smile that said *he had me this time* breaking out on his face.

I had to give him his credit. "You story telling bastard," I said.

Jack sat back, enjoying the moment. The storyteller always loves it when he knows you're hooked. "You see, Clair, the Colonel was surrounded by his dopey operatives. He hadn't given much thought to Joe's ingenuity, his persistence, or his persuasive ways.

"Right after the avalanche of flowers, after Mia My said *yes*, Joe has no choice but to go right for the heart of his troubles. He knows he is out of time and that they will be coming after him. He catches Ba Nguyen just as she is storming out the door. He begs, he pleads, he argues…*We can't wait—it's got to be now! Please, Ba Nguyen.* Even with Mia My pleading the cause of true love and that Joe is the only one for her, the elder tiger lady still looks like she is about to wash her hands of them.

"It seems hopeless, but nobody has counted on Joe's persuasiveness…or the fact that he knows too much about what had gone on before. He makes his last, desperate plea, 'Don't take my love from me the way our enemies took yours from you!'

'What?! How dare you!' she shouts, the tiger lady showing her fangs. If looks could kill, Joe would be a dead man. If she'd had a pistol in that moment, he would have been shot on the spot. Again, it is dear Auntie Kai who comes to their rescue. 'Stop pretending,' she tells Mama Nguyen. 'They took your dear *presidente* from you. It's no secret. We all know…everything. And that man at the church—he said he did it.'

'Everything…!' Ba Nguyen says. Her voice is weak, the wind out of her sails.

'Everything,' Auntie Kai repeats. 'He admitted it. And one worse thing—our Joe's boss is the one we all know as The White Serpent.'"

"Don't ask me how they knew that," Jack said, shaking his head. "They always knew everything. Why do you think the rockets and the mortars always were aimed at our barracks at the 3rd or the White Shack? Anyway, once Mama Nguyen has the picture, her mission becomes clear. Nobody had any idea how fast an angry tiger lady can work when she's motivated. In no time at all, a dozen seamstresses are swarming around Mia My, shaping the white silk wedding dress to her slim figure.

"So they were married before Joe got on the plane!" I exclaimed.

Jack nodded, "I was at the wedding. Everybody was concentrating on what they would do if the Zip generals took over. And, using my customary guile, I managed to sneak out of the 3rd RRU and off base.. They were married in the Saigon Cathedral. Mia My got the wedding she'd always wanted. She walked down the aisle in her beautiful white dress with the 20 foot long train of silk trailing behind like the fluffy white foam of a waterfall. Joe wore a black tuxedo, the classic kind like the men wore in the movies before James Dean and Marlin Brando. Little Vietnamese girls were in attendance. Little Vietnamese boys threw flower pedals. And, at the last moment, Mama Nguyen got me a tux as well, a bit of a tight fit, but nice for all that. Myette and Yvette sang a duet in Vietnamese and the cathedral organ thundered and rumbled happily in the moist and heavy tropical air. Yes, my sweet young Clair—for once good triumphed over evil in that nasty time of bloody terror and uncertainty.".

Jack was still for a long time, looking at the bees buzzing their busy work outside his big slab glass windows for nearly a minute before he continued. "It was so unexpected and wonderful, all that hope and beauty, right in the middle of that dark and ill-conceived war…my war, you know. Mia My and Joe came down the cathedral steps and the guests cheered and threw rice. I heard everybody who was anybody in Saigon was there. When I finish the novel, I'm going to say the sun came out and glinted on the rooftops, and for a brief moment the sky was blue over Saigon. I don't know for sure if it did or not, but it felt like it did."

"Well, I want to know more," I said.

Jack looked at Mia My, and then smiled at me. "What more is there to tell? Joe Bates got his honorable discharge in less than a month. Mia My Nguyen took an Air Vietnam DC-3 to Thailand, and caught a commercial 707 for San Francisco…and they lived happily ever after…"

This just wasn't finishing right for me. I'm no storyteller like Jack, but I've watched my share of soapies and I read my Nora Roberts. "What about Mama Nguyen?" I asked.

"Oh, Joe brought her over and sponsored her as a citizen. She started a company in real estate…she died suddenly, a heart attack."

This was like time, speeding up. I had been so involved with Saigon in the 1960's that I couldn't get my head around the fact that decades and decades had passed.

"And Auntie Kai…?" I asked in a faint voice.

"Is slowing down a little in her nineties," Mia My said with a proud smile. "She lives in an apartment in Paris and comes to California every year. She went back to Saigon three years ago. She did not like it very much, I'm afraid; she was always complaining, 'They call it Ho Chi Minh City now, and she says they make better *Pho Ga Dac Biet* in Paris and San Jose.'"

Jack took a dusty book off of a shelf behind him. It was a green photo album, full of pictures of young Jack and young Joe in Saigon. "Here, Clair," he said, starting me at the beginning. I saw three young *co gai,* one with frighteningly bad teeth, greeting incoming G.I.s with flowers at the airport. There was the entrance to the 3rd Radio Research Unit. Downtown bars and restaurants, peanut girls at the zoo, street vendors and street urchins, funny old French automobiles and cyclo-peddlers with stout legs, colorful cigarette stands and groups of Saigon Cowboys, crippled newspaper kids at Chez Brodard and the Arcade Edan, the Maison

Blanch dress shop itself…and pictures of the wedding, Mia My looking radiant in her beautiful gown, the twin singers standing on either side of Jack…

"Whatever happened to your two pals?" I asked. "The two singers…remember you met the night you got your knife wound?"

Jack's face clouded, and he was silent. Now there was something I thought I'd never see—Wild Jack Larch without any words coming out of his mouth. After a while, he looked to Mia My, who nodded with a faint, sad smile on her face.

"You should tell her everything, Jack," she said. "Clair is your woman, now. You must tell her everything."

"There was a terrible explosion," Jack blurted out, and I thought he was going to cry. Yet another surprise in The House of Jack in what was to be a day of surprises.

"At the wedding?" I asked, startled by the hesitation and then the sudden tumbling of words from his mouth.

"No, no," he hurriedly corrected me. "Some years later. I was already back in the States, churning out my first Dunk novel. Myette and Vyette were singing in a hotel lounge, the Rex; if memory serves.. It was a big step up for them, some officer had bribed the restaurant owners to set it up, and there was supposed to be a tour, and they were going to America…to New York and San Francisco…but there was this terrible explosion and beautiful Vyette was killed and her brother Myette was maimed horribly, he could never sing again—he never *wanted* to sing again." Jack shook his head, lapsing again into silence.

"And when did he die?" I asked.

Jack again looked at Mia My, but this time he was out of gas. "You tell her," he said.

"Myette is still alive," Mia My said. I did not realize it until only a few days ago, when he did one of his old *ju jitsu* tricks on Dorothy. These days, he falls asleep on the lawn mower and drives it in little circles," she said.

"Myette is Ong Vung?!" I'm afraid it was my mouth that fell open on that one.

"What was I to do?" Jack said softly. "His beloved sister was my close friend. Myette had no one to take care of him, and nowhere else to go."

I didn't know what to answer. And, as I was trying to absorb that one, things got even crazier in The House of Jack. Maria, the maid, came screaming into the room. "Dead person!" she yelled, crossing herself over and over and pointing to the front door. She held a bag from McDonalds with our sausage egg MacMuffins dangling like a purse from one hand. "Dead! Dead! Dead!" she screamed.

We all ran pell-mell to the front door, and, certain as rain follows drought, there was another dead person on Wild Jack's estate. It was Jack's ex-wife Dorothy, lying like a crumpled sparrow on the front steps. Her silent body was hunched over in a pool of dark red blood, and there was a huge combat knife stuck in her stomach.

CHAPTER 33

"Cell phone!" I yelled, running for the kitchen and hoping Jack's phone would be on his big slate desk where it always was, buried in the clutter, the piles of paper, the dueling sabers and the Chinese steel balls and the rest of his writer's stuff. I don't know what I was thinking. In the brief glimpse I'd had, Dorothy looked like she'd been lying there for some time, so she wasn't going to get up any time soon. Still, dead people with big knives stuck in them don't show up on the doorstep more than once or twice in a lifetime, if that, and so I was in hyper-drive, moving fast as I could. As I reached across Jack's computer for his phone, a voice said, *"Top. Top, hai la chet!* Stop. Stop or you're dead!"

And in the next moment Ong Vung—*Myette*—stepped into the room from the English Garden. *Crazy times!* I'd never seen Ong Vung in Jack's house, not even once. If he had to talk to Jack about fertilizer or bug spray, he would stand silently on the patio and insist with an underhanded scooping gesture of his good arm that Jack had to come outside. So his presence inside the study was oddly out of place, and made even more strange by the dirty old straw cone hat on his head, the hand clippers that dangled from his crippled right hand and the small, silvery automatic pistol he held firmly in his left.

"Get out of here, you creep!" I yelled.

"No need for to call police," he said. "I make my confession right now with no torture. Yes, I do kill every one person who take from my lovely Jack. Every one bad person always take and take and take from lovely Jack, and he not know it, he is a stupid, stupid man. So I do what is necessary for him."

"But that's not true…" I tried to protest, but Ong Vung continued as if I was the crazy one.

"It is my fate, I love a foolish man who has no sense in his head. I do *chet* to his first wife many years ago, nobody ever know. Life goes on. I *chet* his third wife, Joanie greedy song woman—she think she can take my place? No songbird sing like me. And last night, it is the end of his evil witch. I think I hate her most."

"You stabbed Dorothy?" I don't know why that startled me—after all, he'd just admitted to killing two other people.

"That one very…symbol-like, no? Vietnam person believe in fate. The knife is how I met Jack when he take bad stab in his arm."

He hobbled a few steps toward me. "And now is your turn."

"But I don't take from Jack!"

He angrily waved the silver pistol in my direction, "You take most of all! You take Jack's little house in back!"

"I paid for that house! I saved him from going bankrupt!" I shouted, trying to get through to the insane old man.

"*Khong. Khong phai.* I see all, Clair," he said, the spite adding a roughness to his cracked and reedy voice. With some effort, he raised the twisted hand to hold the hedge clippers as high as his shoulder and shook it at me in a threatening gesture, "You think I just clip the bushes? I am here, I am there, I am everywhere. You the worst Sneaky Pete of all! You worse than Saigon bargirl! You and your two football Cowboy Dance girlfriend, you steal all Jack money to buy houses!"

"That's not true, Myette! That's my money! From my—my football dancing!"

"*Khong. Non.* No, no, no. American woman not so smart as like that! You not make enough money to buy house as a dancer! A lucky bargirl, maybe yes…but no, Football-dancer-lady, you a nasty, bad thief like the others…and I see you know my real name. That not so good for you, Clair."

I figured I'd better keep him talking or I was a dead lady ."You were a singer in Saigon. Jack met you at a night club."

"He met *me first!* He met me! He fall in love with me! But then he meets Yvette, and he is in love with her! I tell him, 'Jack, is all the same thing.' But he shake his head. He say stupid thing to me like, 'Sorry, but my train not wired that way.' Jack is a very

confused man. He not see that love Yvette, love Myette, it all
same-same love."

Keep him talking, I'm thinking, *just keep the crazy man
talking.*

"Jack was a true friend to you," I argued. "After your
accident, he didn't forget you. He paid to get you well, and he
brought you here."

"To be his low-life peasant worker!" Myette spat out
bitterly. "I offered to have operation to make all perfect for Jack!
I would do anything to be with Jack like fate said we must be!
Ngung ma, when I tell Jack, he just shake his head no. '*Khong
phai,* Myette. No, Myette, no, no, no, Jack train of love not wired
that way.'" Ong Vung's single good eye narrowed to a little slit.
I thought he was going to kill me right then and there, but he
waved me back from the cell phone. "*Khong,* Clair. No
policemans now. Just a few more moments you give for me, I want
Jack see me shoot you in the eyes, and then we all find our peace."

It may sound heartless to describe what happened next as
such, but from then on, the events in The House of Jack played out
like the Keystone Cops in Horror-land. Jack and Mia My came
tumbling into the room, Jack yelling, "Did you call 911?"

They both pulled up short when they saw Jack's old
gardener with his stained clipper in one hand and a silvery
automatic in the other. Maria, who was out of her wits with fear,
ran into them from behind, propelling them all forward into the
room. Myette thought they were rushing him, and he panicked.
He raised the small automatic pistol and fired, and the bullet struck
Jack in the chest. I'd always thought of Jack as being as invincible
as Dunk Stingray, who had dodged thousands of bullets, but Jack
toppled over like a falling boulder.

"Nooooooo!" Myette shrieked in a high scream, horrified at
what he'd done. "Not you, my lovely Jack!" He waved his pistol
in the air pointing it at the rest of us, "You! You! You make me do
that! Now you all die!"

Maria, whose actions had unnerved Myette enough so he
had shot the Larch-ster, threw up her hands with a wail and fled to
a guest bathroom where she locked herself in, probably saving her
life. But Mia My wasn't in a retreat mode. She waved me back
with one hand while she herself advanced on the withered old

cripple, whose scarred face was twisted in grief and rage.

"You shameful piss-ant peasant," Mia My said, and she moved toward him like a predator cat that was twice her size. "*Xao lam*, you miserable, low-life, flat face, monkey-brains idiot! *Xao Nhet!* You're the ugliest thing in the world!"

Myette raised his silvery automatic and shot her in the chest. The bullet seemed to have absolutely no effect on her, and I thought he'd missed.

"You rotten, butt-crab, filthy old man," she said, her voice rising to the roar of a tigress as she took another unflinching step in his direction.

His eyes widened and he began pulling the trigger, again and again, without thinking. It was a small caliber weapon, but she was a small person and I saw red blooms appearing on her pastel blouse.

Except for the crimson blossoms on her chest, it was as if no bullets had touched her. Mia My was possessed by that mythical entity, the essence of the tiger now come real, as she stalked her prey. He fired and fired, and then we heard the dull clicks from his automatic.

"Now, Clair, he is out of bullets." Mia My said. "Now is time for your true tiger lady to come out."

But before I could think to do anything, Myette fumbled inside one pocket of his old jacket, coming up with an olive colored ball the size of an orange. *He had a grenade!*

I don't know how my part happened the way it did, but I didn't have to think about it at all. A wordless roar escaped unbidden from my lips. As Ong Vung fumbled for the ring on the grenade, my throwing hand reached back and connected with one of the big Chinese steel balls that Jack used when he was doing his pacing and thinking. In one smooth motion, I picked it up and tossed Myette a high, hard fast one to the head.

It was the pitch of my lifetime, and there was no way I could miss. That odd musical chimes note rang out as the steel ball connected squarely with the center of Ong Vung's forehead. His wig flew off and he staggered back and crumpled like a straw man, never to get up again. The grenade hit the tile floor and rolled into a corner with the detonator pin still intact. I turned to Mia My, who was still standing, a strange smile lighting her face. "Nice throw, tiger-woman," she said. "You be good to our Jack." And with that, the spirit of the tigress left her and she sank to the floor to lie on the tiles near Jack and Myette

Well, it was one thing to say *Be good to Jack,* but the bullet had lodged dangerously close to his heart, and our champion storyteller nearly died on the way to St. John's Hospital, and then, a few hours later, again on the operating table. Actually, he told me he *had* died, had floated up over the operating table and seen his body below him, chest open to the world while the surgeon plucked out the bullet and they hand-massaged his heart to get it started again.

I don't know if that was just more of his storytelling, but the truth is, the old Jack, Wild Jack, actually did go away, to heaven or hell, and neither of us believe he's coming back.

As for Mia My, impossible as it seems, the tiger lady lived, as well. Even with all those bullets in her, she came through with fewer complications than Jack. Once she was well enough, her eldest son, Dinh, met her at the hospital and they flew back up to Northern California together. I took them to LAX, and as they walked down the departure tube for their plane, Mia My was railing at him to be sure about something, probably *Sell, Sell, Sell!*

It was some months later, late September in Southern California, which meant the Santa Ana winds were riding in off the desert. Jack was at his desk, as usual, putting the finishing touches on The Freight Train of Love. I was in the Ghost Nook, looking over the stock market. I'd put a lot of money in natural gas and conservative health care REITS, and they were doing okay. My Cowboy cheerleader Gal Pals hadn't done so well. As Mia My had warned, that was a bad time to buy. They'd come begging for me to bail them out, but my money and my mind were already tied up in other directions.

"I thought you promised Connie the manuscript yesterday," I said to Jack.

"Joe Bates," Jack said, gazing off in the distance where a trail of smoke over the tan-brown hills behind my pool house told of brush fires somewhere north of Simi Valley. "Joe did it right. He saw the freight train. He took the ride." Jack slapped the cardboard box containing his new manuscript, whacking it affectionately with the palm of one hand.

There it was, The Story of Joe and Mia My, all typed up and ready for the presses.

"And what about you, Jack?" I asked.

"Me? Well, you know all about me, Clair. I've got everything else…success, money, divorces, even a kid who hates me—who, by the way, isn't really mine."

"You mean Paul? Of course he's yours."

"No, he is not my son," Jack said, glowering at me. But then I saw a glint in his eyes and a twitch of a smile, just a hint of the devilish old Wild Jack, who would perhaps never quite go away. "I had him DNA-ed," Jack said. "And Dorothy knew it. That's another reason she resorted to desperate measures."

"You're kidding," I said.

"Would I kid you?"

"It's been ten years, Jack, and I'm still not sure about that one."

"It's been that long?" he said.

"I guess that freight train you're always talking about came for us and we were looking the other way or something…"

"I don't see it that way, Clair," he said. "The way I see it, it's all my fault. I'm really good at writing about other people, but not so good with knowing the basic things about myself. I think I'm like one of those Beavers…"

"A Beaver?! Jack Larch is a Beaver?"

"Yeah, you know, I'm an old, beat up airplane roaring around like a bumble bee, old and slow and low over the land, looking for love in all the wrong places and all dinged up and patched over with my Purple Hearts."

"Poor Jack," I mused.

" Then too, I guess I've been too scared to land."

That amused me, in a bittersweet sort of way. "Well, great for you, you get to fly around, getting all that honey or whatever. But what about me?"

He pushed down his spectacles, looking at me like a professor of biology studying some strange new bug for the first time. "You, Clair?"

"Come on, Jack. You know enough to write twenty best-selling novels. I'm asking you—what about me? What about us?"

"Twenty-two best-selling," he corrected me. "And several over a year on the New York Times best seller list."

I smiled and the good silence spread between us as he thought about it. "You know, you've always been the heroine in all my stories, even before I knew you."

"How could that be, Jack?"

"Here's how I see it, Clair-Bear: I'm this crappy old airplane, buzzing around and looking for direction, for understanding, for meaning and purpose in my foolish, bumbling life. And then came you, Clair…I didn't really know it until Ong Vung shot me, and I looked over in that last minute and saw the horror on your face. I knew then… I am the battered old Beaver and you, Clair— you're my landing field."

And that's when he asked me to marry him. Being the Larch-ster, he didn't get down on one knee and shove a ring in my face. That would have been too ordinary for Jack, and with his bad knees, I don't know that he could have gotten back up. Instead, he asked me if I would, and when 'Yes' popped out of my astonished mouth, he asked me out on a date. Right. After ten years, a date with Jack.

A few days later, a limo picked us up in the late afternoon for what he said was going to be a splendid dinner and a night on the town. I wore a pale lavender gown, and the Larch-ster was splendid in a brand new tuxedo that he claimed he found in the back of his closet. On our way to a night on the town, he had the driver stop at Chopard on Rodeo Drive. You don't know Chopard? That's the place that furnishes a lot of the bling to the stars for the Academy Awards. It looked like it was closed, but Jack wasn't worried. They unlocked the door and let us into their house of glittering splendor.

"Anything you want, Clair," Jack told me.

He gulped a little at the size of the emerald ring I slid on to my engagement finger, but I just grinned and kissed him on the cheek. "I know you can afford it," I said.

As we were being driven away, Jack asked where I'd like to be married.

"How about a nice big cathedral?" I suggested. "Maybe the one downtown so all your show biz pals can look at me and go green with envy."

"Let's do that," he agreed. "With lots of flowers and everything. I always wanted a wedding like Joe and Mia My."

"Deal," I said. But I was sure I detected a faint gleam of Wild Jack in his eye. "What?" I asked.

"Well, we're actually still married from Las Vegas."

Yes, there definitely was the hint of that tricky old Wild Jack grin twitching at the corner of his mouth.

"What? But Jack—that makes you a bigamist!"

"Well, maybe technically," he said, "But I loved you too much, Clair. I never could bring myself to sign those divorce papers."

And now, a special excerpt from the
EPIC Author's Award
Best Action/Thriller Novel
by John Klawitter

HOLLYWOOD HAVOC
The Trouble With Fatboy

Available as an e-book in all formats from
www.double-dragon-ebooks.com
and as a best-selling trade paperback
from www.amazon.com

CHAPTER 1

The icy black water hit me like a cold body slam. I rolled over and over, panicked in the dark with blind-folded eyes and air bubbles frothing around my ears. Which way was up? I had no idea. You know, the experts always tell you the bubbles go up, but in the inky blackness it's all up…or down, or sideways.

My hands were tied, but I could kick some with my feet. One foot struck the hard edge of a slippery ledge. Okay, maybe that way was down…or sideways. I felt for the rocky ledge, crouched, gathered myself in a ball, and pushed off.

I'd guessed right; the surface came with a rush. I managed to suck in a quick gasp of air. I shook off the bath towel the bastards had taped around my head for a make-shift blindfold, and saw the dark line of the shore directly in front of me—and the black outline of my two assailants standing there, laughing like I was some new electronic sports game and expectantly hopeful I would sink out of sight, never to be seen again. I kicked desperately and shook my head, an attempt to clear the water from my ears.

"What shall we do, do you think?" I heard the one on the left say, as if they were discussing dinner plans or who might take out the garbage. Yeah, that's me, the garbage.

"I say pop him," the one on the right replied.

"No, no, no. He's too close to shore. He'll just drift back in."

"Well now, old chap, I could not disagree more. After all, he'll drift, either way."

Wait a minute. What the hell was I doing here? Me, Matthew Havoc. Okay, they call me Hollywood Havoc, but this is way past some of the minor schemes and scrapes I get into. I am a small-time Hollywood movie producer. Small beans, very little sauce. I work for Berger Royal, and we do schlock movies. We don't even own our own stages, for Christ's sake; we rent space on the Raleigh lot below Sunset in what is affectionately known as

'Old Hollywood'. And I certainly wasn't here to star as the drowning man in my own movie.

"Wait," I gasped in a bubbly, confused shout. "It's not my fault. I don't really pick the scripts!" That was a lie, of course. At least part a lie. I do help pick the scripts. Okay, I'll admit it. If anybody deserved to be shot for producing imitative, cheese-ball movies, it is me.

Oh, oh! I see a yellow flash and the sharp bark of a pistol. Jesus H. Christ! The crazy-ass *mudder-humpers* are shooting at me! Why can't they just get their refund at the box office? Yeah, I know. This isn't about the movies. This is too serious. This is attempted murder. Hell, this is about to *be my murder*. But making movies has been my life and I can't figure out what else it could be. I pay my taxes, I don't do dope, I don't have any powerful enemies. Another quick gulp of air and I kick down and away. The dark water wraps icy fingers around me, and I do my best to put distance between the shore and myself. My arms, of course, are useless bound the way they are. By now, I'm desperate for air. I force myself, I kick, kick, kick, giving it that old Havoc try, even though I can feel the burning pain surge through my lungs.

But the gods are smiling on me, at least to the extent that there is a favorable undertow, and this time when I come to the surface there is about ninety feet between me and my two friends, the nonchalant shooters making a game out of taking me out. Just ninety feet, the distance from home plate to the pitcher's mound. Still, better than nothing.

"Oh, sporting chance!" the one waving the pistol says.

"Allow me. I'm the better shot," the other replies, and they grapple for it.

"No, idiot. I am."

They're wrestling over the pistol, and I judge that to be a good thing. . I gulp air and pump my feet while they amiably wrestle for the right to kill me.

I shouldn't have to repeat that I don't deserve this. But they're not listening, and my complaints aren't true in the first place. Off-hand, I can think of a dozen reasons you should find some slow and horrible way to kill me. Look, if you're going to shoot me for anything, it should be that doomed scene in

Dragonfly Madness where the fake model helicopter (possessed by demonic influences) comes down on Metropolis like a limp beetle. On the other hand, I didn't have the budget to do anything better, and we had to finish the picture or lose a payment, and we at Berger Royal never miss our play dates or our pay dates. Or maybe you might want to send me to the torture chamber for that rotten tomato film we did called Klish Clash, with its garbage can lid musical numbers, one of our few attempts at social parody. The miserable failure of these individual productions aside, I stand accused—and rightly so—of living for my job, but there have been times when I've thought it's a great job. I'm assistant jack-of-all-trades to the great Hollywood mogul of B-movie schlock, the one and only Vincent Berger, known in the trade as Slick Vinnie or Vinnie-the-Cheap. To me he's just Vinnie, a skin-flint at spending money on his pictures and a heart of gold for every sob-story starlet who comes his way.

I'm Matt Havoc, Hollywood Havoc, the solver of all problems cinematic, the *sho-biz guy who gets things done*. They should give out an honor like that at ShoWest. Maybe they would from now on, in honor of me and my watery death.

Flashes from the pistol are starting up again, so I gulp more air and head back down to my bad ending. My enemies in the business will tell you I deserve this.

They say the life I lead is crap, and that the movies I help turn out are basically stupid and unwatchable. I will admit this much: At Vinnie's shop, Berger Royal Pictures, we create nothing but low-budget exploiters. Yes, that's what we do, and we're the very best at it, and there's a market for it. Come on, I'm supposed to be ashamed for making a living? As Vinnie's fond of saying, *Art, schmart, who gives a fart?*

As I am down there underwater thinking these and similar thoughts, I somehow come out of my confusion long enough to allow the immediate panic to subside. My lungs, I realize, aren't actually bursting and I can probably go a ways before I have to surface again. Yes, it is dark and cold and scary, but as I kick along I try to review how I could possibly have gotten into this mess. How did I, the cleverest low-budget guy in Hollywood, a guy who could create budgets as if by magic, dodge location fee cops, satisfy cast sexual appetites (My black book is legendary), find free parking and feed a cast and crew on the run, ever allow something this stupid to happen?

Earlier in the afternoon, just a few hours before, I'd been in Little Saigon looking for locations for a new picture that wasn't even green-lighted. I didn't find anything half-way decent or even exciting enough to snap a digital, and I'd driven back south to Newport Beach where I lived. I was returning to my condo, absent-mindedly ambling along the short gray cobblestone walkway that I share with my long-time neighbor Bertrand Burke, semi-affectionately known as 'Old Bertie' or 'Old Grampers,' when out of the corner of my eye I noticed the shattered frame of the old coot's front entrance, where his sturdy door used to be. For a moment the image didn't compute, and then I had what the Hollywood story guys call the *bad inkling*, the hero's first hint that things are not quite as they should be.

Let me move this along and try to sum it up here for you before I drown. I'm a thirty four year old journeyman Hollywood producer. I can do—have to do—everything. I know how to write and direct. I've been called on to shoot film when the cinematographer gets the runs or the flu or doesn't come back from a hot weekend in Acapulco. Yes, I am the complete film maker, a MacGyver of the silver screen, the guy who pulls off the impossible shots with bubble gum and a ball of yarn. You know, *My mind is the secret weapon.* Well, enough of that. Obviously, it isn't, or I wouldn't be here, sinking to the bottom of the bay. Let's get back to more Hollywood gossip about me.

I am divorced, a half-dozen years or so ago, from a self-absorbed, gum-chewing, teenage vixen…at least, that's who she was when we took our vows. I guess I knew. Like the country-western ballads lament, *What was I thinking?* Actually, I wasn't thinking, at least, not with my brain. It was one of those spur-of-the-moment Hollywood weddings doomed to failure from the first…well, read the gossip rags while you're standing in line at the supermarket, you know how it goes in show biz. Still, ours wasn't your usual bang-and-run story. We were actually destroyed by success…hers, not mine. Soon after our wedding, the career of the lady of my affections began to blossom, and she forthwith lifted herself like a gaudy hot air balloon right past my cheapie flicks to her present rarified altitude as one of America's most ogled and

highly paid set of tits available on the silver screen, that is, short of
triple-X. Today she's known as Joy Benefeté, but when I first
knew her she was Madge Sacknall, an auburn-haired theater and
drama major with a great body and a wicked grin, a gorgeous
starlet who couldn't sing a single note on key. Not that she didn't
try, but it was painful. I affectionately called her Peanuts, and in
the beginning I was glad of the singing because it meant she wasn't
perfect. The other cracks in the dam showed up a little later.

Okay. Another gulp of air, another bit of my story. About
the time Peanuts married me, fat, bald, Big Vinnie introduced her
to fat, bald, little Super-Agent Harry "Horny" Hyatt. It was
Christmas, and Vinnie was in one of his magnanimous moments.
However, since Berger Royal Pictures had been the kiss of death
for many a young star, Horny's HHH Agency repaid the favor by
christening her Joy Benefeté and moving her out of our shop.

Of course, Vinnie resented the move. He thought of Berger
Pix as one of the few training grounds for greatness, and maybe he
was right. If Steve McQueen could rise above his performance in
The Blob, Peanuts ought to be able to gain artistic recognition with
the lead role in Mission 998, a hot babes in wet T-shirts in outer
space spectacular we had planned for her. Vinnie was moved to
righteous indignation. He would have loved to squeeze another
picture or two out of that magnificent set before she moved them
on to the silk and caviar mob.

I'm not the best judge of these things, having lived too
close to the feisty fact of Peanuts in person, and there may have
been a certain sense in which you might call my ex-wife morally
weak, perhaps lacking in strength of character—but you would
never call her weak-willed or lacking purpose. Strong as iron
comes to mind. Relentless and even reckless in pursuit of her
career, certainly. She knew what she wanted, and she knew how to
get it. That made me something of a way-station on her golden
path.

When Horny Hiatt told her she was ready to walk around
the next bend, she believed it. And the rest of our relationship was
Extra-Extra history, that is, food for the *paraparazzi,* Extra Extra
and The Insider. Madge Sacknall emerged from her cocoon as the
beautiful, generally nearly-naked butterfly Joy Benefeté. Her exit
from Berger Royal Pictures and my bedroom, was followed by her

steady and relentless climb to a sort of lower rung stardom. Cheap, that is to say, because my ex-wife became known and appreciated for the lift, weight and luminosity of her perfect breasts rather than for her acting. And frankly, I believed that was unfair; I knew her better than most, and I saw that, somewhere inside all those curves and that wicked smile, and devious, unrelenting thirst for stardom, my girl Peanuts really had acting ability. How much, I wasn't sure. But the director in me sensed something there that went considerably beyond the luminosity of the flesh..

I told her just that, a time or two, but by then it was too late. She said things like, *I was just trying to hold her back. I was cruel, uncaring, selfish.* And, to tell the truth, after a few months of that, I gave up trying to make a go of it. I had my own grueling schedule. Schlock films wait for no man. Things having become what they had, the two of us were less and less an item around town. Busy lives, separate directions. We drifted apart and separated after a year or two, but we didn't seem to get around to the divorce until a half dozen years later, and when it finally happened it was almost an afterthought. She'd been about to dive into matrimony in the classic Hollywood manner, tying a hasty knot (not unlike we ourselves had, but this time) with some dark-haired and flashing-eyed Italian cinematic heartthrob. And then the Enquirer took an interest, researched the files and found out she was still technically married to me. As they say in the big scene where the complication becomes clear, *Oh, oh.*

Give me a moment here; oxygen seems to be at a premium. A few kicks, another gulp of air, a few more flashes from the now receding shore. Okay. Better now. On with the narration: Long time before, my father, Jack Havoc, was in the film business, too, but he worked for the studios, and he had better credits than I do. Vinnie had known him, and that's how I landed my first job as Vinnie's go-fer, back when I was just out of film school.

Let me tell you about Vinnie Burger. Yes, he's that important. Vinnie, himself, is a larger-than-life personality. He tops over six foot five inches. He carries an enormous girth, and an ability to be amused in the direst of circumstances, and an even bigger talent for squeezing production money out of hitherto untapped sources. Greece. Romania. South Africa. A giant used car dealership in Pomona.   All this, combined with a huge appetite for spending his production monies on Bentley sports cars, big sailing boats, and lavish gifts for wannabe starlets he finds…well, everywhere. Yes, he spends on those splendid luxury items rather than on the production itself, and with my help, he manages to hide the financial drain. Our movies look decent on paper but for these and other reasons turn out to be potboilers that play in the last three or four drive-in theaters in Canada and Mexico and then ship directly to Hong Kong, Seoul and Jakarta. Vinnie's a rogue—but he's got a sense of honor, life alternately outrages and amuses him, and, as had my father before me, I have the bad judgment to like him very much.

I guess I am drifting here, things getting a little fuzzy. I don't see the light yet, though. Jennifer Love Hewlett, the lady who wears those skimpy negligees on Ghost Whisperer, says that when you see the light you are to go for it, and then I guess you pass through the veil or something and you're dead but happy. I was thinking maybe you don't see the light if you're headed to hell, and, after all, only dogs and Oscar Winners Go To Heaven.

Right, right, my story in a martini glass…let's see if I can gulp it down, get through it before I'm fish food. After over a decade of doing hard time as Vinnie's right hand man, I've arrived to where I'm pulling down the producer or co-producer credit on almost every crap film we do. It's a little strange, because I always thought the producer's title would be the end of the world for me, my golden ticket. But when you do great B movies, that isn't necessarily so. Lately what the literary novelists call *malaise* has set in on my normally indomitable spirit. I find that more and more I want to write, not just screenplays but short stories and novels. Less crap, more meaningful stories.

I even daydream of retiring from my career as the clever slave-laborer who cleans up Vinnie's messes. In my dreams the serious people, those who make their way in the world of real ideas and literature, take me seriously. I don't have shouting matches over putting the key light at boob level, I have conversations about literature and art, and a New York agent who doesn't always ask Okay, guy, how many sex scenes we got here?

I know you're not asking, but in case you were, Sure, Hollywood agents love me, at least the lesser known ones do (Dogs are even attracted to guys who have smaller yummies to

hand out). But in my dreams, I'm a long way removed from
here—no, not underwater—far removed from my current position
as co-captain at the helm of inconsequential Berger Royal bubbles
of action/adventure and pot boiling sexual fantasy. You've got it
by now—I'm lost in what Vinnie calls the Fairyland of Tits & Ass,
the land where sex, dope and even blurbs in the Hollywood
Reporter can be negotiated for a screen credit. That means, of
course, the immortal soul (or at least the carefully hoarded life
savings) of a famous used car dealer in Pacoima may be sold for a
name above the title. I know where I want to end up, and this is
not it.

Enough about me. After all, I'm drowning here. You can
read the obit in The Hollywood Reporter. On the other hand, I'm
sure Bertrand Berke, my neighbor, is the one who got me into this.
Old Bertie's your ordinary, garden-variety, querulous semi-retired
old fart living on a fixed income of maybe slightly larger than
normal proportions. I would cast Walter Matthau, if he was still
around and hadn't already walked happily into the light. I may
sound cruel, but I like Bertie too, more than I will ever admit in his
presence. In a way, for him it's all over, his life is a finished
history rather than any blank new pages to be filled. At least,
that's what I thought, up until this afternoon. Ironic, isn't it? I'm
the guy drowning here and I'd been thinking Old Bertie was the
gone goose.

A widower for the last five of his 80 years, Bertrand's
backed away from his middle-aged twin sons, who nearly
simultaneously decided to go for the gay life, though not with each
other. Not that they didn't fool around, but they never made it
official. That would have killed Old Grampers. right there. The
twin pervs, Bertrand calls them, trying for light-hearted malice.
Back when he first got the bad news, he recoiled like a man with a
couple of spiders in his soup. Today, the twins are out of range,
both drifting quietly along in long-term relationships somewhere
on the East Coast. Or at least that's the going story, and as The
Man Hemingway would say, it would be pleasant to assume so.
You wouldn't think Bertrand was a person who could get himself
tangled in a dangerous and deadly mess and then pull me in with
him—but real life has an enormously unpredictable plot-line, have
you noticed?

I cannot recall how many times in the early morning I'd be staggering in from pulling a post-production all-nighter at MatchFrame or Pacific Video, and Old Bertie would be out there in front of his condo in his multi-colored Bermuda shorts and Wall Street Journal T-shirt, the one with the spotty white bleach stains. Like as not, he'd be staring up at the gutters, cursing the pigeons or the bats. Some decades before, Bertrand had invested in a clothing company appropriately named Crazy Wear, and he had stacks of cardboard boxes in his garage crammed full of gaudy clothing you couldn't even sell for profit in third world countries that had never heard of Ralph Lauren or Hugo Black. Lord knows he'd tried.

"Paper in the banana tree again?" I'd ask. But no, this time it was the bats.

"Bats are filthy creatures, Matthew Havoc. Pestilence. Spawn of the devil. And it's not a banana tree, it's a bird-of-paradise gone wild."

"You think all plants would go wild if you didn't drench them in Miracle-Gro."

That's all it took. Old Bertie would launch from there, selecting from his list of the many things large and small that provoked him, sputtering about cruel and unusual property taxes, the growing hordes of greedy wetbacks up from every province in Mexico to take California back, and the inferior quality of the potted plants the condo gardeners—notice the sneaky bastards all speak Spanish when nobody is looking—stick in our front flowerboxes to mark the passing seasons (Coral, cream and light-purple geraniums in February and orange and yellow-and-brown chrysanthemums in August, Southern California being a two-season place).

"Right, Bertrand," I would say. "You got a point there."

"Jesus-God-Damn right, I do," he would agree, grumbling as he moved off to water his spindly over-fertilized citrus tree with a garden hose.

I'm too busy to be Mister Nice Guy, but I found it impossible to ignore the crusty old fellow who, in all fairness, had to walk around the heavy stacks of film cans, video cassettes and scripts that FedEx dumped at my doorstep on a fairly regular basis. I don't think Bertrand minded, because it was some proof that I did real work, though I think he assumed I was more responsible for the shipment, rather than the creation of, the films and videos inside the parcels.

I knew him to a greater degree than I'm saying. At Bertrand's insistence, we had a procedure in case of his business emergencies, and once I'd even had the chance to put it to the test. He was in Mexico City when a man called from Brazil desperately needing a bid on a mobile X-ray unit. I tried to get through to Bertrand, but you know the South-of-the-Border telephone system. Hey, the guy needed a bid, and he needed it right away. I made up a page of numbers, figuring a piece of machinery like that being mobile and all might cost about as much as a six or seven minute Willie Nelson music video or a short but highly sensuous promo film for my ex-wife's latest flick.

I must have been in the ballpark, because the guy gave Uni-Amer Industries that particular piece of business, though for the next six months Bertrand was griping about the size of the kickback. I guess he was grateful—he gave me a watch that told time in three zones that he got for Christmas from some Norwegian shipping company.

"Set it for Tokyo and Singapore," he advised, "any hour of the day you could know what those tricky damn foreign skunks is up to."

Before he left town this last time, he'd switched his incoming faxes over to my machine, so all I had to do was glance at them…that is, when I remembered, and for a long time it was mind-numbing stuff about the functionality of the AZ-37 desktop radiation mode, or the exact dimensions of the trundle bed carrier, that uncomfortable cot-on-wheels that people laid down on before you swung them under Madame Curie's invention for peeking at bones.

And now somebody had broken down his door. I suppose I should have quietly tiptoed inside my own place and called the gate guards the minute I saw it, but curiosity got the best of me. That's the problem with us movie guys. We always want to know the whole story. I walked up to the door and gave a little push. But, instead of opening, it came off its remaining hinge and toppled over with a crash. There was a sudden rustle from the spare bedroom that Bertrand had converted into his office, and before I could retreat, two men came out and surrounded me with their extremely persuasive selves.

Their complexions were black as midnight onyx. They wore shiny business suits that I would have chosen as wardrobe for the successful gangster-businessmen from Hong Kong in Klish Clash, one of the countless Vinnie Berger chop-sockies, that is, the cheapie martial arts films that were among the Berger Royal staples. These black-as-onyx guys had broad shoulders and a collective scowl on their faces.

"Are, perhaps, you Bertrand, himself?" the one on the left said, giving me a little push for emphasis.

"Noooo…" I said uncertainly, pressing for time to think of something clever or at least get my gears in reverse so I could motor on out of there. I started babbling as I tried to back out the way I'd come in. "Bertrand, himself, is an octogenarian with a bad temper. That's obviously not me. I'm not even 35. And I'm fairly even-tempered. You have to be, in my business. Say, did you guys see who broke in here?"

I thought I'd leave them an out, they could say they'd seen a white guy in a funny hat running away, but even that last was the wrong question, at least, coming from me. As it would turn out, there were no right or good questions.

Skin tones on Negroes in America tend to shades from light peach to cherry red and various shades of chocolate brown. Not on these guys; these were blue-black men from the old country, men so dark there was a depth and a luster to their skin that made it shine like polished hardwood. Really, although it was quite beautiful, skin like that will give a lighting director the fits. Even the newest fine grain 35mm can't stand the contrast between an ebony sheen like that and, say, the whites of the eyes and teeth, and no matter what the film schools tell you, video isn't any better.

"No, why do you say that about breaking in?" The first one said. The anger was apparent in his voice.

"This door was hanging open from before we happened here," the other said with a sly half-smile. He looked like the wolf about to jump Little Red Riding Hood.

"Ahh, yes, right. We thought our dear friend, Mr. Bertrand Burke, might be injured," the first added helpfully. "So, of course, we entered this domicile to come to his aid and rescue."

"Bertrand isn't here," I said. "He's away on business."

I don't like crowds in the first place, and these unpleasant refugees from GQ Africa were pressing in too close for my comfort level. Heavy scent of Old Spice trying unsuccessfully to overcome body odor and all that. Nothing an occasional shower couldn't handle, but that wasn't the point. Far worse for my particular situation, the shared entranceway to our condos was isolated from the general view.

In hindsight, I see I should have been a little more concerned a little sooner, but Sea Garden Cove is a quiet, gate-guarded enclave. We don't encounter real trouble, situated as we are, a half-mile inland from the spangled neon glitz of the Coast Highway. Our gate guards aren't much, but in general their obdurate presence is enough to discourage the garden variety of local evils like Jehovah's Witnesses and grade school kids selling overpriced milk chocolate bars with almonds.

"Can you tell us, perhaps, where Mr. Burke got himself off to?" the guy on the right asked. They both were broad-shouldered and athletic looking, but shorter than I was, and I'm barely six feet in my stocking feet.

"Well," I said doubtfully, "He said something about Budapest."

"Budapest!" They gave each other a startled look and then glared at me. I could see further conversation would be required.

I brought it on with a rush.

"Come to think about it, guys, I'm not sure he actually went to Europe…Bertrand is an import-export guy. He goes everywhere, but, as he works for himself, he doesn't report to anybody, and when he does say where he might be going he's not very big on the details."

That explanation didn't really seem to satisfy, either.

"So, then, inform us. Where are the actual business offices of Mr. Bertrand Burke?"

What a snappish little dictator! We could have used this fellow in Klish Clash, where we'd been panned for lack of authenticity. There was a big scar authentically indenting the bridge of his nose. I wondered how he'd gotten it. The only explanations I could come up with were unpleasant. Of course, there I was again, type-casting.

"Yes. Yes, precisely where are they?" the other added like an evil echo. "The offices of Mr. Bertrand Berke of Uni-Amer Industries?"

Maybe it was my overactive imagination, but I sensed an arch indifference and the hint of a foreign accent in their voices. *I was just meat to these guys—they were treating me like I was playback from the dead.*   I thought their speech pattern might be French Colonial rather than German or English, but I'm not really an expert in that sort of thing. In the Berger Royal school of low-budget filmmaking we go for broad impressions rather than literal accuracy.

"Here." I replied simply. "Right where you're standing. This is the broken doorway of Bertrand Berke and these are the offices of Uni-Amer Industries, LLC, *Excellence in X-ray Exports.*"

"Impossible!" The wide black man on the left looked around skeptically, as if Old Bat-brain Bertie might be hiding under the fallen door, or in the nearby hall closet. "I say, I mean to ask you, *Where are the actual offices of Uni-Amer Industries?*"

It's always hard when dreams come crashing down to meet reality. I don't know what these guys expected, but Bertrand's little shell of a company certainly wasn't it.

"I thought you just asked that?"

The fellow gave me a glare that would have crushed an ordinary mortal, but, of course, I'm on the low end in show biz and I take a lot of crushing.. But I didn't need my directorial genius to recognize the increasing coldness in his voice and the dark granite set of his chin. He wasn't asking, he was demanding.

"Hey, don't shoot the messenger," I said.. "This is Uni-Amer, and it's not my fault they don't have a pretty secretary, but with cut-rate shipping, this is what you get. Bertrand works out of this condo, right here where he lives."

I suppose I should have been more on my guard; after all, tricky and unexpected things are always happening in our flicks, which are invariably full of heart-thumping action even if they come up lacking in motivation or real meaning—not that Big Time Hollywood does much better with three times my crew, four times as many shoot days and a hundred times my puny budgets. But the point is, I don't expect adventure in my own pathetic little mess of

a personal life. Adventure is something Vinnie and his schlock
writers and hack directors and I invent and then present to the
forgiving masses as entertainment.

Still, in the back of my mind something about my present
situation reminded me of the time in Dragonfly Madness when the
corrupt Harrigan Matre's henchmen (who were themselves the
Demon-spawn of the Dark Chop-man), anyway I was reminded of
the time these guys had surrounded brave Tran Le just before they
jumped him. Not a good sign, and then, just about when I decided
I'd better be doing something about that—oops, it was too late.

I never had a chance. I'm nearsighted, myopic, you know,
and, even with my Calvin designer eyeglasses, I have terrible
peripheral vision. So I didn't actually see the cold and heavy
object that struck me on the side of the head. And after that, I
suppose I slumped to the ground without saying anything
significant or even out loud. Suppose, but wouldn't really know.

www.ingramcontent.com/pod-product-compliance
Lightning Source LLC
Chambersburg PA
CBHW032302070726

47590CB00015B/288